BLOODLINES

BLOODLINES

A DARK MAFIA ROMANCE

UNRAVELING SERIES
BOOK 1

C.E. SARROW

ISBN-13: 979-8-9942558-0-3 (eBook)

ISBN-13: 979-8-9942558-1-0 (Paperback)

Book cover by Haya In Designs.

Edited by Beth Hudson, Ink, and Amber.

Published by Shadow Walk Publishing LLC.

www.cesarrow.com

For Jay

CONTENTS

Content Note   ix

1. Emory   1
2. Amelia   5
3. Amelia   11
4. Amelia   19
5. Amelia   25
6. Amelia   34
7. Amelia   38
8. Amelia   45
9. Amelia   55
10. Amelia   62
11. Amelia   74
12. Emory   82
13. Amelia   95
14. Emory   107
15. Cal   119
16. Amelia   130
17. Emory   139
18. Emory   146
19. Mirabelle   155
20. Emory   167
21. Emory   174
22. Emory   179
23. Emory   188
24. Cal   195
25. Amelia   204
26. Amelia   214
27. Amelia   220
28. Emory   232
29. Emory   241
30. Mirabelle   251
31. Amelia   260

32. Emory   273

33. Amelia   284

34. Amelia   292

35. Emory   296

36. Emory   301

37. Amelia   308

38. Emory   316

39. Amelia   325

40. Emory   331

41. Amelia   336

42. Emory   339

43. Amelia   345

44. Emory   349

45. Emory   353

46. Amelia   364

47. Emory   375

48. Cal   383

Join My Newsletter   391

About the Author   393

Acknowledgments   395

CONTENT NOTE

Thank you for picking up *Bloodlines*. I hope you enjoy reading it as much as I enjoyed writing it!

Bloodlines is the first book in the Unraveling series, which will follow the same couple, Emory and Amelia, throughout.

While not a pitch black romance, *Bloodlines* is a dark mafia romance intended for mature audiences and contains content and themes that may be upsetting to some. Please take care and check out the content warnings before reading.

To see a full list of warnings, please visit my website (link below):

https://www.cesarrow.com/content-warnings

With love and gratitude—
C.E. Sarrow

ONE

EMORY

Emory Holt looped the necktie around his fist in a makeshift garrote and torqued until the man's face turned red. "Manual coercion," he called it because he couldn't tolerate the chit-chat of interrogation.

The blubbering. The begging. The bargaining with God.

Richard Dauer did none of that. Instead, he clawed at his neck to loosen the tie. Downstairs, music blared as partygoers rose in breathless fervor, bewitched by the night and the storm raging outside. The din disguised the scuffle in Rich's home office. Emory counted the beats bumping against the soles of his dress shoes.

Eight. His shirt was too expensive to chafe that bad.

Nine. God, how he relished squeezing the rarefied air out of Rich's lungs.

Ten. Emory dumped Rich onto the floor.

Legs akimbo, he gasped for a breath. "I don't have what you want."

Emory expelled a quiet laugh. That's what they all said, as if ignorance shielded them from his scrutiny. He squatted and jabbed his gun beneath Rich's chin.

"I hate Portland, hate this weather." Emory tipped his head to the ruckus downstairs. "Hate these pompous fucks you run with. You think I'd be here if you didn't have what I want?"

Rich's glassy eyes drifted to Jack, Emory's second-in-command, and two other men from the Moriarty syndicate guarding the door.

"They're not your saviors," Emory said. The reminder drew Rich's gaze. "I cut you a fair deal, better than most. It's time to deliver what you promised."

Rich licked the blood from his bottom lip and winced as he righted himself against the bookshelf.

"I don't have it, but there's someone here who does." He paused, a tussle with his conscience, perhaps. Rich was as shameless as he was crooked, though, and proved it as he whispered, "Amelia Havick."

Emory smiled at the bitter irony. Of course, it'd be her. The night, so riddled with oddities, demanded another cosmic jest. And what a fucking riot too.

"Amelia," Emory repeated with no right to the familiarity he put on her name.

He hadn't met the girl, not truly—just a fleeting touch, handful of words, and whatever they'd had going from across the room. He could easily pick the stunning redhead from the crowd downstairs, though. Few women could claim such bone-crushing beauty.

Amelia played at timid rather well and had that intangible quality that drove him wild, alluring only when it was genuine. Sexy in an uncertain-of-herself way; doe eyes, dulcet voice, gorgeous body she probably didn't know how to use. What a goddamn dream. It'd heated his blood and sent the room faintly spinning.

A lesser man would kid himself that only he could show her what to do with those long legs and full lips, that she'd bloom beneath him and him alone. Emory was no ordinary man and planned to prove it to her by the end of the night.

There was a colossal problem, though.

"She's Cal's daughter," Emory said and settled uncomfortably on his heels.

Cal Havick—federal prosecutor and self-righteous prick—was hell-bent on decimating Emory's organization. If he only knew how his daughter had eye-fucked Emory from across the room. At his silent command, Amelia had even put on a show for him, her fingers discreetly skimming the tops of her breasts and the inside of her thigh. Sweet thing wanted to be fucked hard by a dangerous man, it seemed.

"What does Amelia have to do with this?" Emory asked Rich, because it wasn't just her looks or the magnetism between them that had garnered Emory's devout attention. From the sidelines, Amelia had observed the festivities with solemn dread and noticed what the others were too drunk or high to see.

"She knows everything and will sing like a bird, but you don't have much time."

"Why?"

"She leaves for Arizona in a few days. Probably thinks she'll be safe there."

Rich scowled as if he derided Amelia's naiveté, as if he weren't the one battered bloody with a gun to his head.

"I counted at least six men from the Velasco syndicate stalking your party downstairs. Are they here for her?"

Rich nodded. "They'll do to her what they did to Burt."

Emory bristled with an abrupt chill. Concern complicated his desire for her. No one deserved the Velascos' indiscriminate brutality.

"They'll do far worse," he said with grim prediction. She'd sing a song, all right; one where death was a mercy and she begged for its kiss. "You're feeding your best friend's daughter to the wolves. If Cal finds out—"

"I don't give a fuck about Cal or his daughter!"

Blood dribbled from Rich's nostril onto his dress shirt. He ripped free an elaborately folded pocket square and held it to his nose. Emory stood with a mirthless chuckle. That was low, even for Rich.

Jack shifted impatiently by the door. "What's our play here, Em?"

Shit or get off the pot. Emory had come for answers. If they were tucked away in sweet Amelia Havick, so be it. His motivations were messy, but business wasn't always done clean.

He holstered his gun and turned to his men. The lights flickered with a boom of thunder, the music momentarily killed.

"Get the girl."

TWO

AMELIA

Two Weeks Earlier…

T he first nettle stings the worst.

First heartbreak. First betrayal. First death.

Amelia Havick couldn't say how often her mother had offered that saying as an antidote to life's little let-downs.

Getting fired.

Amelia might soon add that to the list of formative firsts, but the prospect didn't scare her like it should. Nothing—not even losing her job—could compare to the deep unease coursing through her. Her body stiffened and heart pounded like a drum as she white-knuckled the steering wheel.

What the fuck was he thinking?

Amelia glanced at the manila folder in her passenger seat and punched the gas. The sooner she off-loaded it, the better. It wasn't her fault. She didn't know. It was a simple mistake she'd laugh about someday. She'd tell her friends over cocktails how she bolted out the door at midnight in an oversized t-shirt—no bra— and sleep shorts to deliver the folder to Burt, her scatterbrained boss.

The weight of it was wrong, though.

Simple mistakes didn't deposit dread that sat in her stomach like a sack of bricks. And Burt was clear-headed and sharp despite his age.

Then how did this happen?

Fingers of moonlight silvered Lake Oswego as Amelia's sedan raced along an empty road. A mile back, she had killed the radio to soak up the silence, all but the breeze whipping in from the open window. Amelia's hand trembled as she swatted away tangled strands of hair. Honeyed by the summer sun, ribbons of gold had emerged amongst cinnamon red. It had grown long too and skimmed past her shoulders sun-kissed with a glow her mother called healthy.

Rain freshened the cool air, and the trees stood sentry as Amelia navigated the switchbacks. She breathed deep the scent of petrichor and crushed pine needles.

She wouldn't miss much of Oregon, perhaps only these quiet nights. There was no comfort in it now, though. Sweat slicked her palms and she burned up despite the damp chill.

The folder should've had case law in it, a real snooze-fest. Leave it to an old man to hoard secrets in an unmarked folder tucked amongst other files for review. She wanted it gone just as badly as Burt wanted it back.

Another text pinged. The screen's pale aura filled the darkness. Amelia glanced at her phone in the center console.

Almost here???

Triple question marks. Burt reserved those for only the direst circumstances. Amelia's heart thrummed a frantic beat, and she sped the rest of the way.

Burt met her at the door. He must have seen her headlights cutting through the fine mist that enveloped his two-story estate. One of Portland's most revered defense attorneys, he lived more modestly than most of his ilk, but his home still dazzled Amelia. She hurried up the brick steps, her flip-flops slapping the soles of her feet as she went.

Burt hushed her with a knobby finger pressed to his lips and ushered her into his study. Lamp light pooled on the floor, but shadows consumed the edges of the room.

"Leave it there," he said and pointed to an armchair in the corner.

Amelia offloaded the folder with a quiet breath. *Done.*

She could apologize and promptly leave. It was well past midnight, and the ordeal had gotten Burt out of bed. He paced the room in a tatty robe and striped pajamas, his snowy hair a disheveled mess.

She'd never seen him that out of sorts before. He was brilliant in the courtroom, hawkish but affable. Judges respected him, prosecutors envied him, and Amelia admired him but never wanted the internship. For the first time she could remember, Burt wore his years, all seventy-something of them.

"Burt, it was an accident," Amelia said and caught sight of herself in the mantle mirror.

If he was a mess, so was she. With a clammy hand, she brushed away strands of frizzy hair plastered to her cheek.

"It was careless," he said, sounding eerily reminiscent of her father, right down to the clipped tones and vague disappointment. "Careless of me to misplace it. Careless of you to rummage through it."

"I know. I'm sorry."

The transgression seemed beyond apology, and Amelia figured it was only fair that he fired her. She was moving to Arizona soon, anyway. In three weeks, none of it would matter.

"How much did you see?" Burt asked, unusually pallid as he massaged the base of his neck.

At a loss for how to quantify, Amelia shrugged. Enough to know it wasn't for her, enough that the folder sat in her work bag like a telltale heart pounding on her morbid curiosity.

She'd sensed the wrongness of it, the soft chime of something amiss. That chime wailed with a warning as Burt inched closer. He dropped his voice as if the walls themselves might absorb his secrets.

"No one can know about this. Not even your father." He paused and added forcefully, "*Especially* not your father."

"Why? He might be able to help."

Burt shook his head and motioned to the newspaper on his desk. "He can't stop what's coming."

Amelia skimmed the headline. *Crime Syndicate Suspected in Spate of Gruesome Murders.* Violent crime made for splashy headlines, but something sinister had cast a long shadow over the summer as rival crime syndicates, the Velascos and the Moriartys, courted war after a decade-long truce.

And that was the crux of the folder's contents—a wealth of sensitive information on the Moriartys. It seemed benign at first, nothing that wouldn't be uncovered during discovery—a roster of Moriarty associates, known locations and patterns of life, vulnerabilities to exploit. That wasn't what piqued her curiosity, though. Page after page, she encountered a name on repeat.

Emory Holt.

Amelia had said it out loud once and felt silly after. On her lips, his name started with a hum and ended on a sigh, the syllables perfectly lyrical. The enigma sparked Amelia's intrigue, and it spread like wildfire when she found Emory Holt's mug shot in the folder.

He was strikingly handsome with bronze skin and long, jet black hair framing quintessentially masculine features—strong jaw, high cheekbones, heavy brow. A smoldering intensity gathered behind piercing amber eyes. Those eyes were hypnotic, she decided, but that felt silly too.

Why then did she keep going back to his name, to his picture? A girl like her knew when to quit, and yet she scoured the folder for more of him but got more than she bargained for.

Whoever Emory Holt was, the Velasco family wanted him dead, and the folder's contents detailed how they planned to do it. The Velascos didn't intend for it to be a fair fight or his death to be clean. Amelia had seen enough of the folder then and wanted no more dirty knowledge of Emory Holt and his grisly fate.

"Are you in some kind of trouble?" Amelia asked Burt.

They waltzed along the edges of something dangerous, but Burt refused to acknowledge it. His distraught gaze dropped to the parquet floor.

"The police…" Amelia began gently, but Burt sunk the suggestion with a bitter laugh.

"Who do you think pads their payroll?"

Amelia didn't honestly know, nor could she say if he meant the Moriartys or Velascos. Maybe both. She had so many questions. Why did Burt have the folder? Who was Emory Holt? And why did the Velascos want him dead?

Burt rummaged through the liquor cabinet beside the fireplace. "Do you drink?" he asked but had already fetched two glasses and poured a finger of scotch in each.

"Not really," Amelia answered as Burt handed her a glass.

"In business and in life, I close the deal with a drink," he said and lifted his glass in salute. "It's ceremonial. Sacred. Secrecy is sacred too. Sometimes our lives depend on it. This is one of those times. You will forget what you saw in that folder. No matter what happens or who asks. Your father, the police, anyone. And I do mean *anyone*."

A chill grew in Amelia's chest that not even alcohol could burn away. Her stomach soured and saliva filled her mouth. She'd be sick if she drank. She nodded her assent as Burt sipped.

"When do you leave for Arizona?" he asked.

"Three weeks."

Saying it out loud somehow made it feel less real, as if she was hurtling toward a horizon that would forever elude her, and her dreams of escape were just a fickle mirage.

Burt took her glass and set it on the mantle. An age-spotted hand rested heavy on her shoulder. Amelia couldn't place what gathered in his eyes. Regret, perhaps. Fear, most like.

"Leave sooner. Please."

His desperation disarmed her. Light-headed, Amelia swayed subtly on her feet. "I can't. I have loose ends to tie up."

That she was leaving at all had carved a chasm between her

and her father. It'd been two weeks since their fight with scarcely a handful of words spoken between them.

Amelia didn't bother to explain any of that but didn't need to. Burt squeezed her shoulder hard as fear whittled his voice to a whisper.

"Amelia, you're fired. Make peace with your father then get the fuck out of town."

THREE

AMELIA

At the funeral, someone asked Amelia what she liked best about working for Burt. Polite small talk often yielded dumb questions and doubly so at funerals. Then again, everyone strangled grief in their own way.

Her answer was just as polite, just as dumb. She liked that he kept a bowl of Jolly Ranchers on his desk. He'd suck on the green ones and confess his regrets, that he'd squandered his best years in the rat race. Criminal defense wasn't for the faint of heart, and his ticker had been due for another coronary. "The widow maker," he'd called it.

In the end, it wasn't a coronary that killed Burton Shaw. The newspaper reported that he hung himself with a blue tie, and it seemed a ghastly oversight that his family buried him in one too. If he cared, his corpse hadn't let on, and Amelia thought he looked rather peaceful in his casket.

On her way out of the church, she said goodbye to the other interns for perhaps the last time. They hadn't acknowledged her in the best of times and didn't acknowledge her then. Law students had no time for farewell fanfare. She was the baby, fresh out of undergrad and twenty-three. If they'd gotten her a cake on her last day in the office, it would've read "Good Riddance" in thick, sugary icing.

There'd been no cake and no goodbyes, and Amelia drove home hardly sated on sweet escape. She carried Burt's mantle now, but secrets were like blood stains. Water might wash them away, but shine the right light and you'd find them there. They never truly scrubbed clean.

In the week since Burt's death, Amelia had been trying to come clean with hot showers and guided meditations of blooming daisies. Behind closed eyes, the daisies never bloomed. Instead, she saw the fear on his face when he issued his plea. *Get the fuck out of town.* His death had delayed her departure. If he were alive, he would've busted a gut at the irony.

In her childhood bedroom, Amelia slipped out of her funeral attire and into a white cocktail dress. Only Richard Dauer was tacky enough to throw a party on the night of the funeral. He should've canceled out of respect for Burt, his business partner and friend.

Then again, Rich didn't just throw parties. He hosted galas. God forbid anyone confused the two. Nothing offended Rich like downplaying his importance, and the annual gala was important enough that every Portland lawyer, politician, and socialite attended the lavish event held at the Dauer estate.

Amelia plugged in her phone and checked the time. Late as hell. Ever ephemeral, poetry couldn't wait. She uncapped a pen with her teeth and, in her notebook, captured the turn of phrase niggling in her mind. Someday soon she'd bind her poems together in a proper book and have something to show for herself. Her muse was a flake, though, and fled as her father's voice swelled with rising heat from down the hall.

"Tell me you weren't involved in this, that you didn't know."

Amelia had never witnessed her father work his magic in a courtroom and didn't need to. She knew intimately well how he verbally eviscerated and pitied whoever was getting an earful. She snapped her notebook shut and navigated the moving boxes crowding her room. Her father hated how she'd packed. That was about all he said of her leaving—pointing out the nonsense of spatulas boxed with purses, curios with cold medicine.

"Don't lie to me! A man is already dead."

Amelia leaned into the hall and held her breath to listen. *Who the hell is he talking to?* Someone from the office, no doubt. Callum Havick only name-dropped death on work calls.

"What does being a federal prosecutor entail?" Amelia had asked him once.

Death, he'd told her. Big death, to be precise, the kind West Coast crime syndicates deified. They left a body count he wouldn't reveal, only that it was big, capital "B". His job was to end those organizations. "Crush them" was the phrase he used. Big death made her father a harder man.

These days, work followed him home like a shadow through the door as he indicted the Velasco syndicate. Smaller and flashier, the Velascos ran the drug and sex trade in Las Vegas. They were a thorn in her father's side, but nothing more. The Moriartys were his white whale, his obsession.

They possessed ironclad control over their territory from Seattle to San Diego and called themselves a family, but weren't by bloodline, only ritualistic oaths. A violent brotherhood steeped in dark mythos, they bucked the old-world traditions of the Irish mob but formed traditions all their own. When her father whispered "crush them" with vitriol in his voice and hate in his heart, she knew he meant the Moriartys.

"I won't make it tonight," he said, the disappointment too personal for a work call. "Enjoy your little party, Rich."

The diatribe ended with the thud of something—his cell phone, probably—hitting the desk. The scratch of vinyl came next. Amelia's father was a sensible man—stoic and wise—but predictable. After troublesome days, he vanquished his vexations with *The Dark Side of the Moon*.

Amelia slumped against the doorframe. It'd been a month since their fight, a month of existing like strangers. The bass line of "Money" thumped louder than usual. A clarion call for compassion, it thrashed on her heart. Someone had to budge first. As always, that someone would be her.

Down the hall, Amelia hesitated at the threshold of his office where dust motes glittered in the golden hour. With his back to her, her father stared out the window at a thicket of trees. Their lush canopies swayed in splendid unison against a violently blue sky.

For late June, Portland was downright balmy. The sultry novelty wore off a week ago, and the city sweltered beneath a dome of unrelenting heat. Cool reprieve had rolled in today on cotton puff clouds.

"You don't have to knock, Amelia," her father said before her knuckles met the door.

With a glance over his shoulder, he frowned at her dress hitting mid-thigh. Fatherly disapproval came wrapped in cellophane she saw right through. He knew better than to say anything, though, so they did their little dance. He smiled stiffly. She tried at levity.

"Nothing says 'I'm here to party' like a vintage sweatshirt, Dad."

He shrugged at the halfhearted joke and spared just as little humor. "Nostalgia dies hard, I guess."

His Harvard Law sweatshirt had gone threadbare years ago, and the ink faded years before that. He wore it in stark contrast to his dark hair, combed and side parted, and a salt-and-pepper beard trimmed neat against his chin.

Amelia motioned to his phone unscathed from its tumble. "Everything okay?"

The coffee mug at his lips obscured a scowl, but his steely gaze said the rest. No, absolutely not.

His friendship with Richard Dauer was in shambles. They'd met in law school, but Rich's charisma led him down a path as the city's most prominent defense attorney. "A high society man," her father called Rich, all too pleased to pin the moniker to his old friend. What started as an innocent jab had sharpened with time and could cut to the bone with bitterness.

"It's fine," he said but contemplated his desk. "I need to work anyway."

Amelia eyed the tatty folders and chicken scratch notes, most bearing the Moriarty name. Then there was her father. His hair greyed at an alarming rate and dark circles permanently rested beneath his eyes. The case would be the death of him, and their fight just seemed petty.

Amelia almost said as much, but a photograph slotted in the keyboard caught her attention. In it, an older man flashed a candid smile on the razor edge of laughter. It was a bizarre memento amongst court filings and affidavits.

"Who is that?" she asked.

Her father took another swig from his mug and set it down hard. Coffee splattered a nearby folder.

"Liam Moriarty."

"He's the one you're after?"

"Not quite. He ran the organization for decades but stepped down. I'm after the man who took his place."

With a knot in her belly, Amelia came closer to his desk. The question on her lips didn't need asking, and it wasn't her place to pry.

"Who took his place?" she asked despite herself.

"A man named Emory Holt."

Her father spit out the hard "T" like venom, so at odds with the sweetness she'd put on the name. Amelia saw it coming but still nearly lost the floor. She swallowed hard and scrambled for some composure.

"That's his son?"

"Not by blood, but important enough that he inherited the empire. Emory Holt is something else. Calculated, deliberate, secretive."

"Would Burt have known him?"

Quiet frenzy tinged Amelia's question as the pieces abruptly came together. The folder wasn't bits and bobs of random information, but a dossier on Emory, a man exalted in the criminal underworld. Shame shaded her fascination of him, those nights she found her way back to that folder, back to him.

Her father circled his desk and sat at the edge. The prosecutor's pose, he did it when he needed to coax out the truth. Maybe he thought it disarmed or tempered his severity. It didn't.

"I don't think so. Why? Did he say something to you about Emory or the Moriartys?"

Amelia eyed the door with the instinct to bolt. She inched toward it in a shuffle and conjured a flimsy explanation.

"No, I was just curious. On the phone with Rich, you said…"

"Yeah, about that." Her father slowly rose from his desk and stuffed his hands in his pockets. Amelia knew that move too. He was gearing up to drop a bomb. "Burt's wife is disputing his cause of death. The FBI has agreed to investigate. I doubt it'll amount to much, but they may ask you some questions. Routine stuff, nothing to worry about."

Heat exploded across Amelia's cheeks and spilled down her chest. "Disputing how?"

No longer impassive, concern carved a canyon between her father's brows.

No, not this.

Amelia needed him to cosign her denial, to tell her that Burt really was a sad old man who took his own life, that it had nothing to do with that folder or his warning to her.

"She thinks it was foul play."

Amelia's throat ached with the promise of tears. "You mean murder."

She should've seen it coming. People said funerals were for the living, but so too were the questions because "why" and "how" didn't matter to the dead. Everyone knew the "how," but why would Burt take his own life?

He wouldn't. He hadn't.

"Amelia, is something wrong?"

Her father edged closer. His searing gaze could take her apart, overturn every piece until he was satisfied she had nothing to hide.

Some nights, Amelia sat at the dinner table with Burt's warning rattling in her head as her father ate his supper in small bites. She wanted to carve out the secret like a malignant growth and drop it onto his plate. This was his world, not hers.

He'd given her a chance, but what could she say? The folder told one tale—the Velascos wanted Emory dead—and one her father probably knew well, so why promise her silence?

Amelia didn't know. But then there was Burt and how she dreamed some nights of his secrets poisoning him. What if those secrets could poison her father too?

A thunderclap rattled the window, and they both turned to a darkening sky. Outside, the trees bent against the assault of rising wind, the canopies in chaos.

"I'm fine," Amelia said and buried her tears behind a phony smile. "I have to go. The weather's turning, and I'm already late."

She started for the door, but the cold snap of her father's voice stopped her.

"Why are you running?"

She swung around, certain of his anger, but found hurt etched on his face instead. "Dad, I told you. I—"

"That's just it. You used to tell me everything, and now there's a part of you I can't reach. Are you that angry with me that you have to run from home? Why pack like a maniac just so you can leave early? And why Arizona, of all places?"

He meant the randomness, the way she seemingly closed her eyes and pointed to a map. That wasn't far from the truth. For good reason, he called her his wildflower and saw in her something hard to tame. Amelia flourished in places he couldn't understand.

But home had always been elusive, a state of the heart more than a place to put down roots. Arizona promised belonging she had yet to find and an escape from the secret she held inside. It burned him up that she wanted to leave so badly.

"Not every decision I make is anchored to you," Amelia said and licked the tears from her lips. "I'm leaving in two days, and there's nothing you can say to stop me."

Her father drew a deep inhale and conceded with his chin tucked to his chest. "You're right. I should let you go."

Amelia didn't know if he meant the party or her. She saw him clearly for the first time since their fight; not cold and needlessly cruel but devastated and reeling. He finally seemed to see her clearly too; not a darling disappointment but lost at sea and sinking.

She waited for something, anything other than his impassive stare. His lips pressed together, though, and in a rare moment, he curated his words with care. Amelia took the silent blow. The things he didn't say wounded her worse than those he did.

"A storm's coming, a bad one too. You and your mom be careful tonight." Insult to injury, he dug in his wallet and handed her three twenty-dollar bills. "In case the food sucks and you wanna stop for something on the way home."

Amelia took the money with nothing else to say. They talked in circles around what they were after—a sweeter past where they didn't exist like strangers.

He turned to his computer, a go-to conversation ender, and Amelia took her cue to leave. In her bedroom, she snatched her purse and slipped into a pair of flats then collected her mom before heading to the car.

When she fired up the engine, the radio babbled "Bad Moon Rising," the DJ's homage to nasty weather.

Up above, powderpuff clouds yielded to the black mass marching in, the sky no longer violently blue.

FOUR

AMELIA

Little Red—her father's name for the family sedan—rattled up the steep road toward the Dauer estate. Somewhere a bolt was loose, so it *rap-a-tapped* with too much gas and whined whenever it rained. Amelia gripped the wheel as wind rocked the car.

"Momma, I don't think Little Red is long for the world."

"Don't tell your father that," her mom said and flipped down the visor mirror. She ran a comb through her auburn hair a shade darker than Amelia's and inspected her teeth for lipstick. "He was on the phone when I went to say goodbye. Did he say why he's not coming?"

Work was the enduring excuse, but one her dad was judicious in wielding. He'd never missed the gala despite his growing disdain for Rich's opulence. Last year, he'd sulked in the corner while Amelia shuttled him champagne and crudité.

"Something to do with Rich. I overheard them talking."

Talking was an understatement, one that sopped up the distress in what Amelia had overheard. At Rich's name, her mom hummed a response and gnawed her bottom lip.

Someone once told her that married couples look alike after a while. That didn't happen to Amelia's parents. Instead, her mom inherited her husband's moods, so silent gloom lived on in the passenger seat as the car puttered through the Dauer estate's iron gate.

Nestled against Lake Oswego, the estate was impressive enough that Charlotte Dauer named it Lake Rose Manor. Amelia found that a strange thing, naming a house. Then again, some places demanded it, palaces with heritage and bloodlines erected in stone and splendor. Lake Rose Manor wasn't that.

It was a modernist monstrosity, boxy and sharp and lacking a soul. To Richard, a home had to be an artistic investment, so he commissioned a house that menaced over lush grounds while he dwelled in a pied-à-terre in the city. Amelia found that just as strange.

Despite its charming name, Lake Rose Manor didn't tolerate warm flourishes, only open spaces and lonely echoes. Even the hedges were pruned in unnaturally straight lines. It'd always been at odds with itself, but tonight tried at softness with sweet touches on an austere canvas.

Peony garlands festooned square columns flanking the entryway. The blooms burst in vivid color against grey stone, and their delicate scent infused the night. A dozen tall, wrought iron candelabras lined the walkway to the manor's entrance, though only a few still radiated hazy globes. The wind snuffed out the rest.

"You think it's me?" Amelia asked halfway to the door. "The reason he didn't come?"

Her mom slowed her pace. The chiffon layers of her skirt whipped around her slender frame and her hair lifted on the wind. "Of course not, my love. Why would you think that?"

Why wouldn't she?

The letter from Harvard Law came one rainy spring morning, and the weight of the paper alone said she was in. Harvard didn't send rejections on linen paper signed with a fountain pen. Her father had read the only word that mattered—congratulations— and exhausted his black book with the news.

"My girl got in," he'd told anyone who'd listen.

For Amelia, cold doubt had crept in unannounced. She

smiled big and put it to bed, but on sleepless nights, it tore her to ribbons from the inside out. When she confessed she wasn't Cambridge-bound, he raged with words he couldn't take back, and Amelia could've died on the spot but cried instead.

No one dies from rejection, though, and tears pass like rain, so she stood her ground but learned a painful lesson. Fathers only tolerated self-discovery in sons. "That's my boy making his way," they'd say. Trailblazer. Groundbreaker.

In daughters, it was the primrose path to ruin. Poor baby. Lost little soul.

"He probably told half these people about Harvard." Amelia motioned to the guests up ahead dressed in their finest. "If he came, people would ask, and he'd have to tell them I dropped out."

"It's none of their damn business, and I'll tell them that myself!" Her mom was soft-spoken with a gentle heart. There was fire to be found in her, though, and it burned bright with fights not yet had. She composed herself then asked, "You sure you wanna go?"

"Arizona? Of course. The job's lined up and everything."

The job was an editing gig at a local newspaper. The pay was decent, the hours reasonable, and she'd have the freedom to make a serious run at publishing her poetry. The work didn't matter so much as the escape.

Some nights, Amelia dreamed banal things like flat tires or missing paperwork thwarted her plans. The moment felt a bit like that, and her mom smiled as if sorry to dredge up bad dreams.

"I meant the party."

Amelia glanced back at the winding driveway as lightning cracked the sky. There was the rip cord if she wanted it, but the valet had already left with Little Red, and in polite society, no one ditched a party that early. Then again, Amelia didn't belong in that echelon. In a clearance rack cocktail dress, she didn't even look the part.

"What if we make our rounds for an hour then leave?" she offered, and her mother promptly agreed.

THEY SPLIT up inside to divide and conquer. Amelia cut through the kitchen or the mausoleum, as her dad called it to mock Rich's brutalist taste. With its sparse countertops, the room wanted for a pulse that it only achieved during Rich's parties.

In the great room, a sea of people milled about in glittering gowns and tailored suits. The hollowed-out space opened to the second and third-floor halls above and light installations reflected dully on polished concrete floors below. At the far end of the room, a tuxedoed man played a grand piano next to tall windows overlooking the lake.

Amelia edged along the museum-like walls accosted with abstract art but stopped at a new addition. Rendered in blood red and black, the painting depicted a demon, its face vaguely human except for luminous eyes that pierced the canvas. A gold plaque at the bottom of the frame read "Philippe Velasco Collection."

Of course. The painting was salt in a wound for her father to find.

Several months ago, Amelia's father secured a grand jury's indictment for Philippe, the man at the helm of the Velasco family. "Flip-Flop Philippe," the papers called him when he sought a plea deal. Rich Dauer was known for his defense of indefensible people, most notably Philippe. It'd caused strife with Amelia's father, their ideological differences too much to overcome.

"It was a gift," a man commented behind her.

Amelia turned to a barrel-chested stranger with a gap-toothed smile. He slicked back a tuft of unkempt brown hair, and fleshy belly peeked through the buttons of a wrinkled shirt.

"Philippe's been offloading assets since the indictment." He tipped his champagne flute to the painting and studied it up close. "Bold of Rich to flaunt this."

"You must not know him very well."

Rich would call it high art. He'd said that about his twelve-foot tall, blinding white canvas with a fist-sized red circle in the middle. "Looks like a Maxi-Pad on a light day," Amelia had joked, but it'd gone over like a lead balloon, up in flames when it hit the floor.

"I know him well enough. Martin Kranski," the man said and offered a limp handshake. "You're Cal's kid, right?"

"Yeah. Amelia."

"He's a good man, your Pop. I've known him for years. Burt too." He pursed his lips and shook his head. "Shame what happened."

Amelia agreed with a nod and an awkward beat of silence passed between them. Martin seemed pleasant enough but sipped his drink that looked unnatural in his hand—the glass too small, champagne not his drink of choice—and shifted unsteadily on his feet.

"Actually, I'm glad I ran into you," he said and fumbled in his back pocket. "I was planning to reach out. I've got some questions about the work you did for Dauer and Shaw."

Slotted between his index and middle finger, Martin handed Amelia a business card. A gold seal caught the light and glossy black letters announced his title—FBI Special Agent.

"I understand you were one of Burt's interns and may know about a sensitive matter he was looking into at the time of his death."

Warmth drained from Amelia's cheeks, and she skimmed the room for a friendly face. Anyone would do. She stared at another wallflower a few feet away, an older gentleman in a paisley waistcoat eating a bacon-wrapped scallop. *Please.* The man glanced at her but wandered off. *Fuck.*

Amelia cradled her elbows and feigned ignorance. "I did basic research, case law and whatnot. I don't know about a sensitive matter."

The best lies were woven with truth. Yes, she did his research, made his coffee, listened to his stories. But there was also that folder and how Burt had somehow become dangerously entangled in the Velasco-Moriarty feud.

Martin narrowed his eyes and drifted closer. His thin lips sunk in a frown. "It's very important we talk."

Amelia stumbled into the demon at her back. She gripped the gilded frame to steady herself. Burt had warned her not to tell the police anything but said nothing about the FBI. Amelia didn't know the conversion rate between the two, but it didn't matter. She'd promised to keep his secret and would.

"It was nice to meet you," Amelia said and meant to duck away, but Martin blocked her path.

"I know about the folder. Burt didn't want your name attached to it, so he told you to leave it alone. He had the Velascos' war plans, knew who's pulling the strings from the great beyond, and now you do too. You need to understand the target this puts on your back, the danger you're in."

Amelia calmly shook her head with a wooden smile, but the business card crushed in her fist, and her voice wavered.

"I don't know anything about that."

"Come by my office on Monday. We need to talk."

"I'll be gone by then. Besides, you seem to have what you need."

Amelia thrust the crumpled business card into Martin's clammy hand and turned to leave. She had even managed a few brisk steps, but the boom of his voice stopped her.

"Emory Holt."

Amelia's pulse pounded in her ears. She should have walked away but turned around instead. Martin downed the rest of his champagne with an annoyed flick of his wrist.

"I see that name rings a bell." Pleased as punch, he grinned and ambled toward her. "Burt destroyed the folder. That means you're the only person alive who knows what was inside it."

"Why are you telling me this?"

"If I were Emory, I'd want to know what was in that folder. His private jet landed at PDX this afternoon." Martin hovered close, the booze thick on his breath. He wasn't smiling anymore. "Emory Holt is coming tonight. Dollars to donuts, he'll be dying to meet you."

FIVE

AMELIA

Amelia fled along the wall of grotesque art and reached a less visible pocket off the great room—a sunroom that overlooked the estate's manicured gardens.

Anger coursed through her and settled in her belly with a resounding ache. She never wanted any part of her father's world. He forced her into the internship. *But you agreed.* He put her in an impossible position. *You could've said no.*

With shaky hands, she groped in her purse for her phone. She needed to leave before Emory Holt arrived and the storm did its worst. Amelia dug past a tube of lip gloss and her wallet. The purse was suspiciously light. She pried it open and surveyed its insides.

No phone. At home. On the charger.

Fuck.

It was too late. The storm arrived with a rumble of thunder, and a familiar face cut through the crowd. It was typical of Brian Burrows to come for closure at a time like this. Amelia's childhood friend, he lived next door to Richard but rarely attended the gala. Dressed in jeans, a t-shirt, and Chucks, he conceded only a black suit jacket for the occasion.

"Hey," he said with a smile that used to give her butterflies and smoothed a fall of loose brown curls from his eyes. "I hoped I'd see you here. It's been a minute."

"Yes, it has," Amelia agreed with a stiff smile, though forced platitudes were reserved for strangers. She'd known Brian before memory and relied on her parents to tell her all the adorable things they'd done together as toddlers.

As Brian summoned something to say, Amelia scanned the crowd for a natural exit. The party was too dense, though, and the dance floor packed with guests.

"Can I borrow your phone? I need to text my mom."

"Sure." Brian unlocked his phone and handed it over. "I didn't know if you'd already left town."

"I leave Sunday," Amelia replied offbeat as she tapped a hasty message.

its Amelia meet me out front we need to go

"Sunday," Brian repeated, vaguely dispirited as Amelia returned his phone. He never could commit to a feeling. "I meant to reach out, but time just…"

"Vanished."

And so had he.

Last summer had sizzled with balmy heat against bare limbs, swinging on the hammock with his hand up her shirt. They'd shared soft kisses in velvet moonlight, and her clothes had ended up on his bedroom floor.

The connection had faded with the fall, as most things do, and reality had chilled with a cold snap. They were better off as friends. At least, that's what he'd said and Amelia agreed, but her heart had broken bigger than she let on.

She'd mostly mourned the loss of her senses, that she'd conflated the comfort of a true friend with the intimacy of great love. Brian wasn't her great love, so she'd moved on and he hadn't even noticed.

"Arizona. I feel like I might never see you again." Brian stuffed his hands in his pockets and shrugged. "I'm sure Portland has editing jobs too, you know."

Amelia firmly shook her head. Every goodbye landed like a

ploy to make her stay. It only ignited the instinct to flee and forget the nightmarish interlude. Something nagged with screaming urgency to leave and that perhaps she was already too late.

"I can't stay here, Brian," Amelia whispered beneath the jovial thrum of conversation around them. Thunder boomed and rain lashed the windows. "I have to go. The sooner, the better."

"I guess I don't blame you. I'd get the fuck out of dodge too if the guy I worked for was 'suicided.'"

Brian's fingers crooked in air quotes, and his green eyes glittered with the bit of gossip.

Amelia tempered her interest with a slow exhale. "What did you just say?"

"Burt. I overheard someone here saying he was mixed up with the wrong people. They wanted him dead, so they made it happen."

Amelia gripped the strap of her purse and parroted the logic she'd used to console herself on sleepless nights. Looking back, it just seemed naïve and absurd.

"The police would know if he was murdered."

"Depends what side they're on." Brian gestured to the room where the driving beat of music replaced the piano dirge. "These people are morally fucked, Amelia. We both know the ends they go to for money and power."

Amelia studied the guests gulping down cocktails and crowding the dance floor. The party pulsed with a grim undercurrent. There was always tension between the eclectic rich and glossy public figures, but a certain darkness united the clashing castes of the disgustingly wealthy.

As if to prove it, a drunk woman doubled over with laughter and sent wine sloshing from her glass. She reached for her companion to steady herself but lost her footing and tumbled into Amelia before hitting the floor.

Amelia might have gone down too but stumbled into a solid mass behind her. Strong hands gripped her bare shoulders and guided her away from the shattered wine glass and people rushing over to help.

Amelia needed no more cues to leave. She turned to thank the man behind her and be on her way, but her heart nearly slammed to a stop when she saw his face. Nothing could have prepared her for the savage collision of reality and daydreams.

Emory Holt towered over her, taller than Amelia could have imagined, or perhaps she had no anchor to what a man of his size looked like up close.

His mugshot was a poor approximation of how utterly handsome he was, but it'd done him justice in one way. He peered at her with sharp intensity, his eyes the color of warm honey.

"Hi," was all Amelia could manage on a dumbfounded breath as the room faded at the edges in soft filters.

A gorgeous smile unfurled on Emory's lips and betrayed a warmth that surprised her. She couldn't reconcile it with his history of dark deeds.

"Hi." He laughed, and his gaze swept to her mouth, along her cheekbones, and back to her eyes.

Numbness spread in Amelia, starting at her knees. Turncoat legs went wobbly and weak and her constitution even weaker. They were close enough that she discerned his cologne—spicy and faintly sweet—mingling with the scent of clean laundry. Raven black hair hung in loose waves past broad shoulders, and he was swathed in well-defined muscle with thick arms and long legs.

"I'm so sorry," Amelia said with more weight than a mere pleasantry. Her contrition plumbed perilous depths, those nights she laid awake wondering what had come of him.

For the moment, she apologized for her hands resting lightly on his forearms inked in black tattoos. In a white dress shirt, Emory flouted pageantry with a few buttons undone and the sleeves rolled to his elbows. An unfastened black tie was draped around his neck, and he hadn't bothered with a suit jacket.

"You're fine, sweetheart. I don't mind." His subtle flirtation disarmed her. So too did the resonant rumble of his voice, deep enough to sink into. "Are you alright?"

Emory loosened his grip on her shoulders but let his palms

skim the length of her arms. Their eyes met with the quiet intimacy of his stolen touch.

"Yes, thank you."

Flustered, Amelia righted the dress strap that'd slipped from her shoulder. Emory watched her, seemingly transfixed by how she put herself back together. Or maybe he liked how she came undone, the way her hand trembled and breath hitched.

"I'm good for it anytime," he said with a wink and moved along.

Only then did Amelia notice his companions, two men on his left and one to his right. Across the sunroom, they lounged on the sofas in a close group with Emory central among the other three.

"Who was that?" Brian asked.

Amelia shook her head. "No idea."

The lie came easier than she would've liked, but the secret she hid was the ecstatic rush that left her reeling. His picture had planted the seeds of intrigue, and Amelia nourished them neatly until they bore strange fruit. Indulging in it would be a mistake, her better angels warned.

But the feeling of being watched was universal, primal even. It stuck to her skin and refused to be ignored. With odd affliction, Amelia gathered some gumption and glanced in Emory's direction. Sure enough, he studied her as if memorizing the shape of her body, her face, the way her lips parted with a shaky exhale.

Emory bowed his head and listened intently to the man on his right. With enormous blue eyes and dirty blond hair slicked back, he dressed much the same as Emory with tattooed forearms exposed and a dress shirt half-untucked. Whatever was said, Emory nodded slowly and stared at Amelia from beneath his brows.

She felt on display for him, entirely exposed and frozen beneath the weight of his gaze. Heat seeped across her cheeks and down her chest. She couldn't help the way her body betrayed her. Her heart beat wildly, the pulse settling between her legs.

I'm a good girl, she reminded herself.

But good girls didn't get themselves off to the mug shot of a dangerous man. They didn't fantasize about how he fucked or the damage his lips could do. They didn't crave someone like him who'd wreck her for sport and leave her in ruins.

Emory was a killer. Her fear of him should have eclipsed his allure. It *should* have. And yet, something compelled Amelia to keep his stare as she brushed her fingertips along the tops of her breasts in an exploratory touch. It was sensual for having been subtle, a moment everyone else in the room might've missed.

But not Emory.

No, he noticed, so the corner of his mouth lifted in a smile. Fiendish delight resided mostly in his eyes, though, as if he alone held audience to her most salacious thoughts.

And he wanted more.

With a slight tip of his head, he urged her to go on. In the middle of the party, he wanted a show. Amelia didn't know him and owed him nothing. And yet, she obeyed. She bit her bottom lip as her fingertips skimmed her thighs. Was it an invitation or just a ploy for his attention? Amelia couldn't quite say.

A man like Emory could have any woman he wanted, but he wasn't looking at other women. He was looking at her. Emory kept her eyes and nodded slowly. He wanted more, demanded it with the heat of his gaze and his jaw set firm.

Amelia's heart slammed in her chest. How far was she supposed to take this? As far as he wanted, it seemed. Her fingers crept up the inside of her thigh, just beneath her dress, and her lashes fluttered with a quiet sigh.

No longer smiling, Emory licked his lips and his Adam's apple bobbed with a hard swallow. He narrowed his eyes with a look that said, "I will eat you alive then fuck what's left."

And what if she let him? She could chalk it up to all the anger, fear, and confusion coiling inside her. The truth would claw its way out eventually, though. She wanted it, wanted *him*.

"Go on. Go talk to him," Brian said and scrolled through his phone's notifications. "Dude's eye-fucking you. He clearly wants you over there."

What the fuck am I doing? Amelia shook her head and

collected her composure, though her cheeks burned and hands trembled. Yes, Emory fascinated her, but some things were better left alone, and she was heading in the wrong direction. She needed out of this mess, not dragged farther in.

"No. I *have* to go," she insisted. "What did my mom say?"

"She's upstairs. Said she'll be down in ten. That's plenty of time to go talk to him." Brian grinned as he shoved his phone in his pocket. "Who the hell is he?"

"No one."

"No one, but not a nobody. Rich seems to know him. Look."

Amelia glanced over her shoulder. With one arm slung along the back of the sofa, Emory glared at Rich Dauer.

In years past, Rich planted himself at the party's epicenter to soak up the attention. His roaring laughter would echo through the mansion, a reliable indicator of both his whereabouts and drunkenness.

Tonight was different.

He rushed through the horde with his eyes downturned and lips contorted in a grimace. Rich had always been a handsome man with sandy hair and a syrupy Georgian accent, thick despite his years in Oregon.

Ashen-faced, quiet horror unseated his sly charm as he gaped at Emory, whose attention turned to two men across the great room. The men looked the part in black suits fit for the occasion, but the façade ended there.

They didn't drink or smile or speak. There were more men; two near the piano, a few more by the bar. All around the room, they stalked the sidelines like wolves encircling oblivious prey.

A black figure shifted in Amelia's periphery. She peered out the window beside her, across low-grown hedges, and into the kitchen. Like death in the mausoleum, a man stood at the window in a black coat with the hood obscuring his face. He turned his head and stared at Amelia with one coal black eye. The other was missing. A heinous smile festered on his lips.

Icy dread spilled down her spine. Amelia spun from the window as thunder exploded through the mansion. The lights cut out, plunging the party into darkness, and shrieks replaced the extinguished music.

Amelia dashed forward, ready to flee just as the lights and music returned. The crowd cheered. Her pulse flooded her ears. It was wrong. Something was wrong.

On high alert, Emory was on his feet and stared down the others invading the room. He issued what looked like an urgent command to his companions. The four of them rushed from the sunroom and followed Richard, who scurried up the stairs.

"What's wrong?" Brian asked, his face a mask of concern.

Amelia didn't know how to quantify. The night, the pit in her stomach, the strangers who shouldn't be there.

All of it was wrong. Horribly wrong.

"There are people here who shouldn't be," was all she could manage.

Brian scrutinized the great room. What was there to see? The drunks danced with dizzying delight, blithely unaware of something she couldn't put into words.

"We never know who most of these people are," he laughed, but the humor dissipated as Amelia gently nudged him away.

"I need to find my mom and get out of here. You should leave too."

"Leave? Amelia, what's going on?"

She didn't answer. Her legs compelled her forward, and she sprinted up the stairs. The lights flicked out, and the crowd gasped but broke into whooping applause when they powered on again.

Amelia rushed along the third-floor corridor and rounded a corner to another hall. Loud thuds and a pained scream sounded from the room next to the service staircase. Behind the closed door, angry shouts punctuated scuffling, as if two people struggled against one another.

She tiptoed to the end of the hall and ducked out of view a few steps down the service stairs. Behind the door, Richard pled on strained heaves. Amelia leaned in close to listen. The step beneath her groaned. The shouting stopped.

She silently slipped down the stairs, out of sight to the second floor just as the door above flew open and footfalls pounded down the steps. Amelia closed her eyes and crushed herself against the wall. The stomps stopped halfway down.

After a few seconds of agonizing silence, a man shouted, "No one's out here, Chief!"

She relished a sigh and sunk against the wall as the man retreated. A few moments later, the door above slammed open again and someone hurried down the steps. Her limbs locked as Richard rounded the newel post and barreled toward her, his face red and swollen and blood staining his dress shirt.

"Move! Let's go!"

Hot bursts of his breath hit her cheek, and his fingers cinched her arm. Amelia squealed and dug her heels into the runner rug as he dragged her down the second-floor hall.

"Stop! You're hurting me!"

"They're here for you," Richard said through clenched teeth, his eyes frenzied and unfocused. "You wanna die tonight?"

Wrenching her arm away, Amelia crumpled to her knees. Richard abandoned her and limped down the hall. She ran in the other direction, down the service stairs and to the great room where the music had stopped, but not from the storm. Soft confusion rippled through the party with excited murmurs and exchanged smiles.

"A surprise guest?" someone speculated.

With her heart beating out of her chest, Amelia opened her mouth to tell everyone to run, go, get out.

But it was too late. Gunfire erupted in the great room followed by blood-curdling screams.

SIX

AMELIA

Gunfire ripped through the crowd, and white-hot flames licked up the walls. Amelia choked on plumes of smoke as the petrified throng swallowed her up.

A palm sticky with blood collided with her cheek. An elbow cracked into her back. She screamed, one voice lost amongst the cacophony.

"God, help me!" a woman howled, half her face a bloody ruin and the skin sloughing from her skull.

Someone lurched forward.

Then another.

Three more.

Then four.

A stampede ensued. Amelia crashed to her knees. Her throat burned as she shouted for help like all the others. Her eyes stung and welled with tears. She couldn't see and tried to stand, but a man hurled into her, his knee slamming into her ribs.

Amelia landed belly down on something soft. A body. She was laying amongst bloodied corpses on the floor. Martin Kranski collapsed beside her with the back of his head wet with blood. Amelia closed her eyes and screamed for her mom.

A hand reached through the veil of smoke and grasped her forearm. In one firm tug, it pulled her from the tangled mass of bodies. Amelia slid across the blood-slicked floor but contorted in a desperate bid to regain her feet. When she did, the horde swept her up again as it crushed toward the foyer where men in black suits fired into the crowd.

A violent tangle ensued as half the crowd turned to flee from the foyer and the other half still plowed toward the front door.

A man yanked Amelia in front of him as a shield. She ducked as a bullet whizzed over her head and lodged in his throat.

"Amelia!"

Her eyes snapped to the sound of her name and Brian fighting his way through the crowd. His hand latched with hers. "Out the back!"

They ran through the great room where flames spread with blistering heat and billowed sooty plumes. In the kitchen, the desperate dying cried for help. On his knees, a man clawed at his throat and tried to speak. Nothing came, only blood oozing between his fingers.

"My mom! Where is she?" Amelia shouted as gunfire tore towards them and smoke rolled into the kitchen. Between the bullets and the blaze, they didn't have much time.

Brian shook his head and licked blood from his lip. "I don't know. I ran. I just ran."

"I have to find her," Amelia pled and tried to free her hand, but Brian squeezed hard and yanked her toward the back door.

"Amelia! We have to go."

"No!" she screamed and wrenched her hand away a moment too late.

Behind them, glass crunched.

Amelia whipped around. Emory approached with a gun drawn and trained on her. A spray of blood stained his cheek, and he looked every bit the brutal monster his reputation painted him to be.

Before she could run, he closed the distance, and his fingers clamped hard as a vise around her arm. Amelia writhed in his grasp, kicking and screaming as he tightened his hold. Her fingernails cut into his forearm, and her elbow rammed into his stomach.

Emory groaned, and she slipped from his grasp, but only managed two wobbling steps before tumbling to the floor. He was on top of her quicker than she could've imagined and tried to pull her up, but Amelia flailed, kicked, threw fists. Her knees and palms slipped against the tiles slick with blood.

Before she could crawl away, Emory flipped Amelia to her back. He sat on her legs and pinned her arms over her head. Amelia squirmed beneath him and whimpered as glass dug into her skin.

"Please! Please, don't!" she cried.

"Stop, or I'll kill you." Emory pressed the gun to her forehead and squeezed her wrists. Amelia froze, paralyzed by the fury in his eyes and the cold metal meeting her skin. "Get up," he commanded as smoke filled the room.

In the haze, Brian glided toward them with a paring knife and swung as Emory shifted his weight. The blade sliced his back. With a groan, Emory gnashed his teeth and Amelia freed her legs from beneath him. She stumbled to her feet and fled with Brian out the back door.

Outside, rain lashed her face, and the squall howled in her ears. Wet earth filled her shoes as they sprinted through the gardens, wove through shrubs and trees, trampled over flower beds.

What was it that bid her to look back? Gruesome curiosity. Panic and fear. Emory. Surely, he'd be coming after them. Amelia turned to look, but he wasn't there, and the gunfire slackened as she and Brian ran down the hill and slipped through a small break in the fence.

They hurried across his yard and through his back door to the kitchen. Soaked and shaking, Brian slumped against the wall, and Amelia huddled next to him. His mouth opened and closed, but only heaving breaths spilled out.

Bursts of lightning lit up the dark. A clap of thunder soon

followed, but a handful of sounds went missing—a yapping bark and scampers across the tile floor.

"Where's Minnie?" Amelia whispered.

Footsteps creaked above. Someone was there.

"Your parents?"

Panic pooled in Brian's eyes that locked to the ceiling. He shook his head.

"Let's go," he mouthed.

In quiet movements, he freed his keys from his pocket, but they slipped from his clumsy fingers and hit the floor. The pacing above abruptly bounded for the stairs.

In one sweeping motion, Brian snatched his keychain, and they ran for the garage. In his car, he fumbled with the keys, his hands violently trembling.

"Brian, hurry!"

The engine turned over as the garage door opened behind them. Amelia's breath caught in an agonizing pang in her chest. In the driveway, a silhouette of a man was set against the volatile sky. He dropped the hood of his black coat and lifted an assault rifle.

Brian threw the car into reverse and slammed the accelerator. The engine roared, and the car smashed into the man who careened to the cement.

He sped down the winding hill, cutting through water that gushed from the storm drains and breeched the road. They raced past the Dauer estate, indiscernible amongst the blaze, and shot onto the main road where felled tree limbs lay in a tangle.

"Look out!" Amelia shrieked.

Brian jammed the brakes. The car spun into the oncoming procession of bleating sirens and flashing lights. Tires squealed and horns blared. Amelia cradled her head in her arms and braced for impact.

SEVEN

AMELIA

The car jostled to a stop.

Nothing came.

No mangled mess of metal.

No broken glass.

Just the sirens screaming up the hill and Amelia's breaths exploding from her lips. She cracked her eyes and peeked through the sliver of space between her arms.

On the shoulder of the road, the car had missed the guardrail by mere inches. Amelia peered over the edge to the lake water lapping at jagged rocks below. They sat in heavy darkness and even heavier silence. Amelia didn't know how long it lasted, long enough that her panting breaths slowed and Brian's hands mostly ceased their shaking.

"What the fuck happened?" he asked so softly Amelia wasn't certain if she was meant to hear, much less answer.

"The storm knocked the trees—"

"I don't mean that."

Acidity hit the back of her throat as horror snapped into focus. Amelia spun in her seat and ignored the sharp sting of glass that'd buried in her arms and legs.

"My mom! Give me your phone!"

She held out her hand, but tears wet Brian's cheeks as he shook his head.

"I dropped it when they started shooting. Maybe she got out."

Out.

The word gutted in a way Amelia hadn't accounted for. Her mom had been upstairs. She could have hidden from the gunmen, but the fire was inescapable. Amelia's hand flew to her mouth and muffled a gasp.

"Oh God. This isn't happening."

In a daze, she stared out the windshield. Reality escaped her, and she tried to anchor herself to anything tangible. Even pain eluded her, buried beneath surreal detachment. She bit her lip hard just to prove it wasn't a dream but to no avail.

The wipers struggled to keep up with rain pelting the glass and, across the road, trees thrashed with the wind. The night had gained shades of dark with thick clouds and streetlights knocked out by the storm.

"You said there were people at the party who shouldn't have been there," Brian said. "What did you mean?"

Amelia rubbed her arms to drive in warmth, but her icy fingers accomplished little. Neither did her mouth that couldn't summon an answer. It was too much to explain with her head a mess and thoughts muddled.

"I—I don't know."

A flash of lightning illuminated Brian's scowl. In the dark again, she still felt his heavy stare.

"You knew something, Amelia."

Yes, she did, enough to know they needed to leave, enough that she could've done more, said more. Weighed down with shame, she slouched in her seat.

"There were people there who didn't belong. Richard panicked when he saw them."

Brian hesitated and, for a moment, nothing manifested on his parted lips.

"They didn't just come in right off the bat killing everyone. I think they were looking for certain people."

For me. Amelia studied the empty road. It offered no reassurance but unnerved with eerie exposure. Her stomach soured and hands wrung in a grip so tight her knuckles ached.

"Brian, I think I'm in trouble."

The leather seat crackled as he fidgeted. "Trouble how?"

"Burt knew things he wasn't supposed to, information about the Moriartys and the Velascos. War plans, apparently. It was in a folder. I saw it by accident."

"Why would he have that?"

A question for the ages, Amelia shook her head. Another police car barreled past them in a blur of whirling lights. *We need to leave.*

"Who else knows?"

"No one. Burt made me swear not to tell anyone. I didn't, but I don't think that matters now. They already know I've seen it."

"Who? The Velascos or Moriartys?"

"I don't know. Probably both."

Brian fixed his eyes on the rearview mirror as a downpour battered the car.

"The tall guy with the black hair. I know you know him. Who is he?"

"Emory Holt," Amelia whispered and instantly understood the contempt her father put on his name. "He's Chief of the Moriartys."

"Jesus *fucking* Christ. What if…"

The thought hung unspoken like forbidden fruit neither would pluck. There were too many "what ifs" to ponder.

What if Emory found her? What if they planned to do to her what they did to Burt? What if it wasn't the end?

That seemed certain. The events were connected in a fated tapestry and Amelia could follow the thread that warned it wasn't a tragic one-off.

"We need to leave," she said. "You can drop me off at home."

Brian gaped at her. "Are you out of your fucking mind? I'm not doing that!"

"And I'm not putting you in danger! If they want me—"

"Then they'll find you exactly where they expect you to go. Something awful is going on. We both know that much. It's not safe to go home."

Amelia battled the instinct to argue. It was the watershed moment that read from the margins the thing they hadn't yet said. Only the hunted hide. There was no going back.

"We should go," Amelia said and glimpsed the lake waters below that churned in tandem with a restless sky. "We'll get as far as we can until we're safe and then reach out for help."

"As long as we stay together, we'll be fine."

Brian said it like a pact as he pulled from the shoulder, but it resonated like an ill omen. Along the lake road, the comedown from adrenaline abandoned them both in static shock. Warm air blasted from the vents, but Amelia couldn't shake the chill that soaked to the bone.

"South?" Brian asked when they approached the main highway bisecting Portland.

She fiddled with her purse strap. North meant passing the exit to her house. Everything she loved was north. South led nowhere.

"Yeah," she whispered and rested her head against the window. The condensation wet her throbbing temple.

Brian navigated the on-ramp, and they journeyed with a gulf of silence between them. It continued past Eugene and farther still when the radio crackled with the twang of a lovelorn cowboy.

Eventually, the rain let up, but in its place, thick fog enveloped the road, and the lamp posts dotting the highway thinned. The only light illuminating the car was the dashboard and occasional high beams from passing travelers.

Brian examined the rearview mirror and slowed until a lone car passed. When it did, he flicked off the radio and glanced at Amelia.

"I need to tell you something."

Amelia sat up and winced as glass cut into her with a painful throb. "What is it?"

"I overheard something at the party. These two guys—cops, I think—were talking about the Velascos. They said there's something strange going on. It's like their whole MO changed."

"Changed how?"

Fear washed over Brian in stunning fashion. It momentarily staid his tongue before dampening his voice.

"It's dark. Like, bad juju or something. The brutality of the things they've done." He withheld whatever it was for her sake. "They seemed pretty spooked by it."

It must've spooked Brian, too. He nervously cleared his throat and rubbed the back of his neck.

It didn't make sense. To Amelia's father, the Velascos were the known quantity. They were flashy and prone to flaunting their connections and wealth, which meant they got sloppy. The Moriartys were the ones to fear with their doctrine of death and ruthlessness that couldn't be tamed.

"Are you sure they weren't talking about the Moriartys?"

"Positive."

"Did they say why it's happening?"

"That's the thing. No one knows what's changed, just that they're more violent and depraved, like someone else is calling the shots. Tonight had to be them, right? I mean, did your dad ever mention anything about this?"

Amelia shook her head. "He thought the indictment was a done deal, that he had Philippe Velasco where he wanted him and that was it."

"Clearly, not."

Unease crept in with goosebumps that blanketed Amelia's skin. Headlights flickered behind them once more. The engine roared with Brian's foot heavy on the pedal until the gas light flicked on. Brian stared at it like the cause of catastrophe.

"It'll be okay," Amelia said. "I saw a sign for a station a mile back. It should be coming up."

At the next exit, Brian pulled off the highway and released a shallow sigh when the car behind them continued into the fog. A mile down a country road, he turned into a vacant gas station.

A corroded tin overhang feebly sheltered four pumps, two of which were out of order. A metal sign hung on rusted chains and groaned with the wind. "Frank's Fuel and Auto Repair," it announced in paint-chipped letters. Next to the pumps, a mechanic's garage looked abandoned with its windows coated in a greasy film.

Brian killed the engine and scrutinized the tiny gas mart attached to the garage.

"Let's hope someone's in there," he said. "We won't make it to another station."

Minutes stretched on, but the attendant hadn't appeared. Brian thumped the steering wheel, and his foot tapped the floorboard. They'd have to go in, that was clear, but he refused to budge.

Amelia patted his knee. "Come on. We'll go together."

Outside, her bare legs prickled against the night's chill. Amelia peered through the garage's grimy window. A single bulb hung from the ceiling and revealed shelves filled with dented canisters, rusted tools, and piles of junk. Whoever Frank was, he wasn't repairing cars anymore.

Amelia led the way inside the gas mart where fluorescent light cast a dingy glow. It looked as though the place had been left to rot. Dust blanketed a handful of sparsely filled shelves. The only sign of life was the mournful warble of "Ramblin' Man" pouring from the speakers. They loitered at the counter covered in yellowed plastic. An ashtray next to the register overflowed with stale cigarette butts.

"Hello?" Brian shouted.

Shuffles sounded from behind a door labeled "Employees Only." It flung open, and a hulking man settled beneath its frame in tattered jeans and a sweat-stained shirt. Greasy grey hair framed a bloated face.

"I'm closed," he barked but leered at Amelia.

"Sir, we really need gas," Brian said. "We won't make it to another station."

"You got cash? No cash, no gas. And I won't pump it for you."

Spittle gathered at the corners of the man's cracked lips. Brian's eyes darted to Amelia, and his skin paled as she shook her head. She never carried cash. The attendant pointed to the door for them to leave and turned back to his hovel.

"In case the food sucks and you wanna stop for something on the way home."

"Wait! I've got it," Amelia called after him and fumbled through her purse.

She handed the attendant two twenty-dollar bills. He snatched them from her, but his beady eyes gleamed with greed.

"All of it."

"This is all of it," Amelia insisted.

For a moment, he looked poised to call her bluff, but grumbled to himself and jabbed at the register.

Brian discreetly slipped Amelia the car keys. "Get in and lock the door."

She obeyed and, from the passenger seat, supervised Brian's scrimmage with the clerk until a car pulled in. Her eyes shot to the rearview mirror where headlights beamed from a beat-up Buick. The driver rummaged through the glove box before kicking open the door.

Amelia scooted down in her seat to go unnoticed. Gravel crunched in deliberate steps. Maybe they just needed gas. Why then did they park at an out-of-order pump? The steps stopped behind Brian's car. She squeezed her eyes shut.

Go away. Please go away.

The slow crunch started again, then something lightly tapped the top of Brian's car.

Tap, crunch, tap, crunch.

The sounds came closer until the driver stopped outside Amelia's door.

EIGHT

AMELIA

A knock cracked at the window.

Amelia knew it was coming but still flinched. With another knock, she opened her eyes. A man stared through the glass, his eyes buggy behind thick glasses. A chipped tooth left a small, jagged hole in his smile.

He looked like her high school science teacher—goofy and affable with a flannel shirt stuffed into jeans. The similarities ended there. Something not quite harmless stirred in his eyes.

When he circled his wrist for Amelia to roll down the window, her panicked gaze snapped to the door lock.

"Sorry if I scared you," he shouted and acquiesced with lifted hands. "I was wondering if you could give me some directions."

He flashed a hopeful grin, but Amelia tucked her elbows to her side and dropped her chin to her chest.

"Miss, I just need some help. I'm not from here. Where I'm from, folks help each other out. It's what our good Lord would want."

Don't be rude. Isn't that what he meant? Do what he said or burn in hell branded a bitch?

Fissures formed in his righteous placidity. His smile vanished, and the man abruptly stalked off but only to take a call.

He paced next to his Buick with a smartphone pressed to his

ear, and an uneasy pit formed in Amelia's stomach at the request. No one with an iPhone needed directions from another human being.

Brian hurried from the gas mart to the pump. He fussed with the nozzle and slid into his seat.

"What did he want?" he asked with heavy scrutiny on the Buick and its driver.

"He said he's lost and needs directions."

Amelia couldn't remember if she'd seen him at the party. If he'd been there, he made quick work putting himself to rights.

"How is he lost? We're right off the highway." Panic on the rise again, Brian reached in his pocket for his phone that wasn't there. "Fuck, fuck, *fuck*!"

"It's okay," she said calmly. They couldn't both lose their shit. "Let's get off at the next exit. We can make some turns and see what he does. If he follows us, we'll find the nearest thing open and call the police."

Though Brian agreed, the plan was swiftly moot. The man climbed into his car and disappeared down the country road. If he meant to find his way again, he was heading in the wrong direction.

They left the station as the clock hit one-thirty. The numbers burned in the veil of darkness behind Amelia's eyes. Leaned against the window, she twilighted in and out of restless sleep and woke worse for the wear with sore legs and a splitting headache. She'd lost time too, a couple of hours' worth.

Along the empty, southbound highway, fluorescent signs dotted the service road, every icon of American consumerism standing tall and proud in the night. Columns of light bled through the windshield and refracted through drops of fresh rain.

Amelia glanced at Brian with his eyes trained on the rain-slick road. "Where are we?"

"Medford."

Medford was the last real town before they ventured into the wilderness, yet Brian barreled past its exits.

"Where are we going?"

"Sacramento. My parents are there for the weekend. My dad will know what to do."

The stretch ahead wound through hilly terrain. With the rain returning, their travel would only become more treacherous.

"Brian, Sacramento is another five hours, at least. We should stop and get some rest."

He stirred in his seat as a lone car passed. "Let's get into California. We can stop at the first town over the border. It's not that far."

Not that far, but so far from home. Leaving Oregon felt like leaving behind the known world and the promise of safety.

"Okay," Amelia reluctantly agreed, "but only if you let me drive."

Brian put up no fight. On the shoulder of the last Medford exit, he stumbled to the passenger seat. After ten minutes, he was out, but his limbs jerked and head tossed. With every twitch and groan, he surely relived the nightmare in his sleep. Soon enough, Amelia would too.

The suburbs thinned, and Medford's glow faded. The road curved through craggy slopes, and the hills beyond were black giants in the night. Every so often, passing headlights illuminated the road before disappearing into the folds.

The world around them had gone silent and dark, as if she and Brian were the last souls on earth, running from fleeting shadows and monsters made real.

The rain eased to a drizzle as Amelia crossed into California, but thick fog blanketed the road, and the first handful of exits snaked off into pitch-black hills. A few exits down, Amelia spotted a sign for a town nestled in the valley.

That town boasted only a church, gas station, and school. At its edge, an abandoned factory loomed with broken windows and graffiti-covered walls. Piles of scrap metal and decaying cars made up the perimeter. Across the street, neon lights announced a motel. Amelia pulled into its parking lot invaded with weeds.

The place probably hailed from the sixties and had changed little since. Painted in faded pastels, twelve rooms—six to each floor—opened to the outside. Out front, a rusted fence encircled a small pool, its sagging cover green with algae. She parked next to the only other car and killed the engine.

Brian rubbed his eyes and squinted at the vacancy sign.

"You've got to be fucking kidding me."

"You said the first town in California." Amelia motioned to the featureless horizon around them. "This is it. The first *real* town."

Brian pinched the bridge of his nose and sighed. "Shit. Alright. Let's go."

Out of the car, Amelia winced as she stretched, the glass nagging beneath her skin. Brian shucked out of his suit jacket and rummaged through the backseat.

"To hide the bloodstains," he said and offered Amelia his blue and grey striped sweater.

Amelia yanked it on and followed him into the motel office. A door chime trilled off tune as they entered but didn't rouse the young clerk behind the counter. He puffed on a cigarette and swirled the antenna of a tiny TV as "I Dream of Jeannie" bounced in and out of signal.

Everything about the place was frozen in time. Their steps squelched across a pus-colored linoleum floor, and an old calendar hung on a wood-paneled wall.

At the counter, Brian cleared his throat. The clerk's eyes drifted between Brian and Amelia. A tawdry implication was baked into his sly grin, though his voice remained impassive.

"You want the hourly rate?"

Brian glared at the clerk, but before he could reply, Amelia handed over her last twenty. "How long will this get us?"

The clerk cupped his chin and mulled it over. "Two hours, but I'll give you three." He took the cash and slid a room key across the counter. "You'll be in six, other end of the lot."

"Thanks. I appreciate it," Amelia said and collected the key. "Also, do you have a pair of tweezers, by chance?"

With a sidelong glance, the clerk examined the dried blood on her fingertips. Unfazed, he sifted through a drawer of random junk.

"No tweezers," he said but waved a pair of needle-nose pliers. "Will these work?"

Amelia didn't rightly know. The ends were blunt and not made for picking out glass. With no other options, she took the pliers and thanked the clerk.

Outside, Amelia scanned the empty lot and discerned the factory through the fog. Beyond that, she couldn't see the road and listened for passing traffic, but heard nothing, just moths flitting against the light outside their room.

Amelia unlocked the door and switched on a floor lamp. Stains splotched the room's mauve carpet, and an air freshener did little to mask stale smoke. A room was a room, though, and they needed to sleep.

Brian must've had the same thought. He flopped to the bed, unbothered by the pilled comforter dusted in crumbs. Amelia peeled off the sweater and tossed it next to him.

"I'll be back in a bit," she told him and disappeared into the bathroom with the pliers.

A fluorescent light above the sink buzzed as she studied her reflection in the mirror—skin wan, hair tangled, mascara smeared beneath exhausted eyes. Blood and wine stained her white dress.

With trembling hands, Amelia flipped on the water that gushed from the spout. She dunked a sliver of soap beneath the stream and scrubbed the dress's skirt. She dunked again, scrubbed again. Water sloshed from the sink and flooded the counter. All that mess and the soap didn't help. It just made it worse. The stains were set. They'd never wash out.

Hot tears spilled down Amelia's cheeks. She hadn't cried yet. *What kind of monster doesn't even cry?*

With a gasping breath, she scrubbed harder, the skirt soppy and sudsy and the stains stubbornly refusing to lift.

Mom will know how to get them out.

Amelia stopped. The thought surfaced so casually cruel.

Water babbled in the drain and the soap crushed in her fist. She went down hard with sobs deep and keening.

On her hands and knees, she cried like a child. Like the time she lost her mother in the grocery store. Like the first day of kindergarten waving from the school bus with a backpack twice her size, those see-you-soon moments of gone momentarily.

She cried because there was always a last goodbye, and the lucky ones saw it coming. She cried because she knew in her heart she wasn't so lucky, and no one expected the end to come like that.

Brian hurried into the bathroom and blotted out the vanity's garish light. He pulled Amelia from the floor and held her against his chest until her cries lulled enough that she could breathe again.

"We should get the glass out," he said, his breath humid against her temple. "You'll feel better."

Amelia nodded, though better was relative. Maybe it was catharsis for them both. The pliers met Amelia's skin with pain and left with relief as Brian meticulously pulled the glass free.

When he was done with her arms, he crouched to the floor and started with her calves. Amelia steadied herself against the edge of the counter until he was done.

"There," Brian said, still squatted behind her. "The smaller pieces will work their way out. I'll leave you to it."

He ducked from the room, though there wasn't much to leave her to. Amelia ran a wet washcloth over her limbs. She was still a mess, but it'd have to do.

Out of the bathroom, the room was dark, all but the muted TV that spilled blue light across the floor. Amelia slipped out of her shoes and onto the bed next to Brian.

Against the headboard, they sat shoulder-to-shoulder. A lone cricket chirped in the corner and the room hummed with the sleepy buzz of late-night TV.

"That Moriarty guy," Brian said haltingly. He cleared his throat as if there were more, but the statement floated in the static.

"Emory."

"You've never met him before tonight?"

Amelia didn't answer at first. She stared at Brian and tried to discern why it mattered. He probably only meant to fill the silence, but the question probed uncomfortably.

"It's just...it seemed like you two knew each other."

He didn't mean the eye-fucking, she knew, but the moment that preceded it—her and Emory's hands on each other like a muscle memory and locked at the eyes with the indelible sense of having already encountered one another. Amelia could step outside herself and bear witness to the magnetism that suggested she and Emory were far more than strangers.

Amelia toyed with the snap of her purse still draped across her body.

"No. I don't know him."

But she knew that Emory was born in Puerto Rico on New Year's Eve. She knew he had a faint scar that started at his top lip and ended at his nostril and was more visible when he smiled. She knew how her heart pitter-patted and body hummed with him near. She knew how his weight felt on top of her, how their bodies fit together, how he pinned her arms over her head.

She also knew he was possibly involved in no less than seven murders but, ever a mafia boss, had no direct ties to any. She knew that he invested in commercial real estate through suspected offshore shell companies. She knew he traveled frequently to San Juan where he funded gambling rooms and nightclubs as a possible front for arms deals.

Did Brian believe her? Amelia couldn't say. Regardless, he withheld judgment with a sleepy smile.

"I wanted to tell you at the party, but I guess now's as good a time as any. I met someone and it's gotten serious. I'm looking at rings. She's nice. You would've liked her. You *will* like her."

Brian rocked into Amelia, a gesture meant to soothe, but there wasn't any heart left to break, and his confession came with less calamity than he probably expected.

"I'm sure I will," Amelia said, and it wasn't meant to placate.

Someday the horror would fade, and they'd stitch together some semblance of normal. She'd meet the girl who won his heart and be happy for them both.

Brian interlaced his fingers with hers and squeezed to draw her gaze. "Amelia, you're my best friend. I'll always love you."

Before she could respond, a knock pounded on the door. Amelia yelped, and Brian bolted up. They waited in petrified silence until a voice filtered through.

"It's Eric from the front desk. I need you to move your car."

Brian crawled from the bed and, with the chain fastened, cracked the door.

"Yeah, sorry. Rain's coming and our lot floods," Eric explained. "Just park down here and you'll be fine."

"Sure thing."

Brian grabbed the keys from the nightstand but was gone before Amelia could protest, out the door before she could follow. After he left, she pulled on his sweater again and watched the curtained window.

Minutes passed, and nothing came. No tires crunching. No headlights beaming. Amelia climbed from bed and slipped into her shoes but stopped as she reached the door.

Take the pliers, some instinct warned.

She obeyed and crept into the chilly night with the pliers in hand. Brian's car hadn't moved, but the engine hummed, and headlights pierced the dark. The open door whined with an incessant chime.

Amelia hurried to the car, but a groan stopped her. She spun around to the sound.

On the ground near the pool enclosure, a body stirred. Brian, it was Brian. Brian contorting in pain. Brian seeping dark liquid across the gravel.

Amelia ran over and collided to her knees by his side. His cheeks glistened with tears, and blood oozed from his belly.

"Brian! Brian, please! Look at me!"

With shaky hands, she cradled his cheeks, but his head lolled to the side and blood spilled from his mouth.

"No! Brian, please don't!"

Amelia laid her head on his chest. Her heart raced, and she confused the pulse in her ears for his. When she lifted her head, his vacant eyes were fixed on the sky. The light was gone.

It came then, just like before. A crunch of gravel. A shuffling step.

Amelia's head snapped up. No longer bug-eyed, the man from the gas station had removed his glasses and ditched the flannel for a white t-shirt. He flashed a sadistic smile and pointed a gun at her.

"Come on. Hands up. Do what I say."

Amelia scrambled on all fours. Jagged rocks sunk into her hands and knees until she regained her feet. The man charged at her and hollered something she couldn't understand.

She sprinted across the lot and then the street, her feet slipping on rain-slicked grass as she bounded toward the factory. The man laughed as Amelia darted between rusted cars and ducked for cover, though he didn't shoot.

"Give it up, Amelia!" he shouted. "You know how this ends."

She broke from the maze of decrepit vehicles and bolted onto the road. A pair of headlights hovered in the distance but grew larger as the car sped toward her.

"Stop! Please!" she screamed and waved her arms with the pliers clutched in her fist.

The car screeched to a stop, and the front doors swung open in unison, but the men who climbed out weren't strangers. They'd been at Richard's party as part of Emory's cohort.

"Fuck," Amelia whimpered and turned to run but collided with the man from the gas station.

The hard hit knocked the air from her lungs and the pliers from her hand. His fingers clamped down on Brian's sweater, loose against her body, and he hurled Amelia to the ground.

She thrashed against his weight on top of her and clawed at the mud, reaching for the pliers until her shoulder screamed in pain. Her fingertips brushed the rubber handle.

Amelia grabbed hold and swung hard. The pointed end

burrowed in the soft flesh of the man's cheek and ripped it open. He howled in pain and toppled off her.

"Stupid fucking bitch!"

His fist cracked against her cheek in a powerful blow. Pain seared, bright and blinding, and Amelia's vision blurred as she collapsed again. Her body lifted from the ground.

I'm floating, she thought as her limbs hung loose and weightless.

Something wet her cheek. Blood or rain or tears, Amelia didn't know as she closed her eyes and surrendered to the inky dark.

NINE

AMELIA

Amelia swung her arms in the dark. She found a wall and mapped it out until she reached a door. Faithful fingertips followed the wood grain down until a cold kiss of metal met her touch.

Through the door, she was out of the dark. Lamp light pooled on a desk covered in coffee-stained folders and tattered papers that rustled in a phantom breeze. Through a large window, gnarled trees swayed against a bedeviled sky where night yielded to crimson dawn.

A man stood in front of the window. Even with his back to her, Amelia recognized the weight of the world on his shoulders and the burden of duty heavy on his mind. She staggered toward her father, but her limbs moved like cinder blocks through water.

He turned around, but it wasn't her father she found. Emory flashed a sinister smile. Cavernous holes existed where his eyes should've been. Blood bubbled from the floor vents and streaked the walls. The dead weight in Amelia's legs lifted. She turned to run, but a shadow gathered her hands behind her back.

"Wake up, you fucking bitch!" the shadow screamed with piercing cruelty.

The ruby-hued darkness faded, and Amelia opened her eyes.

Through groggy vision, she discerned the man from the gas station straddling her in the back seat of his Buick.

By the sweater clenched in his fists, he yanked Amelia up then slammed her down again. She groaned through the assault and struggled against him, but a thin rope bound her wrists and sliced into her skin.

"That's enough, Damon."

One of Emory's men ripped Damon off her and dumped him outside the car.

Amelia's consciousness ebbed and flowed like a black tide closing in, and her temples pulsed with every heartbeat. One of Emory's men pulled her from the backseat and expected her to stand, but her useless legs couldn't hold her weight when he propped her against the car. Amelia slid to the ground and squinted against the light.

A desolate two-lane road stretched in a straight shot toward both horizons. In the distance, a mountain range towered over the barren desert dotted with tufts of greasewood bushes and cactus scrub.

Where the night had been chilly and humid, the sun rode high and sweltered with suffocating heat. It had to be midday, but where exactly was she? The desert spilled into California from Nevada. If they drove through the morning, she could be burning alive in Death Valley.

Amelia tried to stand but instead slumped against the Buick roasting in the heat.

"Please. Just tell me what you want," she pled, but Emory's men ignored her.

An eternity passed beneath the angry sun. The men wiped sweat from their brows and scrutinized the road. West or east, Amelia couldn't say. The twin horizons boasted the same shadowless features. Eventually, a black car emerged in the distance.

"It's about goddamn time," Damon said.

The car grew from a wavy mirage and kicked up plumes of dirt as it pulled off the road. Through heavily tinted glass, Amelia couldn't see the occupant, but her stomach dropped when the driver climbed out. At Rich's party, he'd sat next to Emory with amusement then dread filling his big blue eyes.

His blond hair was still greased back, but he wore all black—snake-skin cowboy boots, a plain t-shirt, and jeans with a handgun tucked in the waistband. A wallet chain jangled with each step he took toward them. On his arms, sleeve tattoos displayed colorful pin-up girls nestled amongst a patchwork of strange symbols and bolded letters.

"Well, I, for one, didn't dress for this weather," he laughed. "It's hotter than Satan's asshole out here."

Amelia struggled against Damon, who dragged her to the driver and shoved her to the ground at his feet. Dirt and rock scraped her knees, and her dress shifted up her thighs. With bound wrists, she frantically pulled it back down again.

"I want my money, Jack. Ten grand cash. And I expect to be compensated for the trouble."

Damon pointed to the gash on his cheek. The driver, Jack, strode to the Buick and poked his head in the backseat.

"Where's the boy she was with?" he demanded to know from the other two men.

One shook his head regretfully, but not for the life taken. To them, Brian was just a messy little tidbit. Amelia seethed at the thought but kept her mouth shut.

"That's just *fucking* great." Jack slammed the backdoor shut and paced to Amelia but pointed at Damon. "And you have the stones to demand payment?"

Crouched in front of her, Jack brushed his fingertips beneath Amelia's chin. She flinched at the contact and refused his stare.

"I'm not gonna hurt you. Just let me see."

As Jack scrutinized her collection of injuries, Damon's assault on Amelia turned verbal. He peppered it with slurs—slut, bitch, cunt, a few she'd never heard—and detailed the ways he could have violated her body but hadn't.

Amelia's stomach lurched. What was to say he hadn't? She'd lost time, hours unaccounted for where he had full control.

Jack stood with his fists clenched at his side. "Where were you two when he did this?"

Once more, the question went to the other two men who couldn't summon an answer, so they looked away.

"You get paid when she's delivered," Jack told Damon. "That was his agreement."

Damon shifted on his feet, and his gaze darted between the three men before returning to Amelia. He hurried to the Buick and flung open the passenger door, but Jack hastened after and wrestled a pistol from Damon. With one arm coiled around his neck, Jack pressed the gun to Damon's head.

"Wrong move. We're going for a ride."

Jack dragged Damon to the Mercedes, shoved him screaming into the backseat, and flung the door shut. He chucked Damon's gun at the other two men.

"Get rid of it on your way back. Chief's in a mood, so decide amongst yourselves who's gonna take the lumps for this shit show."

The men retreated—one to the Buick and the other to the car they came in—and rolled out in quick procession down the dusty road.

Amelia swung one leg out from underneath her and tried to stand. With nothing to hold on to, she stumbled to the ground again and sucked in deep breaths that filled her lungs with dead heat. Jack helped her up and regarded her with curious eyes. While he didn't leer, his gaze loitered all the same as he led her to the car.

Amelia wrested from his hold, but he snatched her by the elbow and pushed her against the car. She went limp until he loosened his grip then threw her weight in the other direction.

Jack corralled her again and shoved her harder the second time. He no longer regarded her with pity, only frustration that dangled on the precipice of anger.

"Listen, there are no two ways about it. You're coming with me, okay? That's it. That's your option. You can make this harder by struggling, or you can get in. If it's all the same to you, I'd rather you just get in the fucking car."

Amelia swallowed hard despite a dry mouth. She'd sooner burn alive in the desert than go with him. She could bluff, tell him he would be in a world of trouble when her father found her—it'd surely be soon—but the road had remained empty the whole time, no other souls in sight. She was alone, and Jack was right. There was no way out of it.

Amelia climbed in but garnered no relief from the cool leather seat against her skin or the blast of cold air from the vents. Next to her in the backseat, Damon mumbled to himself. Amelia cradled her arms to her chest and pressed her knees against the door.

Jack glanced at her through the rearview mirror but turned to Damon and said, "If you try anything, I will slit your throat and watch you bleed out."

The warning went ignored. Damon chewed a fingernail and bobbed one knee with a nervous tick. When Jack started down the desert road, Damon's rambles grew louder, and he clawed at his cheek that seeped blood anew. Jack cranked up the music until Johnny Cash's baritone drowned Damon out.

The benefit before was drugs, whatever they'd given her that robbed her of time and ushered in the darkness. At least Amelia didn't suffer in silent panic then. The pain returned too. The thin rope rubbed her wrists raw, and her limbs throbbed with a dull, relentless ache.

She closed her eyes and thought of home, silly little details to distract herself—just how many moving boxes crowded her room? In how many family photos did her dad wear that one sweater? And what was he doing? He must know something horrible happened, but a terrifying notion occurred to her.

What if he didn't know? What if they sifted through the ashes of Rich's party and told him she was dead?

The car shifted as Jack sped through turns. Amelia tried to memorize them, but inertia pushed and pulled, and she lost track of time. They must've driven for an hour before the sway of each turn became less forceful and Jack pulled into a garage. Light streamed into the car when he climbed out.

He spoke with two, perhaps three, other men. Amelia strained to listen, but something cold nicked her neck. Her eyes darted to Damon holding a knife to her throat. Every muscle tensed, and she fought the instinct to jerk away.

"I could kill you so easily," Damon whispered against the shell of her ear. "Wouldn't you like that?"

Amelia squeezed her eyes shut and huddled against the car door. *Do it then,* she wanted to scream. It'd be better if it were quick, but the door swung open, and she tumbled out at Jack's feet. He helped her sit and pulled a folded buck knife from his pocket. When he lifted her bound wrists, Amelia scooted away.

"I'm not going to hurt you. Give me your hands."

Twice, he'd said that. He could say it all he wanted, but bound and taken against her will, he was insane to expect her trust. Bent over with his hands propped on his knees, Jack hung his head in tired resignation.

"You wanna be tied up all night? Not my thing, but to each their own."

Laughter filled the garage from four other men. Amelia scanned the space and the other three vehicles parked beside Jack's. Fluorescent lights hung on chrome chains, and the other end of the garage boasted a heavy steel door.

Amelia licked her bottom lip and tried to control how badly she shook. If she offered her hands, Jack might cut her open and laugh with the others as her blood bathed the floor.

He waited for her answer. That alone must've meant something. *You can't fight. Just do it.*

Amelia offered her arms and held her breath as Jack sliced through the rope. The men observed with something between sympathy and concern. It was their concern that terrified her the most, as if they were privy to her fate.

Jack led her to the door at the back of the garage. Two men followed, while the other two fetched Damon from the backseat. He held open the steel door. It led to a dimly-lit corridor long enough that Amelia couldn't see where it ended, the underworld perhaps. She hesitated at the threshold, and her eyes darted to Jack.

"Come on. Emory's waiting," he said.

Amelia shook her head as if she had any say. "What does he want?"

The question momentarily stumped him, the answer perhaps complicated.

"You," Jack replied with a sinister smile and nudged her into the hall.

TEN

AMELIA

The corridor echoed with the footfalls of Amelia, Jack, and the others following close behind. A series of single bulbs overhead offered meager light. Amelia inhaled shallow breaths that smelled musty and alkaline like asphalt after the rain.

The hall ended at a heavy wooden door where conversation filtered through. The rhythm bantered, but the words were muddled, and the tone straddled the divide between boisterous and subdued. Something in the middle ground unnerved her, and Amelia meant to be brave but couldn't manage the task as Jack shouldered open the door.

Alarming normalcy existed on the other side. A basement lounge exuded shabby elegance with brick walls and distressed wood. Gas lamps imbued a steady amber glow, and mismatched oriental rugs laid in a patchwork against wide-plank floors.

The space fit the two dozen or so men milling about but still managed stripped-bare intimacy. A handful of men gathered around a large, oval table, their voices rising over the pulse of moody music.

A mahogany bar ran along the longest wall. A few men nursed cocktails there between drags of cigarettes, and a handful more swayed with pleasured intoxication. The camaraderie flowed as freely as the booze, it seemed.

Jack regarded the room with evident pride. "We shadow walk tonight," he told her as if Amelia should know what it meant.

She didn't and only assumed it was an obscure reference to the horrors ahead. Her head spun, but she didn't ask and tried to keep pace as Jack cut across the room. Curious eyes followed like falling dominos as she went. A secret passed from lips to ears, ears to lips, and manifested on puffs of smoke, the haze of which hung thick and pungent in the air.

In the corner was an alcove closed off to the rest of the room. Jack stopped at the gossamer drapes in its entry way and assessed Amelia's injuries. With the pad of his thumb, he wiped the trickle of blood from her throat but gave up the effort when she jerked away.

"In here," he said and held open the drapes.

Amelia planted measured steps inside. It was a noble effort not to slink in defeated, but her heart thumped a frantic beat when she saw Emory there.

He engulfed the leather wingback he sat in. Like Jack, he wore black—t-shirt, jeans rolled at the ankle, motorcycle boots—and his inky hair hung loose about his broad shoulders. A handgun and rocks glass laid on a coffee table in front of him.

Time and terror had distorted Amelia's memory and diminished the piercing quality of his stare. His eyes gleamed citrine in the muted light, but agitation unseated stoicism as his gaze roamed her battered body.

Amelia abandoned her stubborn commitment to bravery. She could stand firm and speak loudly, but Emory would see the truth of what she was—caught and petrified. She turned to flee, but Jack blocked her path, and a hoarse laugh sounded from the corner.

Amelia hadn't noticed the other man sitting there but recognition clobbered her. Unlike the photograph in her father's office, Liam Moriarty didn't smile, only observed in a pressed black suit and his grey hair parted to the side. The cigar he puffed flurried ash, and he muttered something to Emory.

Amelia expected an old man to have handed over his legacy,

but Liam looked to be in his late fifties. Then again, the Moriartys weren't dusty La Cosa Nostra with rigid traditions. The mixed identity of ages and ethnicities in the other room proved that. So too did Emory, in his early thirties and capable enough to inherit an empire.

"What happened to the other kid?" Emory asked Jack, his voice as deep as distant thunder.

Brian. Jack sighed small and shrugged even smaller. He spared so little, but an almighty inferno raged in Amelia. Soon, she'd erupt, but Emory beat her to it, and his fury flooded the alcove for all the wrong reasons.

"Who's cleaning it up?" he demanded as if it mattered to him.

Yes, who sopped up the blood with a dirty dish rag? Who retrieved Brian's body from the pot-holed parking lot? Who sewed his eyes shut so his parents wouldn't have to tuck him into a casket with milk-foam pupils peeled to the sky?

When Jack didn't answer, Emory shot from his seat, snatched his gun, and tore through the gossamer veil. The din beyond dampened with his presence, all except Damon ranting maniacally.

Jack tugged Amelia toward the lounge, but she pinned her heels to the floor and turned to Liam because somewhere on her father's desk was a picture of a kind soul with a warm smile.

He offered no warmth, only a solemn nod as if to say, "This will go better if you obey."

In the lounge, Jack pushed a chair against the wall and gestured for Amelia to sit. One man shoved Damon to the floor, and the others circled around. Emory squatted in front of Damon and hoisted him up by the front of his shirt.

"What did I tell you before you left?"

Blood seeped from Damon's cheek and dribbled down the front of his shirt. He glanced at Amelia.

"You said you wanted her alive. So what I broke her pretty face? That bitch got far less than she deserves."

"Wrong part. What did I tell you?"

Quiet at first, Damon's huffs devolved into deranged laughter. When he didn't answer, Emory shouted over his shoulder.

"Jack, what did I tell Damon?"

"We don't tolerate messes. You wanted it done quick and clean. No blowback on us."

Emory stood, but Damon also sprung to his feet, crashed through the circle, and lunged at Amelia. A scuffle ensued as Amelia braced for impact. Emory snatched Damon by the back of his shirt and hurled him to the floor. The other men broke with laughter, and Amelia lost her last shred of composure.

I can't do this. She buried her face in her hands, which reopened the cut there, and released a gasp at the blood on her fingertips. When the men turned to her, she averted her gaze to the tips of her shoes clumped with dirt. The circle opened to let Emory through.

Towering over her, he evaluated her for a moment then freed a pristine white handkerchief from his pocket and flung it into her lap. Amelia dabbed her cheek with it and didn't care that her blood splotched the cloth. He'd made a mess of her life. She'd make a mess of his.

Back in the circle, his boots thumped a bellicose beat as he paced in front of Damon.

"I said quick and clean, and what did you do? Ice the kid, leave him there, and bring her to me a bloody mess. Now, we're left cleaning up after your sloppy shit show. Everything I told you not to do, you did."

Damon scrambled to his feet. "I want my money!"

Emory seized him by the throat and slammed him into the wall. "You're a fucking lunatic."

Legs thrashing, Damon clawed at Emory's wrists and, with what must've been his last full breath, spit in his face. Without hesitation, Emory dropped Damon to the floor, aimed his gun, and fired. Damon's right knee exploded with a spray of blood.

Amelia squeezed her eyes shut. With another deafening pop, Damon expelled a blood-curdling scream. She opened her eyes to a gory sight.

Damon squirmed on the floor, blood pooling beneath the pulpy ruin of his knees. The other men watched with grim satisfaction as he cried for help. It was nothing to them. Damon was crazed, no doubt, but was also bleeding out and howling in pain. Emory looked on without remorse, and the other men venerated him because of it.

He turned to the two men perched against the wall. "Shut him up."

One man removed his shirt and gagged Damon with it. The other dragged him across the room to the door at the back. A dark smear of blood followed. Emory ripped the stained handkerchief from Amelia before trailing after Damon and the other two men.

A hand rested gently on her shoulder. Amelia craned her neck to Liam standing next to her. He was shorter than she expected, and his pale grey eyes betrayed fraught weariness.

"You've seen enough," he said and frowned at the bloodstains on the floor.

In the alcove, Liam motioned for her to sit. Amelia eyed him as he sunk into his armchair and retrieved a half-smoked cigar.

"I don't have the stomach for that shit anymore," he said. "I'd rather sit on my ass and talk to a lovely woman like you."

Amelia stared at the dirt and dried blood beneath her fingernails. Everything—back, limbs, head—throbbed with pain, and she struggled for something to say.

"Thank you. That's kind."

Was it kind? Or simply a lesser shade of awful? She fumbled with the sleeves of Brian's sweater scratchy against her skin. Liam exhaled wisps of smoke and studied her as if passively gleaning what he could.

"I have no reason not to be kind to you."

"I can think of a few."

Charmed, Liam chuckled, but the amusement quickly fled. "Careful now. That shit won't get you far with Emory."

As if on cue, a single gunshot fired from somewhere beyond the lounge. Not long after, Emory tore into the alcove. Amelia's back peeled from the chair as he tossed his gun to the coffee table and resumed his spot across from her. Jack followed him in, and they exchanged a few hushed words.

Amelia's eyes drifted to his gun. She'd never fired one before. How hard could it be? Aim and shoot. He was engrossed, distracted. She slipped to the edge of her seat. Liam stirred as well. When she glanced at him, he shook his head.

"The clip's empty, and you're not that brave," Emory warned with an icy stare from beneath his dark brows. "Go get Mirabelle," he said to Jack, who cantered off as music resumed in the lounge.

The prodding beat didn't preclude conversation and yet there they were without words. Amelia took the opportunity to study Emory up close, and he did the same.

She searched his face for vestiges of regret. His jaw—sharp and well-defined—set firm in a scowl, and the weight of his gaze had changed, but Amelia couldn't define the delta. Curiosity, maybe; questions that sizzled on the tongue but expired there too.

With blood-stained fingers, he scratched at the dark stubble peppering his chin.

"Amelia Havick," he said with false reverie that mocked her outright. "I'm sure Cal is proud; his baby girl following in his footsteps all the way to Harvard."

The irony deserved laughter Amelia couldn't manage. She found some nerve and held her head high when it mattered most.

"That information isn't hard to find," she said, but a tremor ran through the declaration that popped like a sad balloon.

Emory conceded with a wry smile. Amelia couldn't discern the faint scar on his lip in the low light but searched for it as if it might lead her back to his good graces; that moment they shared as strangers and his touch warm against her skin.

"You're right, except you backed out. You're nothing like him, never could be. Where are you heading again? Arizona? You want your freedom, an escape, a place to hide and pretend this never happened. I saw you at the party and you know what I thought? Lost. You looked lost. No one and nowhere to belong to. Why else were you so eager to touch yourself for me? You need someone to claim you, make you whole. Is that it?"

His statements calcified and pelted her like rocks, one after the other, until the last few crushed like boulders. Tears surfaced, not for fear but humiliated exposure. He might as well have stripped her naked and read her like a poem, the ones she'd written, but never shared, the ones buried deep.

Voyeur to her misery, Emory watched her cry. He leaned back and clasped his hands behind his head. Tattoos inked the outside and inside of his thick biceps. Beneath them, a collection of long, thin scars had healed and marred the images that adorned his skin.

"Your old man isn't the only one keeping tabs. I keep up with him too."

Amelia licked the tears off her lips and let the rest dry on her cheeks. She could unravel later. Now wasn't the time.

"He isn't like Richard," she said. "He won't have the kind of money you're looking for."

Emory's brows lifted with genuine surprise. "You think I wanna ransom you? No, that's not why you're here."

"Why then?"

His gaze roamed her body, peeling back layers again with cutting precision. Something like fondness softened his eyes momentarily, that gauziness of sweet recollection. On him, it just looked deadly. Amelia yanked on Brian's sweater to cover more of her thighs. Emory smiled at that.

"You tell me. Something was off last night. I know you felt it. The people who shouldn't have been there, the ones watching you. It's why you ran, wasn't it? Anyone else would've gone home, but you ran. Why?"

Faltering again beneath his unremitting gaze, Amelia said nothing.

"Residual haunts," he answered for her, plucking the words from her lips, though she had no intention of speaking them. "Burt and his big, bad secret. Nice of him to offload it onto you. He didn't kill himself, by the way. The Velascos murdered him."

Still comfortably seated with a smirk, Emory observed her

closely. She meant to rob him of the reaction he wanted, but she was easy to read in the best of times, and it seemed Emory Holt had a knack for laying her bare.

Amelia steadied her breath and looked away, but it only stoked his curiosity. Emory leaned forward and rested his forearms on his knees.

"You don't look surprised. To most people, that'd be shocking news. Not you. Why is that?"

It didn't matter how little she gave. He already knew how she wore shock and horror, the way it stole her breath and painted her face. Amelia cleared her throat and clung to the lie for dear life.

"I didn't know he was murdered."

"But you suspected it. The way it happened, the timing. It didn't add up. Burt uncovered something important enough that the Velascos wanted him dead. Whatever it was, you know it too."

They arrived at the heart of the matter, and Amelia stood trapped in a minefield at the center. One move too sudden, he'd blow the lid. She pursed her lips and shook her head.

"I don't. I was just his intern."

Emory slid to the edge of his seat, and his long fingers stretched as if he considered placing a hand on her knee. He dipped his head to force her stare, but Amelia refused. Still, he dominated her downturned vision. She glimpsed the ropes of defined muscle slatting his forearms and recognized the subtle sweetness of his cologne.

Ensnared once more, her eyes flicked to him, but they weren't on even ground. He was beautiful and awful, and she was a terrified mess. Amelia looked away and sunk back in her chair until the spindles dug into her spine.

"Look at me," Emory rasped.

She obeyed but focused on how the dim light played against his cheekbones.

"You know, and you're here because you're gonna open up and show me all those secrets you have inside."

Worse than his explosive anger was the slow simmer of a dangerous man and the calm that slackened his voice to a gravelly whisper. If only exhaustion could turn her fear into flippant resignation.

The closest she came was indignation. Amelia's dirty fingernails dug into her palms. She held the tension in her body until it was tight as a bow.

"Why would I tell you anything?"

"Because you know who I am."

"I don't," she lied again.

"You do. Say it."

Amelia's heart pumped with a fresh flush of adrenaline. "Emory Holt."

Studious in his fascination, he watched the way his name left her lips then settled back with a satisfied smile.

"I know more than just your name," Amelia added defiantly. "My dad told me about the things you do."

Emory sipped his drink with a bitter laugh. "I'm sure he did, sweetheart, but you don't fucking know me."

And he intended to keep it that way. He'd know every intimate inch of her being, but she could never hope to do the same. Her fear, intrigue, and desire for him unraveled and gave way to loathing.

Amelia hated his certainty, his stoic composure that claimed the upper hand, the handsome smile still soft on his lips. She summoned her bravery and pummeled him with the dirty truth, the ways she knew precisely who he was.

"I know you had something to do with what happened last night and the innocent people who died at that party. I know you had Brian killed, and I know you'll do the same to me. I know enough to know what kind of man you are."

Smile wiped clean, Emory slammed his drink to the table and looked like he might come across it to beat her bloody all over again.

Good.

She'd make it easy.

Amelia gripped the armrests and shifted to the edge of her seat. Emory did the same with cheeks flame red and chest heaving.

He opened his mouth to unleash vitriol, but Liam lifted a hand to intervene.

"Okay. Enough." Liam shed his placidity as he turned to Amelia. "Think twice before you sling accusations like that. We had nothing to do with last night. How dare you accuse us of something so heinous."

"I saved your life," Emory added. "A little gratitude would look good on you."

Amelia's eyes shifted between the two men, stunned at the absolute absurdity of their demands. She understood now her father's chimerical dream for the hard hand of justice to squeeze out the Moriartys' last breath. For the past few years, he'd chased down a man who eluded him at every turn. Amelia sat in front of that same man and pegged him for more than just his name.

"You're a monster."

Hands on his knees, Emory's knuckles flushed white, though he didn't stir. His visage darkened as if a shadow passed over, but he spoke quietly for only the room to hear because someone hovered outside the alcove's veil.

"You don't know what a true monster is, the kind who want to rip you apart and watch you suffer through every breath, the kind who want you, specifically, Amelia Havick. I'll happily send you to them and we'll see then if you still think I'm a monster. I don't give a fuck what happens to you, if you live or die."

He leveled his furious gaze at her, and Amelia's chest tightened, but she didn't look away. She also didn't take Liam's advice to mind Emory's temper because there was a glaring flaw in his fuming diatribe.

"If I'm nothing to you, then why come after me?"

Emory's lip twitched and nostrils flared. The longer Amelia refused to kowtow, the more incensed he became. If that was her only stand, she'd take it.

Tension infused the space between them, and the room stifled with rising heat. Locked at the eyes, neither looked away. Someone had to back down.

It wouldn't be her.

She refused.

So did he.

"Answer me," Amelia demanded and leaned in close. "Emory Holt," she added, soft and artificially sweet.

Brows furrowed, he looked equally confused and aroused.

"Don't play that game with me," Emory warned and met her ingress with just a sliver of space between them. "You won't like how it ends."

"You don't know what I like."

"Then let me find out." With a lick of his lips, he tilted his head and narrowed his eyes. "You gonna eat your words, baby?"

Head swimming, Amelia's heart nearly pounded out of her chest. The pulse at Emory's neck fluttered just the same. It was madness, a foray with fire, and they'd both go down in flames.

Amelia tipped her chin and uncrossed her legs. "Are you?"

"Sit on my face and let's find out," he fired back with a wicked grin and stared between her bare thighs. "I hear I'm great at eating pussy."

Amelia opened her mouth. She meant to refuse, to tell him he was disgusting and awful and she'd *never* let him go down on her or anywhere for that matter. Nothing came, though. No clever comeback or staunch refusal; just Emory's husky laugh, so evidently amused at leaving her speechless.

A woman breezed into the alcove on a rhythmic click of heels. Mouth agape, her amber eyes bounced between Amelia and Emory.

"What the fuck happened? She looks like hell." The woman gently squeezed Amelia's shoulder. "I'm sorry, honey, but you do."

Slim and tall, the woman looked to be in her mid-twenties. Her jet-black hair—pin-straight and glossy—fell to mid-back, and heavy, blunt bangs framed her heart-shaped face done up with winged eyeliner and red lipstick.

"Damon," she said and pointed a red-manicured finger at Emory. "I told you not to trust that psycho. You're too goddamn stubborn for your own good, Em."

Liam chuckled, and Emory didn't argue but pushed from his seat and collected his gun.

"Take her upstairs. I'll come get her after shadow walk."

Emory loomed over Amelia but waited to speak until she acknowledged him. If that were the condition, they'd be there all night. With a massive hand, he roughly gripped her chin and tipped her head to meet his stare.

"We're not done," he said on a smoldering hush. "In the meantime, you'd better decide what your life is worth to you."

Emory released her and disappeared beyond the curtain. Though out of sight, his presence and warning were still very much felt.

ELEVEN

AMELIA

The woman took the steps in a hurry, bouncing up them like a bright-eyed school child. Amelia gripped the rail and refused to match the rhythm. In the middle of the staircase, she stood at a crossroads with the devil she knew down below and the one she hadn't met up above.

"I'm Mirabelle," the woman said and loitered on the top step. "Sorry you were with the boys for so long. If I'd known, I would've gotten you sooner."

In a polite gesture, she extended a palm, but Amelia refused that too and let the sleeves of Brian's sweater swallow her hands.

"I'm Am—"

"Amelia. I know. He told me."

Mirabelle's red lips curled in a sly smile as she pushed through the door at the top of the stairs. It deposited them at the end of a long hall adorned with framed photographs and exposed wood beams up above.

Amelia trailed after Mirabelle and eyed the images they passed —black and white pictures of uniformed men, women with victory-rolled hair, leather-bound youths. *This is someone's home,* she realized.

Mirabelle cut through a parlor tastefully appointed with woven rugs, furniture carved from dark wood, and a rounded stucco fireplace. Pocket doors opened to a foyer equal in its warmth and splendor. Its eggshell walls offset vibrant Spanish tiles lining the risers of a staircase that spiraled to a second and then third floor.

Up above, a stained-glass ceiling gleamed in jewel tones. It depicted wildflowers, vines, and vaguely humanoid figures rising toward a central sunburst as if ascending to the heavens.

Through the foyer's arched windows, the sun expired in pink and gold. The same time yesterday, Amelia had stood in her father's office. *The hell he must be going through.*

Mirabelle marched up the stairs to the second floor and down another hall. Her swaying hips kept beat to the tune she hummed. Amelia didn't know what to make of her or how she fit into Emory's strange underworld.

Somewhere the filter between mind and mouth dissolved, so she asked, "Are you his wife?"

Mirabelle stopped at a door halfway down the hall. "Why do you ask?"

"I don't know. I guess how you talked to him."

"Smart girl. Not everyone gets to mouth off to Emory. You'd do well to remember that."

Twice, Amelia had heard that; first from Liam and then Mirabelle, who didn't follow the advice either. Then again, it wasn't really advice, but a directive, maybe even a threat. They dipped into a bedroom, immaculately clean and filled with the scent of fresh-cut roses.

"Mother, sister, wife," Mirabelle said and disappeared inside a walk-in closet. "That's who gets to mouth off. It's a privilege not even Jack, his deputy, is afforded." She returned with an armful of clothes that she heaved to the bed. "Obviously, I'm not his mother, and I'm sure as shit not his wife."

"Sister," Amelia said, though it went without saying. The resemblance to Emory was obvious—jet-black hair, bronze skin, striking amber eyes.

"You got it." Mirabelle plucked a few items from a dresser drawer and tossed them to the bed. "We're about the same size.

Everything should fit." She gestured to an attached bathroom. "Get cleaned up. I set some things out on the counter for you, but use whatever you want, and take your time."

With sweet smiles and soft touches, Mirabelle exuded warm hospitality. Perhaps she expected it to mask the bitterness of Amelia's situation. Heap on the sugar so the horror goes down. Her overtures, however sincere, rang hollow.

"Do you live here?" Amelia asked.

Charming as the room was, it didn't look lived in. With a few empty suitcases stacked in the corner, it had the liminal transience of a hotel room. It was a simple question, but apprehension occluded Mirabelle's bubbly confidence.

"For now. It's complicated. We probably won't be here for very long."

We. The word unnerved with how it forced Amelia into a collective she wanted no part of. Before she could pry any further, Mirabelle fluttered from the room, and her heels clicked down the hall in a rhythm that no longer pranced but prodded.

Amelia retreated to the bathroom and locked the door. The space was blindingly white and pristine, probably hard to clean. Her mom would've hated it because white exposed everything. Not there, though. It smelled like bleach and the decorative soaps her Grandma Havick displayed during the holidays, the ones no one was allowed to use.

Mirabelle's toiletries lined the counter in neat rows from tallest to shortest. She'd even arranged her make-up brushes like a flower bouquet in a faceted glass holder. Her perfume bottles— not one or two, but three—sparkled in the glittering light. Everything was as pretty as a picture and almost as perfect too.

Funny how things changed. As a teenager, Amelia bemoaned her tiny bathroom with its abysmal lighting and terrible water pressure. Back then, she'd thought it was a travesty. She would gladly take that shitty little bathroom over Mirabelle's spotless one.

She flipped on the shower and peeled off Brian's sweater and her purse beneath. In front of a dressing mirror, her wrecked reflection was almost foreign. No one ever expected to see themselves that way.

A red mark cut across her throat, and there was another on her cheek. Dirt caked the lesions on her wrists, and dried blood flaked from the gashes on her arms and legs.

When steam rolled from the shower, Amelia stepped inside and winced as water rushed over the cuts and scrapes. At least they'd heal with time. The ache in her chest might never. It grew heavier as she watched the water turn pink with blood that circled the drain.

I'm alone.

No, it was worse than that. Alone meant left with strangers or forgotten in an empty room. That was the least of it. She was lost. Her phone was at home, and her hand-me-down purse had stuck with her all the way. No one would find it in the motel room or with a busted strap on the side of the road.

To the outside world, Amelia Havick perished in the blaze. They'd print her name in the newspaper and call her death a tragic loss.

She should've read the tea leaves that warned her. If she'd ditched the party, her mom would have too. Because of her, her mother was likely dead.

And Brian. He'd be alive if they'd kept driving. Instead, he'd died in a weed-infested parking lot. His parents would bury him six feet deep and never recover. Their friends would remember him for his book-smarts but never his bravery that saved her life.

It should've made her sad. Somewhere it did, somewhere far off, like a silhouette on the distant horizon. But a haunting chill prevailed, and Amelia relished how it numbed.

Head against the tiled wall, she stood beneath the shower until the water lost its warmth. Only then did she wash her hair and soap her skin.

Out of the shower, she wrapped herself in a towel, combed the knots out of her hair, and brushed her teeth. In the bedroom, cool air invited goosebumps as she evaluated the clothes on the bed. They were mostly dresses that would cling to her figure or show off her legs. She wanted to hide in Brian's sweater and go unseen.

Amelia ran her fingers over a white, summery sundress, something her mom would have picked out for her. She closed her eyes and conjured her mom's voice and the honeyed scent of her favorite perfume.

Remember, remember. Memories would fade, surrendered to time. One day, she'd forget. *Gone. Poof.*

Amelia opened her eyes and scanned Mirabelle's room. The harlequin bedspread and embroidered pillows, so colorful and bright. Fresh-cut flowers in crystal vases, so joyful and pretty.

Her breaths came hard and fast. It wasn't fair. Glass lamps and beaded shades, the light so supple. Her stomach roiled. She'd be sick. And the exquisite clothes meant for her to wear. They weren't hers, though. She didn't ask for it, didn't want it.

Amelia's nails dug into her palms. *Remember, remember.* It was already fading, a dandelion wish in the wind. *No, no, no.*

Poof. Gone. Goodbye.

With a giant swell of emotion, Amelia came undone.

She swung her arm across the nightstand. The vase of powder pink roses crashed to the floor. The petals scattered, and water seeped along the hardwood's grain. Her throat burned, and tears stained her cheeks. Amelia swung again. The lamp exploded against the wall.

Dark satisfaction filled her up and begged for more. God, it'd feel so good to destroy these beautiful things, to smash them into a million little pieces.

Before she could swing again, Mirabelle bounded into the room. Her baffled gaze darted to Amelia, who stood breathless on the other side of the bed. With guilt written on her face, Mirabelle reached out a hand and guided Amelia to sit on the bed next to her.

"My brother will be back later and wants to talk to you," she said and ran her fingers through Amelia's damp hair. "I could do your makeup. I'm decent at it. I do it for my girlfriends all the time. I know I always feel better when I feel pretty."

With a roll of her shoulder, Amelia unburdened herself from Mirabelle's touch.

"I don't want to be pretty for him. I don't care if he thinks I'm pretty."

"No, that's not…" Mirabelle frowned at her hands wrung in her lap and shook her head. "I didn't mean it like that. I just thought it'd make you feel better. I'm only trying to—"

"Whatever you're trying to do for me, don't. I just want to go home."

Home. It slipped through Amelia's lips thin and quiet.

"Please just tell Emory I want to go home. I need to find my mom. He listens to you. Please."

Mirabelle eyed the open door and chewed her bottom lip.

"I can't. I may be his sister, but I don't make decisions. I know none of this makes sense, and I'm sure Emory will explain, but things will get better."

"You don't know that!" Amelia cried and flew to her feet. In her perfect bedroom with glossy hair and beautiful things, Mirabelle's life was neatly put together. The fucking gall to say things would get better. "You don't know anything about me. My dad is looking for me, and when he finds me, Emory will pay for what he's done. He kidnapped me and had my friend killed. What kind of person are you that you can stand by while he does terrible things?"

Amelia stood tall, but the pride in taking a stand dissipated as Mirabelle slinked toward her, eyes ablaze with her own rage.

"You're what, twenty-two, twenty-three? I hear you've lived a real nice life, and I bet you think your father will swoop in and fix this. Well, I got news for you, baby. Your daddy can't stop what's coming, and just because Emory saved your life doesn't mean he won't put you in the ground without a second thought."

Amelia clutched the towel knotted at her chest and shuffled backwards.

"Careful." Mirabelle pointed to the shards of glass a few inches from her bare feet. "You think Emory's a monster," she said, her anger doused temporarily. "I heard you say it. He's right, though. You don't know what a monster truly is. Our other brother. He's the real monster."

"Is he what's coming?"

Mirabelle contemplated the twin gashes on Amelia's cheek and throat but skirted the question.

"I just meant that things have gotten dark. More violence, more death. Emory's trying to figure out why so he can stop it. If he were truly a monster, do you think he'd bother?"

Though rhetorical, Amelia still declined an answer and asked another question of her own.

"Where's your other brother?"

Fear splintered Mirabelle's façade of strength. She drew a long breath and whispered, "I don't want to talk about him. I shouldn't have brought it up." She snatched a black, long-sleeved dress from the bed and chucked it at Amelia. "Get some rest before Em gets back. You two have a lot to talk about."

Amelia shook her head. She had nothing to say to Emory, not unless he knew where her mom was or would let her go home.

"I don't want to talk to him."

"You have to."

Mirabelle scooped up the other dresses from the bed and leveled a look at Amelia that entreated her to comply.

"I won't tell him anything."

She only meant to test the waters, but Mirabelle dumped the clothes in the closet and laughed at her expense, that she'd be so foolishly brazen.

"That would be a mistake."

"He can't make me."

"He can and he will."

"I'll only tell him if he lets me go home."

That was a lie, of course. She wasn't telling him anything, but Mirabelle ignored her and started for the door. The finality fire-started something in Amelia. That woman didn't call the shots. What could she possibly do? Amelia tried anyhow, frenzied in her desperation.

"My mom, my dad, they need me. Please. I have to go home. I *have* to."

Somber tranquility washed over Mirabelle. Only bad news was delivered that way. It wasn't news to Amelia, though, just the brutal truth that Mirabelle breathed to life.

"You can't. There's nowhere for you to go back to, nowhere that's safe. Only here."

Amelia unraveled with a gasping cry. *Don't let them see you this way,* her dignity warned, but grief battered the walls she'd built. They came tumbling down and so too did Amelia as she fell to her knees. Mirabelle followed her to the floor and pointed to the suitcases in the corner.

"I have a life too, a place where I belong outside of this." She gestured to the bedroom that apparently wasn't her own. "So do Emory and Jack. We're only here because something is happening that we don't understand, something that will tear us apart if we let it. We can't let it."

Cross-legged, Mirabelle sat like a mirror in front of Amelia with enormous sorrow in her eyes. Whatever her past was, she bared a bit of it on the floor, a peek behind her mask of painted smiles.

"It scares me," she admitted and nervously glanced at the door. "The men—Emory, Jack, Liam—they'll never admit it, but it scares them too."

Amelia nodded sympathetically, and her heavy heart slowed its beat. The shadow lifted from Mirabelle, the light in her eyes no longer dim.

"I need to finish dinner before they're back. Rest. I'll bring you food in a bit."

Mirabelle pushed from the floor with a sudden call to duty. What exactly was her duty? Make their meals, tend to menial tasks? Amelia didn't ask about that or what the mothers, sisters, and wives did, or if mouthing off was their only "treat."

On her way out, Mirabelle stopped at the door. "Amelia, you're not as alone as you think."

TWELVE

EMORY

The shadow walk commenced beneath a blanket of stars. With dull flashlight beams guiding the way, Emory and Jack walked in step, their boots colliding in unison against cracked desert. Emory's grip tightened around the hilt of a blade.

Behind them, the twelve Moriarty captains followed in two columns with Liam taking up the rear. At the very end, the initiate walked with his back to the wild unknown.

He couldn't be more than twenty, if Emory had to guess. It was hard to tell these days, and initiates came to him the same—full of piss and vinegar and with some perceived chip on their shoulder.

By the time they shadow walked—the Moriartys' arcane initiation ritual—something broke in them. That vigor was tamed and self-possessed discipline filled the void. They lost something of themselves and severed ties with their old lives.

That was the sacrifice for brotherhood and a small price to pay. Orphaned and ostracized in one way or another, most didn't have families to forsake.

When they were well away from the mansion, a few captains made quick work of building a fire. The initiation struck Emory as a spiritual cleansing more than anything else, but some men swore it possessed supernatural qualities.

Those men claimed something else joined the circle on shadow walk nights, something dark that delighted in their collective sins.

Emory never felt shit, just the night's chill at his back and the fire's warmth on his face. The flames were sacred, though, even he had to admit, and they cast strange shadows as the men circled the fire.

Liam settled behind Emory. These days, he preferred to observe the esoteric rite rather than participate. He stood watch over his legacy, though, and advised where he could, and tonight looked something of his old self—proud of the empire he helped create and less tired too.

Emory unsheathed the ritual blade, all pewter and patina and intricately carved, and handed it to the captain on his left, Pete, who cracked a smile.

All Moriarty men bore a collection of fourteen scars from the blade, one delivered by each captain plus the Moriarty deputy and chief. The scars were a reminder of duty and loyalty. The Moriartys didn't garb themselves in colors or symbols to signify their affiliation. They moved with the shadows and espoused individual obscurity because the organization had an identity all its own.

Some men couldn't handle that obscurity. They wanted to don the prestige and incite fear through the Moriarty name. Those men didn't last long. As Liam always said, "Glory and tragedy belong to the organization, not the man."

Emory stepped aside and allowed the initiate into the circle. The boy expelled a shallow breath and removed his black shirt. Emory stared at the kid, who squirmed beneath the scrutiny. Mirabelle called it soul scrying. Emory called it sussing out rats.

After a few quiet moments, he gave a slight nod and the initiate stood before Pete.

The boy spoke the oath on a timorous breath. "Sanguine inter fratres dedicato."

Blood and brotherhood. Goosebumps blanketed Emory's skin. Jack stirred next to him and Liam shuffled forward.

Pete repeated the oath and drew the blade across the initiate's chest, leaving behind a ribbon of red. He passed the knife to the captain on his left.

On it went, the blade traveling the circle. The initiate spoke his oath to every captain, his voice rising with each iteration and chin tipping higher. His pained grunts dampened to a wince with each slice of the blade, and he reached Jack with blood coating his chest and biceps.

"Sanguine inter fratres dedicato."

The kid's teeth clamped on his bottom lip as Jack delivered a deep cut. Blood oozed thick and dark from the wound. With a smirk, Jack passed Emory the blade.

The boy stood at full height in front of Emory. He looked different. Hardened, less petrified. He stared at Emory with empty eyes, a blank slate they'd mold however they pleased, and puffed out his chest, even if it meant peeling open the cuts. He still looked like a scrawny, bloodied ferret to Emory as he spoke his final oath.

A chilly wind rolled across the desert, and the flames responded, kicking up embers that swirled in the breeze.

"Sanguine inter fratres dedicato," Emory repeated and drew a cut deeper than Jack's.

The kid's nose wrinkled and lip snarled with a grimace. When he was through, Emory plunged the bloodied blade into the ground. From his pocket, he retrieved the white handkerchief.

Blood already marred the ritual cloth, and Emory thumbed the dark red splotch. *Amelia.* He didn't know—and didn't rightly care—if it mattered in some symbolic way.

In a black baptism of sorts, the initiate cleansed his cuts with the handkerchief and a bucket of water. The circle watched his rebirth into brotherhood as he washed away the blood and, with it, his former self. When he was through, he upended the bloody water over the fire.

With the flames doused, the men exploded in an uproar, breaking both the circle and their solemn visage. One by one, each captain clapped the boy on the back, shook his hand, or offered some other gesture of camaraderie. Emory wrangled the kid toward him.

"Remember what I told you," he said for only the boy to hear. The others had already received the same message from him. "Death is your only exit, but you're family now, and we take care of our own."

They headed for the mansion with the boy leading the way and the captains following in clusters.

Liam set a slow pace between Jack and Emory. "Can't help yourselves, can you?"

Emory exchanged a look with Jack. He flashed a smile, lit up a cigarette, and offered one to Emory. He took it and tucked it behind his ear.

"Don't know what you're talking about, old man," Emory said.

Jack tossed the knife in the air. Hilt over blade, the gaudy thing went spinning. He caught it by the hilt and winked at Liam, who glanced at the fire rendered to ash and smoke behind them.

"One of these days, the pissing contest between you two is going to leave an initiate bleeding like a stuck pig and needing stitches."

Jack shrugged. "Worse things could happen."

Emory agreed with a nod. Worse things had already happened. He let that thought go for the moment and admired the full moon riding high.

He never appreciated the light it put off until he moved to the desert. He grew up in a predominantly Latin neighborhood outside of Sacramento, and the moon there never shined that bright.

"Our folk look out for each other," his father always said.

True enough, the ties that bound ran strong and proud and well beyond bloodlines.

Jack's family moved to the neighborhood one summer and were welcomed into the fold with cookouts every other weekend. Emory made fast friends with the crazy fucker, Jack, who lived next door and knew more about baseball than anyone Emory had ever met.

That first summer went by in a haze of racing bikes around until the street lamps kicked on, wading through the creek behind their neighborhood, and pissing off Old Man Martinez, who was all bark and no bite. It was a rare respite from the living hell at home.

As a kid, Emory took his brother Ivan's blows and said nothing about it. When school started again, he showed up one day with a black eye other kids teased him about.

"His daddy did that," those kids whispered, not knowing that Ivan, even at twelve, was a holy terror. Emory's father, on the other hand, was a gentle giant who couldn't raise hell if he wanted.

Ivan expertly preserved the outward veneer of intellect and navigated the world with sly duplicity. His sleight of hand fooled everyone, even their mother. She created a smoke and mirrors show, wrote the script with self-told lies, and applauded even the most basic deeds.

Ivan could shit his pants on that stage of grand delusion, and it'd earn their mother's standing ovation. Ivan pulled the wool over countless eyes, all but Emory, who saw in his brother a distorted pastiche that hid a monster.

"Does Ivan scare you?" Jack asked one night when they were boys camping out in his backyard and having gone quiet with bellies full of s'mores.

Emory had picked at the tacky remnants of marshmallow on his stick.

"Yeah. Mostly for my sister."

His confession had come harder than the hits he endured from Ivan. Sweet Mirabelle followed him and Jack around like a lost puppy with her pink tutu, mussed-up hair in pigtails, and a stuffed dolly under her arm.

She clung to Emory like salt on a pretzel and wailed the nights he spent at Jack's. Where Emory went, Mirabelle was never far behind.

Emory came to the Moriartys with no family to forsake other than her and Jack. With his parents both dead, he'd disowned his brother by then. He didn't need a brother when he had Jack and even told him that the night they shadow walked together.

"Ivan's a stranger to me. You're my true brother, always have been."

"Then I'll follow you to the end," Jack had replied, their bond sacrosanct well before that night. "Until the world burns out and there's nothing left but darkness."

Emory glanced at Jack, who blew smoke out the side of his mouth and laughed. "What?"

"Nothing. Just thinking about old times."

Jack flicked his cigarette into the darkness. "You think too goddamn much. What does it get you?"

"More problems," Liam chimed in and patted Emory's back.

———

THEY SOUGHT refuge in the mansion, the house warm compared to the night's subtle chill. The men descended on the kitchen filled with the savory scents of Emory's childhood. Mirabelle outdid herself with a feast that would've made their mother proud.

On the kitchen island, she'd laid out steaming bowls of white rice and pink beans; a caldero of pollo guisado, a hearty chicken stew; and Emory's favorite dish—mashed plantains served with fried pork.

The men ate like kings then retired to the basement lounge where they'd celebrate well into the night. Jack and Emory would join eventually but retreated to the parlor first, where Emory settled in his normal spot, a sofa against the far wall.

Across the room, Jack flopped into an armchair with his legs dangling over the side. They sat in companionable silence as the clock in the corner kept time.

"Thinking again?" Jack teased.

Emory nodded and chewed his lip. Everyone had invisible

tripwires, the things that set them off. Like all else, he laid his down in parallel pattern easy for others to heed. Those lines were in disarray, a crisscrossed mess that tied him up in knots.

Jack tip-toed the line and went in easy.

"You think Amelia will talk?"

Emory exhaled a laugh so caustic, he was liable to choke on it, and he'd snap his jaw if it clenched any tighter. All the fucking mess—the agony, the explanations, the logistics to pull it off on a goddamn whim—and for what? For her to sit there with her haughty recalcitrance.

Emory boiled on the inside but put a pin in it.

"She's lying to me."

"I'm sure you can get her to open up," Jack said with a wink and a bawdy smile.

If Amelia had intended to melt into Dauer's wallpaper and go unnoticed, she'd done a piss-poor job of it. Emory had noticed her immediately. What wasn't there to notice?

Long legs, perfect body, gorgeous face with big brown eyes and pouty lips.

As Emory got his looks, Jack had savored delivering a bit of trivia—the smoke show across the room was Cal Havick's daughter. Just his luck, but not entirely a lost cause. Amelia Havick had a reputation, after all.

At eighteen, she'd unknowingly met a few Moriarty street soldiers at a house party. They all said the same thing about her— a daydream doll-baby, sweet as a slice of cherry pie. She was an easy target if Cal ever got too close.

Liam had put his foot down, though. Going after the children of their enemies was dirty business, and Emory, not quite chief then, had argued the risks outweighed any benefit.

But Emory was nothing if not a man of his word, even the ones he had to eat. And he did, one after the next, because he'd been dead wrong. Sweet Amelia wasn't the docile little darling he thought she'd be, and she got her licks in well and truly.

Jack sat up and planted his feet on the floor. "Don't you think it's strange how quickly Richard threw her under the bus?"

Threw was a generous understatement. Hurled was more apt and on par for a coward. Emory only had to bloody Rich's nose for him to divulge that Amelia had what he was after.

"I think he would've sold her out to the Velascos too. We just got to him first. Why else would he know when and why she's leaving Portland and where she's going? I think he planned to weaponize that information if push came to shove."

"If the Velascos wanted her, why not something targeted?" Jack asked. The same question hounded Emory. "They could've nabbed her on the street or waited 'til she left town. What was the point of a massacre? And we were there too, man. They could've lit us up and called it collateral."

Emory scanned the door to the hall and leaned forward. Delicate light swathed the room, and faint laughter filtered from the basement lounge below. Jack matched the move toward secrecy.

"It wasn't a courtesy that they didn't," Emory said as quiet as his deep voice could manage. "It was a message—what they're capable of, the risks they're willing to take, how far they'll go. Whoever is at the helm of the Velascos now, last night marked his arrival on the scene."

A chill spread down Emory's spine and hollowed out his belly. Jack slumped deeper into his seat. They both felt it—the haunt in the corner, the shadows creeping in.

The Velasco-Moriarty ceasefire was just a shaky gentlemen's agreement forged between Philippe and Liam a decade ago. With the old guard of Velasco leadership missing, dead, or exiled, the agreement crumbled with blood-soaked spats, and the Moriartys backslid into an all-out war with an enemy they no longer knew.

The Velascos ousted Philippe and welcomed in his place depravity Emory couldn't reason with. Prickly bastard though he was, Philippe understood where to draw the line to keep the peace. Their new chief—whoever he was—clearly did not.

Jack flicked the wheel of his lighter and stared at the flame. "This is just the beginning."

Emory nodded. "Undoubtedly, yes."

Liam wandered in then, smelling like campfire and nursing a drink. Perched at the wood mantle, he struck a match and held the flame to his cigar. When it took, he flicked the match into the fireplace and turned to Emory.

"About earlier," he said between puffs, "who handled Damon?"

Emory peered at Liam from beneath his brow. "I did."

The first rule of conduct—Emory owned the blood on his hands. Tucked in his sock drawer were tally marks of kills neatly penned in a pocket-sized notebook.

It wasn't about conquest, but inventory. Every so often, he looked over the count. He owed apologies to some and remembered the faces of a few. It kept him honest, he reasoned, accountable for the lives he took.

Maybe Amelia Havick might like to know that. Maybe she'd shut that beautiful mouth of hers if she saw the count, far fewer than the heaps of souls she assumed he reaped. She'd think twice then about calling him a monster.

"Next time, hands off," Liam said. "Let the captains or their men handle business. We don't need you wrapped up because you can't control your temper."

"I control it just fine."

Liam slapped his knee with a forceful laugh, more a guffaw, really. Another puff of the cigar wiped his smile clean and his gaze sharpened.

"The whole room watched you blow his kneecaps out. And for what, huh?" He looked at Jack but jabbed a thumb in Emory's direction. "Getta load of Em the tough guy. Big fuckin' brute."

Emory's back peeled from the sofa, but he withheld heat to snub the bait and prove a point. Liam kept a keen eye on him with a Cheshire smile shrouded in smoke.

"You forget how I came up," Emory said coolly, "hands on and they're bloody. I wanted a job done clean. It's not what I got. I can and will still handle business myself. Don't ever forget that."

Liam pointed at Emory and stared down his finger like the barrel of a gun. "Keep your head. It's the last I'll say."

"The last you'll say," Emory chuckled. "Not likely."

In the foyer, Mirabelle hurried barefoot past the parlor door. She carried a dustpan and, by the sound of it, a bag of broken glass.

"What happened?" Emory hollered.

At the sound of his voice, she stopped and padded into the room. With a terse smile, she rustled the bag's shattered contents.

"The girl's got some fire to her."

Fingers laced behind his head, Jack broke with hearty laughter. The humor was lost on Emory. His shoulders tensed, and dull pain radiated down his back.

"Where is she?" he asked.

Mirabelle frowned and picked at the bag's plastic handle looped around her finger.

"She's so scared, Em. She just wants to go home."

Funny how Mirabelle had swept up Amelia's mess and argued on her behalf. She answered the wrong question, though. Emory didn't give a fuck how the girl was.

"She can't go home. *Where* is she?"

"She ate a little and fell asleep in the bedroom across from yours."

"Good. She'll stay there until she tells the truth."

Emory left no margin for discussion, but Mirabelle didn't need him to carve out that space. She crouched at his feet with a plea.

"You need to tell her you're not going to hurt her, that no one here is going to hurt her."

"I'll deal with it."

Liam ashed his cigar in the fireplace and stepped from the mantle.

"Don't forget you have business in Vegas tomorrow. You need to figure out how you want to handle that."

Emory hadn't forgotten but also hadn't expected such a disastrous detour. Second rule of conduct—business was handled in the order it came and delegated accordingly. Vegas wasn't a matter he could hand off to someone else.

"We need to postpone until things cool down," Emory said. "I guarantee the Velascos are hot that we swooped in on their target."

Jack cracked a smile. "Works in our favor. They fuck with us, we fuck with them."

Emory nodded. "If nothing else, she's a bargaining chip."

Horrified, Mirabelle gaped at him. He could deal with her anger but not her disgust. It was the price of doing business around her. She'd see the way he slipped skins into a ruthless man.

"I thought you were protecting her," Mirabelle said, her voice breathy with disbelief. "You didn't say anything about using her to bargain with."

"I'll keep her safe, but she's here to give me answers," Emory reminded. "I need you to get that in her head, Miri. I won't tolerate her being obstinate." He pointed to the bag. "I won't tolerate this shit either."

Mirabelle crossed her arms and sat back on her heels. "You're gonna have a hell of a time with her."

"How so?"

"She's as stubborn as you are."

Emory shrugged. "I'll get what I want."

Jack cut him a lecherous glance. If it were him, he'd play the hand dirty; smooth talk until Amelia parted her thighs and spilled her secrets.

It wasn't as if Emory didn't want that from her too. Amelia was sugar-spun straight from his sweetest fantasies, but his charm didn't work that way and, even if it did, they were too far gone for him to romance her into compliance.

He'd planned to take Amelia himself and even pulled her from the pile of bodies at Rich's party, but his good intentions went awry, as they often did. He had no choice now but to play the part of the beast.

"Eventually, we need to deal with the Vegas issue," Liam interjected again. "When we do, Amelia will have to come with us."

Emory firmly shook his head.

"Absolutely not. Havick's daughter has no business coming with us. I don't want her involved."

"We can't split up our men on her account," Liam said.

"Whenever we go, if she's still here, she'll have to come," Jack agreed. "It's too risky not to."

"No!" Mirabelle protested and sprung from the floor. "Emory, no. She's scared out of her mind. The last thing she needs is to be dragged along while you take care of business."

Outnumbered by Liam and Jack, that was that. The third rule of conduct—Emory listened hard to advice received twice and always asked for ground truth. Sycophants would let him ride off to ruin. If he was wrong, he wanted to know.

He glanced at Mirabelle on the verge of tears. Her bleeding heart would get the best of her someday.

"It's not up to you."

Mirabelle took the ground she was given and dug in again. "No, but it is up to you. I'm your sister, and I'm telling you I don't think it's a good idea."

She only stated their relation in these moments, as if the reminder grounded him when spoken out loud. All too often, it did.

"Fine. We'll give it a few weeks and let things settle, then see where we're at. If she does come, I want you there to look after her." Emory grinned as he stood and motioned to the plastic bag. "Besides, she seems to like you."

Mirabelle rolled her eyes. "Oh, fuck you."

"I'll be outside. Bring her to me," Emory said on the way to the foyer, but Mirabelle got the last word as he reached the door.

"Emory Holt, I swear to God you better be sweet."

Emory did an about-face. Slack-jawed with nothing to say, he stood there dumbfounded as they all stared at him—Jack with a shit-eating grin, Liam who seemed to agree, and Mirabelle with her hands planted on her hips.

"What the fuck do you mean be sweet? I've been perfectly civil." Emory pointed to Liam bailing for the back hall. "You were there. Was I not mostly respectful?"

Mostly. Not hardly. Didn't really try. Amelia wasn't there for him to brush her hair and dry her tears; for hush little baby, don't say a word.

Liam declined a response, just puffed on his cigar that shit ash to the floor.

"I heard you tell her to sit on your face," Mirabelle said, "that you're great at eating pussy."

Emory laughed; so too did Jack and Liam. He hadn't known why he'd said—to test the waters or see the girl squirm. Maybe both. Mirabelle folded her arms over her chest with a pointed stare.

"I *am* great at it," Emory said matter-of-factly. "If she plays her cards right, maybe she'll see for herself."

Mirabelle's nose wrinkled with disgust. "That's gross, Emory."

"Point is," Liam interjected on his way out the door, "listen to your sister and keep your head."

Jack saluted Emory before trailing after Liam. Mirabelle flashed a vindicated smile and followed the other two out.

They got him again with advice received thrice.

Be sweet.

He'd do his best.

THIRTEEN

AMELIA

Mirabelle fetched Amelia long after the sun set, and a terrible darkness rose in its place. Uncanny in its crypt-like quiet, the house was vacuous and gluttonous in its consumption of light and sound. Silent shadows held dominion there.

"He needs to talk to you," Mirabelle announced as if she'd rehearsed where to place the punchy emphasis.

It came down to need.

I don't care what he needs.

Amelia bit her tongue, though she wasn't trying to spare feelings, and followed Mirabelle downstairs.

The black dress she wore was soft and exquisite, and Mirabelle had even rinsed off Amelia's shoes. They squelched with each step through the belly of the mansion, and Amelia peered into the rooms they passed—palatial spaces with giant furniture stuffed to the seams and airy fabrics framing tall windows.

A fountain babbled in the outside courtyard where flowering vines enrobed stone-work lattice. The terra cotta staircase emptied to an expansive terrace below. Just beyond a glittering pool, globes of light dotted the perimeter of a sitting area. Mirabelle motioned to a silhouette at the table.

"He's over there."

Amelia's stomach flipped with a woozy rush, something like racing down a drop-off hill, and her palms were clammy despite the mild breeze. Weighed down with fear in one foot and defiance in the other, she didn't budge.

"Hear him out," Mirabelle urged. "He's not as bad as you think."

Easy for her to say. Mirabelle couldn't see what was right in front of her. Blood affinity blinded, but she tied a blindfold tight for good measure. With nothing more to say, Mirabelle left, and Amelia took a moment to gain her bearings.

The Moriarty mansion perched on a craggy bluff that overlooked black desert, both stunning and frightening in its emptiness. In the valley below, a road cut through like a string of Christmas lights that glittered red and white and wove in a tangle.

I could run. Just follow the road. That would be foolish. She wouldn't make it that far or anywhere at all.

Unlike the trees back home, the palm leaves didn't whisper with the wind but rattled like dry bones. No one built stucco houses with tiled roofs in Portland because the desert existed in only a handful of states, and Oregon sure as hell wasn't one of them. Far from home, Amelia had no choice but to face the shadow in the dark.

Remember who you are.

She was the daughter of Callum Havick, who had to be close to finding her. He had his flaws like anyone else, but he was smart, and he was brave, and maybe she'd inherited the best parts of him or could pretend at least.

Amelia stood tall and drank in the night's crisp air that smelled sweet and clean. A halo of light enveloped the seating area where crickets sang and moths flittered.

Leaned over with his forearms on his knees, Emory stared at the space between his feet. A cigarette's cherry ember glowed as the filter met his lips.

Amelia approached with loathing that soaked to the bone. The presentation of it all would make her sick. Did he like her trotted out with bare thighs in a black dress? Apparently so.

The cigarette paper sizzled as Emory rendered it to ash with a long drag. Head tilted skyward, he appraised her with smoke spilling from his mouth.

Cleaned of gore and with her hair air-dried in glossy waves, she surely looked different, but so did he. A vision of fury earlier, Emory appeared at ease now. He gestured to an empty seat at the table and watched with guarded intrigue as Amelia sat.

"You smoke?" he asked and offered her the lit cigarette.

She shook her head as the chair's cold metal met the back of her thighs.

"Me neither," Emory said and studied the horizon.

The paltry light did little to gentle sharp bones, brooding eyes, and a five o'clock shadow that further accentuated his jawline. He still commanded the space around him, a quality Amelia assumed was immutable, and his imposing intensity hadn't waned. Unwavering and dangerous, it roiled beneath a calm surface.

"Where are we?" she asked.

"Nevada."

So far from home, Amelia shivered with a chill. *No one will look for me here.*

Emory took one last drag and dropped the cigarette to the ground where he squashed it with his boot heel. He opened his mouth to speak, but the words didn't make it past his lips.

"Where's my mother?" Amelia demanded and drew her shoulders back. *Remember who you are.*

Emory's gaze roved her body. "No idea."

"And my father? Is he safe?"

"What the fuck makes you think I know what happened to your parents?" A mirthless laugh escaped him. "Oh, that's right. You think I had something to do with last night."

"Didn't you? Something horrible happens and you're there, by what, coincidence?"

Emory's chest rose with an incensed breath. If Amelia was meant to passively sit and listen, she was making a fine mess of it.

"I told you I didn't. Take it or leave it. I won't tell you again.

You were targeted last night, and you know it. They came for you. Why?"

"I don't know why. I haven't done anything to anyone!"

Emory laughed again at her expense, the derision apparent.

"That's not how it works. Good people get fucked over all the time, and no one cares that they didn't deserve it."

"I care. You're telling me those people, whoever they were, wanted me dead."

"*Want.* They *want* you dead," he corrected with hard emphasis to make her understand. "They don't call it a wash because you disappeared off the face of the goddamn earth. They're coming for you and for me and they're going to keep coming."

"Who are *they*?"

With fiery exasperation, Emory sat up in his seat.

"Who do you think? Who might possibly want you dead?"

Last night, Amelia would've answered with his name. Her father had painted a violent and terrifying picture of the Moriartys—men who murdered indiscriminately and espoused strange traditions that led them down a path of darkness. Central to the mystery was the man sitting across from her.

There was, of course, one other answer.

"Velascos," Amelia said on a hush.

Emory nodded, but his delight in mocking her vanished. He crossed his legs at the ankles and folded his arms over his chest.

"I need to go home. My dad needs me," Amelia insisted. Maybe she'd gain some ground—Emory was human, after all— but he shut it down with a firm shake of the head.

"You can't. The Velascos finish what they start. You go home, you die. Simple as that."

He made it sound so clinical, as if he couldn't summon sympathy for her life upended and hanging in the balance. If it was all the same to him, then why bother?

"You honestly expect me to believe you're protecting me?" Pulse on the rise, Amelia coiled her fingers around the arms of the chair. "My father's entire existence has been to take you down. If you're going to hurt me, then just get on with it and stop with the bullshit."

Emory's eyes flicked to her. Where there was fire before, he turned to ice and cut deep with cruelty meant to wound.

"If I wanted to hurt you, I would've done it already. I could've left you to die, to burn to death like your mother."

Amelia erupted in a flash that propelled her out of her seat. She lunged at him with balled fists. She'd never hit anyone before, never dreamed of it, until then.

Emory sprung up and snatched her by the wrist. He squeezed hard enough that Amelia collapsed back into her seat and trembled in his grasp. Emory lurched over her, seething as he spoke.

"You think you're brave, but I saw you before, and I see you now. You crumble and all I have to do is look at you. Feel that? You're shaking like a leaf. How brave are you now?"

Brave enough that she lifted her eyes to him. Up close, Emory got his look; the fear surely flooding her face and the frantic pulse at her wrist that thumped against his palm. She got her look too; the way he fractured with fickle guilt, gone before it took hold but enough to dispel his anger.

Emory released her and reclaimed his seat with strange affliction. When his eyes found her, he seemed to measure some conflict in himself, and when he spoke again, Amelia didn't know which part of him had won.

"I don't want to hurt you," he said. "That's not what this is about."

Amelia couldn't reconcile his words with the ones that'd come before or the bruises blooming beneath her skin. Then there was Brian; sweet Brian, with disheveled curls and a lopsided smile.

"You already have," she said.

In a feeble effort to put distance between them, Amelia sunk in her seat. Emory ran his fingers through his hair and dragged his chair over until they faced each other. Lunar shadows sharpened his features, and he moved stealthily for such a tall, long-limbed man.

"Here's the deal, Amelia. I'll keep you safe, keep you alive. In exchange, you'll answer some questions for me because there are things I'm having trouble wrapping my head around."

She glared at him. "Sounds like your problem, not mine."

"Don't fuck with me!" Emory snapped, his voice ringing heavy in the night. "I said I didn't want to hurt you, not that I wouldn't. I find it hard to believe you had no idea who came after you or why."

He slipped to the edge of his seat again, and Amelia did the same, the distance between them closing toward collision. If he could rage, so could she. Amelia's blood pumped hot, and the chill of the night vanished along with her fear of Emory so full of false threats.

"I know exactly who came after me. *You* did. You were the one who orchestrated a kidnapping, the one who had your men murder my friend then drug me and bring me here. *You!*"

Emory couldn't argue the logic and, to his credit, didn't try. He stared at her from beneath his brows as a sweet breeze enveloped them. It lifted the loose ends of his hair and carried the warm spice of his cologne. It tempered something in them both.

Amelia drew a shaky breath, and Emory settled in his seat to redraw the space between them. He lowered his voice as if the night itself had stilled to listen. Dead air encased them, and the moths all fluttered away.

"Burt was a fucking clown, digging into things he should've left alone. Martin Kranski tried to help him out of the shit storm. I saw you talking to Kranski last night. You couldn't get away from the guy fast enough. Why?"

Emory stared at her lips with overt fixation. He could take her apart with one look and seemed poised to do just that.

Remember who you are. She was lost and alone in a world where he was God. She'd have to give him something.

"My dad and Richard had an argument before the party. I don't know what about. Martin came over to ask about my dad, and I didn't want to talk about it. That's it. There's nothing else."

Amelia kept his eyes despite the lie. She worked it like clay in her hands. With each iteration, it came easier, softer, more pliable. Emory's appraisal of her changed then, and he regarded her with somber concern before going impassive again.

"Why were you there last night?" Amelia asked.

Emory glanced at the desert awash in a full moon's glow. In the distance, the road lights twinkled like drawn-down stars.

"Rich Dauer owes me something and had more opportunities than most to deliver but didn't. I knew I could corner him at his own party."

"You said the Velascos are coming for you too. Why?"

"I assume to upend this." He tipped his head backwards to the mansion behind them. "Our organizations have had a ceasefire for a long time, but they're backtracking on it. I need to know who's behind it and why. That's what Richard owes me. Answers. All he knows is that the Velascos are unmanageable."

"They're different than they used to be," Amelia mused airily enough anyone else might've carried on.

Not him. No, of course not. Emory responded with a thoughtful nod but seemed to harden with that detail.

"They're different because Philippe Velasco is dead. He went missing a few weeks ago. Body parts turned up in the Colorado River. Yesterday, the medical examiner identified those parts as Philippe. People assumed he bailed after the indictment. Truth is, he was betrayed, killed by his own men."

It made sense, the fight with Richard and her father's words that a man was already dead. Amelia had assumed he meant Burt.

"Why would they do that?" she asked.

"A few of their captains thought Philippe was too dovish when your dad came around. That sentiment grew with someone fanning the flames of dissent. Philippe felt the target on his back and turned rat for a plea deal. Staging a coup is no small thing, though. It means there's a sickness inside. Mutiny, distrust, betrayal. It all falls apart. But they're not falling apart. They're getting stronger, more brutal, more organized."

"Who's in charge now?"

Emory shrugged, but his severity returned.

"That, more than anything, is what I need to know. Someone let the wolf in the door, and now it calls the shots from the shadows."

Leaned forward, he pinned his elbows to his knees and interlaced his fingers.

"I know about the folder, Amelia. I know you saw it."

Her eyes shot to him. *Fix your face.*

Too late. Her lips parted and body responded in ways he already knew how to read.

"So, here's what I think," he continued. "I think Burt figured it out. He named the wolf and paid with his life. Now there's one other person with the same puzzle pieces." Emory lightly traced a knuckle along her bare knee. "You."

Though his touch was tender, brutality remained in his stare. The sentiment menaced in its mismatch. He would sooner savage her than save her. Fading fast beneath his scrutiny, Amelia shook her head.

"No, I...I don't know."

"You seem unsure."

Emory's mouth curled in a smile that would've been painfully gorgeous, except for how it peeled back the curtain and bathed her in limelight. Time to spill her guts and shine. Amelia demurred instead, wilting at center stage.

"I don't know anything about that. I swear. The things I saw didn't mean anything to me the way it did Burt."

It wasn't an attempt at subterfuge. Too captivated by his photograph, she hadn't fully consumed the folder's contents and could only recall a mishmash of information.

"So, you did see something."

Amelia licked her lips and eyed the stairs to the courtyard. With no savior in sight, a searing ache returned to her chest. She'd revealed too much but knew so little. A dog with a bone, Emory wouldn't stop.

"Look at me," he rasped and gripped her thigh. Amelia stared at his hand but didn't move. "You knew enough to run, to know that the Velascos aren't the same. You know more than you're telling me. Just give me a name, Amelia. That's all I need and I will make this go away for you."

Emory's attention lingered on her lips again as if he meant to extract the secrets there. His grip tightened too. *He must know I'm not wearing underwear.* What would he do with that knowledge? Make her spill her secrets in other ways?

Amelia desperately wanted to believe he wasn't that kind of man, but what did she know about him? That he wanted to fuck her. That was inarguable, and he wanted her to know it too.

Emory bit down on his bottom lip as his gaze explored her body. He seemed to take his time at the parts he liked best—her bare thighs, full breasts, soft lips. Amelia squirmed in her seat. Emory relented with a sigh and removed his hand from her leg.

"Alright, I tell you what. I know you're tired. I am too. Sleep on it, and in the morning, I have a feeling you'll remember all the little details eluding you now."

Another false smile graced his mouth. Once more, it didn't match the look in his eyes. The disconnect invited more dread because it wasn't sweet sympathy. A threat prowled in his gently spoken words. Emory put a finer point on it.

"Last night wasn't about shit luck or being in the wrong place at the wrong time. The Velascos have a death warrant for me and now you, understand? The longer you withhold, the less I have to act on. We have a common enemy, and I'm trying to help you."

There it was again, the Royal We. Both he and Mirabelle tried to draw a fated thread between them. Amelia snipped it for good.

"I don't care what you're trying to do."

Emory sucked in an offended breath that he held in his chest. That's right. He wanted gratitude, down on her knees in praise. Amelia refused.

"Then I guess we're done here," he said with a cold snap.

"Yeah, I guess so," Amelia replied, just as frigid.

Emory stood and roughly shoved his chair into the table. In an absurd gesture of chivalry, he held out his hand to her. Amelia contemplated his calloused palm and long fingers but rejected it.

She started toward the stairs and ascended them, keenly aware of Emory close behind.

Inside, he led the way through the mansion to the bedroom Mirabelle had deposited her in earlier. It was sterile and lifeless with stiff bed linens and side tables with nothing but a lamp on each and an alarm clock on one. When Emory nudged open the door, dim light spilled into the hall. Amelia stood beside it and waited for him to leave.

He didn't depart, only demanded with a surly bark, "What? This is gonna have to be good enough. I'm not putting my sister out of her room on your behalf."

"I didn't ask you to. I didn't ask to be here. I didn't ask for any of this!"

Too afflicted with bone-deep fatigue, Amelia didn't care that her voice echoed in the hall. She did a dangerous thing, stepping toe-to-toe with him and causing a scene, though no one was there to see. Without an audience to intervene, Emory walked her into the wall and propped his hands on either side of her head.

In the darkness, his hulking shadow leaned in close, but shadows didn't expel sharp breaths on the brink of coming undone or radiate heat that invaded the shallow void between them. With her back against the wall, Emory's strong arms caged her in, and his breath warmed her ear.

"I heard about the stunt you pulled earlier in Mirabelle's room. You wanna rage? Then rage at me." One hand slipped to her waist and the other gripped her throat. "Fill me up," he said, his nose brushing her cheek. "I can take it. But if you hurt my sister, then I hurt you worse. Pain you can't imagine."

He spoke slowly as to not be misunderstood, and Amelia took him at his word because there lay his boundary—Mirabelle both his virtue and his weakness.

Emory pulled away enough to stare at her mouth and not with shallow interest like before, but palpable desire even the darkness couldn't conceal. His grasp on her throat tightened until Amelia's lips parted with a startled breath.

"Maybe I do want to hurt you. Squeeze until you beg me to stop."

Emory had nothing left to threaten her with that he hadn't already, so her curiosity of him took a morbid turn. Fueled by exhaustion, Amelia discarded her better judgment, the rational part that demanded her fear. Pinned against the wall, what power did she have?

Enough to call his bluff.

"Go ahead," Amelia said and placed her hands on his chest. Against her palms, his heart raced just as wildly as hers. He so clearly didn't know what to do with her—fuck her into submission or deliver on his more sinister promises.

Emory ran the pad of his thumb along her bottom lip and eased into her until their bodies met. Amelia closed her eyes as his thumb caressed her top lip.

"Is that what you want?" he asked, his dick hard and pressed against her. "I don't think you know what you're asking for, the things I could do to you."

Emory released her throat and cupped her cheek. His hand at her waist disappeared beneath her dress and settled on her naked hip.

"No underwear." He smiled wickedly at the observation and leaned in close, his lips nearly grazing hers. "That for me?"

A dizzying thrum coursed through Amelia. Emory couldn't hide his arousal behind walls of steely reserve and something in his brazenness sent her into a tailspin of conflicting desires.

He would fuck her so good, she had no doubt, and seemed the kind of man to take great pride in that. And maybe he wanted to fill her up, to put her on top of him and let her ride to her heart's content, until she came with trembling knees and his cock slick with her orgasm.

Remember who he is.

A monster. A murderer. A horrible man.

Amelia gripped his shoulders. Her fingers dug into the muscle there and she drew him in. With her breasts against his chest, she craned her neck to meet his gaze.

"Nothing I do is for you," Amelia whispered. "Get off me."

Skin hot, she burned alive but shoved him away. Emory laughed, and perhaps Amelia should've been afraid as she hurried into the room where the bed was unmade. How easily Emory could pry open her legs and make a bigger mess of the sheets. And wouldn't he love to find her already wet and ready for him?

Amelia cradled her elbows and turned to the door. Emory leaned against the frame. A faint blush dusted his cheeks, and he ran a hand over his mouth.

"And to think Mirabelle told me to be sweet," he said.

Amelia rolled her eyes. "Great job you're doing."

Emory's anger returned, and the scar on his lip exaggerated its sneer. Good. If he hated her that much, he could leave; let that be that and throw in the towel like Mirabelle had. If her only weapon against these people was driving them to exasperation, Amelia would wield it with all her might because she hated him too.

"I'll be across the hall," Emory told her and, in a miserly demonstration of good will, locked the door from the inside.

The stilted courtesy seemed foreign to him and entirely forced, enough that Amelia just as easily interpreted it as a threat. She managed a nod and mumbled "goodnight," yet another wasted courtesy. The farce of pleasantries only further plowed a gaping chasm between them.

"Sleep well," he said with what seemed like great difficulty and an even greater desire to be unburdened of her.

When Amelia refused a response and wanted him gone, Emory pulled the door shut behind him, locking her inside.

FOURTEEN

EMORY

The next morning, Emory plied Amelia with breakfast she barely touched. A croissant disintegrated in a pool of pineapple juice on her plate, and a piece of melon was left skewered on her fork. He stretched his legs beneath the table. When his calf brushed hers, Amelia turned sidesaddle in her seat to avoid his touch.

Emory created pockets of silence Amelia refused to fill, so the quiet animosity brewed between them. She stared out the window of the breakfast nook and rubbed the inside of her wrist. Self-soothing, he assumed, until he glimpsed the rope marks there.

He tried the next day and the day after that. A week passed where they bickered and brawled. There were afternoons of fraught silence and evenings of bitter dispute. Emory made promises at dusk that he broke come dawn. He tried at softness then turned to stone. He was, in turns, her ally and her adversary.

The only fixed variable was Amelia. Her denial and affront; the way she assumed the worst of him and that every gesture was done in bad faith.

It started to feel like extended foreplay with no avenue for release. Emory had even told her so with no expectation that she'd drop to her knees and be good to him, but the statement must've galvanized something in her.

"I don't want to fight anymore. It's become too personal," she told him that morning, her tender contrition merely a smokescreen.

Emory knew what she meant. It wasn't what was said or that it had gone too far. It was that it felt like make-believe where they maligned each other the way only lovers could. Too personal meant too intense, too intimate, too liable to escape fantasy and become something real.

At the breakfast table, Amelia scooted as close to him as she could tolerate to still keep with the lies. Legs crossed, her interwoven fingers cupped one knee. The pose exaggerated the fullness of her breasts in a loose tank top.

"I think we should clear the air. I heard you have business tonight, so whenever you're free, I'm ready to open up to you."

Open up to me.

She chose the suggestive words with care, but it'd taken her a week to try that approach. A woman adept at weaponized seduction would've already batted her lashes and showed some skin. Out of her depth, the attempt almost endeared, but Emory discerned her intent to disarm and distract.

Still, he drank in the sight of her—auburn hair aflame in the morning light, pillowy lips parting with what he swore was an invitation, and the illusory warmth of her gaze. The last bit bothered him the most, that she'd toy with his heart to earn her freedom.

"Sure," he replied tepidly. "I can't reschedule my meeting tonight, but tomorrow works."

It wasn't a lie per se, just an embellished truth. He had dinner plans with a few associates, nothing he couldn't cancel. As expected, the detail roused her interest, and Amelia flashed a heartbreaker of a smile.

A lesser man would've shattered. If only she meant it. She didn't, and that was her fatal flaw. She overplayed her hand, and when he left for Vegas in the evening, she watched him go and even waved goodbye as if she might ache at his absence.

Emory enjoyed a nice meal and productive conversation that would've continued at a members-only gentlemen's club, but he cut the night short. Just before midnight, he arrived back at Liam's and parked in the garage to hide his arrival. With a fine bottle of bourbon from the basement lounge, he crept through the mansion turned down for the night.

In the parlor, he poured a drink and waited in a chair with clear sight of the stairs. At a half past midnight, the doubts arrived as he freshened his glass—maybe he'd misread Amelia's intentions—but a door creaked on its hinges upstairs, and light footsteps padded down the hall.

With his eyes well-adjusted to the dark, Emory watched Amelia tiptoe down the stairs in bare feet, her ballet flats hooked on her fingers and her purse clutched to her chest.

When she reached the landing, he yanked the pull-chain on the lamp beside him. Amelia jumped with a startle and expelled a sharp gasp.

"Going somewhere?" he asked, delighted at trouncing on her great escape.

Poor thing looked devastated as she stashed her shoes and purse by the front door and crossed the foyer.

"You've been waiting for me?" Amelia asked as she entered the parlor.

"What do you think? That I trusted you to stay put?" Emory chuckled as he lifted the bourbon glass to his lips. "You're determined. I'll give you that."

He eyed her over the rim as he sipped and wondered if her choice of attire was deliberate—denim shorts that barely covered a damn-near perfect ass, thin white t-shirt slipping off her shoulder, a black bra visible underneath. She'd have to hitch a ride somehow and showing some thigh to a lonesome trucker wasn't the worst idea.

A thunderbolt of jealousy knocked Emory off kilter. He

downed his drink but poured another finger of bourbon and studied the way Amelia's body moved as she slinked toward him. It drove him crazy; all that doe-eyed innocence he just wanted to wreck.

Amelia wasn't so innocent, though. With the face of an angel, she'd probably fuck him like a fiend. If she planned to seduce him, he wished she'd get on with it. He was tired of the dance and in need of some affection, more than just a warm body in his bed.

Amelia sat on the sofa adjacent to him and didn't seem to mind that his outstretched legs rested perilously close to hers. Emory offered her the glass. He didn't know if she liked bourbon or even drank at all. That was their paradox. The heated exchanges implied depths of knowledge not at all earned.

"I thought you had business tonight," Amelia said and cautiously took the glass.

"Were you counting on it?"

She held his stare and took a sip. "What do you think?"

"What do I think?" Emory knit his fingers behind his head and reclined in his seat. "I think you should reconsider running out on me."

"Don't count on it," she mocked.

With a flicker of defiance in her eyes, she held out the glass. Complicated impulses had convinced Emory that he despised her. It wasn't her, he realized, but the fool for the fantasy he'd become. Night after night, his thoughts faithfully beat a well-worn path back to her. Always to her.

Emory snatched Amelia by the wrist and wrenched her toward him. The glass tumbled from her fingers and shattered against the floor. His mouth hovered close to hers, enough that her frantic breaths caressed his lips.

"Every word from your pretty mouth has been a lie," he said. "Either you start telling me the truth or I turn you over to the other side."

Amelia's eyes darted over his face, panic perhaps that he might crush his mouth to hers.

Maybe he would.

Maybe a hard kiss and rough sex was the watershed moment they needed.

His cock hardened at the thought. She could hate-fuck him for all he cared. What he wouldn't give to have her long legs wrapped around him as he buried himself inside her; on all fours, his hips slamming into her ass; on her knees with her perfect lips wrapped around his dick.

Emory had thought of it so often, craved it night and day, and it'd become the engine to his instincts. It'd drive him into madness if he let it. *Keep your head.*

"Good," she said, her famed fire burning in her eyes. "I'd rather die than spend another minute here with you."

Amelia couldn't lie like him, nor could she see how her body betrayed her. She didn't know that her nipples hardened, chest heaved, limbs trembled as he leaned in close.

Emory called her bluff with a simple act of intimacy—a nuzzle of his nose against hers. Amelia's instincts betrayed her too. She closed her eyes and returned the gesture. Emory released her arm and traipsed his fingertips across the top of her thigh. A ghost of a touch, it elicited from her a gentle sigh as her hand found his shoulder.

"I don't believe that," Emory whispered against her lips. "Give me tonight and you'd die just to spend another with me."

With a shuddering breath, Amelia's head lolled back and exposed the length of her neck. Emory gripped her thigh and drew her onto his lap. She came willingly and didn't object when he pressed his lips to her pulse. He slipped a hand to her ass and dotted soft kisses up her neck. He'd be good to her too. She had to know that.

His lips slowed as his fingers met the juncture between her legs. By the heat coming off of her, she had to be soaked. Emory lifted his head enough to look at her. Wide-eyed, Amelia stiffened as if waiting for him to take more than he already had. Emory wouldn't, not unless she made the first move.

And she did.

Her knees fell open, and her arms snaked around his

shoulders to draw him near. Emory kept her eyes as he hooked his middle finger beneath her underwear and pushed it aside. He traced her slit with his fingertip in a light stroke and stared between her legs.

Her pussy was as perfect as her mouth—plush pink lips he wanted so badly to fuck, to taste. When she didn't pull away, he sunk into the delicious wetness there and slipped a finger inside.

"Emory," she gasped.

He couldn't tell if it was a protest or a moan. It had facets of both as his thumb gently circled her clit. With her eyes shut, Amelia arched into him and rolled her hips.

"Is this what you wanted from me?" he asked and slid another finger inside. Amelia bit her bottom lip to disguise a smile.

She could only lie with one set of lips but seemed to have forgotten that as she unraveled with his touch. Emory dropped a kiss to her bare shoulder and stroked her from the inside until Amelia relaxed against him.

"Look at me," he commanded. Her lashes fluttered as she met his gaze. "Say it. Tell me you wanted this."

"Yes," she sighed and rode his fingers as if she needed it just as badly as he did and was ecstatic they could finally drop the charade.

Amelia came apart right there in his arms. Emory tugged her bra down to free one breast that fit so fucking perfectly in his palm. He sucked on her nipple that was already hard.

"Is your pussy going to take my dick this good?" Emory demanded to know.

Amelia didn't respond. With her eyes squeezed shut, she struggled for full breaths as Emory pumped slow and deep. She was so close and could have her orgasm but would have to answer him first. Emory wrapped her hair around his fist and tugged.

"Answer me."

"Yes."

"Good girl."

Emory swiped her clit and resumed his rhythm. Amelia rewarded him with another moan, and her beautiful face contorted in pleasure. He watched her, memorizing the tremble of her lips and the pulse at her neck flickering beneath her skin. Another flush of wetness soaked between her legs and coated his fingers. Such a sweet thing, she came so beautifully with his name on her lips and stunned in the afterglow with her cheeks flame red.

Emory unzipped his pants and freed his cock. "Take what you want," he said.

A startled breath escaped her, and a torrent of emotion surfaced on her face. Part scandalized, part enthralled, poor baby didn't know what to do. She stilled and clamped down hard on her bottom lip. Amelia hesitated, and Emory almost asked why.

It's not what she wants.

He thought of the fights they'd had; those long nights with tears streaming down her cheeks, and Amelia desperate for comfort he refused to give. She needed him to want her in ways he'd never shown; not just her body, but the parts of her he barely knew.

Emory rested his forehead against hers and combed his fingers through her hair. Amelia came a little closer and steadied herself with her hands on his chest. He only meant to push her to the edge and break her down. He never actually expected her to roll her hips and grind against his shaft.

Amelia did, though. Her wet pussy glided against his cock, and she wrapped her arms around his neck. Another paradox of intimacy, Emory closed his eyes and joined her in the moment, their moans soft and breathy and their lips perilously close to a kiss that never came. If this was her power play, Emory would let her have every inch.

With his hands on her hips, he guided her movements. No longer demure, Amelia ground her clit against the tip of his cock that then slid to her opening. One thrust, and he'd be inside.

"Go on," Emory commanded. "I know you want more."

His chest heaved and body tensed, every part of him struggling to maintain control. Once more, though, Amelia wielded soft power that bested him with ease.

"No," she said, so sweet and commanding in her own right.

Emory narrowed his eyes and tightened his hold on her hips. It was his turn for a power play. He hadn't forgotten her master plan, nor could he forgive how she'd wanted to fuck with his heart.

"It's funny," he said, his mouth hot against hers. He nestled two fingers between her pussy lips. "If you can't stand me, then why are you so wet for me?"

That he called her out dumped them back into reality. Amelia's knees clamped shut against his hips, and she righted her clothing. Emory had seen and felt too much of her. She'd retreat behind her denial and remind herself how much she abhorred him.

"You can't have me," Amelia insisted.

"We both know I already do," Emory laughed and placed a soft kiss to her lips before sucking her cum off his fingers.

His boldness ignited her anger. Amelia shoved off him and stormed from the room. Emory watched her go and tucked his dick back into his pants. For most men, a blow to their pride rendered them fools. Emory was no different. The sting of rejection propelled him from his seat, and the booze emboldened, so he trailed after her as if Amelia was his to follow.

"You really think you can survive without me, baby?"

Emory's question boomed off the walls and echoed up the stairs. God help anyone trying to sleep. On the warpath, he didn't care.

Amelia shot him a look of pure venom as she slid into her shoes and scooped up her purse. "I'm not your baby, and I don't need you."

Another barb that stung, Emory pounded across the foyer and ripped open the front door. With an outstretched arm, he presented her exit.

"I don't need you either."

Amelia evaluated the black wilderness beyond, no stars to light up the sky and myriad monsters stalking the night. Her eyes raked over his body as if sizing him up. The fight would never be fair, though, so she played her only hand and marched toward the door.

In the end, desperate men all looked the same, and Emory couldn't lie to himself that he'd ever let her go. He caught her by the arm and wheeled her around more forcefully than intended. Amelia yelped as her ankle buckled. Her arm shot out to break a fall, but the heel of her hand connected hard with his nose.

In a blinding flash of pain, white dots spangled Emory's vision. He stumbled backwards and lifted a hand to his face. Blood trickled from one nostril and splattered his palm. Horrified, Amelia's hand flew to her mouth. They stared at each other in stunned silence until a door upstairs slammed open.

"What the hell is going on?" Mirabelle demanded and flicked on the foyer light. Her satin robe billowed behind her as she rushed down the stairs.

Amelia locked eyes with Emory. A question for the ages, neither had an answer or knew what game they played, nor did they truly understand the rules. Emory answered on both their behalf with a one-shouldered shrug and wiped the blood from his nose.

Mirabelle surveyed his busted face and tutted with a click of her tongue.

"You two are unbelievable. I'll get some ice."

When the whisper of her slippered feet disappeared into the kitchen, Emory exchanged another look with Amelia. Guilt fragmented her features, and she looked primed to apologize, but Emory cut her off at the pass.

"Go to bed, Amelia," he said, more capitulatory than commanding, and shut the front door.

Defeated, she retreated up the stairs as silently as she'd descended, and Emory returned to the parlor. He stuffed a tissue in his nostril to stop the blood. The droning pain burned as much as it ached and began to spread across his cheeks.

Emory eased into the armchair, mindful of the blood staining his hand and the glass shattered on the floor. Liam shuffled in from the hall of photographs. He chomped on an apple and eyed the tissue hanging out of Emory's nose.

"Where've you been?" Emory asked.

"Book club," Liam said and smacked on another bite. "What happened to you, tough guy? Get into a bar fight or something?"

Before Emory could answer, Mirabelle hurried in with a bundle of ice wrapped in a dishtowel.

"Let's hope she didn't break it," she said and thrust the towel into his face.

"Careful." Emory took the pack and wriggled his nose to assess the damage. The bone didn't crackle, and the pain was present but bearable.

Liam shook his head and laughed. "Ah, sweet Amelia. Happens to the best of us."

"I doubt Francisca ever clocked you."

"No, but we were married almost twenty years. I'm sure she wanted to."

Mirabelle cut Liam a sidelong stare and might've laced into him about encouraging Emory's "bad behavior," as if it was his fault. She didn't, but instead turned to Emory and pointed toward Amelia's bedroom upstairs.

"You are losing control with her."

"I'm losing patience, not control."

"Look at you!" Mirabelle flung a hand at Emory holding the ice pack to his face. "This girl's got you on your knees and twisted up in knots. You are coming undone."

He had no recourse to deny it. The house kept secrets, but not that well. The others had heard the arguments and bore witness to Emory's foul moods. But he had bodies buried in the walls too, the things he'd deny if they were ever exhumed.

He walked an ever-narrowing path between lust and loathing, and while he might not need Amelia, he wanted her; wanted her warmth and her smiles, her lips pressed to his, her body curled against him as they slept.

It wasn't just about sex. He craved her affection. As the days wore on, his frustration deepened and not because she harbored secrets, but because the harder he tried, the more the rift between them grew.

"Figure it out," Mirabelle said and headed for bed.

After she left, Liam sunk into the sofa and set his apple aside.

"Miri's right. Amelia's gotten under your skin. You need to stay the course."

"That's not the issue. I've been banging my head against the wall for a week straight. I'm frustrated. I want movement, progress. I need intel to act, but I'm tired of waiting."

The ice clacked as Emory pulled the towel from his face. He rubbed a splotch of blood staining the terrycloth.

"What if she's telling me the truth? We don't know what else was in that folder. It could've been filled with fluff. What if she doesn't have what we need?"

Days ago, he'd briefly considered the possibility. Too blinded by anger, he'd dismissed it outright. The logic crystallized as Emory said it out loud. Amelia wasn't a master of resiliency, nor had she brilliantly crafted a charade of innocence. She withheld because she had nothing to give.

"That was always a risk," Liam said. "I thought she admitted she saw something, though."

"She did, but what if she doesn't understand what she saw or forgot?"

Liam snickered. "How could she forget?"

Until then, Emory hadn't considered how trauma erased memories in nonsensical ways. He remembered only snippets of his mother before she died. Like a damaged picture book, grief tore out the pages at random and time ravaged the rest. Perhaps it was doing the same to Amelia.

"She's been through a lot."

"We've all been through a lot. She doesn't need to understand what she saw. She needs to tell you, so *you* can understand."

Emory shook his head. "I think we're too far gone for that. Even if she remembers something, she sure as shit won't tell me now."

"Time heals all wounds, even hers," Liam said and collected his apple as he stood.

Fingers steepled beneath his chin, Emory peered up at him. "I don't know. I may have shit the bed on this one."

Liam patted Emory's shoulder the way his father used to. The gesture bid him to listen hard to the wisdom that followed.

"You and Amelia need a breather. Cool off on her for a few days. She'll come around."

FIFTEEN

CAL

Callum Havick stabbed at the potatoes on a paper plate, careful not to poke through the grease-soaked bottom. Funeral potatoes, they were called. Other cultures revered death as life's only guarantee. Americans made cheesy potato casserole with a morbid name. Damn if they weren't good, though.

Cal's roommate from law school and one of his oldest friends, Paul, leaned against the kitchen counter. With a crumpled paper towel, he dabbed the sweat beading his brow and spoke over a box fan buffeting in the corner.

"I see you found your appetite."

"The start of it, at least," Cal said between bites.

Grey hair sprouted from Paul's mostly bald head, and a couple more crow's feet cracked at his eyes. His infectious laughter was the same, though. Time didn't wear on that.

Cal hadn't seen him since last summer when they, along with Richard and a few others, had celebrated their thirty-year Harvard Law reunion with a trip to Monterey.

As the sun set on Big Sur, the men and their spouses had reminisced on their youth, and Cal had fallen in love with his wife all over again. Butterflies had bloomed in his belly, and he'd gone tongue-tied and clammy. He'd decided then to renew their vows the following summer.

This summer, he realized and swallowed down the last bite of casserole.

Paul's wife, Susan—a plump woman with florid cheeks and Midwestern sensibilities—shuffled into the kitchen with a vase of wilted lilies.

"You can't exist on potatoes," she said and set the vase on the counter before clearing away the empty casserole dish.

Says the Kansan. Potatoes were all Cal could stomach. Everything else either sat like a brick in his belly or sent him dashing to the bathroom.

"I'm going to dry the flowers and make the most darling little trinkets with them. Keychains, paper weights, whatever you'd like."

Paul fanned himself with the newspaper.

"What the hell is Cal gonna do with all that?"

"It's a memento. It'd be a shame to throw them out."

There were a dozen more arrangements rotting in Cal's living room. They'd arrived in droves from colleagues, friends, people whose names didn't have a face in his memories.

"I'd love that," Cal said with a smile. It was the least he could do.

When Paul and Susan had heard the awful news, they'd taken the red eye from Chicago and set up camp at the house. The rest of Cal's Harvard crew had done the same and descended on Portland to make casseroles, arrangements, distractions.

"You two visit," Susan said and shooed Paul and Cal toward the deck off the kitchen. "Paul, we need to leave in about twenty minutes."

Paul saluted his wife and followed Cal outside where the evening air was thick and warm, but a hell of a lot cooler than inside. Yesterday, the air conditioner had thumped and bumped and finally given up the ghost, so the house baked in another heat wave. *When it rains, it pours.*

"You know you're more than welcome in Chicago," Paul said and pushed leaves off the deck with the tip of his shoe. "Suze and I wouldn't mind. Shit, she'd be delighted. It'd give her someone else to fuss over."

Humbled by the gesture, Cal glanced at the kitchen window. Through the glass, Susan scrubbed the casserole dish in the sink.

"I appreciate it, but I can't. I need to stay."

His fingertips swept over his cellphone stowed in a belt clip. For the first few days, it rang off the hook and Cal had answered with his heart lodged in his throat. Amelia was never on the other end, though, only mournful condolences. He collected them graciously gutted and wrecked.

"Look, you're just gonna keep beating yourself up," Paul said with forceful affection, the kind that barges in with good intentions. "I think getting away would do you some good. You've just gotta—"

"I've gotta what? Cope? Wait for another pile of ashes to show up at my door?"

Everyone had opinions about Cal's grief. Cal had opinions too. These days, they zipped from his lips far faster than he could stop them. Paul shook his head and tried again.

"That's not what I meant. I love you like a brother, and I hate seeing you this way, but no one has seen Amelia since the party. I don't know that you're going to find her in the..." Paul cleared a catch in his throat. "Well, in the way you think you are."

Paul couldn't say it. No one could. Dead. Amelia Havick was dead. That's what everyone wanted to say, and Cal was suffering, not stupid, so he heard the whispers and read the room.

"My daughter isn't dead," he'd told anyone who'd listen. With rubbery smiles, they indulged it like a lunatic delusion and threw him a bone to say that they tried. It was only human to be so knee-deep in denial.

"You think she's dead," Cal said with a sinkhole in his chest. Shoulders hunched, he collapsed into it. One day, it'd swallow him whole.

Paul fixed his eyes to the far end of the yard where sunlight and shadows met on the overgrown lawn.

"If she were alive, she would've come home by now."

The point stood, but Cal stubbornly refused to believe it.

"I'd know if she was gone. It'd be like a light turning out in me."

"I know what it's like to lose someone without making amends. What happened between you and Amelia wasn't your fault."

Wasn't it, though? The trees beyond the fence swayed in the gentle breeze, not unlike the last time he saw his daughter. His carelessness had driven a wedge between them by then, and Amelia stood in his office no longer a little girl, but her trust in him fading like a dying star.

Most nights, Cal dreamed of her. The years of her life played like an old movie until the film ran out at dawn and he laid alone in the morning light.

"I shut her out," Cal said, the words thick with shame. "She needed me, and I left her out in the cold. And for what? My own pride. I was so hard on her. Maybe if I hadn't been."

Cal grounded the thought before it got away. He couldn't rewrite the past, so he turned to Paul and voiced what mattered.

"This isn't about the things I didn't get to say or what I would've done differently. Amelia isn't dead. I can't prove it, but I need you to believe me. She ran from something that night."

"From what, though?"

"Burt warned me that Rich was in over his head with Philippe Velasco. I've got this sick feeling that Rich knew more about Philippe's death than he let on."

Paul folded his arms and sucked on his teeth. "Fuckin' Rich."

He didn't know the half of it and took up the cause because Cal had made it clear that Richard Dauer wasn't the man they used to know. And he was missing—not identified amongst the dead and his beloved Ferrari unaccounted for. The implication was clear. Richard survived but made no attempt to reach out, not to Cal or anyone else.

"Something bigger is going on," Cal said, "and I think Amelia is caught up in whatever it is."

An uncanny calm blanketed the yard as the world went quiet.

The birds stopped chirping, and the leaves no longer rustled. Tension tangled in Cal's stomach.

"Listen to me, Cal. If you're not gonna come to Chicago, at least consider leaving town for a while. It's not good, you staying here alone."

"I'll think about it." Cal mindlessly patted the phone at his hip, his only lifeline to Amelia. "I appreciate all that you and Susan have done for me. You have no idea what it's meant."

Paul squeezed Cal in a tight embrace and huffed in a way that Cal knew he stifled tears.

"You can't imagine how sorry we are."

Cal's chest ached, and he clung to his friend who'd stayed longer than anyone else. At the kitchen table, Susan plucked petals from the lily arrangement and placed them in a plastic bag. The clean casserole dish sat beside the barren arrangement.

"What am I supposed to do?" Cal asked tearfully.

"You carry on because you're Callum Havick, the most decent man I've had the pleasure of knowing, let alone calling one of my oldest friends. And damn it, we're getting old, aren't we? What the hell happened?"

A hearty chuckle rumbled from Paul, and Cal wiped away the tears as he laughed too. Susan smiled at them and tapped her watch.

"The offer always stands," Paul said as they headed inside. "You give your HVAC guy some hell. If he ain't here by tomorrow..."

"I know. I will."

Cal bid his farewells to Susan and Paul, shed the last shared tears, and watched as their rental pulled from the driveway. Paul honked three times and waved out the window.

After they left, Cal sat on the porch until twilight delivered him into darkness. He went inside then and took up his spot at the end of the kitchen table with a clear view of the front door.

When Amelia turned sixteen, everyone told him to expect long nights waiting for her to tiptoe inside after curfew. He never had to. Amelia was always a good girl. Even as a child, she'd been soft-hearted and eager to please; his little daydreamer with daisy-chains in her hair and poems in her heart.

He'd worried that she needed thicker skin to weather a world that could be cruel. In the end, the cruelty had come from him. He deserved the punishment he received, the nights he listened as she cried herself to sleep and her icy retreat in the days that followed. The words still played on repeat, that moment of anger he couldn't take back.

Cal's phone trilled. The chair wobbled as he flew to his feet and answered the call.

"This is Cal," he nearly shouted. The outburst left him lightheaded and faintly breathless.

A man on the line was polished and polite, a silver-voiced stranger who introduced himself as Special Agent Kingsley Bright with the FBI's Portland office. Pleasant enough, Agent Bright offered his condolences without the stuffy pretense of a fed but pivoted to business with little intervening chit-chat.

"I work in our organized crime unit," Agent Bright explained. "I picked up an investigation from my colleague, Martin Kranski. You know him?"

"I've met him a few times."

Slovenly but sharp had been Cal's impression. Agent Kranski would show up late to meetings in wrinkled suit jackets stinking of Pall Malls and meatball subs. He got the job done, though. That counted for more than the slick special agents murdered out in black and with an almighty ego to match.

"Agent Kranski was investigating Burt Shaw's death. He was at Mr. Dauer's party for unrelated business." Agent Bright paused a beat. "Unfortunately, he didn't survive."

"I'm sorry to hear that. Look, I don't mean to be crass, but what was there to investigate?"

"That's why I'm calling. I'm sure you already know that the Velascos have reorganized at the top."

That was a delicate way to put it. Philippe and his deputy were executed in brutal fashion. For the remaining ranks, it should've been a violent scramble to the top. Instead, someone had orchestrated a stunning and orderly transfer of power. Cal had never seen anything like it. Even the hand-off from Liam Moriarty to Emory Holt had its growing pains and a few flickers of discontent from other captains.

"What about it?" Cal asked.

"Burt was tangled up in things he shouldn't have been. He knew about the Velasco overthrow before it happened and likely knew the identity of the man involved, the one holding power now. I understand your daughter interned for Burt. Did she ever mention anything to you about the work she did, anything she might've seen?"

Cal stared through the sliding glass door. The backyard was dark, and the shadowed trees bobbed with the breeze. He drew the vertical blinds shut and killed the box fan. The house went deathly quiet as he paced the kitchen.

"She rarely talked about it. What does she have to do with this?"

Soft static filled the line. Cal pulled the phone from his ear. The call timer ticked along for three, four, five seconds more.

"Amelia saw the information Burt uncovered about the Velascos and—"

"That's why she's running."

Cal collapsed to the chair not unlike the night the medical examiner called with the news. Yes, the remains were Helen. No, he'd have to wait a few more days to collect her.

"Running," Agent Bright repeated incredulously. "You think your daughter is alive?"

The question was innocent, but Cal was heartsick and tired and doing his level-best to keep it together.

He'd made the phone calls, picked the hymns, assigned the readings, lit the candles, minded the flowers weeping petals to the living room floor.

He'd said hello to distant friends, tolerated stupid stories, and amassed condolences that boiled down to the same fucking sentiment.

Be strong, Cal. Be brave. Smile. Heal. Move on. She's dead. They both are. She's dead. Your baby is dead.

"No, I don't think!" Cal erupted with his fist pounding the table. "I know she is. I know it like I know my wife died a cruel, senseless death. I understand the crime scene is still being processed, that most victims won't be identified for weeks, if ever at all. I've got the Portland police telling me it's pointless to open a missing persons investigation, and now you're implying she was targeted because of some stupid internship she never wanted in the first place, one I pushed her into. So, which is it, Agent Bright—is Amelia in danger, or am I a moron for believing my girl is alive?"

"Woah, woah. Cal, listen," Agent Bright broke in and departed with the polished façade. "I believe you. I do. I think Amelia is alive."

Dizzy again, Cal steadied himself against the table. "You do?"

"Yes, and I want to help you find her. Do you know where she might've gone, where she would've run to if she knew she was in danger?"

"I don't know." Cal raked his fingers through his hair, still at a loss no matter how often he asked himself that question. "But I don't think Brian Burrows's death was a coincidence. He was Amelia's best friend and at that party. They must've been together at the motel. That boy who worked there, the clerk, he would know for sure."

"Well, if he wakes up," Agent Bright replied gravely. "The doctors say it's not looking good. I asked the sheriff's office to go back to the motel and search the area. They found a pair of bloody pliers on the side of a nearby road. It looked like a struggle."

"She was taken?"

"Possibly."

Cal's elbows dug into the table's wood grain, and he cradled his forehead in his hand. When he didn't speak again, Agent Bright continued with urgency lacing his voice.

"I have more to share, but it's better if we talk in person. In the meantime, I really think you should get out of Portland. Do you have any family you can stay with?"

The question stung. Cal's brother and only sibling, his parents, in-laws, and his wife were all dead, and Amelia was missing. *I'm alone.*

"I appreciate the concern," Cal said. "I'll think about it."

Cal hung up the call with a promise to stay in touch and began his nightly ritual of turning off the lights and trudging upstairs. And where he normally hurried past Amelia's shuttered bedroom door, he stopped at it now. Someone had shut it. He didn't know who, only that it was a kind gesture from one of his friends. Cal cracked it open, and grief followed him in like the house guest that never left.

The bed was unmade, and Amelia's phone sat on the nightstand plugged into the charger. He wouldn't dare see how many times he'd called, how many frantic messages he left.

His fingertips swept over her notebook of poems, but her brush, of all things, did him in. Perhaps it was the strands of red hair colored just like her mother's or how it'd been tossed to her bed as though she were coming right back.

She's not coming back.

With that thought, Cal collapsed with the weight of sorrow and regret. On his hands and knees, he glimpsed a moving box labeled 'Family Memories.' Bile hit the back of his throat. Cal dashed to the bathroom and vomited up the potatoes. He cleaned himself up, then went to his office and turned on a record for sonic relief.

He laid on the floor and stared at the ceiling as "Wish You Were Here" ripped at his heart. Quiet tears trailed over his cheekbones and gathered warm in his ear. He reset the needle and did it all over again as the hours passed him by.

At a half-past midnight, Cal crawled into bed but tossed in a twilight state of sleep. It wasn't the vacant space next to him or Amelia's empty bed down the hall that kept him up. Without the air conditioner's white noise, every sound roused him—a creak then a thump, the gust of wind, the tick of his watch. Cal checked the time.

2:32 AM.

He gripped the sheets, afraid of the dark for the first time since childhood and explained away the sounds. The creaks were just the house settling. It was nearly three decades old. And the groans? The wind had picked up. As for the thumps, well, he didn't know about that. Maybe a tree limb had shaken loose. Just as that thought came and went, a tremendous crash slammed against the deck outside.

Cal shot up in bed. His heart pounded as he threw open the nightstand drawer and pulled out his loaded gun. He crept to the window and dropped to his knees to peek at the deck below.

The motion sensor light was on, but no one was there. No shadows moving about. No animals dumbfounded in the light.

Cal stood and slid into his loafers. Downstairs, he clutched his gun and stared out the sliding glass door.

Nothing.

There was nothing.

He stepped outside as the wind picked up again and scrutinized the tree line. Curiosity trumped fear, and Cal walked down into the yard, but the hair on his arms stood on end as he scanned the woods. Still, there was nothing, just the swaying silhouettes of trees.

I'm being watched.

Someone lurked out there. It moved in the shadows, and he stared into the face of something he couldn't see. The motion light clicked off and plunged Cal into darkness. The sensation creeping over him intensified.

They're coming.

Cal dashed inside. He slammed the sliding glass door shut and flipped the lock. After a beat of panicked silence, he heard it.

The record player.

Upstairs, "Wish You Were Here" blared and brought with it a cold shock of terror. Sick with heartache, he almost sprinted to his office.

Don't go up there, Cal. Whatever you do, don't go up there, a voice warned within.

He bolted through the laundry room, into the garage, and yanked at the car's door.

Locked, it was locked.

Keys.

He needed the keys.

Cal bounded back inside. His palms collided against the kitchen table, and he upended stacks of paper that tumbled to the floor.

Music blasted through the house in an awful symphony. Delirious with fear, Cal's vision blurred, but his hands met his keys, and he snatched them up along with his wallet before sprinting to the garage.

With the car in reverse, he jammed the accelerator and sent empty trash bins sailing through the air as he peeled from the driveway. He watched in horror as Amelia's bedroom light flashed on, and the drapes rustled in the window.

Cal fled Portland. He ran from a threat that had no name or true manifestation beyond the unearthly terror it imparted. He understood something of his daughter's fear, the reason she ran from home.

Cal had no choice but to do the same.

SIXTEEN

AMELIA

Mirabelle broke the news.

"I'm so sorry, love. Your momma didn't make it," she said through glistening tears.

Amelia denied it at first.

It was a trick. A ruse. A sick joke.

Haunting silence came next, that moment before the surge, and then grief took her under with a wail she didn't recognize as her own. Her knees crashed to the floor, and the rest vacated her memory with shades of black. Black behind her eyes at night. Black from the curtains drawn shut by day.

That first night, Amelia sobbed into a pillow so hard she nearly smothered herself. Mirabelle had been there to remind her to breathe and, in the days to come, cradled her, cried with her, drew hot baths, hummed sweet songs.

Liam Moriarty offered his condolences with white peonies and a kind note. Even Jack apologized for her loss. His bright blue eyes had gleamed with sincerity, and Amelia accepted it politely but asked to be left alone.

They all came, all except Emory.

Like a pebble in her shoe, his absence grew more obvious with each passing day. That she craved his comfort added complexity to the pain. Amelia wanted to curl up beside him and sleep for days, but it was foolish to seek shelter in such a hard man.

She saw Emory only once in passing. So engrossed in his inner world, he hadn't seen her sipping tea at the kitchen island. She tried to make herself small, but even her diminished presence disturbed him. Emory turned to her as if expecting someone else. Whatever he meant to say perished on parted lips, so he tipped his head and let her be, and Amelia thought that was just as well.

After a week, her heartache hardened to a dead calm. Amelia laid awake most nights and stared at the ceiling until pastel dawn spilled through the window.

Horrible questions kept her awake. Had it been quick? Quick enough her mom wasn't afraid or in pain? Had she been alone? Was her father alone now too? Some nights she tried to sleep but saw Brian in her dreams choking on clots of blood and with the light leaving his eyes.

Tonight, sleep was hard won for different reasons. Emory had business in Las Vegas tomorrow and planned to take her with him. Mirabelle had told her that afternoon and even echoed Emory's logic: "It's safer this way." But that wasn't Mirabelle's truth, only Emory's, so she faltered when she said it, and Amelia dwelled on that fracture of doubt.

She tossed to her side and stared at the clock.

2:32 AM.

The numbers glowed like red embers. Another day and night in the underworld. Time marched on, but that hardly seemed to matter. Amelia pulled the stiff covers over her head.

Everyone there meant well in the worst ways. The bed's starchy sheets were pulled taut against a hard mattress and chaffed her bare legs.

Brian's sweater had mysteriously vanished too, whisked away to the dry cleaners, or so Mirabelle speculated because she didn't honestly know. What a useless gesture. It'd come back smelling like any other striped sweater, but not like Brian.

In its place, Mirabelle had taken Amelia's measurements and ordered clothes. Boxes came for days on end, big and small and filled with beautiful things. It was a grand luxury in the confines of a nightmare.

"You'll want for nothing. Even Emory agrees," Mirabelle had told her.

Oh, how she'd beamed at that last bit, a bold effort to engender trust. She hung her fragile hopes on it, and Amelia whacked them down with a biting retort.

"You mean nothing except my home and family, right?"

Mirabelle had excused herself then and came back later with puffy eyes and a sniffly nose, but a fresh round of bright smiles and another big box. Amelia had burned with shame and apologized, but Mirabelle feigned ignorance at the slight.

Amelia shot up from the sheets. The clock with its colon-for-eyes blinked flatly at her. She swung her legs over the side of the bed, got on the floor, and, beneath the nightstand, yanked the clock's cord from the wall.

A muffled conversation filtered from down below. Emory's deep and commanding voice was unmistakable to her after her time there. Amelia often heard it rumbling through the mansion and sometimes his resonant laughter too. She pressed her ear to the floor and steadied her breaths to listen but couldn't make out the other voice.

With a pang of curiosity, Amelia pushed from the floor, and the voices melted into the darkness as she tiptoed across the room. She cracked open the door and hovered beneath the frame.

Angry footfalls paced the foyer below. She knew the cadence of Emory's stride and the way his boots hit the floor. He'd once pounded after her like that.

The night he held her in his arms and slid his fingers inside. The night he almost kissed her. The night she almost ran away.

"The road to hell is paved with good intentions," Liam said. "Damon murdered that boy, and if you didn't have a vested interest, he would've done the same to Amelia. The very thing you were trying to protect her from would've happened anyhow."

Brian. Like his sweater, Amelia assumed they forgot. Her heartbeat hastened as she crept into the hall.

"I already admitted Damon was a mistake," Emory argued, "that I should've done it myself. What would you've done?"

"Oh, good! No harm, no foul then. It all goes away."

"What do you want me to say?"

"A prayer that the motel clerk doesn't get chatty when he wakes up."

"*If* he wakes up."

Eric. Amelia didn't know that Damon had hurt him too. The poor boy was so young.

"From your lips to God's ears," Liam warned. "You better pray he kicks it. Her being here set something in motion we're not prepared to deal with."

"It was already in motion."

"Don't be so fucking naïve. There's something else going on. You and I both know it. The things the Velascos are doing, have already done, are beyond the pale. Philippe was a lot of things, but never a butcher. If he weren't dead, I'd say it reminds me of—"

"Enough!" Emory barked. "Leave it alone."

The hallway darkened, Amelia could've sworn. Emory stopped pacing, and silence stretched on. She coiled her arms around her middle to ward off the chill, and the starchy bed seemed a splendid comfort, but her legs carried her farther down the hall instead.

"Answer my question," Emory said. "What would you've done?"

"You know my thoughts. You brought Amelia here, went through all the trouble. Make her sing, Emory."

Amelia's stomach twisted. Dressed as a threat, it hid the depraved. A bad man might've seized on it as permission to do awful things, whatever those might be.

"Answer the fucking question. If you'd been at that party, seen her huddled in a pile of bodies and crying for help, what would you've done? Left her for them, left her to die? Is that the kind of man you are?"

Judgment dripped from Emory's questions that came

wrapped in so much affront. Something gave way in Amelia. A softening of the resistance, a fissure in the barricade.

She slumped against the wall with a winded breath, as if all the air had been knocked from her lungs. What kind of man was Emory Holt? She couldn't say anymore.

Emory exhaled a quiet, scathing laugh. "Nothing? Alright. I'm going to bed."

"My point still stands," Liam said. "I told you to cool off a bit, not ice her out. You've made no effort to speak to her since she decked you."

"She doesn't trust me."

"Why the hell should she? Try harder. You're down here raising hell on her behalf. Look at you, tough guy. You're up my ass about it. I would have helped her, by the way. Fuck you for thinking otherwise."

"Fuck you too, old man."

Their voices rose with dueling heat, so close to fisticuffs, but they called a truce with laughter, and the tempo of their banter turned on a dime. A patting sound followed, the telltale way men embraced—hard hugs with open palms whacking each other's backs.

Emory muttered something Amelia couldn't hear before his boots sounded up the stairs. She froze, suddenly aware how far she'd drifted down the hall, too far to make it back to bed.

Emory rounded the corner in quick strides but stopped with a shuffled step when he saw her there. His hair was combed back and gathered neatly at the nape of his neck. In a white t-shirt and jeans, he smelled faintly of cigarette smoke and whiskey.

Amelia didn't know what his business outings entailed, only that they mostly occurred after dark and kept him out late.

She remained rooted halfway down the hall in an oversized t-shirt that barely covered her ass. At least she was wearing underwear unlike their first encounter in that same hall.

"I couldn't sleep," she explained, though Emory hadn't said anything and refused to come closer.

He stared at her impassively, but in the pale moonlight, Amelia swore he looked mildly relieved.

How convenient for him to have revealed his motivations indirectly. He could divulge how he felt in a confessional of his own making as she listened through the veil. Emory wasn't a coward, though. He withheld deliberately.

That pebble smarted again, sharp and paining her more than she cared to admit.

"I imagine not," Emory said flatly. He crossed his arms and chewed the inside of his cheek.

"It wasn't the noise. I was already awake."

"I know." He glanced at her bedroom door cracked open and probably glimpsed the sheets in a tangle. "I hope you can get some rest."

Emory resumed hurried strides and breezed past her on the way to his bedroom.

"Why didn't you come?" Amelia demanded more than asked as he reached his door. She tried to banish the hurt from her voice but couldn't match his stoic detachment.

Emory turned to her with a look of confusion, but his shoulders tensed as if steeling himself against accusations. For such a strong man, he couldn't carry the weight of his guilt. He needed her to relieve him of it. Amelia refused.

"My mom died," she said and inched toward him with a lump in her throat that she swallowed down. "I missed her funeral. My dad buried her alone and probably expects to bury me too. My entire world has crumbled, and you have nothing to say to me."

Emory clenched his jaw and sucked in a deep breath that filled his chest. Amelia imagined he did that on purpose. He made a show of how he tamed his anger, and she was supposed to be grateful that he didn't unleash it on her.

"You heard me down there," he said, his voice raspy with fatigue. "You want me to repeat it?"

Amelia shook her head. They'd already been down that dead-end road. He could touch her but not console her; was generous with his passion but austere in his affection. She knew his boundaries and wanted no part.

In prowling steps, Emory started down the hall to her. He approached with the confidence of a man who got what he wanted, always and without exception.

"Then what the fuck do you want from me? You want me to turn myself inside out for you? Down on my knees to tell you I'm sorry? To beg your forgiveness that your life turned out this way?"

Emory loomed over her, and Amelia craned her neck to meet his eyes.

"Yes," she answered honestly and noticed the gun tucked into his waist band and the flecks of blood on his shirt.

That same blood marred the tattoos on his forearms. She knew on instinct the blood wasn't his and, by that same instinct, backed away.

"See, this is the problem with you and me," he said. "You think you know what you want when it's far away. The closer I get to you, the less you want of me. I don't go by halves. You get all or nothing. I'm not built for the in-between."

Under different circumstances, Amelia might've appreciated his brutal honesty. He made clear what kind of man he was, and Amelia wondered what kind of women he'd had before, if they were anything like her. How could they be? Emory promised a zero-sum game where his love was the prize for total surrender. What kind of woman accepted that?

Plenty, it seemed.

Emory opened his bedroom door and stood with his back against one side of the frame and his hand casually propped on the other.

"You in or out?" he asked and tipped his head to the inside of his bedroom.

Amelia studied him and sifted through his outward apathy for a shred of anything else. Backlit by moonlight, his intentions were harder than ever to decipher. She didn't know what he was offering—sex or something more—and made no move in either direction.

Indecision would be her answer because he demanded to know what she wanted but said nothing of his own desire. Night after night, she had laid herself bare. It was his turn to do the same.

He wouldn't, of course. Not Emory Holt. He'd keep the high ground to remain out of reach.

"I'm not that kind of girl," Amelia told him but came closer. That she contradicted herself confused him, she knew. It confused her too, the need to be near him then the urge to pull away. It came in waves she failed to predict.

"That's not what I want from you," Emory said as Amelia stood in front of her bedroom door.

She sensed a lie or perhaps his own contradictions. He'd brought her there for one thing but held onto her for another, and neither knew the reason anymore.

"Then what do you want?" Amelia asked as they faced one another on either side of the hall.

It wasn't an accusation of anything, just a simple question that she'd asked countless times before. And countless times, he'd given her some version of the same answer—for her to come clean, spill her guts, sing.

With his hands in his pockets, Emory leaned against the doorframe and contemplated her. His eyes drifted down her body, skimming her hair tousled from sleep, her breasts in a thin t-shirt, the length of her bare legs. His gaze settled with some weight to the floor between them. Brows knit, he thought it over with a shake of his head.

"I don't know anymore."

Emory looked deeply troubled to be at a loss. His uncertainty gentled something in him, though. Drenched in lunar light, Amelia spied the cracks in his resistance too.

For tonight, that was all she wanted. She stepped into the hall, and Emory did the same until only moonbeams remained between them. When he freed his hands from his pockets, Amelia wondered if he meant to hold her and if she might let him. On either side, the answer never seemed clear.

"Maybe that's our problem, you and me," she said with another step closer until they met in the middle, close enough to touch. "That neither of us know anymore."

Emory peered down at her, his boots adding to his height as she stood barefoot before him. Up close again, his presence consumed with less of a threat, and his chest rose and fell with quick exchanges of breath.

"Maybe," he replied off-beat and distracted, as if he'd just found his answer but still refused to confess.

Whatever it was, he carried it with him across the hall in backwards steps, and Amelia did the same. They paused momentarily, each at their door, but the distance between them remained. How long it'd last, Amelia couldn't say.

It was dangerous, the incessant talk of wants and needs. Neither could help themselves, though, so they kept coming back to disturb the space they shared, the only common ground between them.

"*I don't need you,*" they'd each declared at one point or another but barreled toward the day they no longer meant it.

SEVENTEEN

EMORY

Emory woke with the sun. It wasn't ritual, just memoriam. In the quiet respite of morning, he'd think of his father, but the memories were forged in absolutes. He remembered everything or nothing; the recollections larger than life next to the lost years.

Even at thirty-one, he could still taste the cold winter mornings of his childhood when the sun hadn't yet warmed the sky and frost coated the windows. In the kitchen, Emory would sit atop the air vent billowing heat as his father tugged on work boots.

And he could still feel the swampy heat of summer nights helping his dad in the garage. With his father elbow deep in a Pontiac GTO, Emory would hand off tools until Ivan wandered in.

By then, his older brother had taken an interest in torturing small animals with their father's tools. In the room they shared, Ivan would torture Emory too with the grotesque details of his new hobby. Emory slept on the couch thereafter until his mother made good use of the switch. Then he didn't sleep much at all, sometimes at school, but that landed him in trouble too.

Ivan eventually advanced to the sledgehammer as his tool of choice. With their father distracted in the garage, he'd admire it with a silent threat. One day, he'd crush Emory's skull. Ivan would leave then, and Emory was always slow on the uptake after.

"Get outta your head, son," his dad would say, "and don't worry about your brother. That boy is broken in ways even God can't fix."

True enough, worrying hadn't solved anything, and God never fixed Ivan.

By seven-thirty, Emory had showered and dressed in black jeans and a t-shirt with his long hair tied back. By eight-thirty, he got to work in an unused office on the third floor. For shame it wasn't with his hands. He'd be happier if it was. Turn a wrench and free his mind.

At a half-past eleven, Jack's noisy trinity sounded in the hall— boots stomping, wallet chain rattling, the whistling of some goddamn tune sure to stick in Emory's head. Jack cantered in sporting a devilish grin and flopped into the chair across the desk.

"Mornin,' sexy," he said and picked his nails with a pocketknife. "Rough night?"

"Just about."

Three, maybe four hours of fitful sleep. Another fight had in the hall, though, that one had felt different. On the ropes, he had nothing left for Amelia and thought she might've been pleased.

She wasn't. Amelia wanted him contrite, not defeated, but his pride couldn't bear to bend the knee. Something had shifted in him and in her too. It burned him up that he couldn't tell what, so that rough night bled into an early morning. If he didn't sleep, too fucking bad. The world kept spinning.

"I heard Liam lighting you up last night. Everything alright?"

Emory shrugged and snapped shut his laptop's lid.

"It's fine. What's done is done. Damon is—"

"In pieces."

Jack's perpetual amusement vanished and left behind a fearsome visage. He was just as dangerous and brutal as the other men but charmed with humor they couldn't quite manage. He leaned in close. An errant strand of hair fell in his eyes and grazed the crooked bridge of his nose.

"About the motel clerk. We can make that problem disappear."

Jack pitched cold-blooded murder with the sleazy grease of a car salesman and a toothy smile to match.

Emory shook his head and asked, "For what? What did he see? Amelia? Okay, so he saw Amelia, places her with the Burrows kid."

"He can place Damon there too. That will track to us."

"Damon had no loyalty. He was in a lot of pockets, not just ours."

Jack folded the knife and acquiesced with lifted hands. His instincts had accuracy, though, enough that Emory picked up the thread to see where it ended.

"What are you concerned about?" he asked.

"We don't know what the clerk knows. Could be nothing, could be everything. We get rid of him, we get rid of an unknown."

"True, but the more you pick at a wound, the more it refuses to heal. Might be best to leave this one alone."

Jack mulled it over with a nod, though clearly unconvinced. At an impasse, Emory offered no promises, just consideration.

"Let's find out more about the hospital the kid's at. If it'd be an easy hit, okay; a production, I don't have the appetite."

"Fair enough. For today, I already briefed the men. Ten are with us. The rest will stay behind with Liam."

"Good man. Thank you."

"You know I love you," Jack said with a wink and hopped to his feet.

"So you say."

Emory grabbed his gun and tucked it into his waist band. Down the hall, he and Jack walked in step.

"I want another captain with us and a few more men too," Emory said. "I'd rather have more and need less. We can spare the numbers."

"How 'bout Pete? He can bring a few of his soldiers."

"Perfect."

They took the stairs to the first floor.

"And Amelia?"

"With me."

Jack grinned. "She still hate your ass?"

"Probably a safe bet."

Who could blame her? And those walls she put up, Emory would've put them up too. Hell, he had put them up, but bitterness breached, an assault in broad daylight, and he traced its lineage back to blame. Amelia blamed him for her misfortunes, and Emory inherited guilt that grew wild like weeds he couldn't pluck out.

Outside, he and Jack waded into a wall of dead heat with no breeze to call reprieve. The tiled terrace out front offered pockets of shade but couldn't make up for a sun that raged toward its peak. In the distance, craggy earth met bright blue sky, and popcorn clouds ambled along.

They were early. The men wouldn't show for another fifteen minutes. In these moments, Emory indulged the break; no duty or planning or expectation to bury his fear for the sake of others.

In these moments, he and Jack unearthed old memories. Jack had a way of glossing over tragedy with detours back to happier times—riding bikes, skipping rocks, staring up at the stars those summer nights as kids, wondering how it'd all pan out. *Not like this. Never like this.*

And in these moments, Emory had nothing left to do but laugh. *"Suck it up, buttercup,"* his old man would say. It was the hand he was dealt.

Jack leaned against a stucco archway and lit a cigarette. "This plan will work?"

Emory knew better than to peg a sure thing. Plans were simple, people were unpredictable, and business was always personal to a degree. He wanted the organization sleek, trim, and tight. That meant consolidating assets and lobbing off the dead weight; in that particular case, a bloated gambling establishment whose revenue wasn't worth the trouble it caused.

"Hopefully," Emory said. "Plans have a way of going sideways. The point is to be prepared. Are we prepared?"

Jack cocked his head back and exhaled a mouthful of smoke. "I'd say so."

They kept conversation light and inconsequential until Liam joined them. He bummed a cigarette from Jack and settled beneath the archway.

"You boys be safe today," Liam said. "Do what you need to and come home."

Home.

The mansion wasn't Emory's home, as much as Liam wished it was. The house was too big, too lavish. Part hacienda, part Spanish mission, it'd been homage to Francisca Moriarty and might've been a sanctuary under better circumstances.

For Emory, it was strictly temporary, and he hadn't the heart to foot stomp that, so he paid Liam a dull smile, and Jack did the same, though it wasn't his home either.

One by one, the Moriarty men gathered in the circle drive out front. Emory greeted them with an iron handshake and ensured they understood their orders. At any glint of confusion, he went over the plan again. Jack bullshitted and cracked quick-witted quips that maintained morale and settled nerves.

"Figure your captains out. Play to their strengths," Liam once told Emory. He heralded the advice and read the fine print in others. It meant knowing himself too, though; what he was and what he wasn't.

He wasn't Jack with all that bantering swagger, but when Jack couldn't muster the muscle to discipline, Emory stepped in with a stern hand. The balance worked.

In the sweltering heat, his men waited and Emory checked the time. It was close enough to noon to put up a fuss. He dug out his phone, but before he could fire off a text, the front door opened and Mirabelle dazzled with a smile that doubled as a talisman against his agitation.

"You're late," Emory said.

She rolled her eyes. "Your watch is fast."

Behind her, Amelia slipped through the door. She looked the way Emory remembered from Dauer's party—bone-crushingly beautiful with full lips, upturned nose, and auburn hair cascading over bare shoulders.

It wasn't just the length of her bare legs in a sundress or the slope of her hourglass shape he found so utterly alluring. Amelia disarmed with Bambi eyes and smiles so sweet.

Up close, the girl had claws. Push too hard, she had bite. It intrigued and infuriated him, and it was the hot blast against his skin as he approached.

"Amelia," he greeted tepidly. "You'll ride with me today."

Her eyes darted to him, the electric shock of her name passing his lips perhaps or maybe the arrangements she had no say in. Without a word, she flounced down the steps to the circle drive below.

"She's got some fire to her," Mirabelle once said.

All Emory ever saw was ice. Amelia wouldn't protest with passion and panic, only biting aloofness and willing estrangement.

Mirabelle frowned, apparently shattered it wasn't roses between them, just a wasteland of salted earth that bore no understanding. Emory would happily call it a red zone and have that be that, but Liam pointed at him with a stark reminder.

"She'll come around. When she does, you know what to do."

Make her sing. Emory balked but bit his tongue.

The men divvied up. The ones staying behind ambled inside while the others hustled to their cars. Arms crossed, Amelia stood stiffly next to Emory's car and eyed him warily as he approached. Every time he came near, she braced herself that way.

Emory didn't invest in lost causes, so he'd stopped coming around, but their time apart only made things worse. Amelia couldn't bear to be near him, and he couldn't stomach the rejection.

"You don't have to look so heartbroken," he said and tried in earnest to mask his resentment.

There was no disguising it, though, as he tore open the

passenger door. She peered up at him, her eyes searching his face for something more. Emory understood well enough that he intrigued her, that she wanted to take him apart just to figure him out. She puzzled on what he just said, and her head went on its side as if she didn't comprehend.

"You're not what's breaking my heart."

"Well, you might be what's breaking mine," Emory replied, half a joke, and even laughed to prove the humor. Of all things, that made the difference.

Amelia uncrossed her arms, and her gaze flicked to his chest before meeting his eyes again.

"Oh. I'm sorry," she said with surprising softness, a departure from her usual defiance.

For the moment, Emory could believe she meant it too. The tension dissolved in her shoulders, and she came closer with less affliction than before.

"It's a long ride," he said. "Plenty of time to tell me about your broken heart, and maybe I'll tell you about mine."

EIGHTEEN

EMORY

They rolled out along the highway, a pejorative for two dusty lanes with nothing to see and nowhere to go except Las Vegas. Emory glanced at Amelia in the passenger seat. Grief had imparted a haunting stillness in her. She wore it like armor and settled comfortably in the silence between them.

When she lost her mother, he said nothing about it because his words would've come out of order. Demands before apologies, upside down and inside out. She made his pulse rise and blood boil, so Emory withheld condolences lest he dish them out hot and jaded.

It wasn't as if he hadn't once been knee-deep and sinking in the same devastation, though. He owed her something. Commiseration, at least.

"About your mom," he said and shattered the silence, "I lost mine too. I was eight."

"I'm sorry to hear that," Amelia replied but declined his gaze.

"I wasn't looking for sympathy. I just mean I know how hard it is."

She looked over at him and even went to speak but must've thought the better of it. Emory waited. Nothing came, though, only the rising tide of frustration on his end and a vast sea of reticence on hers.

"Look," he said forcefully, "this will go easier if you try, even a little, to trust me."

Emory trained his eyes on the road, but in his periphery, Amelia crossed her arms and stared. What did he expect? Some ground, maybe more frigid resistance, but certainly not her honeyed voice firing back a piece of her mind.

"*This* will go much easier if *you* understand that kidnapping people and forcing them to go on your little field trips doesn't inspire trust."

Emory faltered, flat on his face and tongue-tied too. He licked his bottom lip and gripped the wheel.

"I didn't kidnap you, and this isn't a field trip."

"You kidnapped me."

"I didn't."

"Well, I don't want to be here, so what would you call this?"

The sun pounded through the windshield. Emory cranked up the air, as much to buy time as battle the heat.

"An obligation," he said with as much authority on the matter as he could muster. "Sometimes we gotta go places for our own good. Like, fuck, I don't know." He scratched his chin and sighed. "I don't like going to the post office, but I do it 'cause I have to."

The reasoning was weak, the explanation flawed, the analogy stupid. He knew that, even without Amelia's perplexed look that seemed slightly embarrassed on his behalf.

"This isn't like the post office. Besides, you don't go to the post office."

Her certainty incensed. What the fuck did she know about him?

A bead of sweat trickled down Emory's temple. He swiped it away with a rough hand and snapped on a short fuse.

"I buy stamps just like everyone else!"

She laughed then.

Amelia Havick laughed at him.

No one laughed at him.

No one.

They supplicated, placated, measured every word, regulated

each movement. Curated to appease, it drove him insane. Not her. She didn't give a shit who he was, so she laughed; not mocking, just gently amused. It dispelled enough of the tension that Emory conceded where he could.

"Fine. I brought you here against your will."

"It's call kidnapping."

"It's your turn," he demanded, more churlish than intended.

"My turn for what?"

"Compromise."

Amelia unfolded her arms and traced her fingertips along the hem of her skirt inching up her thighs. Emory's heartbeat quickened as his eyes followed her fingers. *Fuck, don't start that.* At the end of his rope, he couldn't handle the tease.

He remembered well the way she tasted, how her beautiful face contorted in pleasure when she came. That memory existed on the edge of his thoughts and waited for quiet moments to invade.

"Compromise." Amelia lingered on the word and studied the barren horizon dotted with brush. "For right now, I believe you're probably the least likely to hurt me of the people who want to."

Emory expelled a quiet laugh. "Any more caveats you wanna cram into that statement?"

"Fine," she said and rubbed her arms blanketed with goosebumps. "I acknowledge that you're protecting me."

Amelia turned to him with a shy glance through dark lashes. When the road demanded his attention, Emory looked away and turned down the air conditioner.

"Mirabelle told me you have a brother," she said, the statement imploring with a latent question she didn't have the nerve to ask.

"Had. I *had* a brother."

"Is he missing?"

Emory shook his head and scanned the rearview mirror where the black caravan carried on like a funeral march.

Missing implied they wanted Ivan back because hearts ached for those who'd never come home. Ivan would know. How many girls had been plastered up on posters because of him? "MISSING," read bolded letters from desperate families, and Ivan the Butcher more than earned his epithet. He claimed those girls' lives then took their stories to his grave.

"No. He's dead."

Amelia's lips pursed and eyes darted across the dashboard as if chasing a thought.

"I'm sorry. Mirabelle made it sound like he was still alive. I must've misunderstood."

"You didn't. Mirabelle could stand over his rotting corpse and still not believe he's dead."

"What was his name?" Amelia asked, too intrigued by the topic for Emory's liking.

"Ivan," he reluctantly replied.

Like his dad, Emory believed to name evil was to conjure it. Ivan's name was a malediction, and his brand of evil particularly heinous. Amelia didn't know that, though her outsized reaction of worried eyes and knitted brows might have suggested otherwise.

"You know him or something?" Emory chuckled to lighten the mood.

She shook her head. "No."

Liars overcompensated. They said too much, reacted too big. Amelia did neither but still sheltered something worth protecting. If he pushed, she'd deny, so Emory filed that away for a revisit once he paved clearer in-roads.

"Enough about him," he said. "Tell me about you."

"What about me?"

"Whatever you want to tell."

"You mean the things you don't already know from keeping tabs?"

Emory sucked in a sharp breath. Another battle of wills, was it? He readied the calvary for all-out war, but Amelia's words were empty of the accusation that could've been there.

"It's a joke," she assured with a pretty smile. "A bad one, but maybe you shouldn't tell people that you keep tabs on them."

"Sounds like you're telling me how to do my job."

"Sounds like someone needed to."

Emory laughed, oddly enchanted as the girl doled out jabs sweetened with humor.

"Fair enough," he said. "So, what's Amelia Havick's story?"

She shrugged and eyed him with the last vestiges of apprehension.

"There's not much to say. No adventures unless you count college in Eugene. That's the farthest I've been from home."

"You regret not going farther?"

"Not really. That place was good to me. I used to go to the library, to this secluded spot by the reference books no one reads. I'd study, write, daydream. It overlooked the woods, and the fog rolled in whenever it rained. It felt safe, peaceful. I think of it sometimes when I can't sleep."

Emory soaked up the sound of her voice—timid in some ways, bold in others; calm and captivating. Mirabelle claimed he and Amelia were alike, and if he'd just come in easier, he'd see it too.

He sweetened on her with a stomach flip and an exchanged glance where she regarded him more gently too.

"I like that," Emory said. "I grew up in Northern California. I miss the coast, the redwoods." He gestured to the arid landscape. "This isn't my scene."

"I can see that."

Amelia shifted toward him. The sunlight caught in her hair and warmed her perfume. Emory breathed in the floral sweetness, something like ice cream in a rose garden.

"Alright, what else? You break any hearts in Eugene?"

Amelia thought it over until a conspiratorial smile formed on her lips. "Almost. I have a secret."

Make her sing. Her song would start like that, the willing surrender. Emory wouldn't have to coax it out of her. All he had to do was cede the stage and listen.

He put some grit in his voice and charm in the glance he gave.

"Let's hear it."

"My junior year, I won first place in the pie contest at the county fair. I entered as a joke and forgot I was on the hook, so the pie was store-bought. Everyone raved about it, thought I was an amazing baker. I'm not. It was a scam."

Amelia broke with effervescent laughter. Even her secrets were saccharine. Maybe that's why she invited him in, batting her lashes for the beast at her door. He'd normally ridicule that kind of naiveté in others, but she wasn't stupid, and it wasn't a ploy.

"Unbelievable. Were you exposed?"

Amelia nodded with mischievous pride. "Oh yeah. Big scandal. Broken hearts."

She bit her bottom lip so full it had a crease at its center. More shy than seductive, it suited her so goddamn well; that nervous flutter of her lashes and the flustered breath passing her lips. It fucking wrecked him.

Your move. Make it count.

With his elbow resting next to hers, Emory leaned a little closer. He had her where he wanted. Why then did it feel so cheap?

"I'm sure you spared your old man some heartache if the worst thing you've ever done is rig a pie contest."

Amelia's joy, fleeting as it was, disintegrated, and she stared at her hands clasped tight in her lap.

"He'd beg to differ."

"Why's that?"

"I didn't want to go to Harvard. My dad arranged the internship with Burt, said it'd put my doubts about law school to rest. It didn't. Halfway through, I told him I'd already dropped out and had an editing job lined up in Arizona."

"Why Arizona?"

"I don't know. I liked the light there and the heat. I thought I'd feel better with warmer weather. Maybe I sensed it'd be good to me. I wanted somewhere to belong, the freedom to write and breathe and just *be*."

Shame came like a blow to Emory's chest. He'd gotten off on a technicality—no, he wasn't the one who kidnapped her—but had no claim to innocence. He'd derailed her life and mocked her dreams.

"What do you write?" he asked, atonement for the mess he'd made.

"Mostly little poems. The things I've seen or places I've been. Nice memories. The people I love. Dreams I have. That sort of thing."

"Not so little."

With sorrow in her eyes, Amelia smiled. "Not to me."

"But to Cal."

She nodded. "God, he was so angry, the things he said."

"What did he say?"

Amelia stiffened with cool poise. No one ever hid their pain as cleverly as they thought, though. Emory read her fine print—Cal had fucked up good—but everyone had their limits, the things that hurt too much to speak. That was hers.

"Look, I'll never be pals with your dad. Nothing you can say will make me hate him more than I already do."

Amelia drew a long breath then spoke quietly, as if it were the first time she'd repeated her father's words.

"He said I was a failure and a disappointment and that he couldn't wait until I was some other man's problem and he could wash his hands of me."

The cruelty stunned, even for Emory. God only knew how many times his temper had bested him. Still, he couldn't imagine saying that to someone he loved.

"Fucking prick. What'd you do?"

"Nothing. I cried and didn't talk to him for weeks." Amelia smoothed down the hem of her dress, and Emory battled the instinct to reach for her hand. "He was out of line, but he's a good man."

Everyone knew what kind of man Callum Havick was—tenacious and unwavering in his convictions, the way he chained himself to the blind might of justice. A good man, maybe, but who was she trying to convince? Not just Emory, it seemed.

"A good man wouldn't make you cry," he said out of spite, though the hypocrisy wasn't lost on him.

"You made me cry."

"I don't claim to be a good man."

It was half a joke, but Amelia studied him as if weighing what little she knew of his heart against his sins.

"I'm not sure you're a bad man either."

"The jury still out?"

"Might be," she laughed.

A grin deposited some ache in Emory's cheeks. "I guess I gotta win you over then."

"What's the plan?"

He glanced at her and answered sincerely, "To be sweet to you."

"I'd like that," she said with a smile.

Unrehearsed, it went much better. Amelia must've thought so too and relaxed in her seat. The lines on the road had melted into a daze, but the highway gained lanes, and the traffic picked up too. They'd arrive soon, and Emory owed her more than just sweetness.

"About that night," he said, vaguely aware they'd had so many rough nights and he ought to specify. "The first one. What I said in the basement lounge. I'm sorry. I didn't mean to hurt you."

It tasted like a lie, sounded like one too. Hadn't he meant to break her down? Apologies chased with lies were as good as useless. On her level, he said all that mattered for him to say.

"Okay, I did mean to hurt you, and I'm sorry for that too. You didn't deserve it. I was a dick."

"You were," Amelia agreed, no bullshit on her end either, "but I forgive you."

"Good. And, for the record, I like your stories."

"Really? They're kind of simple."

"That's the appeal," Emory said and took their exit. At the end of the off-ramp, he stopped at a red light. "People make things too complicated. Simple is better."

In his world, others tried to impress with stories of death and darkness, a means to relate as if the scars they wore were prizes to be won. He dealt with enough darkness. Lonely at the top, Emory craved the light.

Amelia stared at him with placid curiosity and perhaps divined the parts missing in him, his soul sick of violence.

"Your life is awfully complicated for a man who likes simple things. Could you ever leave this and have a simple life? That's what you want, isn't it?"

No one had ever asked him that before—not Mirabelle nor Liam, not even Jack—and he'd never answer honestly if they had. The sacrilege would be too great, the cost of walking away too staggering. Emory contemplated the cracked and broken landscape out the windshield. He thought of his home, where he belonged in the world, and it wasn't there.

"I'm sure it's not that easy to just leave," Amelia continued, a gracious means to skip past that part because he was the one folding in now with pain he couldn't talk past. "I guess that's why you like simple things. Maybe sometime you can tell me your simple stories, if you have any. And if not, just make them up, and you can pretend for a little while that things aren't so complicated."

"I'd like that," Emory said and regarded Amelia with renewed fascination.

On his level too, she paid him no deference in hopes of currying his favor or seducing his affection, and Emory no longer wanted anything from her either. Enough was enough. She didn't have to sing.

Behind them, a car blared its horn.

The light was green.

NINETEEN

MIRABELLE

Outside of Vegas, the convoy rolled into a vacant lot behind a small strip of shops. The quaint street was lost in time, the prelude to a ghost town on the cusp of charming and sweet. Safe behind the car's tinted glass, Jack leaned over the center console. His lips swept against Mirabelle's, and a calloused palm caressed the inside of her bare thigh.

"Someone might see," she said and lifted a hand to his chest.

Jack fumbled with her underwear. "You said that this morning."

"No, I said someone might hear."

She had woken up to his mouth between her legs, and while the pillow muffled her moans, that didn't matter in a house that echoed. Jack hadn't cared and always took whatever he pleased. Sometimes he'd pull her into an empty room, and their lips would crush together, and his hands would tremble, and it was all a dizzying rush of beating hearts and limbs entwined.

"I want you," he whispered.

"I'm wearing lipstick, and we need to be careful."

Mirabelle nudged him away. Sure enough, his lips were red and dick was hard. She tossed him a napkin from her purse but couldn't do much about the rest.

"Jesus, Miri, who fucking cares? It'll come out eventually. You

155

know what I'll say when it does?" Jack pointed to a sun-bleached fence post beyond the car's hood, a stand-in for Emory, perhaps. "Fuck you. She could be with a scumbag but ended up with me."

Mirabelle crossed her arms and dropped her eyes. There was nothing to say that she hadn't already, and they only ever fought about that.

"Alright, you got me," Jack sighed. "Consider me careful."

Mirabelle tapped the tip of his nose, crooked for having been broken too many times.

"I consider you cute."

"Don't call a grown man cute."

Jack craned his neck to the rearview mirror and wiped his lips with the napkin. He'd always had boyish good looks, a veritable dreamboat with baby blues, sandy hair, and a blinding smile of straight white teeth.

And he hated it.

His tattoos were something like dousing a clean canvas with dirty dish water, anything to wreck the pristine gleam.

"Get your fine ass out of the car," he commanded with a throaty laugh and stuffed the crumpled napkin into his pocket. "Slow," he added when Mirabelle opened the door.

She bent over and let her red-thonged bottom peek from beneath her black skirt. Jack always liked that, the naughty exploits when no one was looking.

"I'm not a whore," she'd told him their first night together as she slipped out of a silver dress as glitzy as a low-hung moon.

Only a whore would say something like that while doing her own undressing. Jack had prowled across the room, and she'd told him not to get too excited. She wasn't a virgin, either.

Over the years, she'd heard from the girls in the inner circle that he liked it rough. Those girls were the chosen ones who earned their keep for more than just a night. A few married into the organization. A few more held out hope. All had stories they swapped as eagerly as the men they sometimes shared.

But Jack was deliberate in his conquests. There were certain things he wouldn't do. Mirabelle was one of them. For years, she'd nursed the bitter sting and rebuffed him when he finally came around. She didn't need his pity, but it wasn't pity, and his redlines were only business, not personal.

He'd been gentle that first night, more lover than madman. Either the other women had lied or Jack had assumed she was fragile. Maybe both were true. Mirabelle never asked.

She approached Emory's car across the lot. Her duty was simple—mind Amelia. The ease of the task depended on the mood he'd left the girl in. The journey was long and their misunderstandings plenty, but Emory climbed from his car and strode to the passenger side with a lightness uncommon in him. When he opened her door and offered his hand, Amelia took it without reservation.

Men weren't observant of these things, so the others didn't notice the break in the clouds. They'd say Emory was only being polite, but Mirabelle saw the sleight of hand; Emory's fingers that lingered, Amelia's soft little touch.

The group headed for the front of the building. Pete, the captain of Los Angeles post, occupied Amelia a few steps ahead. In the sunlight, her hair gleamed like peaches and gold, and she glanced over her shoulder at Emory who smiled in response.

"I see the Cold War is over," Mirabelle said and kept pace with him. "How'd you manage that?"

"Maybe I was sweet."

"For the right ones, you can be."

"And the wrong ones?"

Mirabelle laughed. "They come crying to me."

Yes, with giant tears and mascara staining their cheeks. God, how they blubbered. To hear them tell it, Emory was cold to the touch and out of reach. They said he was unknowable, but most enigmas weren't one thing, so Emory was, at times, witty with dry humor then guarded and aloof. With him, it was either keys to his kingdom or quickly shown the door.

To be fair, Emory was his own contradiction. Their mother raised him to love and cherish women; not just the treasure between their thighs, but their feminine mystique. From their father, Emory inherited not just handsome looks, but also his brooding and blustery self-reliance.

The odd amalgamation meant Emory revered the women he loved as if they hung the moon. The women he took home were different. They were his queen for the night, but by morning, the cold came in again. Less than a handful ever reaped the benefits of his absolute love and devotion, but those women had bailed when his world became too much.

The group gathered in a store marked M.L. Berneski and Sons Prescriptions. Liam secured the spot decades ago and assigned a retired captain, Giovanni, to handle the front-facing business.

An outsider would rightfully wonder how a place like that still existed. Its checkered floors were well-worn but kept free of dust. Red-topped soda stools lined a laminate counter that ended in a pie case offering slim pickings. Only a few shelves with basic medical supplies gave the place any legitimacy as a drugstore.

A tenor bellowed from a record player behind the counter, and Gio beamed as the crowd filled in. A broom tumbled from his age-spotted hands and he approached Mirabelle first.

"My girl," he said and embraced her with strong arms despite his old age. "You waited too long to visit. You got taller, yeah?"

"Doubtful, but I'll take it."

Gio's fingers—nearly as crooked as his back and the knuckles swollen into knobs—slipped from Mirabelle's shoulders. He stared at Amelia doing her damnedest to go forgotten in the corner.

"Who is this girl?" Gio hollered at Emory propped against the soda counter.

"This is Amelia," Emory said as Gio approached her.

"Ahh-Melia. Your name sounds like music. You like music?"

With all eyes on her, a blush painted Amelia's cheeks. She ought to get used to it. Girls like her never went unnoticed for long.

She nodded and cleared her throat. "Very much."

A buffeting fan swallowed up her voice, so soft and sweet, music in its own right.

"Roberto Murolo. You know him?" Gio asked, but Amelia shook her head. Like pledging blind allegiance, he closed his eyes with a hand over his heart. "Oh, he's wonderful. He sings 'Malafemmena.' It's about a beautiful woman, a heartbreaker. You're too sweet to break a man's heart, yeah?"

Amelia's lips curled in a playful smile. "Can't say I've tried, so I guess we'll see."

Gio roared with laughter and turned to Emory, who looked on with a swell of pride. The others would call it amusement. Mirabelle knew his subtleties, though, and the shades of emotion that bridged stoic restraint and fevered passion.

"She's funny," Gio said and pointed at Emory. "She's your girl?"

Mirabelle buried a smile and averted her eyes. Jack did the same. He wouldn't dare look at Emory in a time like that. The room was divided as the oblivious gawked and the wise looked away.

Even Amelia stared at the tips of her shoes. She wasn't a damsel, though, and delicate fire like hers burned with slow heat. No wonder it tempted Emory. He had a taste for her kind and surprisingly soft finesse that'd dote endlessly on a woman like her. Rattled, Emory crossed his arms and shook his head. Gio ambled over and clapped him on the back.

"Sing 'Malafemmena' to her every day, and maybe she'll go easy on you. Amelia," Gio called out and picked up his broom, "if he gives you trouble, ring your friend Gio, and I'll come straighten him out."

Gio mimed a one-two punch that sent a wave of laughter through the store.

"I've got business in the basement," Emory told Gio when the ruckus died down. "You get to spend time with the girls. Try to behave."

Gio shooed Emory away with the broom's bristled end, and all but three men retreated downstairs. At the counter, Gio served up pink lemonade and cherry pie and hummed along to his records as he swept the floor. When "Malafemmena" came on, he abandoned his chores and insisted they dance. Each in turn, he twirled Mirabelle and Amelia around the room and chuckled when both stepped on his toes. After a few songs, he excused himself to the back room with a newspaper and a hand-rolled cigarette but let the records play on.

Mirabelle suggested they sit outside, and Amelia followed her to the door, but one of their minders shot from his perch by the window. A young one, he could barely fill out the patchy mustache sprouting from his upper lip and did his best to look intimidating.

"Oh, keep your dick in your pants," Mirabelle said. "We're just sitting outside."

"Stay where I can see you," Scumstache replied and returned to his post.

Mirabelle ignored him. Everyone saw defiance in her, a wild streak they couldn't tame, so they clipped her wings and worried about migration. Where the fuck did they think she would fly?

On the steps out front, they lounged in the shade of cotton-ball clouds. Mirabelle liked to go there in spring when the wildflowers thrived for a little while in an inhospitable environment. Beneath an oppressive summer sun, those flowers had burnt up weeks ago.

"What is this place?" Amelia asked and studied the storefront sign.

"A haven for high rollers. The ones who care more about money than a flashy venue. They come here to avoid taxes on their winnings. For profit, of course."

"Of course." Amelia sipped her lemonade and asked cautiously, "Why are we here?"

Lie with a smile. It's what you do best. Emory would never divulge his secrets to Cal Havick's daughter. Then again, no woman should be reduced to "some man's daughter," so Mirabelle offered the truth.

"Emory wants the gambling operation off the radar. The guy who runs this place pushes drugs through here. The Moriartys don't fuck with the drug business."

"How come?"

"People in high places will turn a blind eye to a lot of things. Drugs aren't one of them."

With a deep frown, Amelia set her glass on the step and surveyed the street.

"Don't look so surprised," Mirabelle said. "There are crooked people everywhere."

"I know."

"Do you?"

"Yes." Amelia lifted her forearms and, with the grace of a pageant queen, twirled her wrists. It mocked with an elegant display of cuts and bruises still healing. "Do *you*?"

The pointed question came with an equally pointed look. When Mirabelle declined a response, Amelia asked, "What's your role in all this? Do you get a say in things?"

The loaded question pried too much. Mirabelle narrowed her eyes and issued a warning to sweet Amelia so coyly sipping on pink lemonade.

"My role is to shut the fuck up when people ask me questions."

The straw tumbled from Amelia's lips and rolled along the edge of the glass.

"Let's say a man like your daddy comes sniffing around. You know what I say? I say that I don't know Gio from Adam. Or him or him or him." Mirabelle pointed to each of the Moriarty men inside the store. "I can't remember names, places, phone numbers. Nothing. My role is silence."

"And the wives and girlfriends, that's their role too?"

"The good ones, yes. It takes a special kind to be so ride-or-die for your man that you're willing to sink with the ship. It's why Emory wants me to find someone on the outside, settle down, be happy."

It wasn't just a want. He'd made her promise with the same gravitas as things spoken on deathbeds.

Amelia scooted a little closer, dug a little deeper. "Why don't you?"

Mirabelle noticed Scumstache at the window scrutinizing the street. There was nothing to see out there, just weeds sprouting from cracked asphalt and a Lays potato chip bag flattened in the middle of the road. With no breeze, it hadn't moved.

"I'll tell you a story," Mirabelle said. "I grew up in a house that backed up to woods thick enough to get lost in. Whenever things got bad with Ivan, that's what Emory and I did; got lost back there. Jack lived down the street, so he'd tag along too.

"One day, Ivan found us. He'd come for me, to do things a brother should never do to his sister. Jack and Emory fought him off, but I knew then the price of my freedom was Ivan's death. I guess I've earned it now, but I don't believe he's really gone."

Mirabelle took a heavy gulp of lemonade. The memories were chaotic—screams and grunts and Jack jamming his pocketknife into Ivan's eye. As Ivan howled in pain, Emory had put Mirabelle on his back, and he and Jack ran like mad for home. That was Mirabelle's last day in the woods.

Amelia stared at the uneven slab of sidewalk in front of them. Even in the heat, her skin paled. "Emory said he's dead."

"Emory says a lot of things."

"And what about him and Jack? What's the price of their freedom?"

Mirabelle had been asked the same question before by lovelorn girls with foolish dreams of luring their Moriarty man away. No pussy was phenomenal enough to break blood oaths. That wasn't what Amelia was after, though. Her face betrayed resigned sorrow on Emory's behalf, Jack's too, all the lost souls trapped in the machine.

"Death," Mirabelle said. "At the end of the day, this is the only family most of us got. It's why the men stay. Besides, where are they going if they leave? They have nothing outside the organization. Inside, they have brotherhood, loyalty, and girls like me who'd move heaven and earth for them."

Amelia propped her chin in the heel of her hand. A stray breeze rushed down the street. The potato chip bag puffed with air. Free to leave, it tumbled on, and Amelia watched it go.

"Don't you want out? To live your dream, whatever it is?"

Mirabelle lifted her eyes to the clouds sailing by overhead. Was that the dream? She didn't know. The outside world scared her more than it should. A strong, fearless girl inside the Moriartys, she didn't know who she was on the outside.

"I never really thought about it," she was ashamed to admit. "This is all I've known. It's easy for Em to say I should get out. He doesn't understand. I have reasons to stay."

"Jack," Amelia said with a dreamy smile.

Mirabelle sat up stiffly. How the hell could Amelia have seen? And if she saw, Emory must've too. *Lie with your eyes.* Mirabelle tilted her head and regarded Amelia like a class-A moron.

"Aren't you two together?" Amelia asked.

"Why would you think that?"

"I'm sorry. I thought I noticed something. I—"

"You didn't. I've just known him a long time is all. What about you? You got a boyfriend back home who's gonna come save you?"

Amelia shook her head and sorrow surfaced in her eyes. "No one's gonna save me. Only me."

"Well, what about your dreams? You're Harvard-bound, right?"

"No. I called it off. It wasn't my dream."

"Cal's dream?"

Amelia nodded and, with her fingertip, traced a deep crack in the cement step where a single dandelion grew. "I was backed into a corner and forced into the role he wanted me to play. It didn't matter what I wanted."

"It's what men do. Put you in a role and cry foul if you quit."

That was the delicate take. Small fires existed in all women. It started as sadness that kindled the rage. It burned and it burned and they called them crazy. No woman wanted to go up in flames.

"So, here I am." Root and stem, Amelia ripped the dandelion out. "Free, I guess. Trapped again."

Mirabelle drew a long breath of dead heat. She had no words of comfort or priceless advice but tried for Amelia's sake.

"It won't be like this forever. This is just a detour."

Quiet with her thoughts, Amelia picked petals from the dandelion. She lifted her eyes to Mirabelle with fresh resolve and chucked the flower to the steps.

"A detour means there's a way out. I've told Emory everything I know. There isn't any song to sing."

"I know there isn't," Mirabelle said and not for the first time. Emory wouldn't hear it from her, though. He had to see for himself.

"Thank you for believing me." Amelia smiled with what might've been the end of it, but she bypassed the natural exit. "The motel clerk, the one Damon hurt. He's in the hospital. What will happen to him?"

Mirabelle shrugged, uncertain of where Amelia was going. "Same thing that happens to everyone in the hospital. He'll either live or die."

"And who decides his fate, Emory or God?"

The blunt question pulled no punches. Amelia wasn't the first and wouldn't be the last to put Emory and God on equal ground, but it didn't impress Amelia as it did the others.

On the surface, she was harmless and sweet, but then the gloves came off and she was discerning and sharp. She didn't fit the mold nor would she flit about with glamorous ambition to fuck her way to Emory's side, his vapid queen rotten to the core. Amelia already had her thumb to the pulse and felt his heart beating. But she didn't know him and couldn't see what Mirabelle saw. Emory would fall hard for a girl like her.

"Another lesson, know your place," Mirabelle insisted with a sharp stare leveled at Amelia. "Some things are off limits, including questions like that. Now, about the things I've told you today."

Amelia crossed her heart with her finger. "Silence."

"Good girl. Is this a 'fuck you' to your dad?"

"More like a small act of defiance."

"Sometimes it's all we got."

Girlish mischief gleamed in Amelia's eyes. "Then we should take it every chance we get."

"Yes, we should," Mirabelle heartily agreed.

At the window, Scumstache tapped his phone and scanned the empty street again. He locked eyes with Mirabelle and the machismo fled. He looked like a little boy caught with his hand in the cookie jar. A cold flush surged through Mirabelle.

"Let's go," she said. "The men are antsy. That's never a good sign."

Inside, a record played, but the music no longer disguised Emory's voice down below. It rumbled through the floorboards with steady heat.

"Where's the bathroom?" Amelia asked Mirabelle, but the question roused Scumstache's interest.

He peeled away from the window and muttered something inarticulate, a demand, perhaps, that Amelia stay put. She paid the boy no mind and neither did Mirabelle as she directed Amelia down the hall.

Whatever his intentions, they fell apart. In a fluster, Scumstache's hands shook as he frantically typed on his phone. From the back of the store, the two other Moriarty street soldiers noticed.

"Who are you texting?" one demanded and approached Scumstache from behind. The other circled to his side. Cornered, Scumstache shoved his phone in his pocket and turned with his back to the window.

"No one," he answered and crossed his arms with a smirk.

The fucking nerve of this kid. Mirabelle killed the record player and marched up to him with an outstretched hand.

"If it's no one, then give me your phone and let me see."

The boy huffed a derisive laugh and glanced at the street again. Up close, Mirabelle invaded his space.

"I said, give me your phone."

Scumstache sucked in a long breath and stood at full height. Mirabelle had underestimated his size. A head taller than her, he peered down as if he had the upper hand. For a brief moment, it seemed he might comply as he reached for his back pocket. It was the wrong pocket, though. On the exhale, he pulled his gun and steadied it at Mirabelle.

"Drop it now!" shouted one of the street soldiers.

Hands up, Mirabelle froze and so too did Amelia as she returned from down the hall. In shaky steps, Mirabelle backed away. With his gun to her head, Scumstache no longer looked like a little boy.

He wouldn't do it. Fear couldn't listen to logic, though. She stumbled into the soda stool, blood pumping like ice in her veins.

Scumstache swung his gun to Amelia creeping toward the basement door.

"Stop! Stay there!" he screamed over the demands of the other street soldiers to drop his weapon.

Chaos unfolded in the basement too with a scuffle ensuing down below and Emory shouting his own demands. Amongst the mayhem, Gio rushed up behind Scumstache. He jabbed his gun to the back of the boy's neck. His old hands trembled but his instincts were as ageless as the fury in his pale eyes.

"Put it down!" Gio demanded.

The boy lifted his hands but didn't drop his gun. Like before, he held his breath and made himself tall, summoning all the bravery he could manage. Pressure pounded in Mirabelle's ears as Scumstache whipped around. She opened her mouth to scream, but gunfire choked the sound.

At point-blank range, Scumstache buried a bullet in Gio's belly and bolted for the back hall.

TWENTY

EMORY

In the windowless basement, six Moriarty men crammed into a card room where the stagnant air stifled. Gio never ventured down there, so dust gathered along the baseboards, and cobwebs cropped up in the corners. Upstairs, he sang along to his cherished records and sent Amelia and Mirabelle into fits of giggles.

Emory, Jack, and two captains, Pete and Disco, sipped strong tea at the felted table. Two trusted street soldiers perched against a gold-vein mirrored wall while the rest stood watch outside the door.

"It's too fucking hot for this shit, man," Jack whispered to Emory and motioned to the gaudy samovar—a Russian tea urn— at the table's center.

The caretaker, Viktor, had trotted it out to forestall the inevitable. It worked for a little while, and Emory let him dig his own grave with stories of wild excess and lost inhibition.

"More?" Viktor asked and reached for the samovar.

The man's eyes were beadier than Emory remembered and his teeth a darker shade of decay. He was fatter too. His belly hung over his pants, and a wrinkled shirt struggled to cover it, the buttons liable to pop.

Emory shook his head. "It's time to talk."

Viktor pretended not to hear and stood so abruptly that he

bashed his head on the red-shaded lamp hanging over the table. It emitted a jaundiced glow and rained dust motes as it swung on a brass chain.

"Enough!" Emory snapped. "Sit down."

Bent over at the table, Viktor surveyed the room for a friendly face. Finding none, he sat again but gripped the chair's armrests so tightly his knuckles flushed white.

"You know why I'm here," Emory said. "Be straight with me and we won't have any problems."

"Is there an issue with the cash flow?" Viktor asked. "I get regulars. You get your money. I don't bother you for a bigger cut."

Emory pointed at him. "That right there. You never ask me for a bigger cut. Why?"

Viktor chewed a flake of dry skin on his bottom lip and inhaled a breath that wheezed deep in his lungs.

"I deal honest with you. I take my share and no more."

"I'm not talking about padding your cut. I'm talking about the Rolls Royce outside and that shit." Emory flung his hand to the gold chain around Viktor's neck and the jeweled baubles squeezed around his fingers. "I compensate you well, but not that well."

"What's your point?" Viktor tugged a handkerchief from his back pocket and roughly dabbed at the sweat beading his forehead.

What a waste, all the years bleeding money on the joint. It was more than just a bad investment, though. Viktor's duplicity was a dangerous liability. Emory held his composure and kept the room in deliberate suspense until even the captains stirred in their seats.

"This isn't the lifestyle of a racketeer," he finally said. "Cocaine is a lucrative business, though. So is heroin."

Viktor folded his arms over his chest, but his attention drifted to the door. Emory turned in his seat to follow his gaze.

"Am I keeping you from something?" he asked with mock courtesy. It marked the third time Viktor had eyed the door.

The man stalled again. With grubby fingers, he rifled in his shirt pocket for a lone cigarette. He made an equally fine production of fetching his lighter and savoring the first drag.

"You brought a guest," he said and pointed to the ceiling that no longer creaked with footsteps above, though music still bled through. "The girl upstairs."

Amelia. The corner of Emory's mouth twitched in a nervous tick. Everyone had them. He knew his and worked diligently to eradicate them. Too late, Viktor seized on the momentary break.

"My sister."

"No. The red head. I saw you with her out back." Viktor smiled and ashed his cigarette. "Pretty thing," he added on afterthought and stared across the table at Emory. "She's yours?"

As above, so below—all eyes in the room turned to Emory, unified in their scrutiny. Who was Amelia Havick to him? The answer didn't matter, only the vulnerability she might've infected him with. They scouted it out like a sickness in him.

"We both like pretty things," Viktor continued when Emory hadn't answered and lifted a hand to admire his rings. "Except I favor pretty things I can stand to lose. I wonder if you're the same."

The heat of the room moved through Emory. He tore his gun from his waistband and slammed it to the table. With the barrel end pointed at Viktor, his hand rested on top.

"We're not the same. I come by my pretty things honestly. Cartel money paid for yours. I told you from the jump I'm not involved in that business. I wanted this joint run clean, and you swore up and down that you understood. So, here's what it's gonna be. You can keep your bullshit, but we're done here. I expect you out by—"

"That's not what's going on!"

Viktor pounded his fist to the table so hard the samovar toppled and bled tar-black tea leaves onto the felt. Emory gestured to the captain of Las Vegas post.

"You know Disco. He keeps an eye on you, makes sure everything's good. You think he didn't notice that you run the business dirty?"

Viktor rolled his eyes with a huff. He'd pay for the insolence. For the time being, Emory filled the room with the boom of his voice.

"Are you suggesting he's a liar? Tell him! Go on. Look Disco in the eye and tell him he's a fucking liar."

Viktor either had to come clean or double down on denial. Coward that he was, he did neither.

"Maybe you don't know your men as well as you think you do," he said with delight in his eyes mismatched to the scowl on his lips. "You talk about liars, but do you trust these men here?"

One by one, Viktor examined each man in the room, but Emory refused the bait. He didn't need to ponder the question or evaluate them too. These were his brothers. Simple as that.

"More than I trust you. They took oaths. You didn't."

Viktor laughed darkly and squashed his cigarette in the ashtray. "Your blood oaths won't protect you from what's coming."

"And what's that?"

"You wouldn't believe me if I told you."

"Try me."

Viktor's yellowed teeth split his lips with a sinister smile. "Your brother."

"My brother?" Emory asked, the breathless question useless filler. He'd heard just fine.

Viktor leaned forward and whispered, "Ivan."

Emory's grip tightened on the gun, and his free hand curled into a fist, the nails digging into his palm. *Name your demons. Make them real.*

"Ivan," he repeated, just as quiet. "You've been chatting up ghosts?"

That earned a round of laughter from the room. Viktor found no humor in it. Neither did Emory.

"I'm not lying. Ivan said you'd deny it, so he told me to tell you this. Remember the girl in the woods, the day it was just you and him. Do you know what that means?"

Emory nodded vacantly as the memory assailed his senses.

The taste of blood in his mouth. The sun beating hot against his neck. Face down in the leaves. God, how they'd reeked of wet rot. No one knew about that day, not a soul on earth except Ivan and him. Emory's stomach roiled, and he swallowed down a crippling wave of nausea.

"Ivan's alive," Viktor added, almost apologetically, "but you knew that, didn't you?"

Emory shook his head. It loosened a bead of sweat that rolled down his temple. Hadn't he known, though? How could he not? The same blood coursed through Emory's veins as his brother. Maybe that meant something in a primal sense because Emory discerned Ivan's existence in the ineffable; the shape of the night and the horrors that it hid.

"He asked me to pass along a message," Viktor said. "He promised you something the last time you saw him. He's ready to deliver."

"We're done here, Em," Jack broke in and reached for his sidearm, but Emory stopped him with a raised hand.

"You tracking?" Viktor asked.

Emory didn't respond. The room pulsed in a funhouse distortion where the mirrored wall seemed to creep closer, and his chest tightened, each breath more labored than the last. *I can't fucking breathe.*

Four years ago, he took the helm of the Moriartys, and Ivan slithered from the shadows to congratulate him. On a cold winter's night in Northern California, Emory walked to his car, but a presence followed. He led that presence beneath a lamppost to force it out of the darkness. Ivan had slipped into the light but hardly looked human. His remaining eye was black and soulless, a killer's stare.

"Little brother," he'd whispered. "Don't assume your place at the top means you and Mirabelle are safe. I will destroy everything you love. Piece by bloody piece, I will take it apart then I'll take you."

Emory never saw him again. Word came his body had been discovered in a burned-out car at the bottom of a ravine. No one claimed that dead man, so they called him Ivan Holt and rendered him to ashes. In Emory's dreams, Ivan's rotten corpse was ripped limb from limb with maggots in his mouth and one goopy eyeball oozing down mottled skin. Rest in torment. What a fitting fucking end.

In death, there'd been paltry relief, so Ivan's ghost remained. Better to be haunted than hunted, though. Emory couldn't live with that affliction again, didn't know how to anymore. He'd lost the skill in these years of fragile peace. *This has to end.*

Emory flew to his feet and sent the chair tumbling to the floor. He racked the slide of his gun and aimed it at Viktor.

"Where is he?"

"You won't find him. He'll find you." Viktor clicked his tongue and added with a wicked grin, "And your pretty things too."

Emory rounded the table in a few pounding strides. Fury blackened the edges of his vision. He seized Viktor by the front of his shirt and hurled him to the floor.

"On your knees!"

Still smiling, Viktor clambered across the floor as the room stirred. Everyone scrambled from their seat. Someone entreated him to stop. Emory didn't know who. He didn't take commands from others. He'd earned this. Viktor huddled against the wall. Kindling to the rage, Emory relished the sight. *Make him beg for his life.*

"Get on your *fucking* knees!"

Viktor tried but not quick enough. Emory yanked him up by a fistful of hair. It loosened in clumps from his scalp. With one hard kick, he stomped Viktor's jaw to wipe that fucking smile clean. Viktor's head snapped back. On hands and knees, he spit up blood before collapsing to the floor.

"Where is he?" Emory bellowed and straddled Viktor.

His fist smashed into the man's jaw; once, then twice, three times, four, until he lost count; until bones broke and Viktor's face was a mess of shredded tissue and gold teeth glinted on the floor. In the mayhem, a body landed on top of Emory, a voice screaming in his ear.

"Em!" Jack shouted. "Em! Stop!"

Emory tossed Jack off of him. His blood-slicked hands cinched Viktor's neck. He squeezed until bones popped against his palms. With another dump of adrenaline, he slammed Viktor's head against the floor.

"Where the *fuck* is he? Answer me!"

Viktor's eyes rolled to the back of his head and mouth gaped open. Out poured more blood and broken bits of teeth. Emory let go. Viktor gulped down hard breaths and rolled to his side. His cheek rested in a shallow pool of blood. Hands shaking, Emory pressed his gun to Viktor's temple, and his voice trembled just the same.

"Tell me where he is."

Viktor pointed to the ceiling. Up above, the music had stopped. Amelia and Mirabelle didn't laugh. Gio didn't sing. In their place were muffled shouts. A single gunshot. Mirabelle's scream. The storefront window shattering.

Viktor lifted his hands in surrender. "I'm sorry. Please. I—"

Emory pulled the trigger. Blood, bone, and brain exploded out the back of Viktor's head as mayhem unfolded outside the door.

TWENTY-ONE

EMORY

Gunfire shredded the basement's hollow-core door. Emory ducked as the mirrored wall shattered and rained down shards around him. Outside the room, the walls veritably shook with screams and shouts.

"Everyone out!" Emory commanded and rushed into the lounge, where half a dozen masked men opened fire. He picked off one before diving behind a table for cover.

"Emory!"

His vision blurred with Mirabelle's scream from upstairs, a scream he hadn't heard since they were children, a scream reserved for terror only Ivan could inspire. Emory bolted for the stairs, but the pulse thundering in his ears dampened the chaos. Jack shouted something after him. He couldn't hear. It didn't matter.

Upstairs, a barrage of bullets had torn through the store. Mirabelle huddled beneath the counter with Gio bleeding in her arms.

"Amelia!" she shrieked and pointed down the hall.

Emory spun around to the back door propped open.

Outside, a Moriarty street soldier struggled to get Amelia into a car. She writhed like wild, her legs kicking and fingers clawing at the hand over her mouth as she was shoved into the backseat of an

SUV. Emory hurdled over toppled stools and sprinted down the hall.

Legs like lead, he couldn't move quick enough as the car lurched forward. He fired his gun and the bullet broke glass. Another round busted out the back window. It wasn't from him, though. He ran into a hail of gunfire to get to her. Momentum couldn't stop him. He slammed into the side of the car and tore open the back door.

Amelia scrambled toward him. He had her in his arms but, with a violent yank backwards, she broke loose from his hold. The street soldier, one of his own, had her by the hair, his hand around her throat. In a crimson haze, Emory landed a fist against the kid's face. His nose cracked with a spray of blood, enough to momentarily stun.

Emory couldn't say how he got her out, just that she desperately clung to his shoulders as his knees buckled. They tumbled to the ground as bullets ripped around them. Emory huddled on top of Amelia. She curled into a tight ball beneath him. There was nothing left to do but wait. Wait to die. Wait for it to end.

We won't get out of this alive. Emory tucked his arms beneath her and drew her into his chest. Amelia shook against him and gripped his shirt to pull him closer. They'd die like that, fused together for someone else to pull apart.

The salvo slackened, though, and the car sped off. Emory didn't know how long he and Amelia held onto each other. Long enough that others stumbled outside and some feeling returned to his legs. He rolled off of her then, his teeth gritty with dust as he squinted at the sun.

His vision cleared, and he pushed from the ground, but his lungs burned with each frenzied breath. As his men piled into cars around them, Emory pulled Amelia to her feet. The back lot was empty and so too was the street beyond.

Gone. The same old story and nothing ever changed. Ivan vanished, and Emory reeled in the aftermath. Mirabelle dashed toward him, but the flurry halted with the rattle of Jack's wallet chain. Tears wet his cheeks, and he hurried across the lot with Gio's limp body in his arms.

"Stubborn fucking bastard!" Jack cried and placed Gio in his car's backseat.

The world went deadly quiet then. All eyes landed on Emory as they awaited his command. Everything came apart at the seams, and they looked to him to stitch it back together. What the fuck did they want from him? Battered and bloody, he just wanted an escape. Instead, he swore he drifted from his body as a calm, unifying force stepped in.

"Get him to Dr. Gordon. He's on call a couple miles north," Emory told Jack then turned to his captains. "Corey, take six men and go with Jack. Disco, work LVPD for damage control. Give them my apologies and tell them to expect my call. The rest of you, follow me back. I'll call Liam and tell him to lock it down."

Without argument, the men moved in solemn concert. Lost in the squall, Amelia stood motionless as the men scrambled around her. Emory slipped his hand in hers and drew her gaze with a squeeze.

"I need to get you out of here," he said and led her to his car where Pete already waited.

"Give me your keys," he hollered from the driver's side. "I'll drive back."

Emory tossed his keys to Pete and slipped into the back seat with Amelia. They peeled out of the parking lot and sped down the street. The highway burned away like wildfire in a race against time, even as the noises still rang in Emory's ears—the screams, the gunfire, the pounding of his heart.

His phone rang with shrill insistence, each call quicker than the last and voices shouting through the other end—Liam locked down the home front; Gio likely wouldn't make it through the night; the Velascos had blood on their hands and hell to pay.

The scenery slipped by in a blur, and Emory stewed in the tattered pieces of his thoughts. He should've seen it coming. The signs were there, the writing on the wall. He was too stubborn to see. It was his fault. He'd shoulder the blame but had only paid part of the cost, the debt not yet settled.

Beside him, Amelia stared in a daze until everything gave way all at once and a sob escaped her. She buried her face in her hands and swiveled away from him. Tears were an exhibition only a privileged few were allowed to see, and he'd trained her well not to seek comfort from him. That divide had kept them apart long enough.

He reached for her, his fingertips sweeping across her back to cup her shoulder. She stilled at his touch and lifted her face from her palms.

"Come here," he said and pulled her toward him.

Amelia slid across the seat with little coaxing and nestled against his chest. Emory held her close, his cheek resting atop her head.

"I'm sorry, Amelia," he whispered with a sigh that rustled in her hair. "I'm so sorry."

He felt her nod against him, but she had the grace not to ask what he was sorry for. *"Everything,"* he would've told her; sorry for her losses, too many to count; sorry for the road ahead because it'd only get harder.

Amelia lifted her head to look at him. Blood coated her bottom lip. She licked it away and gripped his forearms. *I want you closer,* he thought, and it must have occurred to her too, so they moved in unison until their foreheads rested against one another.

"You're shaking," she said through sniffles.

He hadn't noticed, and perhaps that was the point. Ignore the fear until it showed itself out. He knew better than to search for something steady to hold onto, but it was right in front of him.

"Are you okay?" Amelia asked, probably of the blood staining his shirt and skin.

With a question that simple, Emory came undone. He didn't answer, and she wouldn't make him, and so she came to him first. With her arms wrapped around his shoulders, she drew him into the warmth of her body. Emory soaked it up; in dire need of her heat and the comfort it brought.

She said something, whispered it for only him to hear. Emory couldn't remember what it was or maybe didn't register it in the first place. All he knew was how she felt; the brush of her hair against his forearms slatted along her back; the smell of her perfume and the heart notes of blood; her chin perched on his shoulder and how in the back seat she let him hold her.

Amelia kept at bay every twisted thought he might have had, all but one, and so it remained, singular and taunting, out of order but still on cue:

Piece by bloody piece, I will destroy everything you love.

TWENTY-TWO

EMORY

When the parlor clock chimed nine, Emory counted his blessings with each resounding toll. They returned to an unscathed home front. The fallout was contained. The battle won.

But fate was sufficiently tempted with the ticking of time and whispers of gratitude. Dr. Gordon, physician to the Moriarty family, called with tragic news. Gio didn't make it. He was too frail, the injuries too severe, the blood loss too much.

Midnight approached, but no one found solace in sleep. Emory walked the halls and observed luminous distractions on repeat—bedside light spilling beneath shuttered doors, the blue bleed from TVs, cigarette flickers in the dark.

When the sun went down and the other lights—those desperate beacons for some kind of peace—came on, most Moriarty men just wanted to forget. The ones with wives found comfort there. The ones with no one to call their own plucked a pick-me girl waiting in the wings.

Years ago, Emory had thought their open arms and parted thighs had everything to do with him. Mostly, it hadn't, not until he achieved some status in their eyes.

He'd long since departed with burying his fear and frustration between the legs of a woman he hardly knew. Of the ones he did know, he'd loved deeply only a few. Their tolerance of his world invariably faded, though, and when they wanted out, he set them free.

Emory sought refuge in the courtyard. It was a shadow space, shaded by day and forgotten by night. With nowhere to sit and no reason to linger, it functioned like a thoroughfare that connected the house's wings and the terrace down below.

In the courtyard, the wind danced amongst the honeysuckle vines, and the stucco walls bled back warmth from the day. Beyond the courtyard's fountain, he found Amelia perched at the railing overlooking the terrace. Barefoot, she drowned in an oversized t-shirt that doubled as a nightgown.

She didn't stir at his startled double step but stared in tranquil fascination at the desert road where headlights glittered. Not so long ago, she would've stiffened at his approach as if bracing for a fight.

Amelia patted the railing beside her for him to join, the gesture a bellwether to how far they'd come.

"I was just wondering where that road leads," she said and twirled the end of her ponytail around her finger.

Emory had pondered it himself a time or two, but some other thought—duty and business and who's killing who—pummeled his daydreams until they stopped coming around. All he knew was it ran like an asphalt artery through dying towns. The years went by, and the heartbeat faded. Ashes to ashes, they'd all turn to dust.

"It leads out, I guess," he said and folded his forearms on the railing.

Amelia scooted closer. "That's as good a direction as any."

"It was always my favorite."

She lifted a hand to present the road, but Emory shook his head.

"I'd have to figure out how to get down from up here. The logistics are messy."

Messy, yes, but treacherous too. A free fall from these heights meant sure death. If he survived, it'd be broken at the bottom, carrion for crows. Amelia regarded him with a doleful smile as if searching for some consolation to offer. Emory spared her the hunt.

"Can't sleep?" he asked, though it seemed obvious. Earlier, she'd absorbed the news of Gio's death with quiet poise, but the sun set on troubled times that undoubtedly haunted her too.

Amelia shook her head and bent forward against the railing. The thin t-shirt rose up the back of her legs and revealed the slope of her ass. Emory's blood heated with typical visions; her clothes on the floor and his mouth grazing the inside of her thighs. The fantasy had evolved, though, and he entertained how she'd feel curled against him as they slept.

"What's the opposite of claustrophobia?" she asked.

"No idea."

"I have whatever that is."

"You fear open spaces?"

"Not so much the openness, but that there's nothing to hold on to. It's like being dropped in the middle of the ocean with no anchor. You're just lost in all directions and at the mercy of the tides." Amelia studied the courtyard for a moment then added, "This is an anchor space."

Emory shifted nearer to her, both intrigued and bemused at the paradoxical places where she sought solace. He admired her up close—the faint freckles that dusted her cheeks, the way one auburn brow arched more than the other, the crease in her bottom lip he was dying to kiss.

He shook his head with a soft chuckle. Amelia laughed too, a rarity he'd come to cherish. He could stay there forever just to soak up the sound.

"You know," he said, "Arizona is about as wide open as it gets."

Amelia mulled it over with her eyes to the terrace below. The pool's murky glow didn't quite reach the table where she first met him in the dark. That past seemed so distant.

"Arizona was about escape. I was feral for freedom. From Oregon, my dad, the internship. My mom used to tell me not to wish time away. Burt was always good to me. I feel bad that I wished away my time with him, with everything."

She stood from the railing to face him, and Emory did the same.

"You were right, and I was wrong not to tell you," she said. "There was a folder, and I saw what was inside. If it could've prevented what happened to Gio—"

"Amelia, this wasn't your fault. I brought you with me today. That's on me, not you."

"And it's me they came for, whatever they think I know." She laughed again, this time without amusement. "The irony is it's nothing. You could've asked me at the party, and I would've told you, and you would've said, 'That's basically worthless,' and we would've gone our separate ways, and this never would've happened."

Her take on their imagined conversation endeared. In reality, she might've sidled up to him, and he might've done the same, but it would've been over before it began, as soon as Emory told her his name. When he was a street soldier, women readily dismissed his sins. As a captain, that task grew harder. As chief, his role was too big to overcome.

Amelia chewed her lip and looked as though one weight lifted from her shoulders while another piled on.

"Today in the car," Emory said, "you reacted to my brother's name. Did you see it in the folder?"

Amelia nodded. "It's uncommon enough that it stood out, but it was just a name. I didn't know who he was or how he fit into anything."

"No reason why you would."

Emory drew a hand over his face and through the length of his hair. Tendrils of unease spread as the worries and what-ifs amassed. They didn't pay him the dignity of an orderly onslaught but came in an unrelenting barrage. War was war, but that was the bright line he'd be a blind fool not to see. Ivan had crawled from a shallow grave and was comfortably seated at the top of the Velascos.

Leaned against the railing, Amelia's gaze skimmed his forearms, tracing the ink there with heavy interest.

"Nothing I saw in the folder made sense to me, except..."

"Except what?"

"You," she quietly confessed, and even amongst the shadows that shrouded them, Emory discerned the blush painting her cheeks. "Your picture was in the folder and details about you. The places you go, the people you're close to. I knew who you were at Richard's party. I knew the things you've done."

A part of Emory wanted to believe her and invest in a fairytale where their paths crossed one fated night and, behind her soft touch and sultry gaze, she understood him in his totality. Emory couldn't keep with that narrative, though. Amelia didn't know the extent of his crimes, the ones that earned him his reputation. In his world, no one rose to the top without blood-soaked hands.

"What else did you see?"

"They want to kill you," she said on a worried hush as if to let him down easy.

Emory laughed, the revelation hardly a surprise, but the irony too good to ignore. Her secret laid bare was hardly a secret at all.

"Somethings never change. Anything else?"

"No. I didn't make it past you."

Amelia peered up at him through her lashes, and the corner of her mouth lifted in a smile. Though she said nothing else, Emory understood that that was her ultimate confession, the one she'd safeguarded so fiercely.

He sidelined his flattery and asked, "You sure there's nothing else?"

"Not from the folder, but there is something that happened at the party. Martin Kranski said someone is pulling the strings in the Velascos from the great beyond. It didn't make sense at the time. He meant Ivan, didn't he?"

Emory nodded and, unsteady on his feet, looked to the sky, but there was no anchor there, only clouds that blighted the moon and delivered a chill. The abyss below beckoned, and the fall seemed less treacherous. Broken at the bottom was perhaps a kinder fate.

"Emory," Amelia ventured softly, "my first night here you told me there are real monsters, ones who would tear me apart if they got the chance. Both you and Mirabelle talk about Ivan that way. Why?"

Emory eyed the terrace steps with a bullish need to take his exit. A worn-out voice within warned him not to breathe this to life. Then again, it was easier to talk to strangers. Maybe he'd trot out a little tale like some fucked-up vaudeville.

"You can tell me," she encouraged with a hand on his forearm, her palm warm against his skin.

Good women promised their silence, but it wasn't about that. It was about trust. Hadn't he asked the same of her, to put faith in him when she had no reason? And Amelia wasn't a stranger anymore. Strangers didn't look primed for heartbreak on his behalf or part their lips with words of comfort at the ready.

"I was ten," Emory said and stared at the tips of his boots, though they held no particular fascination. "It was the first warm day of spring. I went to the woods where Jack and I had built a fort. I wanted to see if it'd survived the winter."

That day, the wind moved tender through the trees, sweetened with clover grass and morning dew. Emory had darted down a path through the woods, besotted by the sun that felt like warm bliss. When he rounded a grove of trees, the contentedness vanished in one catastrophic instant.

"I found Ivan there. He was on the ground and gyrated in this strange way, grunting like he was hurt. The sun broke through the trees, and I saw a flash of blonde hair and a body beneath him. It was our babysitter, a girl from school. Her face..."

Emory closed his eyes. It only made the flood of memories worse. Amelia caressed his forearm.

"Her face was bloody and broken. Her belly had been cut open. It took me a while to realize she was already dead. When I did, I ran, but Ivan ran faster. He dragged me back to her body, told me to lay down in the leaves, and made me watch as he finished raping her.

"If I looked away, he'd get up and kick me in the ribs. I didn't care about the pain, just that I could see her insides. Somehow that was worse. So, I laid there on the dead leaves. Her eyes were open, staring at me, and I stared back. I don't remember how long it lasted, but when he was done, we hid her body behind a fallen tree and covered her with leaves. He told me, 'You and I, we did this together as brothers. If you tell anyone, I'll say you fucked her too.'"

That night, the family had celebrated Ivan's fifteenth birthday. As Ivan blew out his candles, Emory silently sobbed at the dinner table and was sent to bed for making a fuss. Thereafter, the world was cold and stinking, no longer ripe with better days to come.

Sick to his stomach, Emory wavered on his feet. Amelia stared at him on the verge of tears. He didn't want her sympathy, didn't need her feeling sorry on his behalf. Plenty of people got a raw deal. Plenty.

"I've never told anyone that," he whispered and hid shaky hands in his pockets. "I don't talk about it or Ivan because people get the wrong idea, try to draw parallels between us or weigh my sins against his."

Amelia nodded but couldn't meet his eyes. He shouldn't have told her. He should've lied, said he was fine and sent her to bed. Maybe they should both just walk away and call it a wash.

Emory collected his reserve to do just that, but, like a bolt from the blue, Amelia flew into his arms. Her cheek burrowed against his chest, and her arms coiled around his middle.

"I'm sorry," she said, her tattered breaths warm as they seeped through his shirt. "You're not a monster. I never should've called you that. It's not what I think. You're nothing like him."

Emory froze on delay, processing the feel of her body and the affection she gave so freely. That was her off-ramp, her reason to reject him and stand firm in her disgust of his world. She didn't but consoled instead with her hands caressing his back.

Emory returned the embrace with his heart racing. Surely, she felt it humming against her as he held on tight. As she let go, Amelia slipped her hands to Emory's forearms and pondered the tattoos there.

"At Rich's party, someone pulled me from the crowd. It was you, wasn't it?"

Emory nodded. "I thought you knew," he said but wasn't so sure anymore. In the chaos, she probably hadn't seen him trudging through bodies to get to her.

Her brows furrowed, and she licked her lips. "No, if I'd known..."

"I know. I wanted to help you. Still do."

Amelia swayed to the cricket's song, an excuse perhaps for her arms to slip around his neck and fingers to weave in his hair.

"Even though I have nothing left to tell you?"

Emory cupped her cheek. "That's not the only reason I brought you here."

"What's the other reason?" she asked and tilted her head to find more of his touch. Her face fit so neatly in his palm, every piece of her constructed to match with him, or so it seemed.

Emory dipped his head until his mouth hovered close to hers, their lips brushing as he whispered, "Because I know what it's like to feel unsafe and alone."

Their lips met in a light kiss just as boot stomps hurried across the courtyard. Emory and Amelia turned as Jack rounded the fountain but halted mid-stride, his eyes shifting between them.

"Miri wants to talk," Jack told Emory and backed away in an awkward offer of privacy but loitered near the fountain.

"Fuck," Emory sighed and kissed her forehead. "I'm sorry."

With a crestfallen smile, Amelia released him. "It's okay. You shouldn't keep Mirabelle waiting."

Emory left her in the courtyard but turned back before he reached the door. Ignoring Jack, Amelia blew him a kiss. It thrilled Emory far more than several real kisses had. Those were cheap, ephemeral bliss. Nothing like his heart still racing, dizzy as he drifted inside.

"What was that?" Jack asked as they ascended the stairs. He reeked of cheap whiskey.

There was no easy way to package it. The comedown left Emory sapped but sated, a bit like the ecstatic fog after incredible sex.

"Progress," was all he said.

"She sang?"

"She confirmed what Viktor told us. Everything else we already knew."

"Good. We can cut her loose then."

The declarative incensed. Emory shot daggers in the dark. Jack didn't notice, only delighted himself at the brilliant dig.

"I'll make that decision," Emory said curtly. "Not you."

TWENTY-THREE

EMORY

In Emory's office, the desk lamp cast misshapen shadows around the room, and Mirabelle sat coiled up like a spring in the desk chair. With her legs wrapped tight over one another, she hugged her knees to her chest.

"What's going on?" Emory asked.

Jack leaned against the edge of the desk next to a half-spent bottle of whiskey. He wouldn't be the one to say it—whatever *it* was—so he glanced at Mirabelle who regarded Emory with familiar heat. It simmered behind her eyes first, then fired up the breath from her lungs.

"We shouldn't have been there today! This wouldn't have happened!"

Emory shut the door and met her searing accusation with hushed austerity. There was no need to raise voices in a house of restless souls.

"You're not that naïve, Mirabelle. It could've happened here and could've been a lot worse. What happened to Gio—"

"Could've been avoided!" Mirabelle sprung open, her legs and arms unwrapping all at once. "Scumstache is a rat. He sold us out. He murdered Gio! I want him dead!"

"Enough," Emory said, and his distorted shadow moved across the room as he paced to the window behind his desk.

"Disco and Corey are looking for him. When they find him, we'll make him talk. Once we have answers, we can take the fight to the Velascos."

With two fingers, Emory separated slats of the blinds and peered through the crack. He didn't know what he expected to find. The night revealed nothing of consequence, just a streetlamp struggling to fill the dark, not unlike the last time he saw his brother.

"Miri doesn't know what Viktor told us," Jack said. "You need to tell her."

Emory turned from the window. Mirabelle was already staring at him.

"Tell me what?" she asked with a haunting stillness, as if something in her already knew.

Emory took Mirabelle's hands as he knelt in front of her. Malformed and twisted, the shadows at the edge of the room seemed to darken. He hadn't rehearsed how he might tell her the news, and perhaps that was for the best.

"Ivan. He's—"

"Alive," Jack cut in with biting precision. "He's alive."

Mirabelle's petrified gaze darted between Emory and Jack. "How?" she whispered.

"I don't know," Emory replied honestly. "All I know is he wanted it this way. He knew we'd drop our guard if we thought he was dead."

"This was him," Mirabelle said as angry tears flooded her cheeks. "It's always been him. I told you he wasn't gone, Emory! I told you, and you never believed me. Why couldn't you believe me?"

Emory accepted the blame with a solemn nod. "I will find him and end this for good."

The assurance fell flat. Ivan promised pain and would deliver in spades. It was only a matter of time. Mirabelle yanked her hands from Emory and cradled her knees, child-like as she rocked in her seat.

"Why can't he just leave us alone?"

All their lives, she'd asked Emory that same question and always the same way—through tears and exhausted from unrelenting terror. When she was four and Ivan snapped her arm, she asked Emory why. When she was six and found her bunny, Cotton Ball, a mess of blood, guts, and white fur in her bed and Ivan in a fit of laughter, Mirabelle sobbed so hard she couldn't breathe and asked Emory why. He'd never had an answer.

Emory stood and sat at the edge of the desk next to her. "I won't let him get to you. He'll have to get through me first."

"And me," Jack vowed on the other side of her. "It's what's kept him away. He knows Em and I won't let anything happen to you."

Emory exchanged a glance with Jack. Neither man really knew what kept Ivan away or why he'd slithered back. Mirabelle nodded vacantly and stretched her legs. Liquid sloshed as Jack grabbed the whiskey bottle.

"You need to tell Em what you told me." Mirabelle pointed to the bottle at his lips. "And you need to lay off that. You've had enough."

"It's never enough," Jack sighed but put the bottle down. "Cal Havick is missing. He hasn't shown up to work. His phone goes straight to voicemail. Big Johnny said the Portland police can't reach him. The dude just vanished."

Emory quietly listened, though a source at the Portland Police Bureau had already slipped him that information.

Mirabelle craned her neck to Emory. "If she lost both her parents..."

Her voice trailed off as if speaking the possibilities might manifest them.

"Someone probably talked sense into him, told him to lie low. Jack, see what else Johnny can dig up, and we'll go from there."

"Amelia can't know about this," Mirabelle said.

Emory disagreed with a firm shake of his head. "She has a right to know. I'll deal with today's fallout first, then see what I can find out about Cal."

"Em, she can't—"

"I said I'll deal with it!" Emory snapped and shoved off of the desk. "Amelia will stay with us until it's safe for her to go home. Until then, I'm bringing her into the fold."

Jack snickered at that. "So, what, she's one of us now?"

"Jack, stop," Mirabelle pled.

"No, I wanna know. You brought her here for one reason. Isn't that what you said? What's that reason now, Em?"

The tip of Jack's tongue flicked lasciviously across his top lip, and he winked with no humor, only spite. Emory's fists clenched until his knuckles popped, and his breaths shallowed to hot spurts through gritted teeth. *Keep your head.*

"We both know what Ivan would do to her," Emory replied with icy restraint. "I'm not letting her leave. She's mine, so she stays with me."

Mine.

Jack and Mirabelle both pondered the possessive. Emory used it so seldomly to describe women. They were never his; he rarely wanted them to be. He and Amelia had hardly shared a kiss, and yet he'd gone ahead and marked her as his own.

Jack lifted a finger and opened his mouth to spit fire again, but Mirabelle intervened.

"Both of you stop. It's fine. Amelia will stay here until this ends. For tonight, she can sleep in my room with me. She's too scared to be alone."

Amelia was many things—contrite and listless—but afraid to sleep alone wasn't one of them. Emory let it go and nodded his assent. With a sudden push, Jack hopped from the desk, snatched up the whiskey, and retreated to the door with a sway.

"Hey, you're not going anywhere tonight," Emory called after him. "You've had too much."

Jack stopped halfway to the door and turned over his shoulder.

"I'll stay," he said but was looking at Mirabelle. "Night, y'all."

An anguished smile flashed across his lips but disappeared, and so did Jack down the hall. The sound of his boots grew faint until that faded too. Mirabelle stood and wrapped her arms around Emory's middle, her body still trembling.

"It's gonna be okay," Emory said. "Ivan's fucked up, but only human. A bullet to the head will end him just fine. Then we can finally move on."

"I hope you're right." Mirabelle's voice fractured with fatigue and dread in equal measure, and she extracted herself from Emory to fetch Amelia.

After she left, Emory shut the door and waited until the house fell silent. In a halo of lamplight, he sat at his desk and opened his laptop. A search of Cal Havick brought up his official portrait seated in front of the American flag in a pressed suit. He didn't smile but stared into the camera, cocksure and determined.

Emory scrolled the call history on his phone. He knew better than to save the number in his contacts and held his breath as the call connected.

A man answered, his voice groggy with interrupted sleep. "Agent Bright."

"It's Emory. I'm cashing in."

Sheets rustled on the other end of the line. A beat later, Kingsley Bright replied, "I can't help you."

Charity didn't exist in Emory's line of work, and he didn't offer his services for free. He'd helped Bright once and accepted as payment a favor in return at a time of his choosing. Bright had either forgotten or grievously misjudged Emory's bookkeeping.

"And here I pegged you as a man who keeps his word," Emory said and clicked onto Cal's personal Instagram page.

The last post—a family picture taken at Amelia's graduation—was almost two months old. In it, Cal beamed with pride next to his daughter. She was as gorgeous as ever in a cap and gown, but Emory saw clearly the heartbreak in her eyes. It seemed unconscionable that Cal hadn't seen it too.

When Bright refused a rebuttal, Emory continued, "I know you have your claws in Cal Havick."

"What makes you think that?"

Emory expelled a husky laugh. Bright's offended incredulity

never failed to amuse him. The man should've known the depths of Emory's connections. His reach had only expanded since they last spoke. Along the West Coast, it wove through the corrupted core of law and order, all those sacred institutions men like Kingsley exalted.

"Intuition," Emory said.

A door creaked on the other end of the line. When he spoke again, Bright's voice echoed, still tetchy but no longer hushed.

"His daughter, Amelia, is missing."

"My condolences," Emory said with no sympathy to spare.

"I'm trying to help him."

"Don't."

"Emory, whatever this is, whatever you're doing, it's not going to end well for you."

Emory's desk chair groaned as he leaned forward and rested one forearm on his knee. His temper flared with Bright's warning. He wouldn't take kindly to threats.

"I could say the same about your predecessor. Kranski."

Bright released a heavy breath then snapped, "What do you want?"

"I need you to keep an eye on Cal. Make sure he doesn't do anything stupid."

"Like what?"

Emory scoffed at the question. Cal's stubborn ambition had eclipsed better judgment. He wasn't rash, just obstinate, and Bright would do well to cull those tendencies in his new friend.

"Like overturning stones that are better left alone. He won't like what he finds underneath."

"If he thinks you know where Amelia is, he'll want to talk to you."

"Then redirect, Agent Bright."

"*Do* you know where Amelia is?" Bright pressed, ever the dutiful law enforcement officer, gathering leads wherever he could.

Emory smiled. "No, but I wish him the best of luck getting her back."

Cal Havick wanted Amelia to be another man's problem, so he spoke it into existence but couldn't dictate how it manifested. Heart, body, mind, and soul, Emory would gladly claim Amelia as his own and watch with delight as Cal choked on his words.

"Jesus fucking Christ," Bright muttered. "Do you want to protect him or antagonize him? Because you can't do both. Not when we both know the Velascos are trailing him."

Emory glanced at his laptop screen and Amelia standing next to her father. The girl was built for love, so eager to pour it into someone else. He thought of the man she deserved and wondered if he was worthy. He could be, but it had to start somewhere.

"I've always liked you, Kingsley," Emory said, "but can I trust you?"

"My word is good."

"Keep Cal close. I'll reach out to him when the time is right." Emory drew a long breath and closed his laptop. "Don't make me regret this."

TWENTY-FOUR

CAL

Cal landed in an old gold-mining town in southern Oregon. He checked into a bed-and-breakfast where the innkeeper showed him to the only available room and commented on Cal's luck. It was tourist season. Give it a week and they'd be booked solid through autumn. Cal had faked a smile. The old man hadn't known the half of it.

The next day, he made a trip to the local Walmart and stocked up on essentials. He could be anyone he wanted. That was a freeing thought in front of a display where t-shirts with stupid sayings exploded from cubby holes and amassed on the carpet tile floor.

He'd never be a man who wore graphic t-shirts, though, so Cal opted for a pack of solid colors and picked up a burner phone too. What it lacked in bells and whistles, it made up for with big buttons for clumsy fingers. Like a phantom limb, he still sometimes reached for his belt clip, though his phone was on the nightstand at home and surely drained of life.

On his fifth day there, no one bothered him much. At breakfast, he kept to himself as couples came and went. They'd survey him with pitiful smiles, and Cal released them from the burden of conversation with his nose in a newspaper.

The fifth day bled into a fifth night as the sun moseyed

toward the horizon. The town's main drag boasted a few restaurants and shops that sold tchotchkes already covered in dust. The tavern was the place to be, though it didn't have a sign out front. Someone told him a storm carried it away and the owner didn't bother with a new one. "Signs say what's ahead. No use if you already know." Tough to argue that logic.

A bell hanging over the tavern door announced Cal's presence. One of the bar backs—a pimply teenage kid—ran a ratty mop over sticky floors and greeted him with a nod. Giant tube TVs hung in each corner and hummed the baseball game on mute. A mold-speckled drop ceiling rounded out the cavernous space.

At the bar, a few locals bullshitted with the owner, Rudy, who'd lived in the town his whole life. He'd relayed that fact with exuberant pride the first night Cal drifted in. Rudy and the regulars never asked questions, but instead would chat with Cal about nothing of consequence as he gnawed on onion rings and sipped pale ale.

Rudy pointed to the back where pock-marked dart boards clung to the wall and an ancient jukebox glowed in the corner.

"Your friend's back there," he said over the buzz of a mostly empty bar. "I'll bring your usual."

Cal thanked him and wove past the high-top tables to where Kingsley Bright watched the ball game in a red t-shirt and faded jeans. A tall, Black man, he greeted Cal with a firm handshake and a warm smile. Cal had never met him before, but over the course of his career, encountered plenty of FBI agents who left a sour taste in his mouth. Most liked to talk in circles around him. Some were difficult to read. Others had an agenda. From the jump, Kingsley seemed cut from a different cloth.

After Rudy dropped off a round of beers, Cal raised his bottle to Kingsley. "Here's to working together," he said.

"To working together." The bottle necks clanked in salute, and Kingsley asked, "You settling in okay?"

Cal took a long pull from his beer and wiped his lips with the back of his hand. "More or less."

It was the polite thing to say. Turmoil had ripped through his life, and settling in suggested Cal had landed on his feet. In reality, he drifted on the wind, lost and unable to catch his breath.

He expected Kingsley to delve straight into business, but casual conversation flowed with little awkwardness. Over beers and hot wings, they chatted about their family lives. Kingsley showed Cal pictures of his wife and two sons. Over a second round of beers, Cal unearthed memories of Helen and Amelia, the ones where humor triumphed over sorrow and he could talk past the lump in his throat. Kingsley roared with laughter, and for the first time in so very long, Cal laughed too.

The regulars paid them curious stares with small-town bullshit easy to read. Two other men sat at the bar but kept to themselves. They weren't regulars or townies, so Rudy served their drinks with a sideways glance he reserved for strangers.

"As much as I've enjoyed this, I think we outta talk business," Kingsley said. "I've pieced together what I can from Agent Kranski's notes but was hoping you could fill in some blanks. First and foremost, I'm wondering about Rich Dauer's friendship with Philippe Velasco. It seems they were close."

Cal drew a long breath. The topic still sizzled with raw emotion, a live wire never buried.

"Philippe was just another client. At least, that's how Rich explained it. Eventually, routine business turned into gifts, dinners, vacations. Attorney-client privilege protected that friendship. I never got far when I asked about it."

"And Rich's relationship with the Moriartys?"

Cal blinked at Kingsley. "I wasn't aware there was one."

"A witness identified Moriarty members at Rich's party. The papers are painting what happened as collateral in the Moriarty-Velasco feud, but someone is doing their damnedest to keep Rich's possible involvement out of the press."

Cal huffed a bitter laugh. There was no better evidence that Rich was alive. Only he would care enough to keep his reputation intact at a time like that.

"As I understand it," Kingsley continued, "Burt was concerned about Rich's dealings with these organizations."

"That tracks. A week before he died, Burt reached out to me wanting to meet. He said it was about Rich but didn't elaborate."

"Burt was ready to call foul on Rich's friendship with Philippe," Kingsley told him. "He thought it created an ethical dilemma for the firm, so he dug into it."

"Dug in how?"

Kingsley surveyed the bar and lowered his voice.

"There was more to Philippe's story than what he offered in his plea deal. He confided to Rich that someone was quietly influencing his most trusted captains. Those captains had plans for a coup then war with the Moriartys. Philippe gathered all the information he could about the coup, the war plans, everything. He compiled it into a folder, handed it off to Rich for safe keeping, then went into hiding. The Velascos must have dirt on Rich because he coughed up Philippe's whereabouts without much cajoling."

"And the folder? I assume the Velascos wanted that too."

"Yes, but by then, Burt had the folder. He found it snooping around Rich's office and confronted Rich about it. Bad timing. Rich had just sold out Philippe to save his hide and had no qualms about throwing Burt under the bus too. When Burt realized this, he reached out to Agent Kranski for help, told him Amelia had seen the folder and was in danger too."

Cal's stomach knotted, sick enough that he eyed the bathroom door to measure the distance.

"Wait. Why would Amelia have seen it?"

"From what Burt told Kranski, she grabbed it on accident. No one knows how much she might've seen, though."

Cal slumped in his seat. "Why wouldn't she tell me? I could've helped her. And why the hell wouldn't Rich warn me about this?"

The questions came louder than Cal intended as the bar went quiet.

"I don't know about Amelia," Kingsley said, "but I do know that Rich's priority was saving face with civilized society."

Kingsley layered sarcasm on the last bit. Above the table, civilized society was a mask of faux outrage. Beneath it, they had their fingerprints all over these organizations. Suggest too much chumminess between the Richard Dauers and Philippe Velascos of the world, and things got ugly.

"Watch who gets a burr up their ass. They're always the most corrupt," Cal said. "My brother, Mitch, used to say that about civilized society. He knew better than most, spent his career in Vegas PD trying to nail Liam Moriarty to the wall."

"So I've heard," Kingsley replied but was polite enough not to repeat the rumor: the Moriartys murdered Mitch Havick.

Cal had heard that same rumor as he put his brother in an early grave. Mitch had tried to fracture the Moriartys at their fault lines and watch them crumble. In the end, it was Cal's family left fractured and crumbling.

On the other side of the room, a stranger ambled to the jukebox. With his back to them, he stared inside the machine and drummed his fingers against the frame. Kingsley turned to Cal but seemed to keep the stranger in his periphery.

"I don't imagine the name Ivan Holt is foreign to you."

Cal shook his head. He hadn't heard that name in over a year. Every so often, someone said it with faltering trepidation, and Cal was never quite prepared for the dread it deposited in him. He took another swig of beer, but his mouth went dry as he spoke.

"When I worked for the district attorney's office, Ivan was under investigation for a series of murders in California, Nevada, and Oregon. Same MO. All college-aged women away from home. Sexually assaulted, tortured, murdered."

"Melancholy Man" crooned from the speakers and sliced through the bar's unnerving quiet. The haunting tune sickened against the backdrop of the conversation.

"I heard the tape," Kingsley confessed with evident shame.

The tape. It wasn't actually a tape. It was just what folks called the recording. Everyone knew about the bodies pulled from rivers and left in fields to rot. The stories made the news, but most never knew the horror behind the headlines.

A college student in Oregon was murdered and her horrendous fate recorded—ninety minutes of begging, sobbing, and wailing until she no longer sounded human. Her murderer never spoke, only grunted as he assaulted her.

"If you don't mind me asking, what happened to the case?" Kingsley said.

Cal interlaced his fingers with his palms pressed together.

"We had enough evidence for a grand jury to indict but were in a race to get to Ivan before Emory did. He was closing in on his brother and hell-bent on serving his own justice. In the end, it didn't matter."

Two years ago, the DA called with the news. They found Ivan Holt's mangled body in a car at the bottom of a deep ravine. Between burns, decay, and scavenging animals, the rotten flesh clinging to his bones was unrecognizable. The medical examiner identified him through dental records and called it a day. *Justice served. You're off the hook,* the DA had glibly told Cal, who'd boiled with rage. A quick death was hardly justice.

"Here's what I needed to tell you, why I insisted we meet." Kingsley stiffened and licked his lips before cautiously proceeding. "Ivan isn't dead. He's very much alive and leading the charge within the Velascos. Philippe wasn't just running from an eventual coup. He was running from Ivan Holt."

At a loss for a proper response, Cal shook his head and stared at his hands that looked folded in prayer, though he'd long ago lost his faith.

"You're sure?"

"Positive. The body recovered from that wreck wasn't him. Ivan knew he was a hunted man. Staging an accident got both you and Emory off his back and gave him time to regroup."

Cal heard Kingsley as if from a distance. Muddled and misty, the words sunk in on delay.

"Why?" he asked.

"A means to an end."

"What end?"

"Emory."

Cal's skin crawled with the name. He never understood the hatred between the Holt brothers. They seemed more kindred than not—one a suspected murderer and the other at the helm of a brutal criminal organization.

"A blood war," Cal said.

"Yes. The Velascos and Moriartys have stayed out of each other's business. Sure, there's heat here and there when territories clash or associates double dip, but this won't be a war between them. It'll be a proxy war between the Holt brothers."

"Why now? Ivan could have ended it before Emory took over."

"The fall is harder from great heights. Emory's enjoyed his life protected at the top. Now, Ivan will usher in that fall and relish every inch of the tumble. It's already started. The Velascos murdered Giovanni De Luca a few days ago. Emory and Jack were there when it happened."

Cal pinched the bridge of his nose as the beginnings of a headache grew from the center of his forehead.

"Jesus Christ. Gio was the goddamn patron saint of the Moriartys." Cal dropped his hand and stared at Kingsley. "Well, is anyone on our side gonna do something about this?"

The idiot who fired up The Moody Blues whistled along, but his face was still obscured as he swayed in front of the jukebox. The two strangers at the bar looked on, but their attention drifted to Kingsley and Cal.

"Vegas PD insists on handling it." Kingsley stared at a water-stained ceiling tile above him and scratched at the stubble on his chin. "It's what I hate most about this job. You get hamstrung with bureaucracy and red tape and then—"

"Evil walks," Cal cut in. "It lives while innocents pay for the misdeeds of monstrous men. The girl from the tape, her father came to my office, flew in all the way from New York just to plead with me. He'd buried the parts of his daughter that were found and wanted closure through justice. I had to turn him away. There was nothing I could do."

Cal's chest tightened, and that lump in his throat returned, but he forced the words that came out sharp and sour.

"I never want to do that again. And I never want to be that man, to bury my daughter while a monster gets to live."

"You won't," Kingsley insisted. "We will find Amelia and bring her home."

We. The sentiment struck a chord more deep, resonant, and moving than Cal could've anticipated.

"So, what does this all mean? Amelia's running, but to where?"

Kingsley shrugged and said, "If the Velascos had caught up to her, we would've known by now."

Dead. She'd be dead. Could still be dead. Chin to his chest, Cal refused to voice the possibility.

"Look, the motel clerk is making progress," Kingsley said. "His doctors think he might pull through. If he does and can place Amelia at the motel that night, my office will open an investigation into her disappearance. Those pliers I mentioned are with the lab. We'll see if they hit for prints or DNA. In the meantime, I know an investigator in Vegas PD who can help us. He's a little out there, but he's got a beat on the Moriartys."

"A dirty cop?" Cal snickered.

"Not quite." Kingsley glanced at the jukebox still singing and lights still whirling. Rudy paced behind the bar as if he sensed some trouble ahead. "Here's the deal, though. You can't stay here."

Cal waved off the notion and drained the last of his beer. He also couldn't live his life on the run. A drunk stumbled from the bar and his stool crashed to the floor, but the two strange men weren't watching the commotion. They instead exchanged a glance with the man at the jukebox.

"These people know who you are," Kingsley whispered. "There's no obscurity in a town like this. Let's get your things and get you out of here."

Cal surveyed his surroundings with fresh perspective. The bar lost its charm and gained an abrupt hostility. The walls looked sallow in the ghastly light, and the floors seemed stickier when Cal went up front to pay.

The two men watched as he waited for his change, and the jukebox fired up again as Cal and Kingsley headed for the door. Kingsley pressed on, but Cal's legs refused as a guitar strummed its melody. A week ago, that tune had brought him comfort.

Cal locked eyes with the man at the jukebox. With a smile, he raised two fingers to his forehead in sinister salute as "Wish You Were Here" filled Rudy's bar.

TWENTY-FIVE

AMELIA

On the third floor of Mr. Moriarty's mansion, a shuttered room held many splendid things, most notably a finely wrought table with iron legs and a green marble top. Gold-vein ran through the slab, but the crown jewel sat atop—a black rotary phone.

The sleek thing teemed with temptation, and Amelia admired it at first because there was no harm in just looking. The cord had coiled on itself, so she righted it, but her fingertips caressed the handset, and the dial tone purred in her ear. *It's just a touch,* she thought, but that touch longed for more.

Amelia dialed the first five digits of her father's number, but there were too many sevens and nines, so the mechanical churn cranked on her heart, and her nervous breath hitched with no words to say.

Hi Dad. I'm alright. I'm doing just fine.

In the end, she didn't complete the call. Shuttered spaces were abandoned for good reason, so Amelia left it alone and straddled a divide bridged by shame. Shame she dialed the first half of her father's number. Shame she couldn't dial the rest.

Four days passed since the abandoned call, and the mansion stirred with Gio's funeral preparations. Each day brought new faces—men with strained eyes and deep scowls; elegant women and their cherub-cheeked children. The men nursed their grief in the basement with cards and booze. The women gathered in the kitchen for white wine and gossip. Amelia roamed the liminal space between.

Most funerals these days were couched as a celebration of life. The dead didn't need anyone's sorrow, and perhaps the living didn't know how to cope with it. Night after night, mourners celebrated Gio's life but ignored the grisly circumstances of his death. In the basement lounge, the men undoubtedly picked it apart and examined it fully. The women, on the other hand, refused to acknowledge it altogether.

"Gio was murdered, and we almost died too," Amelia had reminded Mirabelle. "Are we supposed to just forget?"

"The men haven't forgotten," was her reply. "It's not our place to nag them about it."

Their place, apparently, was to arrange charcuterie boards, chill the wine, light the candles. They created an illusion of normalcy for men who lived in a world that was anything but.

Those first few nights, Amelia obliged the invitation to socialize and smiled with timid grace as she tried to fit in. Most of the women regarded her with staid aloofness that didn't reject her outright but still held her at arm's length. Many already knew who she was, and her story passed on red lipstick whispers when they thought she couldn't hear.

She heard just fine.

The men weren't much better. Their verdict of her was gaussian. The majority middle were apathetic, but a handful paid her hostility that silently warned her to fall in line. The other minority pitied her, but from some distant shore like onlookers to a shipwreck. Then there was Emory. These days, chaos and duty nipped at his heels. He'd linger long enough to tell her hello and ask how she was before something else demanded his attention.

Amelia thought of him in peaceful moments where her heart hurt less. Of all her daydreams, the ones of him were the most comforting and sweet. By night, she thought of him in other ways—rough palms parting soft thighs, kisses lush as he filled her up, warmth as he came inside her. Amelia would fall asleep soaked between the legs but never quite satisfied with her own touch.

As Mirabelle tended to the day's festivities, Amelia shirked her own duty to fit in and curled up with a book in the room of splendid things. When the black phone rang, it scared her half to death only because she still didn't have any words to say.

Hi Dad. I miss you. I dreamt of Mom again.

It wouldn't be him. Of course not. But temptation and guilt were strange bedfellows, and Amelia felt she ought to atone for her dalliance with the phone. She put on a poppy-colored sun dress and made herself pretty for the judgmental shrews downstairs. *"Hold your head high, sweet baby,"* her momma would have said, but Amelia only ever saw her mother in dreams. In the waking world, she carried on alone.

She crossed the foyer where the stained-glass dome above dazzled in a kaleidoscope of color. The parlor clock kept time with her steps, but music pulled her into the hall of photographs where Bob Dylan drifted from the basement lounge.

She hadn't been down there since her first night at the Moriarty mansion. To remember it was like plunging into a past life. The cuts and bruises had faded, but Amelia healed up differently on the inside. The pieces fit together again, but the picture was no longer the same. At the other end of the hall, someone eclipsed the sunlight streaming from the great room.

Emory.

Amelia didn't have to look. His presence spoke for itself in a language she knew well—the grace of his gait unusual in such a tall man and the intensity he wore like a well-tailored suit.

Emory approached with his hands behind his back. He smelled of spiced cologne and the fresh-pressed linen of his white button-up shirt. His skin was a deeper bronze, as if time in the sun had treated him well, and his hair hung in loose waves about his shoulders.

"Don't you wanna be with the others?" he asked.

The question vibrated like long-ago days of solitude on the

swing set and her father's car rumbling up to an empty school playground. *"Why aren't you with your friends, Amelia?"*

She shook her head as butterflies battered her composure and squandered all the clever things she might say.

"Not particularly. Don't you wanna be down there?"

Amelia motioned to the dying lines of "Knockin' On Heaven's Door" lilting from the basement. Emory mulled it over with a handsome smile. There he stood with the ease of a man who'd shed his duty, if only for the night. And there she stood, pulling apart at the seams because her crushes always started the same way—so shy, it whittled her breath to a whisper in her chest then dropped her eyes and stilled her tongue.

"Not particularly," he said. "It's too loud, too..."

"Crowded?"

"Precisely." He drifted closer, his smile fading. "I was actually coming to look for you. Mirabelle said you've seemed distant the past few days. Is everything alright?"

Another echo of paternal wisdom. *"You'd be happier with your head out of the clouds and feet on the ground."* To her father, pragmatism was a virtue. Daydreams were not. She was an aberration under some other man's roof, and like her father, perhaps Emory intended to chide her about it.

Amelia crossed her arms and took up her own defense. "I'm fine. I just needed some space."

It wasn't a lie, just absurd. No one clamored for her company. She was a stranger shoved in the corner, the houseplant someone forgot to water. Did it matter why she wilted? It must've to him. Sincerity gentled Emory's voice.

"Take whatever space you need. I just wanted to give you this."

He revealed what was behind his back—a black leather notebook with *A. Havick* stamped in the bottom corner. On top was a polished fountain pen with ivy leaves carved into the brass body.

"It's for your poetry," he said, his fingers brushing hers as the notebook exchanged hands. "I thought you could use it to write."

Emory stared at her lips but licked his own. It seemed neither had forgotten their kiss in the courtyard, fleeting as it was. Like a precious jewel, Amelia had examined every facet of it—the surprising softness of his lips, his hair sweeping her cheek, his strong arms holding her close. She wanted to gush about it to someone and deconstruct the moment to relive it again. There was no one to humor her, though, so Amelia buried it like a secret by day and unearthed it each night.

"Emory, thank you. It's gorgeous," she said and stroked the notebook as sleek as that black phone and the pen's body gleaming like the rotary dial. Her heart sank with rediscovered guilt, and she cleared a tickle in her throat. "I feel like I don't deserve it."

"Of course, you do," he laughed with a folded brow, apparently flummoxed at her modesty. "If anything, I'd say you deserve far more."

Emory stalled and his hands disappeared into his pockets. Any other day, it would've marked the natural end to their rendezvous, and he'd be on his way to wherever his men had gathered.

"This was always my favorite part of the house," he said instead, and Amelia followed his gaze to the photographs lining the hall.

The confession surprised her. The Moriarty mansion was palatial and lavishly appointed, every part meant for admiration.

"Really? But everything here is so beautiful."

"That's the point, I guess. This part is simple, nostalgic."

There it was again, Emory and his need for simplicity. He studied a photo of a woman cradling a baby on the porch of a bungalow home. She was a paragon of fifties glamour with black curls and ruby red lips.

"Who is that?" Amelia asked.

"Liam's mom." Emory pointed to the next frame where a scowling soldier puffed out his chest. "This is his dad, Joseph, in Vietnam."

"How then did this all start?"

Amelia gestured to the mansion, the symbol of the Moriartys. Everything she knew about them came from her father. It wasn't what he told her that shaped her perception, but his quiet vexation rife with rage.

"Some men wage war in here." Emory tapped his temple as they continued down the hall. "Joe was that way. Even after he came home from Vietnam, the war never truly ended for him, so he built a brotherhood of lost souls, men who were similarly afflicted and had no one to turn to, nowhere else to go. At first, they offered protection to the neighborhood. That led to gambling rackets, shylocking, the like. It grew from there, and they found in each other family and belonging."

Emory didn't have to tell her. Amelia would've figured it out as they passed faded photographs where love, joy, and the pulsing promise of new beginnings radiated from each frame. A monster unmasked, her father surely never knew the Moriartys that way.

They stopped at a photograph halfway down the hall. In it, Liam wore fatigues a smidge too big, and a rifle hung heavy over his bony shoulder.

"Liam was raised in this life," Emory said. "To him, it was the family business. Joe thought military service would instill the discipline Liam needed to lead the organization one day. It did, and Liam eventually inherited it with one rule: our secrets are sacred."

Amelia stilled, but when she met Emory's eyes, the warning she expected wasn't there. Instead, his gaze flicked from her lips to her eyes again, and Amelia's heart strummed a quickened beat. The sun washed farther down the hall and saturated the glossy length of Emory's hair.

He tapped the soldier in the frame standing tall next to Liam. "That's my father."

The resemblance snapped into place. Emory's coloring was darker than his father's chestnut hair and blue eyes, but the striking features were the same.

Amelia beamed as she studied Emory then the photograph. "You look so much like him."

"So I've heard. He and Liam served together in Iraq. They lost touch after they came home but reconnected when my mom passed."

"Where is your dad now?"

"He died of a heart attack when I was thirteen. Liam and his wife, Francisca, took me and Mirabelle in."

Despite his composed delivery, Emory's jaw clenched with old hurts. He looked caught between exalting memories of his father and suppressing the sadness they stirred.

"I'm so sorry to hear that."

"It's okay. That was a long time ago."

"How did your parents meet?" Amelia asked as they passed several more photos.

"After my dad got out of the military, he went to Puerto Rico. He only planned to stay a week but met my mom." Emory paused and glanced at Amelia with a knowing smile. "He got hit with the thunderbolt."

"The thunderbolt?" she laughed and turned the phrase over in her mind. "Wait, like in *The Godfather*?"

He nodded with a chuckle. The reference was to something more consuming than love at first sight and tinged with more madness too. It was also perhaps the most tender moment in a story Amelia remembered was shaded with sorrow.

"They were crazy for each other, and my dad refused to leave without her. My granddad had other thoughts."

"He didn't like your dad?"

"Not exactly. My dad had known my mom for less than a week and wasn't a practicing Catholic. My granddad refused to give my mom away to a man who didn't intend to marry her in the church. So, my dad rediscovered his faith under my granddad's tutelage until he agreed to the marriage. It took four months."

Emory relayed the last bit with evident pride and admiration. The story was worthy of both, that a man would be so devoted to the woman he loved.

"That's very romantic," Amelia said, her cheeks warm well before they dipped into the sunlight.

"He had his moments."

She waggled the notebook. "Seems you do too."

"For you, yes," Emory said and studied her in the fresh light as they reached the end of the hall.

Amelia's heart picked up its rhythm, a steady pounding against the notebook she clutched to her chest.

"Why for me?" she asked but wasn't fishing for a grand gesture.

Plenty of women had appeared over the last week unattached to a man and shamelessly on the prowl. Amelia wasn't foolish enough to believe that none had offered Emory their company and so much more. A man like him could have his pick.

A soft smile spread on his lips, but his eyes conveyed what was in his heart, a steadiness of affection that'd seemingly grown in their time apart.

"Thunderbolt," he said.

"Thunderbolt," Amelia repeated, keenly aware of how far they'd come.

The change had happened unexpectedly in them both. If anyone asked how it began, they'd have no coordinates in space to give, no moment in time to tell, only that they stood in the midst of it now, baptized in new light at the end of the hall.

They stood beside the last photograph, one where Liam Moriarty flashed a candid smile. In Portland, the same picture, tattered at the edges and regarded with contempt, sat on her father's desk. Here, it held a place of honor amongst a proud bloodline.

"I see why this is your favorite part of the house," Amelia said and cast one last look down the hall before they drifted into the great room.

The space was an Elysian dream, redolent with lavender and drenched in golden light. Through tall windows, the sun melted like sherbet on the horizon and spilled across the desert valley.

"Simple things," Emory said and settled next to the window.

Amelia contemplated the scene outside and that lonely road in the distance. "And yet here you are where nothing is simple."

It was only an observation, but Emory treated it like a question to be answered. Shoulder against the window frame, he stared out and Amelia admired his profile.

The poetry I'll write for you, she thought fondly, though her crushes always ended that way, those times she bled her heart onto a page and handed it over. The ones before crumpled it up and said it was too much. *"Not all hearts are built for boundless love,"* her mom used to say as she freed the hair plastered to Amelia's tear-stained cheeks. *"Those poems you write. Darling, save them for someone worthy."*

The scar on Emory's lip twitched with a frown. "I came here without a choice. It was survival, not ambition."

Eyes to the floor, his hair was a curtain around his face and his cheeks a dusky pink. Heavy was the crown upon his head, but Amelia recognized the burden as loneliness, not duty.

She reached up and gently tucked a lock of hair behind Emory's ear. The gesture drew his gaze. He was heartsick over something.

"You ask me the same question every time you see me, but I wonder if anyone's ever asked you, so I will. Emory Holt, are you okay?"

"Amelia Havick, no, I am not."

"What can I do?"

Emory stared up at the ceiling and thought it over with a hum. It was a clever distraction as his arm slipped along the small of her back, and he drew her in close.

"Hmm, well, let's see." Emory appraised Amelia in her sundress and wedge heels. "You look beautiful, like you're ready for a date or something, and I happen to know a place on the third floor."

"Oh yeah?" Amelia laughed, giddy just to be near him again. "You know a place?"

"Yeah, there's this balcony. No one fucks with me up there. I was gonna grab some food and hide away. You wanna hide away with me?"

Offered in earnest, the question came quiet and not for the sake of discretion. Emory drew a long breath and shifted on his feet. *He's nervous,* Amelia realized. It never occurred to her that she might elicit butterflies in him too or that he might fumble his words with his heart on the line. Something in the balance, that they were on equal footing, calmed her frazzled nerves.

Amelia held his hand in both of her own and stared up at him from beneath her lashes. "Only if it's a date."

The blush on Emory's cheeks deepened. Whatever his worries, they seemed to depart. "Yes, it's a date."

"Then let's go hide away."

TWENTY-SIX

AMELIA

Hidden from the courtyard below and terrace farther down, the balcony overlooked the valley and an expiring sun that set the distant mountain ridge ablaze. Amelia and Emory laid out a light spread on the bistro table and shared their first meal together.

As they split the last clementine at dusk, its juice sticky and sweet in the summer heat, Emory looked contented for the first time Amelia could recall and laughed with a lightness that sounded silver to her ears.

Twilight rose and the conversation flowed over shimmering candlelight. Amelia slipped out of her shoes and eased back in her seat.

"So, this is all yours now," she said more than asked and tipped her wineglass to the terrace far below where the others had gathered.

"Whether I like it or not."

"You don't like it. The more I get to know you, the more I see that."

"And what is it you see?" Emory asked with a smile that only partially hid some hesitancy. Not everyone liked being examined that way.

"It's like you've been cut from another world and pasted here, forced to live in two dimensions while the rest of you is somewhere else. An outsider to your own empire."

Amelia wanted to go where the other parts of him existed, that place where she'd find him whole. For the time being, the closest she'd find was the balcony where Emory seemed at ease, relieved perhaps that he could drop the pretense and just be himself.

He savored a sip of bourbon, both the drink and her observation demanding a thoughtful pause.

"You're not wrong. I'm grateful, though. As a kid, I never knew what Liam did for a living. He'd show up at my house in a blacked-out sedan. He was like a superhero, a guy people respected and feared. The night my dad died, I knew Miri and I had no home anymore, so I packed our things and got us out. With Ivan still around, I had no choice."

Emory shrugged as if it were nothing, just a story from his past, but his shoulders tensed as he ran his fingers through his hair and continued.

"I called Liam, thought he was the only one who could protect us from Ivan, and he did. He brought me and Mirabelle here, but I knew the second I stepped outside of this world, my brother would be waiting. I was tired of feeling helpless and wanted to take my power back, so I asked Liam to let me shadow walk. He agreed but only when I turned eighteen.

"He never showed me preferential treatment. Like everyone else, I paid my dues as a street soldier. Eventually, Liam offered me a seat at the captain's table, a small post without a ton of responsibility. I did well in that, so he put me in the post everyone wants, the one with the connections and prestige."

"Las Vegas," Amelia said.

Warm shadows danced across Emory's face where a smile unfurled. He gestured to the chorus of laughter on the terrace below.

"See, you already know more than some of them." He leaned forward, head tilted and looking an awful lot like he might want to kiss her. She wished he would. "You get it, Amelia. You just do."

She brimmed with glittering glee she couldn't explain, smiling until her cheeks ached and soaring with the stars. Emory grabbed the bottle of wine and freshened her glass.

"After I had enough years in, Liam wanted to phase me into his position. He's always treated me like a son, and I owe him my life, so it was the least I could do. When I agreed to take over, I wasn't thinking about my future or living a simpler life."

"And now?" Amelia asked between sips of wine.

"And now, I wouldn't know a simple life if it fucked me seven ways to Sunday. Now, my brother is still alive, and I'm right back where I started, feeling just as powerless as the day I left home."

He shook his head, not quite defeated but humbled perhaps. Amelia dragged her chair over to sit by his side. To think she'd once inherited her father's beliefs of Emory, a man who navigated the underworld but preserved the best parts of himself, the ones Amelia saw so clearly were good and honest and worthy. She finally found the words to say if that phone ever rang again.

Hi Dad. You never knew him. You never will.

"What happens next?" Amelia asked haltingly. Mirabelle had warned her not to pry, but the charade of normalcy couldn't last forever.

"I find Ivan and kill him unless he kills me first," Emory replied with dark laughter, but Amelia witnessed the fear of failure grow in him.

"I won't let him hurt you," she said and placed her hand on his forearm.

Emory stared at her, utterly mystified, it seemed. She didn't blame him. What the hell could she do against Ivan? It didn't matter. The thought must've counted for something because Emory patted his chest with a smile as if taming his heart.

"Thunderbolt?" she asked and pulled her knees onto the chair. It brought her closer to him.

Emory nodded. "Thunderbolt."

"Okay, pretend a simple life *did* fuck you seven ways to

Sunday," she said, her chin propped against the heel of her hand. "What does it look like?"

Emory settled in his seat and contemplated the question.

"Well, I'd make an honest living. I'd settle down somewhere I can see the stars at night. Maybe up north with lots of trees, at the end of a road so it's quiet and secluded, somewhere I can sleep well. Find someone to love forever, just me and her."

His eyes met hers before dropping to his empty glass. Amelia fetched the bourbon bottle and poured him some more.

"She'll be very lucky to have you."

"She'll be worshipped. It's how I love."

Emory studied her in the candlelight as he sipped his drink. A drunken ruckus erupted below and beckoned like a siren to collect those adrift on thoughts of freedom.

"The thing is," he said, "I don't worry about working some nine-to-five I hate or bills I have to pay. I worry if the people I love are going to be alive tomorrow or if the day will come I lose my freedom. It's hard to put someone else through that, and it's never ended well whenever I've tried. This world has a way of tearing people apart."

Troubled again, Emory shook his head as if dismissing bad memories.

"You said some men wage war inside themselves. That includes you, doesn't it?"

"Yes. What I want is solace, but I've learned to accept that's just a dream."

"It doesn't have to be a dream."

Amelia scooted closer, as if dividing the distance could impart some belief. Emory tipped his head to the music pulsing below but held Amelia's stare.

"They think I'm already living the dream. They don't see things the way you do, least of all me."

Amelia took his hand. "I do see you. All of you."

"I see you too." Emory interlaced his fingers with hers and, with a gentleness that surprised her, softly kissed each of her knuckles. A flutter grew in Amelia's belly, and heat bathed her cheeks. "And what is it you want for your simple life?" he asked and squeezed her hand.

"Books and tea and rain. Believe it or not, a small house with lots of trees where it's dark enough to see the stars. To love someone who loves me back. Same as you."

"Same as me," Emory repeated with quiet understanding passing between them, kindred in the way they held a mirror to each other.

He shifted in his seat and leaned in close. His mouth lingered just a breath from contact, as if relishing the intimacy of the moment.

"Are you going to kiss me now?" Amelia asked, a ridiculous question born from another bout of unraveling nerves. Her arms snaked around his shoulders, and she held onto him as a source of strength lest she fall to pieces against his touch.

Emory's laughter warmed her lips and nose brushed hers as he nodded. "That was the plan. Is that alright with you?"

"Yes," she whispered.

Emory pressed his lips to hers, the kiss deep for having been delicate. They both drew a long breath in unison, and their hearts might've beaten just the same. His tongue parted her lips, then slipped into her mouth. He tasted just as she imagined, both masculine and sweet.

A quiet groan rumbled from the back of Emory's throat as his fingers sunk in her hair. His other hand roamed her body—down her back and the dip of her waist, up the rise of her hip, cupping her ass.

"Let me take you inside," Emory said in a shallow pant against her open mouth.

Amelia nodded. "Where did you have in mind?"

"My bedroom," he said between kisses, each more eager than the last.

Competing desires ravaged Amelia—accept the invitation to his bed or let it unfold in its own time. She wanted him desperately, but he intimidated her. Her heart pounded hard in her chest, the pulse thrumming deliciously between her legs.

"If I go there, I'm liable to take off my clothes," Amelia said, her head swimming as Emory trailed kisses down her neck and his fingertips skimmed the tops of her breasts.

"That was the idea." Emory hooked one finger beneath her bra and brushed her nipple in a delicate tease. "I want to go slow, take my time with you. We have all night."

Body humming beneath his caress, Amelia nodded. "Then let's make the most of it."

TWENTY-SEVEN

AMELIA

Emory led Amelia to his room in quiet retreat as if they ought to bank some silence before disturbing the night. *This man will eat me alive then tear me apart,* Amelia had once assumed of Emory but wasn't so sure anymore.

Long ago, she'd loved a man like that with pushy hands and hard kisses that hurt more than they aroused. Her friends had told her it was passion and that men in lust didn't know how to behave. Their advice: collect that token of affection—how flattering to be devoured—and spread your legs.

And hadn't Emory once been the same? Yes, he'd been manic with longing that night in the parlor, and she'd lost her senses right there in his arms. She'd almost accepted his offer to come upstairs and finish what they started, if only to call his bluff. She would have found no bluff that night but no romance either. Just another man dying to get inside.

The intoxication had matured since then. Though heady with complexity, it felt far less like spinning out of control. It wasn't what Emory said, but the way he moved so calm and confident. He was self-assured and not for the conquest, but in his commitment to the moment. True to his word, he didn't go by halves, and she saw what he meant when he said she'd have all of him; a man who'd eat her alive then love her right.

Inside his bedroom, Emory flicked on a lamp, and Amelia stood rooted at the end of the bed. The tidy space spared no excess other than the full-length mirror in the corner. A pleasurable chill pervaded the room that held the faint scent of jasmine and fresh greens, though she didn't know from where. It was pristine, but not quite lived-in enough to know that it belonged to him.

"You looked surprised," Emory laughed as he unfastened his watch at the dresser.

Her stomach flipped at the sound and the glance he gave in the mirror's reflection.

"Maybe a little. It's very clean," she remarked, though that didn't surprise her.

Amelia wasn't entirely sure what she expected and had only caught rare glimpses of his space, just a sliver through a crack in the door. Much like the man, the rest remained a mystery. She existed on the other side of that divide now, and there was nothing left for him to hide. If that scared Emory, even in the slightest, she wouldn't have known as he emptied his pockets and removed his belt.

Like a strip tease, he made a ritual of the wait, and Amelia found herself transfixed in watching him slowly shedding his shirt. Bare chested, he approached in deliberate steps that bid her to remain still. She couldn't move, even if she wanted. Her knees went faintly numb, and thin, shallow breaths issued from her lips, not unlike the first few times they met. In fact, shades of that past flickered, and she trembled as Emory eased up behind her.

"Someday soon I'll take you to my place in Vegas," he said and dropped a kiss to her shoulder.

Amelia stretched her arms overhead and draped them around his neck. "Soon?"

She had no anchor to time anymore. Days, weeks, months— soon could mean just about anything.

Emory nodded as his hands engulfed her waist. "Soon as I can."

With a shuddering breath, Amelia sunk into him. Emory slipped the straps of her dress from her shoulders, and the poppy red fabric pooled at her feet. He didn't seem to mind her mismatched lingerie—a red bra and black thong—and neither did she as they admired their reflection in the mirror.

"We look good together," Emory said, and his lips grazed her cheek.

With his arms protectively wrapped around her middle, Amelia rested her head against his chest. Skin to skin, it was the closest they'd been, and neither rushed through the moment to get onto the next.

Amelia luxuriated in the warmth of his bare chest and closed her eyes as his fingertips slid to the heat between her legs. He touched her sweetly, a gentle tease until she melted further into him. The man was a master at commanding his touch. It could be anything she wanted, and when she wanted more, he sunk a finger inside and then another to fill her up.

"I missed you these last few days," Emory muttered with a gratifying pant against her neck as he worked between her legs, the confession as satisfying as his touch. "Look how gorgeous you are."

Amelia cracked her eyes to the reflection. She looked small in his arms. Her cheeks flushed and lips parted with ragged exhales. With another swipe between her legs, her eyes fluttered shut once more, and a soft gasp escaped her.

This can't be real.

The thought broke loose from a distant fantasy, the feel of her fingers between her legs, imagining what Emory Holt might feel like inside of her; before she ever met him, that time when she came hard with inevitable shame. There'd be no shame tonight. With a roll of her hips, Amelia ground against his hard cock nestled against her ass and watched with delight as he clamped down hard on his bottom lip.

Hand in hand, Emory led her to the bed, and Amelia's heart skipped a beat. There was something wildly intimate about the gesture, that they arrived in the moment joined together. Amelia absorbed the sight of him in the murky light, his body carved in lean muscle and tattoos covering his chest, shoulders, and back.

"Lie down," he commanded with a nip at her bottom lip that softened into a kiss.

Amelia obeyed and relished Emory's weight as he climbed on top of her. Where this once might've intimidated, it thrilled instead.

"I can't stop looking at you," he said as his fingertips traced her curves and his gaze followed.

"Are you afraid if you look away I'll disappear?" Amelia laughed and swept her fingers through his hair.

Emory grinned as he undid her bra. "Little bit."

"I'm not going anywhere," she whispered into another kiss, one burning with heated urgency. She needed him inside of her.

Emory cupped her breast and rocked against her as his tongue plunged into her mouth. Lost in his taste and the feel of him on top of her, Amelia was only vaguely aware of her underwear sliding over her hips and down her thighs and then discarded somewhere nearby.

His touch swept her nipples, enough to make them hard and for the rush to go to her head. Naked beneath him, Emory nudged her knees apart and admired her body laid out in offering.

"You're a work of art," he rasped, breathless as he stroked between her legs. "Fuck, and you're so wet."

"I'm always this wet for you," Amelia told him truthfully and couldn't tell what aroused him more—the statement or that she arched her back and rolled her hips to match his rhythm. "I want you," she sighed.

"Oh yeah?" Emory's mouth hovered over hers. "How bad?"

One large hand settled on her throat firmly, and his thumb pushed against her jaw. Lust darkened his gaze as his fingers pumped inside of her. Amelia meant to respond, but when her mouth opened, moans poured out as pleasure coursed through her, each steady wave building toward her climax.

"Please," she cried out and gripped the sheets. She was *so* close, even gasped it once and then twice.

Unceremoniously, Emory pulled out of her and shed the rest of his clothes with a cocksure smile. She might've pouted and put up a fuss if not for him on his knees before her. Emory's fingers glistened with her pleasure as he stroked his cock. She knew he was big—how could he not be for a man his height—but his dick was perfectly long and thick and slick at the tip as he ached for release.

Until that moment, it hadn't occurred to Amelia to be nervous. Emory was more man than she'd ever been with; not just his size but the voracity of his appetite. Her pulse beat as frenzied as the thoughts racing through her head.

"First," he said, his voice gravely as he eased on top of her. The tip of his cock rested between her legs. He caressed her cheek as his tongue flicked against hers. "You will always come first. Besides..."

He kissed her neck, sucking gently right beneath her ear, the first mark of many he'd undoubtedly leave.

"Ever since that night you tried to run away from me..."

Emory's lips skimmed between her breasts, stopping only long enough to suck each nipple. His hair brushed her waist, tickling on the way down.

"I can't stop thinking about how wet you were."

Amelia steadied shaky hands on his shoulders as he trailed kisses down her belly.

"How sweet you tasted." His lips passed her hips. Emory hooked one arm beneath her leg. "How good you'd look naked in my bed, riding my mouth." He matched her eyes as his lips grazed the inside of her thigh. "There hasn't been a night since when I haven't come so fucking hard thinking about this."

Yes. God, yes.

Amelia nodded eagerly, though he couldn't see. He closed his eyes and circled her clit with his tongue in one delicious swipe. Her legs trembled with another lick that terminated in a deep kiss between her legs. The tenderness disarmed her. No one ever kissed her like that. They went for the kill; too hard, too eager, too ready to be done and on to the next thing.

Emory lingered, no moment too trivial, so he took his time as he said he would, and it started with a kiss. A simple kiss between her legs and then another. The sensation racing through her was unreal. A mere fantasy couldn't have predicted it. With delicate pressure, he sucked on her clit then each lip before his tongue set in again. Amelia lost her breath as she gripped his shoulders, her chest constricting and fingernails digging into his skin.

He'd said he was great at eating pussy. Great. Just *great*.

With a mouth like his, she figured there was some truth to the statement, but he'd monstrously undersold himself. The man was a savage between her legs, merciless in how he devoured her. If this was what being eaten alive meant, she'd die a million deaths for him to do it every night.

"Jesus, *fuck*," Amelia gasped. "Emory."

"That good for you, baby?" he chuckled and stroked her from the inside, his long fingers easily reaching her sensitive spot hidden deep.

Amelia couldn't answer. Words would've failed her anyhow. As with his hands, Emory's mouth commanded her body. He hooked his arms behind her knees and, in one swift movement, rolled to his back and brought Amelia with him.

"Ride my face," he commanded and didn't wait for her to shimmy up his body. With a firm grip on her ass, Emory hauled her up his chest and set in again before Amelia could even straddle him.

Dizzy and disoriented, she held onto the headboard and tried desperately to compose herself as he lapped at her pussy. With every flick of his tongue or caress of his lips, she came undone, her legs trembling and thighs crushing his cheeks. Emory peered up at her and the wickedness in his gaze said he wanted a show. It was her time to shine.

Any lingering inhibitions fell away. Amelia matched his eyes as she swiveled her hips in loose rolls. Emory buried a moan between her legs, his chest rumbling and fingers digging into the back of her thighs. Lost in the moment with his mouth between her legs, Amelia closed her eyes and rode his face as faithfully as she'd ride his cock.

"Fuck, baby, you're so sexy," Emory muttered, his panting

breaths like heaven between her legs. "Turn around and suck my dick."

Once again, Amelia had hardly processed the demand before Emory had flipped her around and positioned her exactly how he wanted. On all fours, she was face to face with his perfect cock. Amelia wrapped one hand around his shaft and glanced back at Emory with a sweet smile. She couldn't say what flashed in his eyes—possessiveness, lust, the need to mark her as his own and keep her forever.

"That's my girl," Emory said and licked her cum off his lips. "Get to it," he commanded with a wink and light slap to her ass.

Amelia's stomach flipped, and she met that command with a tease. She sucked the tip of his cock then placed a soft kiss there.

"Like this, baby?" she asked, her lips deliberately brushing his tip. The gesture drove him crazy. Cheeks flushed, Emory grit his teeth.

Before he could answer, Amelia took him in her mouth and sucked, her tongue swirling and hand stroking. Emory tensed beneath her, and another moan disappeared between her legs as he delved in again. The rush went to her head. Amelia sucked hard and tried to focus, but she lost her rhythm at the sensations tearing through her.

It didn't matter. Emory seemed to like it sloppy and thrust into her mouth, grunting as he restrained himself. His thumb swiped her clit, but his tongue was relentless as it sunk inside her. Amelia steadied herself on her elbows, her body taut and trembling and composure quickly fading.

"Fuck, Emory," she cried, blindsided by her release that came with an exquisite rush.

All the maddening tension they'd shared—the unbearable ache to be near him, to know him, to have him—unraveled in one dazzling moment as Amelia tumbled off of him. Face buried in her hands, she steadied herself for a breath.

"Oh my God," Amelia muttered into her palms.

She could fucking cry and almost did. The embarrassment would've been too much to take, though, so Amelia pulled herself together with another shuddering breath. Emory laughed as he climbed on top of her, positively pleased with himself that he'd made her come so easily, and moved in for a kiss. Amelia could taste herself on him. She didn't care about that, not with his body hot against her and his thick shaft resting heavy between her legs.

"Fuck, that was sexy," he said and brushed the hair from her cheek. His gaze swept over her face, admiring her as he caught his breath.

Amelia held onto him and drew him down for another taste. His mouth was warm, the kiss tender. Falling fast, she needed him close but buried her face against his chest so he wouldn't see.

"You're shaking," Emory said, ever attentive. Of course he'd notice how she trembled.

It wasn't for some claim to chastity. Amelia was instead keenly aware of the sordid path she'd taken to end up naked in his arms. Accepting him into her body meant consummating more than just their relationship, but her place in his world.

"Do you want me to be gentle now?" he asked but seemed to already have the answer in hand.

"Maybe," she replied with a shrug and didn't know how to read his smile or the way he studied her as if seeing her for the first time.

Emory took her hand and threaded it in his, their palms pressed together. "You're so beautiful, Amelia."

He kissed her again, hotter and needier than before. Yes, he could be gentle, but the passion remained in how he devoured her lips with perfect understanding of the intimacy she craved.

"Do we need something?" he asked and rocked against her. His shaft glided between her pussy lips. Amelia sighed at the sensation and almost lost the question, forgetting it was hers to answer.

"I have an IUD," she panted against his mouth as he ground against her clit still pulsing from her last orgasm.

"I wanna feel every inch of you," he said. The tip of his cock rested at her opening. "Is that okay?"

Amelia reached between them and took his cock in hand. For

a man his size, he'd have no choice but to be gentle. Her stomach fluttered at the thought. She wanted him to make her whole as he filled her up, to feel him moving inside her, to be as close as they could.

"Tell me what you want. *Everything* you want," Emory whispered, his breath bathing her skin and his lips soft at her neck.

Amelia squeezed his hand and wrapped her legs around his hips. "I want to watch how you fill me up."

He kissed her pulse. "What else?"

"I want you to come inside me."

"And?"

I want you to love me, not tear me apart. Amelia didn't know how to ask if he knew how, so she dug her heels into his ass and wrapped her arms around his shoulders as if she'd given him all her wants. Emory lifted his head but something in him had changed. *He knows.*

Heart to heart and nose to nose, he kept her gaze as he pushed inside. "Fuck," he sighed and let his head hang heavy. "Goddamn, I knew you'd feel good, but this..."

Emory stayed inside her for a moment, unmoving as they both marveled at the connection.

"You feel so good too," Amelia said with a smile and drew him in.

She captured his lips in a kiss as he worked his way deeper. With each roll of his hips, the sharp sting gave way to a sweet ache between her legs. She bit her bottom lip to stifle a moan but abandoned the effort as he picked up his pace.

She let herself go at the sight of him, a strong man on top of her. Emory cupped her breasts, waist, thighs, anything he could get his hands on. Amelia swiveled her hips so he might feel every part of her from the inside out. That drove him to the brink. His chest heaved and legs stiffened. He was close, and so was she. Emory had found the sweetest spot and knew it too.

In one fluid movement, he hitched her legs over his shoulders and stared down at them joined together. Amelia propped herself on her elbows to watch too. Her lips stretched around his cock, her clit swollen and aching for another touch.

"I knew your pussy would take my dick so good, baby."

"*God,* yes," she muttered and collapsed back against the pillow.

He was so deep inside of her. Amelia's breasts bounced with each thrust. Emory leaned down and took one in his mouth, his tongue swirling against her nipple. Amelia grabbed onto his ass. His muscles contracted and released against her palms each time he bucked his hips. Emory lifted to his knees, gathered her wrists in one large hand, and pinned them overhead.

"You like that, don't you?" he growled.

Ruthless again, he loomed over her and squeezed her wrists. He might've fucked her too hard if not for how diligently he studied her face and watched how she responded. Unable to breathe, let alone speak, Amelia nodded. The pressure between her legs surmounted with a flush of wetness and a rush that left her heart racing. Yes, she wanted this too; wanted him to devour her, claim her, take everything he could.

"Emory," she gasped and reached down to swipe her clit. "Don't stop. I'm so close."

A gentle wave before, the second climax slammed into her. Emory extracted every second of it from her body, his rhythm unrelenting as she rode her release. Their lips met again in a fervent kiss, his moans pouring into her mouth and vibrating against her chest. With one last thrust, Emory collapsed on top of her. Amelia closed her eyes with a heavenly sigh but opened them again when his hand met her cheek.

"Look at me," he whispered.

So often, he'd demanded her gaze, an angry command she never really understood until that moment. If she wanted to be loved, then he wanted to be seen. She met his gaze as his cock pulsed inside her. Amelia could come again from the sensation alone.

She kissed his neck beneath his ear, then whispered, "I want to see."

Emory eagerly obliged and pulled out of her slowly. Together, they watched as his cum seeped out of her and coated her pussy.

"Jesus Christ, you're a fucking dream," Emory said and beamed as if proud to have wrecked her this way. On top of her again, he slipped his arms underneath her. "Come here. I need you."

On a long inhale, Emory breathed her in deep, a breath that filled his lungs, and he held it there just as soundly as he held her in his arms. He released it on a laugh, sincere despite how quietly it departed his lips.

God, and his lips. They were perfect. He kissed her again, and if he meant to eat her alive, he was certainly succeeding. He feasted like a man starved, and when he was through, he shook his head with a sated smile.

"What is it?" Amelia asked and freed the strands of hair that'd stuck to his cheek. Flushed, his body billowed heat, and his skin dewed with sweat.

"Bet you never thought you'd end up like this," Emory said and combed his fingers through her hair.

Amelia shook her head and studied the tattoos on his chest. On the left side was a heavenly host of angels and the right a legion of demons. They looked at war over his heart that strummed so peacefully.

"Did you?" she asked.

"I wasn't sure you'd ever come around." After a pause, a grin unfurled on his lips. "You hated my ass."

"I didn't hate *you*."

He laughed at that and looked primed to call bullshit. She couldn't blame him. Their early days together were mired in complications.

"I hated that I was attracted to you," Amelia said as she traced the tattoo on his bicep and the scars underneath, "that you turned me on, that I wanted you so badly. I hated the guilt and shame I felt because of it. Hated that I wanted to be close to you, and that I wanted you to want me too."

"Of course, I wanted you. I've wanted you for so long."

For so long.

Amelia smiled at the marker he placed. She'd done it too, and neither could escape the nonsense of their timeline. If she could catch her breath, Amelia might have told him that it seemed they'd already spent a lifetime together or perhaps quite a few. His presence conjured memories just out of reach, so it all felt like being roused from the sweetest dream. She couldn't recall the sequence of events, only the feeling of having lived this moment with him once or twice or endlessly before.

"What is it?" Emory asked when she still hadn't said anything.

"What is what?"

"The way you're looking at me." His eyes flicked over her, roused with some mystery she couldn't see in herself. "I don't think anyone's ever looked at me this way."

"I don't think I've ever felt this way," she admitted.

Some men gloated in that singularity because it wasn't enough just to love them. They needed to be the only star to light up the sky, a supernova burning up what had come before and spoiling what might come after. Emory wasn't the sort.

He collected her in his arms as he rolled to his back. "I haven't either. It's not about erasure. I've been in love before, and I know you have too. But this is…" With a thoughtful pause, he searched her face. "Well, you're the poet. Maybe I can tell you how I feel and you can put it into pretty words."

Amelia traced her fingertip along the angelic host tattooed to his chest. Maybe the placement was intentional, his better angels so close to his heart.

"For you, I already have," she said.

TWENTY-EIGHT

EMORY

"Fold," Emory said and tossed his cards to a table too intimate for poker.

The Queen of Hearts sopped up condensation that pooled at the base of his glass. With a coquettish smile, Amelia fanned herself with a straight and scooped up her winnings.

"Are you sure you're good at this?" she teased and organized her chips in mismatched stacks that drove Emory wild, almost as wild as her lips that pursed with a bad hand and fingertips that mindlessly stroked her collarbone.

It was the deal they'd made after a morning of incredible sex—hands off each other for a little while; let their bodies recover as they came up for air. That task grew harder with each successive round of cards.

Emory laughed. "I was until I taught you."

He shuffled the deck and dealt another round. Oddly enough, Amelia's winning streak didn't fan his competitive flame. It ignited other fires, though. With each win, she'd lightly gasp with surprise and bounce in her seat, breasts jostling in the tight confines of a black tank top. Emory collected the sights and sounds and layered it over visions of her in his bed; how she had gasped beneath him with a quiver and quake, clung to his shoulders, clawed at his skin.

Neither could leave it alone, whatever they'd started, so sublime magnetism prevailed. On the third floor, they spent the day listening to music, playing poker, and stealing kisses every chance they got.

The room boasted the fine antiques Liam's late wife had collected—woven rugs that brightly adorned terracotta tile, curios with odd functions, dusty books with well-worn pages. The space was chiefly a grand gesture of love. *"I'll always be her husband,"* Liam had told Emory years after Francisca died, *"and in this room, she'll always find a quiet place to rest."*

Through the window, a balmy breeze carried in the scent of lemon blossoms, and a strip of sunlight laid across Amelia's bare thighs. All afternoon, Emory watched the light roam her body— across her face where it revealed the rich russet of her eyes, along her breasts, pooled between her legs. Soon, his lips would forge that same path down her body.

On the table, his phone buzzed. *SoCal calling...*

"Do you need to take that?" Amelia asked on the third ring as Emory debated whether to answer.

The shadow had already been cast, so he patted his knees and stood with a sigh.

"I do." He motioned to his cards face down on the table. "This is trust. Don't peek."

"Trust," Amelia said and handed him her cards. Back lit in the afternoon light, she gazed up at him with a winsome smile.

Jesus Christ, stop my fucking heart. She'd tossed that look at him all afternoon. It heated his blood and flooded his cheeks with warmth. Emory tucked her cards in his back pocket and leaned down for a kiss, but his mood soured as he stepped into the hall.

In solitude, he led best. His men festered with a feral need for vengeance, though. Over the past few days, all twelve captains had separately sought his private audience. Emory had listened to liquor-induced tirades about retaliation and a few composed appeals for a tactical counterstrike.

Wild dogs needed to be kept on a short leash, though, so Emory stolidly refused bloodletting in the streets. The corpse of an important man trumped a mass grave of nobodies. Once Gio was put to rest, the red shroud would lift and they'd all see clearly what must be done.

In the meantime, Emory sent his most vengeful men on a mission to sate their bloodlust. If Scumstache was smart, he would've skipped town east bound. Instead, he was holed up in a casino hotel waiting to be rescued. No one was coming to save him, though, and there wasn't a stone in Vegas Emory couldn't overturn.

He lifted the phone to his ear without greeting.

"We got him," Corey, captain of San Diego post, relayed. "You know that prick only shadow walked a year ago?"

Not surprising. Greed and glory sent the young bloods off the rails. They weren't slick enough to mastermind schemes or connected enough to guard against blowback.

"If he's that green, how did he know our plans that day? Someone had to've been working him."

"We'll make him chatty," Corey said with glee registering in his gruff voice.

"Please do."

Emory hung up the call with a pit in his stomach. The kid was just the stem. He still had to dig out the roots. Back in the room, the air was honeyed with Amelia's perfume, and the light suffused with cloud cover. In luminous contrast to the dark deeds done in the hall, she beamed at him as he took his seat.

Emory returned her cards and tended to his hand—an ace high, but nothing more. He dropped his chips to the table and sipped his drink to bury a smile. Amelia's brows knit as she studied her cards. She searched Emory's face and chewed her bottom lip. Sweet thing had the easiest tells. She won on luck of a good deal, not a knack for deception.

"Your move," he deadpanned.

Amelia discarded two cards, and Emory dealt two more. She sifted through her harlequin pile of chips and bid three blue. Emory raised two reds, but Amelia's resolve collapsed as she met his impassive stare and folded with a three of a kind. Emory tossed down a shitty hand.

"You tricked me!"

She feigned affront, but merry laughter rang through the room. His bluffs enthralled her almost as much as winning.

"I did." Emory cleared away his chips. "My apologies."

As he shuffled the deck, silence washed over Amelia. She spun a white chip against the table and fidgeted in her seat.

"Emory."

He'd never get over his name on her lips. Even now, it sent shivers down his spine.

"Amelia."

"You know that motel clerk, the one Damon hurt?" she asked and held onto fresh cards like a lifeline.

"Mm-hm."

"Is he okay?"

Emory anted up with a white chip. "He's still in the hospital, I think."

Amelia shook her head and rearranged the cards in her hand with vacant interest. The order didn't matter, only the distraction.

"That's awful." A dissonant pause hung in the air like ending a song off tune. "He was very young; probably just out of high school. He didn't deserve what happened to him."

She couldn't bluff to save her life. Emory set his cards aside and folded his arms on the table.

"Sweetheart, what is it you need from me?"

His casual affection seemingly set her at ease, and Amelia released a shaky breath. Though the cards crushed in her small hands, she matched his eyes with wolfish determination.

"I want him to be okay."

At another table negotiating terms, Emory's worlds collided. He saw the bravery it took to ask, and it both dazzled and disturbed that some part of her still feared him.

"I understand, and I love that you've got such a big heart, but there are risks if he makes it too. I can't rob from the reaper and expect him to call it even, you know?"

Amelia frowned. "I know."

The divide between Moriarty men and women had its function. It wasn't a chauvinistic holdover from Joseph's time as chief, but a practicality meant to guard against that particular quandary. Amelia's compassion was worth protecting, though, so Emory did what all Moriarty men swore they never would.

"Is that what you want?" he asked as if they were shopping for some glitzy bauble or zippy convertible to make her happy. He sensed it would cost him far more.

A radiant smile unfolded on Amelia's lips. Every part of her exuded warm romance as sweet and tender as basking in the afternoon sun. With a face like that—so angelic and with a heart of glimmering gold to match—he'd be hard pressed to deny her anything, and thus Emory backed himself into a dangerous corner.

He took her hand and lightly kissed the top. "I have a feeling he'll pull through."

———

By early evening, the afternoon haze thickened, and overcast clouds blotted out an already sinking sun. They hung dark and low and crackled with heat lightning.

As a simple man with simple desires, it stood to reason that spaghetti was among Emory's favorite meals. As a street soldier, he would drag his exhausted carcass through the door of the apartment he shared with Jack, Pete, and Corey and throw together slop called dinner—noodles and tomato sauce. It'd been a small comfort when he'd known so few.

And because Amelia blessed him with boundless affection, she cooked his favorite meal and even secured an accomplice, Pete, who'd bought the missing ingredients for her that morning.

At the island, Emory chopped vegetables as Amelia navigated the kitchen with heartwarming familiarity of where the spoons and pots and colander all lived. On an empty terrace beneath a sky-stained grey, they shared a quiet, uninterrupted dinner until the wind nearly toppled the table, and Emory decided that that was their cue to head inside.

Amelia packaged up the leftover spaghetti and homemade bread as Emory washed dishes in the sink. When his phone vibrated in his back pocket, he dried his soapy hands and fished it out.

SoCal calling...

Emory excused himself into an adjacent corridor and answered.

"You called it," Corey shouted over buffeting wind before moving inside. "The kid was a go-between. He heard the plans from Torres, who was in the room when Disco went over marching orders that day. Torres instructed fuck-face to funnel information to a Velasco associate. Kid claims he had no idea he was set up. He thought the associate was working for Viktor."

"Fuck," Emory sighed. The boy was expendable. Torres was not. Under Disco's mentorship, he'd been marked for captainhood. "What's left of the kid?"

"A couple inches of life. You wanna close it?"

"Yes. Slowly."

"You wanna do the honors? We'll keep him alive until you can get here."

Emory chewed on the prospect. It wasn't as if bloodlust didn't tempt him too. He kept alive the image of Amelia in the backseat of an SUV with a gun to her head and the kid's hand clamped over her mouth.

That keepsake became his North Star. Guided by its light, Emory walked his own path toward vengeance, tantalized by its violent end. He would carve out the boy's eyes and tongue but leave his other senses. The kid could listen to Emory sharpening his knife, feel the strips of skin leaving his body, taste his own flesh.

In the courtyard, wind ripped the honeysuckle vines from the stucco wall and flower petals swirled in the squall. Amelia loved those flowers. In the kitchen, she hummed as she dried dishes, the familiar melody comforting and sweet.

"No," he said. "I've got plans tonight. But make it memorable. You get me?"

Emory had talked in riddles for so long. The true meaning of things was a dead language. Corey translated just fine and expelled a gritty laugh.

"Oh yeah. We got plans too."

"When you're done, find Torres. I want everything he knows about Ivan; where he is, what's next. I don't care how long it takes or what you have to do. You understand?"

"A few are rolling on him now."

"Good. After Gio's funeral, you'll take over Las Vegas post. Disco will report to you. Pete can cover your territory until Jack and I come up with a permanent solution."

Silence crowded the line long enough for Corey to light up a cigarette and take a heavy drag.

"Disco ain't gonna like it."

"I don't give a fuck what Disco likes!" Emory boomed. "You think I care what he wants? You think his ego means shit to me? I should exile him to Redding post and be done with it." Emory gripped the window frame as thunder rattled the pane. "Tell Disco to get his house in order and call me when it's done."

"Roger. Rest easy, Chief. We'll get it sorted."

Emory ended the call with grim satisfaction. He could stomp the heads off snakes, but treachery was a leviathan he couldn't slay alone. That meant identifying the trustworthy in the ranks.

Back in the kitchen, he sat at the island across from Amelia but stewed in his anger.

"Everything okay?" she asked as she dried a wooden salad bowl.

"Just tying up loose ends," he replied, a bluff she saw right through.

"You're brilliant. I'm sure you'll figure it out."

Amelia put on a darling smile, though concern stirred in her eyes. Somewhere she learned to walk the tightrope between asking too many and too few questions. Mirabelle must've taught her that.

"And you're incredible," Emory said. Though entirely sincere, it was meant to redirect. "Thank you for dinner. It was also incredible."

"I'm happy you liked it." Amelia retrieved a pot from the drying rack and returned to the island. "The key is to roast the tomatoes and garlic for the sauce. Oh, and the secret ingredient is pancetta."

Emory laughed, his dour mood dissolving. "Isn't the secret ingredient supposed to be a secret?"

Amelia shrugged and stared dreamily at the ceiling as she dried the pot. So many moments with her were worthy of committing to memory. That was one—how beautiful she was without make up on, her lips stained red from wine, the way she looked at him as if she was memorizing him too.

"It's my mom's recipe. When she met my dad, he was awful at taking care of himself, so cooking was her love language. She taught me everything I know."

"About cooking?"

"That and how to patiently love a hard man."

Amelia set the pot aside and contemplated the courtyard where the wind toppled a glazed pot. It rolled, unbroken, on its side. Lost in thought, she wrung the dish towel in her hands. Tears welled, but she quickly wiped them away before they spilled down her cheeks.

"Sorry. I'm fine most of the time, but the pain surfaces so fast. There's nothing like it."

Her bottom lip quivered as she tried to temper her grief. It never worked that way. Emory stood and circled the island. He lifted her to the counter and wrapped her in a strong embrace. Amelia held on tight as if she wanted to fall right through.

Cheek to cheek, Emory rocked her in his arms. "I know it hurts. I know it does."

"All I have are memories of her. What if I forget? Then she'll really be gone."

Emory combed his fingers through her hair, the strands wavy from the kitchen's heat. Amelia gazed up at him with tears clinging to her long lashes. He'd once responded to her hurt with callous disinterest. To think of it filled him with shame.

"You won't," he said and kissed each of her tear-stained cheeks.

"Did you?"

Emory shook his head. "I still remember my mom. You'll remember yours too."

Where he'd never been elegant with words, Emory could rely on touch to convey what was in his heart. With a hand at Amelia's cheek, his thumb traced her lips plump and swollen from crying. He leaned in and pressed his mouth to hers in what might've been a kiss too hard, but Amelia softened it as she sunk into him.

His tongue parted her lips with no cajoling, but her fingertips stroking his chest reminded him to go slow and savor. Savor, he did. Her mouth was sweet as he kissed her deeply.

"What a poem you are," he whispered, love drunk and languishing. "I wanna hold you. Do you wanna do that, go lay down together?"

When Amelia nodded, Emory lifted her from the counter and led her by the hand to his bedroom.

TWENTY-NINE

EMORY

In Emory's bedroom, he turned on a movie, and it struck him then how small acts of normalcy settled them both. Like all lovers, though, it was a thinly veiled distraction as he and Amelia kissed in the dark.

His fingers roamed her body in a feather-light touch—a brush across her breasts, down her stomach, between her legs. It wasn't just a tease but exploration he'd never quite taken the time to master. He did then and discovered new parts of her.

Beneath him, Amelia rolled her hips with rising pressure against his hard cock. With warmth rippling through him, Emory migrated his lips to her neck and lightly sucked on the hollow beneath her jaw.

"God, you're a heartbreaker," he said before trailing kisses down her body.

"I'm really not," Amelia laughed. Her fingers sunk in his hair and nails grazed his scalp. He recalled she didn't like being misunderstood in that way. Hearts weren't always broken by malice, though. Sometimes people just got clumsy.

Emory rested his head in her lap and stared up at her. With wide eyes, more Bambi than bedroom, Amelia gazed back as he caressed the silky inside of her thigh. She hummed at the touch and combed her fingers through his hair.

"I won't break your heart," she told him. "Don't break mine either."

"You're safe with me."

Emory sealed the promise with a kiss to her knee before sliding off her shorts and underwear. He tossed them to the floor, and the rest of their clothes quickly followed.

Make her sing had taken on new meaning as she laid naked before him. Emory palmed her breasts that fit so perfectly in his hands. Her nipples hardened with his touch, and he dipped his head to suck each one. The tension in her limbs eased as Emory's tongue swirled each nipple and elicited from her such soft sighs.

His body heated and cock hardened as he rose to his knees. Amelia bit down on her bottom lip and slowly spread her legs before him. In the dim light, she glistened, already wet and ready for him.

Emory ran a hand over his face. "Goddamn," he breathed into his palm before easing on top of her.

His fingers worked between her legs, one and then two tucking inside. His lips skimmed her stomach and, further down, he peered up at Amelia as she held her breath. Propped on her elbows, she watched intently as his mouth arrived between her legs and his tongue slid along each of her lips.

"Emory," she sighed, her head falling back as he savored her taste.

He kissed between her legs just as slowly and sensuously as he kissed her mouth. It was a destination for him, not an inconvenient errand along the way of getting off. He relished the heavenly little pants and moans that escaped her, a whole chorus of sounds that made his heart pound as his lips and tongue worked in concert.

"You taste so fucking good," he panted before diving back in.

He meant it too and had obsessed over far less. If she only knew how savagely he craved her. Most nights, it was all he could think about. Unable to focus at business meetings, deals had been done and decisions made with his blood hot and Emory thinking only of how she'd taste and the ecstasy he could bring her.

Amelia rolled her hips, grinding against his mouth as her knees fell further apart. Her lost inhibitions thrilled him almost as much as the flush of wetness soaking his lips and dripping down his chin. Emory plunged his tongue inside her and swiped her clit until Amelia arched into him.

"I'm so close," she gasped. Another few flicks and she tensed, her thighs warming his cheeks as she came in one shuddering breath.

Everything softened then—her body, the sound of the TV babbling in the corner, the gauzy blue light. Emory crawled up her body, his mouth slick from her orgasm. With the heels of his hands propped on either side of her head, he drank in the sight of her beneath him. Amelia's hair fanned across the pillow, and she panted shallow breaths. A fine layer of sweat coated their bodies. Its scent mingled with the sweetness of her perfume.

"You're fucking perfect, Amelia," he whispered into a kiss.

Some women were scandalized at tasting themselves. Amelia didn't seem to mind as his tongue slipped into her mouth. On top of her, their kiss slowed enough for him to revel in her taste and the feel of her lips plush against his. Emory bucked against her, his cock nestled between her pussy lips and his shaft grinding against her clit.

"I need to be inside of you," he groaned and almost accomplished the task. The tip of his cock slid inside, but Amelia sat up and kept his gaze as she guided him to lie back then knelt between his legs. Emory expelled a rasping chuckle.

"What is it?" she asked.

"You're so eager to please."

She settled to one hip, her hair cascading over her shoulder as she tilted her head.

"For you, yes."

For me. If he could hold a mirror to her, she'd watch her own willing surrender and love in the look she gave. It spurred Emory's possessive streak. She'd belong to no one else ever again. *Mine.*

With one arm propped behind his head, he enjoyed the view

as Amelia wrapped her fingers delicately around his shaft. He covered her hand with his own and instructed her movement.

"Hard, baby," he said and squeezed with steady pressure.

Good girl that she was, Amelia obeyed beautifully and stroked him in slow, hard movements. Emory closed his eyes with a shaky breath as pleasure tore through him, an electric wave that rippled down to his toes. He wouldn't last long, not with her touch like magic. He cracked his eyes. Amelia licked her lips and rose to her knees. She climbed on top and ground against him, her wet pussy teasing his cock as she rolled her hips.

Emory wound her hair in his fist. With a light tug, he demanded in a throaty groan, "You gonna take my cock like a good girl, hmm?"

He bucked his hips to push inside, but Amelia shook her head with an impish smile.

"You have to wait."

"I've been waiting all day," Emory protested and tried to corral her by the waist, but she slipped away and eased down his body.

Her gorgeous lips nestled against the tip of his cock. "Then what's a little longer?"

Emory shuddered with the exhale she gave the moment before she took him in her mouth and sucked. An ecstatic sigh vacated him, and he gathered up her hair in his fist again. Her hand coiled around his shaft and met her lips with each pass. And when he liked it too much and moaned with impending release, she lifted her eyes to watch him.

Emory muttered incoherently into his palms. Whatever he said was lost in a slew of delirious sighs and groans. Euphoria sent the room faintly spinning. He was so close and could've let it ride, but another need superseded simply getting off. Emory reached down and gathered Amelia in his arms. She came eagerly as he hauled her on top of him.

"I need you," he breathed into the crook of her neck as she laid against his chest.

"It's only been half a day," she laughed before sucking on his ear lobe.

"An eternity."

Despite a heated flush, goosebumps blanketed his skin as Amelia sat up again. Emory took a moment to marvel at the sight of her straddling him; the way the pale light played against her smooth skin and tenderness in the way she looked at him. Never had a woman ever looked so stunning on top of him.

Emory gripped her hips as she eased down his length, her head falling back with a gasp as she took as much of him inside as she could handle.

"Fuck, you're so good," Emory moaned.

He already knew she would be tight, warm, and wet but hadn't anticipated the feeling of completeness too. They were meant to be that way, to belong to one another. Amelia must've had the same thought. She nodded, though he hadn't said anything, and Emory mirrored her. *Yes, I'm yours.*

One hand drifted from her hip, and he dipped two fingers into her mouth. Amelia needed no direction from him. With her eyes matched to his, she sucked as she rode his cock. It was a beautiful sight—her thighs trembling and lips stretched around his dick; his shaft slick with her cum; her nipples hard and hair a tousled mess.

The frenzy would start and couldn't be tamed. Emory toppled her to the bed, his heart pounding as he slid back inside. It felt like slipping into silk. Amelia's thighs clenched his hips and arms coiled around his neck. Their breath mingled with shallow pants, their lips hovering a moment away from a kiss.

Emory plunged his tongue into her mouth and, with each thrust, sunk deeper inside. Amelia unraveled like a knot, everything falling to ribbons around him. With her warm body beneath him, he didn't know where to look or touch—her breasts that bounced with each thrust, her pussy wrapped around his cock and revealing her clit begging for a touch, her gorgeous face contorted in pleasure.

Emory spread her legs further apart, licked his fingers, and reached between them to swipe her clit. Amelia fell into the rhythm and gazed down to watch him fuck her. She loved that part. So did he. Emory feasted on the sight until his balls tightened, pressure growing at the root of his shaft. *Not this. No, not yet.*

He closed his eyes. It felt too fucking good. He wouldn't last long. It'd be over before it really began, so he let himself rest deep inside her and covered over her mouth with his own. He indulged in her sweet kisses and the way she wove her fingers through his hair. The closeness swept him away, the moment where their hearts pounded against one another.

"I want you," Amelia moaned with a smile and rocked her hips to take more of him in, a subtle demand to be fucked deeper.

Emory obliged until everything constricted and he felt he might snap. His arms coiled around the small of her back, and he buried his face against her neck.

"God, fuck me harder, Emory. I'm so close."

Emory sat up, pinned her hips to the bed, and pounded into her mercilessly. Amelia cried out as she came, her body squeezing around his shaft. The sensation was all-consuming, enough to take him under, so he surrendered to it.

Emory let it wash over him as his cock pulsed inside her, enthralled at claiming her that way, feeling every inch of her tight around him. He came with a woozy rush. His body buzzed and limbs ached, and Amelia's name escaped him in one heavy groan.

On his knees, his head fell back. Emory scrubbed his hands over his face and sent quiet breaths to the ceiling until the world stopped spinning. Delirious in the comedown, Emory pulled out of her and would've collapsed to the bed, but Amelia smiled up at him. He knew that smile. She wasn't done with him yet and was well-practiced in all the delicious ways she could quite literally bring him to his knees.

She reached between her legs and kept his gaze as she traipsed her fingers through his cum. Emory didn't know what she loved watching more—him fucking her or his cum soaking her pussy.

She had his attention. Emory sat back on his heels as Amelia massaged her clit, her lips, her opening.

Enraptured at the sight, his chest heaved, and he stroked his cock until he was hard again. Amelia bundled two fingers and slipped them inside herself. She was drenched between the legs and reaching for him with her free hand.

"I need you," Amelia sighed. Her small fingers clearly weren't enough anymore, so she pouted about it. Poor baby would never be fucked this good again. He'd ruined her in that way and set the bar too high to reach. *Good.*

Emory took her hand from between her legs and guided it to her lips.

"Suck," he rasped and laid down beside her.

Amelia did as she was told, sucking her fingers clean as he rolled her to her side and entered her from behind. He held her in his arms with one hand propped on her hip to keep her still. The other clamped over her mouth as he buried his cock deep inside, deeper than he'd been before.

"You're such a good girl begging for it like this," he panted. His lips crushed against her cheek and hand slipped to her neck. "Don't you ever forget who owns this pussy."

To prove it, he thrust hard until her breaths escaped her in a sharp gasp, almost a scream. His grip on her throat tightened. He demanded an answer.

"You do." Amelia tensed and clutched his hand at her hip. "Fuck, you do!"

Emory grinned and rewarded her with the softness she craved. He kissed her cheek and slowed his speed, grinding in long strokes until only his tip remained inside her before plunging back in.

"You're so good to me, baby," he whispered and slipped his tongue into her mouth. "Look at me. I want to watch you come."

Out of breath, Amelia nodded and kept his eyes through a heavy-lidded gaze. Her brows knit and lip quivered. A sweet moan caught in the back of her throat, and her pussy tightened around his shaft, the sensation more exquisite and mind-blowing than he could ever recall, as if her body was made for him. *Mine.*

He surrendered to it and came hard with his eyes locked on her. She collected the sight with a hand on his cheek and her lips brushing his for another kiss.

Emory never stayed long in the aftermath and not for lack of affection. It wasn't his speed, but he lingered in it now just to marvel at their connection, the taste of her mouth, the heat of her body. The need to be closer, though, surprised even him. Emory rolled Amelia to her back and eased down on top of her.

"I wanna hold you," he muttered, though her arms were already securely wrapped around his shoulders.

The double-talk existed there too, and Emory didn't know how to carve out the parts of himself that avoided the truth. Wanting to hold her was just a substitute for never wanting to let her go.

Amelia understood. She hitched a leg over his hip and whispered as she cradled his cheek, "I'm not going anywhere."

"Good."

Emory placed a soft kiss to her lips before rolling off of her. Amelia settled contentedly in his arms as his palm roamed her naked silhouette. Echoes of her remained on his body—her smell on his fingers and the fading sensation of her limbs coiled around him.

In the crook of his arm, Amelia propped herself up on her elbow. Her fingertips traced small circles against his chest, and she looked at peace. If his world of death and violence could disappear, he imagined that was how he'd find her—lost in some thought and a faint smile on her lips as she daydreamed in the dark.

"What is it?" she asked. He might've asked her the same.

"This is gonna get complicated," Emory said and mostly meant his phone on the nightstand vibrating with another text. The statement was nebulous enough to apply elsewhere, though.

"How so?"

Amelia rested her head against the heel of her hand. The fingertips of the other continued their caress that might've soothed if not for Emory's heart faintly racing.

"I'm gonna fall for you," he said quietly as if the descent hadn't already started. The future framing was a ruse that Amelia swiftly sussed out.

With an adoring smile, she steadied her palm against his chest. "I think you're already falling."

A culture of fear existed around the grand confession. Give your heart, get gutted in the end. The exposure no longer frightened Emory. He rested easy with it and found safety in Amelia that'd eluded him before. It seemed abnormal that love and fear once came as a pair.

"I am," Emory agreed. "I think you might be falling for me too."

With his fingertip, he traced lines between the freckles dusting Amelia's shoulder. She settled down beside him, her bare skin soft and warm against his.

"I am. Love doesn't have to be a complication, Emory."

"I'm not afraid to love you," he told her as his phone buzzed on the bedside table, this time with a call. They both ignored it.

"Then what are you afraid of?"

The question came sweet as if Amelia intended to chase away his fears, whatever they may be. There were too many to choose from, but they all distilled down to the same thing.

"Losing you," he replied honestly, though it sounded like a cop out.

Anyone truly in love feared it falling apart. That wasn't what he meant. He could withstand the usual pathways to heartbreak, those bittersweet ends of an ill-matched love. But there was another path promised to him, one shaded with tragedy and horrors too far ahead to fully see. *I will destroy everything you love.*

"You won't lose me," Amelia assured with a kiss and, for tonight, Emory could believe her.

For a while, it ended as it began—caresses in the dark and softly spoken words of affection—until Amelia fell asleep. Careful not to disturb her, Emory reached for his phone and returned the missed call.

"My house is in order," Disco said when the line connected, no emotion coloring the lofty declaration. Only time would tell.

"Corey is taking over your post," Emory told him. "For now, you'll be his number two. This will never happen again, understood?"

Muffled static filled the line. "Yes," Disco replied dryly. "I'm sorry, Chief. I had no idea about Torres."

Part plea, part protest, neither was quite contrite. It wasn't about being sorry but saving face. Hit with heat, Emory would've rained down hellfire. Only his temper ever made him stupid, and it might've then, but Amelia stirred in his arms.

Her long legs stretched, and she burrowed close with a slumberous sigh. Emory kissed her forehead and stroked her hair. Her serenity in sleep, the way she held onto him, her small hand placed over his heart, it tamed something in him, and Emory found words far more merciful than he might've otherwise.

"For your sake, that'd better be true. Tonight, I expect you to send a message down your ranks about what happens to rats. The other captains will do the same."

Emory hung up and turned off the TV. As the wind howled outside, he and Amelia slept peacefully in one another's arms. By morning, word had spread in gory detail about the price of treachery.

THIRTY

MIRABELLE

Sheets damp with sweat and orgasm twisted around Mirabelle's legs. The insides of her thighs were sticky and numb, and the bedroom's soupy air smelled like the swapping of body fluids. Not lovemaking. Not fucking. Just sex stripped of ornamental intimacy.

Beside her, Jack puffed a cigarette with an arm propped behind his head. The paper hissed with each drag, and smoke swirled in the haze of late morning. Unblinking and unsmiling, he stared at the ceiling fan whirling above them.

"You think Em's fucking her?"

Mirabelle didn't appreciate the question's maniacal undercurrent or the callousness imbued in his gaze. Like some of the other men, Jack placed the blame for Gio's death squarely at Amelia's feet.

Amelia Havick wasn't the problem, though. It was Amelia *with* Emory that irked Jack the most. To him, she was an iron fist in a velvet glove he'd have to crush while still tender. It was too late. Amelia had already bloomed and, while her petals might still bruise, her thorns could draw blood.

Mirabelle folded an arm over her chest and examined a chip in her manicure. "Does it matter?"

"It does with her. People get nutty when they fall in love, and Em needs to keep his head." Jack's eyes shifted to Mirabelle with unusual weight. "He won't love her, by the way. He'll only think that he does."

Jack dropped the cigarette into his coffee mug where it expired with a sizzle, and Mirabelle didn't bother pointing out the fatal flaw in his logic. In love, perception was reality. To think you're in love was to have already arrived in it.

"Amelia knows we're together," she told him. "She asked me about it."

Mirabelle had meant to keep that a secret—it'd only upset him—but weaponized it now, not entirely sure why. The arm behind Jack's head came free as he bolted upright.

"What did you tell her?"

"Nothing. I denied it."

Jack scrutinized her through narrowed eyes. He didn't believe her, and that didn't matter. Mirabelle's affection for him slipped away like a kite string surrendered to the breeze. She witnessed the escape but did nothing to stop it.

"What else did she ask?"

"Nothing big. Look, she's different, you know—"

"Oh, fucking hell, Miri! No, she's not!" Jack's palm slammed the bedside table as he felt for his cigarettes. "You think she'll keep our secrets when Cal's back in the picture? She's not your goddamn friend."

Mirabelle freed her legs from the sheets and jumped from the bed in a wretched huff. She'd tolerate Jack's wandering eye long before she'd suffer whatever demon squatted inside and nourished the rage.

"Baby, stop," Jack said as she yanked on her underwear and scooped her shirt from the floor.

With an unlit cigarette dangling from his lips, he crawled from bed and wrangled her by the waist. In the morning light, his limp dick looked ugly and tattoos faded. He pulled the cigarette from his mouth and pointed the filter at her.

"It's my job to look out for Em, and right now he's not seeing the big picture. We brought Amelia here because we thought she knew something. She doesn't, and now Gio is dead, and the men are wondering why we're still sticking our neck out for her. And you know what? It's a fair question. I need you to get through to him, Miri." Jack lit the cigarette and took a drag. Smoke billowed from his serpentine smile. "For his sake, not mine."

That part used to captivate her. From across the room, she'd watch Jack work his charm with wit coming out one side of his mouth and lies out the other.

"Don't put me in the middle," she cried. The kite string slipped again, lost to a clear blue sky.

Jack cradled her face with gentle hands but kissed her forehead hard. "Do what I say."

Without another word, he got dressed and left Mirabelle to dry her own tears. A warm shower worked well enough to soothe, but the resolve conceived amongst suds and steam vanished as she donned her funeral dress and put herself together.

She gathered her nerve and headed down the hall to Emory's room. Her heels clacked in purposeful rhythm, and she rapped at the door but marched inside. Dressed in black slacks and a pressed white shirt, Emory fiddled with his tie in the mirror and glanced at Mirabelle in the reflection.

"Barge in like that and you might see something you don't like."

Mirabelle sat stiffly at the end of the bed and caught sight of herself in the mirror. Her shoulders were taut and grief touched her face. *Smile.*

"You sleep okay last night?" she asked.

"Like a rock."

Emory furrowed his brow at the tie's misshapen knot. With one hard yank, it unraveled, and he tossed the length around his neck to start again. Mirabelle hopped from the bed and shooed away his hands.

"I looked for Amelia yesterday," she said and worked the tie with nimble fingers. "She was supposed to come out with everyone. I thought it'd be good for her. A break, some fun. Well, she didn't, and when we got back last night, she wasn't in her room. Know anything about that?"

Eyes pinned to the ceiling, Emory shook his head. "What is there to know? We had dinner and then—"

"And then you spent the night together. Again."

Mirabelle shoved the knot snug against Emory's throat. He murmured a thank you and ducked away.

"Let's call a spade a spade," he said and ran a lint comb over his suit jacket laid out on the bed. "You expect her to spend time with people who whisper behind her back but ignore her otherwise? Of course she didn't want to go."

Mirabelle had forgotten that part. Emory's gallant gestures turned fiery if anyone dared sling arrows at his chosen one. No wonder Jack sent her to tiptoe through the minefield alone. Mirabelle defused with a playful poke to Emory's ribs.

"Fine. If we're calling out spades, you're into her."

He squirmed away. She followed and jabbed him again as he tried to sidestep her advance.

"You never like the chicks I introduce you to, but you like her."

"Okay, enough." Emory grabbed Mirabelle's wrists and gently pushed her away. "You're annoying me."

"Everyone already knows, Em."

"Knows what? And who is everyone?"

"The wives of your men. They think she's yours."

"She *is* mine," he said matter-of-factly. In the corner, he sat in an armchair and polished his shoes. "They should occupy themselves with their husband's dicks and quit worrying about what I'm doing with mine."

"So, you *have* been doing something with her."

"Jesus, Mirabelle! You just don't know when to stop, do you?"

"I just want you to know what people are saying."

"I don't care, and I know that's not why you came in here. Out with it."

On cue, Mirabelle forgot her lines, the carefully crafted call to reason. She wasn't like Jack, though. She didn't have clever ploys devised on the fly.

"Let me take Amelia out," she said on a nervous whim. "A do-over for yesterday. She needs it."

Emory settled back in the chair. One shoe dangled from his finger, and the polishing rag crumpled in his fist.

"Out where?"

"I don't know. *Out.* Not far and just for a couple hours. We'll take some of your men."

Emory ended the matter with a sharp shake of the head. "No. Absolutely not."

"Please. I don't ask you for much."

The shoe hit the floor. Emory closed his eyes and cradled his forehead in his palm.

"Miri, I concede to you more than you realize, but I don't like how brazen you've become. Our brother is back and *now* is the time you wanna go out? No. Absolutely not. You and Amelia stay here."

Now or never. Make him see.

Mirabelle sunk to the edge of the bed closest to him. The sheets smelled sweetly of sex, and she plucked a long strand of red hair from the pillow. Whatever happened between Emory and Amelia, it was leaps and bounds closer to lovemaking than her and Jack's tryst that morning.

"What are we doing here, Emory? You gonna keep her locked away forever and that's it?"

Head still in his hand, he glared at her from beneath his brows. "You know that was never my plan."

"Look, I adore Amelia and, under other circumstances, we wouldn't have this conversation, but she's not some random chick you picked up at a bar. The impact this could have on your men, the business, it's—"

"You think I haven't thought about that, how this could all go sideways?"

"And yet you're still willing to risk everything we've worked for."

Emory abruptly stood from his seat and pointed at her with a harsh warning. "Stay out of the business. I won't tell you again. We're done here."

As always, he drew the boundaries of their conversation. Mirabelle never had a say. She bolted from the bed and stomped to the door.

"Fine. Your world, your rules, right?"

"Don't fucking walk out on me!" Emory hollered at her back. "What the hell is wrong with you?"

Mirabelle slammed the door shut and crossed the room in pounding strides. "This isn't about the business. This is about you being honest with me!"

Emory settled on his heels and momentarily looked poised to dig in at an impasse. He conceded, though, his face contorting with a rare glimpse of pain.

"Fine. You want honesty? Here it is. You know how often I wanna leave my life? Leave you and Jack and Liam and start over in a nowhere town. No name. No past. Nothing."

His voice cracked with a swell of emotion. Emory stood tall and righted himself before it took him under.

"I bury it and hope to God the wound heals before it festers. Then there's Amelia. She takes one look at me and sees what all of you pretend isn't there. The only time I'm at peace or feel like I can finally breathe again is when I'm with her. She's the escape, the starting over, the healing. That's it. That's the truth, which is far more than I ever get from you."

Mirabelle numbed with a chill despite Emory's searing stare. "What is that supposed to mean?"

"You know exactly what it means. I am honest with you. I don't sneak around behind your back. I don't lie to your face as if you're too dense to notice."

He knows. Of course, he did. The timing of the revelation coincided with his and Amelia's time together.

"No, what you do is keep me out in the cold. And I'm supposed to be happy there and play the part you put me in. Say please-and-thank-you then shut the fuck up and smile when I want to scream. How was I supposed to know you felt this way? I'd do anything for you, but what power do I have?"

"You think what I have is power?" Emory laughed bitterly. "You don't know what I've done for us. What choice did I have when we left home? I was thirteen. You were eight. The things I do and the things I've done, they were always to keep you safe, to give us a fighting chance."

As close as they were as siblings, there were things Emory never talked about, including the day their father died. It'd poured chilly rain as Emory hastily shoved their things into his backpack and toted Mirabelle away from home. In a fogged-up bus stop, Emory had made a choice that propelled their lives down this path. Her childhood ended that day, but his had ended years earlier with a secret he still safeguarded.

"You're not always honest with me," Mirabelle said as tears wet her cheeks. "You hold on to things. You keep secrets. What happened?"

"I told you what happened with Amelia."

"I'm not talking about her!" Mirabelle screamed through a sob. "That day in the woods with you and Ivan. Something happened and it changed you. What did he do?"

On a warm spring day, Mirabelle had swung on the swing set in their backyard, but the song she'd hummed disintegrated when Ivan broke through the tree line with a sobbing Emory in tow. Blood had stained both their hands and, that night, Mirabelle snuggled next to Emory and listened helplessly as he cried himself to sleep. A solemn iciness became a part of him after, marked by something that'd broken him. He never spoke of what that something was and wouldn't speak it now.

"Does Amelia know?" she asked with shameful resentment.

Shouldn't she be happy he found in Amelia a confessional, a girl who'd whisk him away with sweet kisses and tender promises? *You can have it all,* she'd say, but little darling blinded herself to how much it'd cost him.

Emory fled behind his stoicism, the only shelter he allowed

himself, and said nothing as he fixed his gaze to the door. *I'll always be the last to know.*

"I don't want to talk about it," he said with a face of stone and a voice to match. "I never meant to hurt you."

His Adam's apple bobbed and jaw tipped high. Even his attempt at comfort came like a winter's chill. Defeated on all fronts, Mirabelle turned to leave. What would Jack say? *You failed.* Another voice joined the choir, soft-spoken from a fawn-eyed beauty. *Small acts of defiance.*

"You know," Mirabelle said as she reached the door, "Amelia asked me what would happen if you ever tried to leave."

"What did you tell her?" Emory asked mildly but with a splinter of hope, as if Amelia had already devised some savvy scheme to set him free.

"The truth." Mirabelle didn't need to elaborate. The price of escape was as simple as it was severe. "Have you told her what you told me, everything you feel for her?"

Emory pressed his lips together and shook his head. For such a loyal and loving man, he had a tendency to bungle that part. He claimed to never have the right words, and yet he had a whole tome of them for Amelia.

"You should. She deserves to know how you feel but also how this ends."

They both knew how love ended for him—locked in a cage without his companion. He always set them free. Emory slowly sat at the end of the bed. With his elbows propped on his knees, he hung his head.

Jack would call that progress and remind her that love was sometimes cruel. *It's for his sake.*

"I have to wonder," Mirabelle said, "if you never wanted this life, then why bring her into it?"

Emory lifted his eyes and crumbled with a resigned smile she knew all too well. When Ivan raged or their mother died or the rainy night they ran from home, he'd said, *"I'm alright. I'll be okay,"* with pain in his eyes and a smile on his lips. When there was nothing else to do, nothing else to say, nothing that could hurt him more than he hurt like this, Emory smiled.

Mirabelle left then and tearfully told Jack it was done. He celebrated the victory but didn't ask why she cried. Alone in her room, she dried her tears and fixed her makeup. Downstairs, she greeted the funeral guests with bright laughter, tenderhearted hugs, and what felt like a gaping hole in her chest.

THIRTY-ONE

AMELIA

The funeral commenced in the sweltering heat of late afternoon. Beside Gio's grave, the men baked in black suits, and the women fanned themselves with the memorial leaflet. Amelia slipped into the shadow of a holly oak and leaned against a pockmarked headstone. Lace-like lichen filled its inscribed letters —a poem perhaps—but she couldn't decipher it.

The priest didn't break a sweat. He had that frozen dispassion required of all Catholic clergymen. Amelia remembered it well. When she was eight, her mother dressed her like a little bride and sent her down the aisle to receive the Eucharist from icy hands. In his golden robes, the priest had stooped to hear the sins of a child.

"I'm not sure God is real," she'd tearfully confessed with communion wine still sour on her lips.

That priest had had no comfort for a sinner like her. He'd frowned and sent Amelia back to the pew, hollowed in her shame.

Across the burial plot, Emory watched her from behind aviators that couldn't temper his stare. A pair of oversized sunglasses sat on Amelia's dresser at home, so she didn't have the luxury of feeling unseen. She had nowhere to hide, not even from the sun that competed with the heat between her legs and excused her blush. A smile crept across Emory's lips as if he divined her thoughts, and Amelia's stomach flipped with a woozy rush.

That morning, they'd had foreplay in the shower and sex in the bed. While the water rushed down her back, Emory had dropped to his knees and dove between her legs. Dizzy from an orgasm, Amelia pleaded to feel him inside, so he hauled her off to bed and tossed her to the mattress.

With his chest against her back, Emory had muttered in her ear, "I want you like this," and gripped her thighs hard enough that Amelia knew to obey him. A soft sigh had escaped her as he pushed inside from behind. She'd never get over how he filled her up and already craved how he felt, how he moved inside of her, how he called her a good girl. *His* good girl.

With hot kisses, Emory had savored her shoulder, neck, and cheek as he thrust slow and deep. It'd left her head swimming as their bodies melded together. Emory had been all over her, existing in every part simultaneously as his consuming weight settled on top. His hands had been in her hair, roaming her curves, palming her breasts.

Closer than they had been before, that was how he liked it, she'd realized. He'd been in control, and she'd submitted to his will, awash in pleasure at his ragged exhales that left her wetter and wanting more. Emory had even slid one hand beneath her to swipe between her legs as he fucked her hard into the mattress. Amelia had bucked against his movements until they'd fallen into a delicious rhythm.

As the pressure rose between her legs, she'd gripped the sheets and buried her face in a pillow while Emory's breaths rustled in her ear as he panted her name. He might have said something else, but it'd been lost in the haze, just a rumble against her back. Amelia's toes had curled and head fell back against his shoulder as she relished her release. Emory had come quickly after, his orgasms just as intense as everything else about him. And though he was ravenous in his lovemaking, his aftercare was just as sweet.

Burrowed against him, Amelia had traced the tattoos on his forearms, more iconography of light and dark, death and the divine.

Let us stay this way, she'd thought but mined for hope as the earth caved in. On the nightstand beside a loaded gun, the texts had poured in as soon as the sun was reasonably seated in the sky. With strong arms coiled around her waist, Emory had held on a little longer, as if letting go meant facing a cruel reality.

When the priest completed his sermon, the mourners filed past Gio's grave and placed a white lily on his casket. As Amelia waited her turn, Liam Moriarty approached in a pristine black suit hardly wilted from the heat.

"There's been a change of plans, my dear," he said and offered his arm in a polite gesture. "Emory will ride back with Jack. You'll be with me."

Amelia knew better than to put up a fuss, so she accepted his arm. As they strolled between the graves, Liam reached into his breast pocket and handed her a prayer card. On it, the Virgin Mary stood amongst thornless roses with her hands lifted in prayer.

"From one former Catholic to another," he said.

"How did you know?"

Liam grinned and patted Amelia's elbow linked in his. "Guilt. All good Catholics are consumed by it."

"And the bad ones?"

"They end up a fair-weather believer like me. Only in crisis do I rediscover my faith."

"And you've rediscovered it now?"

Liam glanced back at the priest, who signed a cross over Gio's casket heaped with lilies.

"As our friend would say, for everything there is a season. A time to kill and a time to heal. A time for war and a time for peace."

Amelia parsed the truth from the gospel. Burying Gio was like closing a book; not just on his life, but the false normalcy they'd all enjoyed. Wine-soaked nights and grief forgotten between the sheets would soon end.

"I take it the time for peace and healing is done," she said.

On a pea gravel path, they passed a marble angel in mourning, its face buried in the crook of its elbow. In its hand were flowers covered in verdigris. Liam veered toward a black sedan third in line behind the hearse.

"Most of the men back there are soldiers trained in peacetime," he said. "They haven't known war. They will soon."

Amelia hummed as if she knew. Maybe she did. Big death wasn't such a distant notion anymore. The concept made contact. These days, she viewed it through the lens of a man whose arms she'd fallen asleep in, his tender touches clipped from her fantasies.

What would dad say if he saw me now?

Nothing.

He'd turn to ice in the stifling heat, the silence of a shattered heart. Still, missing him was a fog that never fully lifted. Amelia roamed in the haze until light broke through with glimpses of her past; the person she was, the people she missed.

"You know why I'm telling you this?" Liam asked.

Not a clue. If he wanted to scare her, he might've said worse. Amelia shrugged and offered the only thing that came to mind.

"So I know my place?"

Liam laughed as if tickled by the honesty and touched by the humility. She hadn't intended either.

"No. You've found your place." He gestured to Emory standing with Jack beside Gio's grave and with the weight of the world on his shoulders. "You need to understand what's coming, though. War is hell, and you're his queen. Emory will look to you for peace and comfort. If you can't give him that, then it's best to stop this before it truly begins."

Liam opened the passenger door for Amelia, and she settled in stiffly with the age-old tale. In it, a wild woman wavers like the open ocean and lures a good man to his grave. What could be done? Silence the siren, and save that good man from himself.

She watched warily as Liam shed his jacket and circled the car with a purposeful gait. It wasn't a chance arrangement, but a decisive strategy to get her alone. He climbed in and fired up the engine, but Amelia stopped him as he reached for the gearshift.

"After the war, what happens then?"

"Life moves on," Liam said. "Emory has always wanted his equal, and he's found it in you. You two will carve out your empire together. With him, you'll have whatever you want."

Amelia smiled but not for her future foretold. Love like that was a limerence, as liable to drive her and Emory mad as it was to bring them happiness and peace.

"That's a romantic take. I'm not sure the world works that way."

"Ours does. You chose Emory. You must choose his world too."

"You mean pick a side."

Amelia knew damn well the ever-widening divide she straddled. One day, she'd face a grievous decision—swear an allegiance or be torn apart. Liam nodded, his stare exacting. It unbuttoned her attempt at neutrality and left her doubts exposed.

"Why?" she asked. "So many of the women here live in both worlds. They weren't made to choose."

"That's an illusion, Amelia. They work their jobs and raise their children, but they don't truly exist in both worlds. Push comes to shove, they know where their loyalty lies."

Liam paused and surveyed Emory and Jack making their way from Gio's grave.

"The road ahead is treacherous," he said and shifted the car into drive. "Think hard and clear if this is what you want."

The funeral procession lurched forward, and the ride home proceeded in silence because Liam Moriarty didn't know her, not really, and it smacked of a not-so-distant past where her father had raged.

"What the hell do you want, Amelia? Do you even know?"

Irony of ironies, she did know. With every beat of her heart, Amelia knew and spoke strong and clear, but her ambitions didn't dazzle, and what was worse than a good man gone astray? A lost soul like her swinging from whim to whim. Amelia could barely stomach that inquiry from her own father, let alone Liam Moriarty, so she kept quiet but fumed in the hypocrisy until they reached the mansion.

Liam parked in the circle drive and turned to Amelia as if already aware she had more to say.

"You ask me what I want," she said, "but have you ever asked Emory that question?"

Liam drew a deep breath and fixed his eyes to middle distance beyond the windshield.

"You haven't, have you? Or maybe you don't need to because you already know Emory deserves so much more than this."

Liam laughed. It made her anxious. She knew so little of how to read the man.

"On that, we agree," he said and killed the engine but lightly grasped her forearm before she opened the door.

"You cannot talk like this with others," he warned with a nod out the window to where the Moriarty men and their families filtered inside. "I know your heart is in the right place, but they don't. Treachery is blood in the water. Mind your cuts."

———

AMELIA SCOPED out a spot in the great room where funeral-goers mingled with food and drink. Most kept eyes on her, the questions amassing in their implacable stares.

Alone in a corner with the prayer card, she waited for Emory. He and Jack arrived a half hour later in mismatched moods. Where Jack beamed, a solemn shadow fell over Emory as a few captains urgently occupied him in conversation.

Amelia would find him later when he was in less demand. She slipped away to the parlor where votive flames danced in ruby red glass on a family altar. She lit a match but hesitated over an unburned wick.

Her grandma had always said death came in threes. If true, whose soul would add to Gio's trine? Or perhaps he was preceded in death.

Helen Havick. Brian Burrows. Richard Dauer.

Death had already exceeded its multiplicity.

A presence entered the room behind her. Amelia shook out

the match and turned around. Sinister in a black suit, Jack's eyes locked on her with severity she'd only heard of in him but never witnessed for herself.

"I didn't peg you as the religious type," he said and crept toward her like a predator approaching startled prey.

Amelia gripped the metal candle rack behind her. The fleur-de-lis trim dug into one palm, and the prayer card crumpled in the other.

"I'm not."

Jack didn't seem to hear her. It wouldn't have mattered if he had. He smiled, delighted to crush her beliefs either way. Amelia turned to leave out the pocket door to the foyer, but Jack darted forward. His palm collided with the wall, and his outstretched arm blocked her escape.

"You care about him?" he rasped with liquor on his breath and malice in his eyes.

Amelia's mind raced for her next move. She didn't know what hurts Jack drowned in the bottle, so she gave him some grace and pushed past the fear thick in her throat.

"Yes. Very much. Do you?" she asked, quiet but accusatory.

Jack smiled a nearly perfect smile. To think, she'd once thought him kind, an ally in the underworld. She'd gravely misjudged him.

"I've known Em most my life. You've only been here a minute. He'll fuck you 'til he takes you home then forget you ever existed. You're nothing to him. *Nothing.*"

Amelia lifted her chin to meet his unfocused gaze. She wasn't forged in fire with a steel spine and sharp tongue. She didn't command a room with golden laughter and effortless charm. She went unnoticed in quiet corners and spoke too softly for others to hear, but she wasn't nothing, never nothing, and stood her ground with a trembling voice and her heart thundering in her chest.

"I'm not nothing to him, and you know that," she said.

Like a curtain coming down, Jack's self-possession fell to the floor. It left him red-faced and fuming.

"You're poisoning him, putting thoughts in his head that don't belong."

"Whatever you're trying to do, I'm not afraid of you."

Jack freed a folding knife from his back pocket and held the blade to her throat. His eyes roved Amelia's body and settled between her legs as if he contemplated fucking her hard just to make a point. It wasn't about desire, just control.

"You should be," he said and leaned forward until his lips brushed her cheek. "I'm not like Em. I don't worry if I'm a good man. I know that I'm not. Stay away from the people I love. I won't tell you again."

Jack eased off and put his knife away. After he left out the pocket door, Amelia collected herself with deep breaths and burning cheeks. On the ledge of a built-in hutch, she smoothed out the prayer card with trembling hands. The Blessed Mother looked on placidly but offered no solace.

Behind her, Emory's footsteps stirred in the hall of photographs. She'd know his cadence anywhere, had committed it to heart. Amelia held her breath and released it as a comforted sigh when his chest met her back.

Wedged between the hutch and him, she gripped his forearms that snaked around her middle. One of his hands slid up her stomach to cup her breast, and the other grasped her waist.

"I feel like I haven't seen you all day," he muttered in her ear and melted against her, his body warm and loose hair brushing her cheek. "I wish these people would leave."

Amelia craned her neck until her lips met his in a soft kiss. "They need you."

"No, they don't, but *I* need *you*."

Emory's tongue traced her bottom lip before slipping into her mouth. Amelia spun in his arms, and he lifted her to the hutch's ledge. The time apart, so laughably brief, dropped a match to their desire.

The prayer card tumbled to the floor as the kiss turned feverish. Emory pushed her dress to her waist, and Amelia straddled his hips with her bare thighs. His fingers grazed the swell of her breasts in a touch that laid goosebumps against her skin. One finger slipped beneath her bra and teased her nipple until it was hard. The other hand cupped her ass and guided her movements. With his hard cock nestled between her legs, each languid roll of Amelia's hips mimicked how she might ride him.

"Let me take you upstairs," Emory panted against her open mouth. "I wanna taste you, feel you."

He pushed her underwear aside and stroked between her legs before sinking a finger inside. His thumb swiped her clit with delicate pressure. Amelia closed her eyes and surrendered to the sensations.

"That's my good girl," she heard Emory say somewhere along the way to her climax.

How was it he knew precisely how to touch her, hold her, make her come undone? She cracked open her eyes as Emory dropped to his knees. With one leg hitched over his shoulder, he went to work with his mouth, and Amelia lifted her arms to steady herself against the bookshelf at her back. A thin book tumbled to the floor.

She meant to protest, to tell him someone might find them that way. It didn't matter. None of it did. Her hesitation was fleeting and swiftly dissolved as his tongue swirled her opening. Emory gripped the back of her thigh, and she relied on his strength to hold her steady.

"I missed you," she sighed and combed her fingers through his hair. He stared up at her and, by the light in his eyes, she knew he smiled between her legs.

No man had ever lavished that much attention on her that way. With his mouth between her legs, he seemed to thoroughly lose himself as much as she did. Amelia's head fell back hard against a shelf, but the sting was lost amongst the pleasure surging through her. The music in the great room disguised another climax that came in one loud, shuddering breath.

"I missed you too," Emory chuckled as he stood. "I swear I'm gonna do that every day."

Eyes heavy-lidded with lust, he kissed her hard, but

something in the promise troubled her. They couldn't go on like that in perpetuity. *Mind your cuts.* Warm tears brimmed as Amelia slackened in his arms and slumped against the bookshelf.

"What's the matter?" he asked.

Amelia gripped his dress shirt and buried her face against his chest. She hated how swiftly the tears came, that they even came at all.

"Look at me."

She shook her head. "I don't like when people see me cry."

"I'm not people." Emory tipped her chin, and his gaze softened as it ran a circuit between her eyes, down to her lips, and back again. "It's just me."

Meant to soothe, it only hurt more. It was just him and her like it had been for days, and where the Queen of Heaven couldn't comfort, the King of the Underworld could. Since when was he the only thing that brought her peace? It must've happened when she wasn't looking. She was losing herself there. Bits and pieces fell off, replaced with things that confused and scared her.

"Why are you crying?" he asked not unkindly, but Amelia still felt called to the carpet to explain.

And she had a perfectly good explanation. Jack had brandished a knife and threatened things he conveniently didn't speak. Some men were clever that way, creating loopholes for their awful behavior, but Jack was also a liar and a better one than she. He'd lie through his teeth to cast her out. Over Emory's shoulder, Amelia glimpsed the hall of photographs and his world built on belonging but only for the chosen ones.

"I don't know where I belong," she said.

Emory kissed the tears off her cheeks. "You belong with me. We belong together."

"Like we have been?"

He stiffened and pulled away enough to look at her. "You mean just us, without all this?"

Emory motioned to the heavenly strum of "Malafemmena"

warbling from the great room. When Amelia nodded, he took her hands and hesitated before speaking.

"We can dream about it, a normal life where it's just us two," he said, a bit of tenderness before the fall, "but this is who I am and what I have to offer. I'll give you everything, but I can't give you that. It's not how this works."

"Then how does this work?" Amelia asked in what was clearly a bridge too far.

Emory removed himself from between her legs and paced to the center of the room. With his back to her, he had the answer, and the hollowness in Amelia's chest warned it would tear her to pieces. Emory turned around and offered it carefully, quietly.

"It starts with you opening your eyes, Amelia. War's on our doorstep, and we just buried one of our own. I'm needed here now more than ever. This is where I belong."

Amelia hopped from the hutch and crossed the room. "Me open my eyes?" she asked incredulously.

With the glacial austerity of a bygone era, Emory folded his arms and clenched his jaw.

"Yes. You see what you want, what we'd be if I made this disappear. What makes you think I can do that?"

It had Jack's fingerprints all over it. No wonder he'd returned victorious while Emory waved the white flag. He was a man at war with himself, and Amelia was collateral in the crossfire as he sorted out his allegiance.

"I had a plan, a life I wanted to live," Amelia said with anger leaching into her words. The tears she'd fought to hide barreled down her cheeks. "Maybe it wasn't prestigious or important, but it was the one I chose for myself, and that meant everything to me. And now here I am; lost again and wondering where I fit in. But I don't fit in because this isn't where I belong, and you know that."

Amelia stood before Emory close enough that he could hold her. He didn't. For all his burning passion, he went cold again.

She pointed to the noise down the hall and said, "Maybe they can't separate the man you are from the monolith you've become, but I can, and I know you don't belong here either. You can lie to yourself about that, but you can't lie to me."

Emory said nothing and refused her stare. It was the double-edge sword of being seen. He rejected the exposure and tended to the gaps in his armor. Amelia reached up and cradled his flushed cheeks.

"I know what I want," she said. "It's you. I want you. I want you out and free and mine, but it can't be like this. You said it yourself. This world tears people apart. It'll tear us apart."

Emory relented and drew her close. A defeated smile formed, then promptly faded, but the agony in his eyes was his answer.

"You're right. It does, and I never want that for you, but I can't change who I am. I've been down this road before, and I know how it ends."

Eyes glistening, Emory lifted her hand and held it against his chest that rose and fell with a rapid exchange of breath.

"It's always fallen apart, and I can't do it again. Not with you. I survived it the other times, but I don't know if I'd survive it with you."

In the corner, the parlor clock started its chimes. Emory tensed as he waited for the tolls to end.

"My captains are waiting for me downstairs," he said and unwound his arm still at the small of her back. "We'll talk more tomorrow night after everyone's left. I promise I'll get you home when it's safe. *That's* where you belong."

With that, he kissed her forehead and let her go. Rocked with a sudden wave of nauseous heat, Amelia closed her eyes and shook her head.

"You said I belong with you, that we belong together," she cried, humiliated again at the swiftness of her tears and how childish she must seem.

Emory dropped his eyes as he reached the door, and he too seemed to straddle a divide that was ripping him apart. He glanced at the hall and then Amelia, weighing his options, and she wished he wouldn't.

She'd done that before too and stitched her heart to her sleeve where it went rejected. Unlike him, though, she'd do it again and again, no matter how much it hurt because some sweet day it'd be worth all the pain.

"We do belong together, sweetheart," he said with infuriating sterility that gave her nothing. No tears shed. No hurt to share. "We met at the wrong time is all."

Is that all?

Amelia bit her lip and put on a charade of strength with a hopeless nod. She watched him leave in case he relented. He didn't, of course. Emory retreated from the room as everything they could've been spoiled on the vine.

Heartbroken and reeling, Amelia remained rooted in the middle of the floor. The last few tears stung as they dried on her cheeks. The funeral dress was itchy, and the shoes pinched her feet.

She stood unmoving through the length of another song, frozen in the callousness of it all and uncertain of who to blame. And perhaps that was the worst of it—the blameless efficiency of how it ended. That was the danger of daydreams and the futility of faith.

Amelia stooped to the floor and collected the prayer card and book that'd fallen. She thumbed through its pages and picked a random one.

"It's only a bruise," read a line inside. She covered that line with the prayer card, closed the book, and shelved her faith for good.

THIRTY-TWO

EMORY

In the basement lounge, Emory held court. All twelve captains, plus Jack and Liam, gathered around the oblong table. The pendant light above had a spotlight effect, so Emory sat exposed at the head.

He had done the needful with emotional amputation. Sever the limb to save the rest. There he was, a hero to his own ego, while Amelia cried upstairs. Hail to the Chief. Emory the monolith was as strong as ever while Emory the man came unglued.

A cloud of smoke hung over the table, shapeless and swirling in the light. Though it stung his nostrils, Emory drew a deep breath.

"Deception and deceit are venom to the organization," he said. "I won't tolerate gossip or lies, so you're here to learn the facts."

He wasn't trying for the dramatic flair of a vague threat, but it still resonated that way. Some men nodded. Others cut sidelong glances at one another. Most had heard a bastardized version of what came out of Torres and jumped to conclusions, either grievously wrong or splintered with half-truths and hearsay. *"Call court and put it to bed,"* Liam had advised.

Emory tipped his head to Corey. "The floor is yours."

Stone-faced, Corey stubbed out his cigarette and sat at attention. He was a good soldier still. The Army had declared him a combat hero and decorated him with medals to prove it but ignored the demons of war that hounded him. He deserted before redeployment and was dishonorably discharged. All the qualities in Corey the military discarded—grit, loyalty, courage—he funneled into the Moriartys.

"Torres confirmed that Ivan is leading the Velascos," Corey said. "Ivan kept a low profile after his 'accident,' but a year ago reached out to two Velasco captains who were already eying a takeover. Together, they orchestrated Philippe's overthrow and murder. Ivan keeps his inner circle tight, only a few captains he sends orders through. The rest admire him as everything Philippe wasn't. Ruthless, action-oriented, a visionary."

Emory exchanged a worried glance with Jack. Ivan's brutality would metastasize into a sickness the Velascos couldn't manage. What they saw as action-oriented was reckless impulsivity. Their visionary would lead them to ruin.

"He'll only be shiny and new once," Emory said. "They may admire him now, but he'll bleed them dry. What's their next move?"

"Torres says Ivan is planning something big, something he promised you, Chief." A sympathetic half-smile twitched across Corey's lips. "Torres didn't know what that meant."

I will destroy everything you love.

"It means something personal," Emory replied and evaluated his men staring expectantly at him. "The Velascos are a whole new beast under Ivan."

"Well, are we going to ice these fuckers or what?" Scotty, captain of Redding post, demanded from the other end of the table.

His bald head gleamed, and crimson colored his cheeks. Where other captains minded boundaries with Emory, Scotty pushed.

"Vegas was a warning shot," Emory said, "and I'm not

escalating on a whim. We strike when I know where Ivan is, and it'll be measured. Ivan is sloppy. I'm not."

Scotty shot a look at Marcus, whose territory shared a border with his, though Marcus was based in Sacramento. Emory spotted the exchange, brief and subtle though it was.

"Vegas was more than a warning shot," Marcus said with mild apprehension and couldn't hold Emory's stare. "They came for the Havick girl, and they'll come for her again."

"What we're all wondering is," Sal, captain of the Bay Area, chimed in, "what are we doing with her? Is she coming or going? Much respect to you, Chief, but she either needs to be in or out. This on-the-fence shit will spell tragedy for everyone. You. Her. *Us.*"

"What are you concerned about?" Emory asked Marcus.

Still unable to look at Emory, he spoke to the wall beside him. "When you cut her loose, she'll go back to daddy and sing like a bird."

Emory counted the nods around the table. Six. His captains were split down the middle.

"Sing about what exactly? She knows our faces and a few of our names. You think Cal doesn't know that already? He keeps tabs on everyone at this table."

"She knows about the shop in Vegas, where we're headquartered, our numbers, our structure."

Marcus counted on his fingers each rapid-fire response and summoned the courage to look at Emory.

"Cal Havick hung his bid as a federal prosecutor on taking us down," Emory said. "If he was gonna drop the hammer, he would've done it by now. Anything Amelia has learned here won't help him."

"You took his daughter from him," Scotty said. "That all might be true for Cal Havick, federal prosecutor, but don't underestimate him as a father."

"We understand your point," Liam said, "but his daughter would be dead many times over if it weren't for us. That won't be lost on him."

"And Gio is dead because of her!" Eli, captain of Reno post, erupted. "I'm sorry, but you're fucking naïve if you think otherwise."

Across the table from Eli, Corey lurched from his seat. "Who the fuck do you think you're talking to? Show some *goddamn* respect. I will bury you!"

Emory lifted an arm to stave off Corey and addressed Eli.

"You want someone to blame? Blame me. I brought her here. Question my decisions and take me to task. I don't give a fuck, but don't get it twisted. What happened to Gio isn't on her."

The table fell silent as contention grew. The seeds of doubt had already been sown, but what they'd reap, Emory couldn't quite say. He eased back in his seat with one forearm resting on the table and the other in his lap.

"We'll hold off on a counterstrike for now and use the white line first."

The room stirred in a simultaneous shift. The blood thirsty wanted to strike swiftly and strategize later. The white line was the peacemaker, a line of communication between the Velascos and Moriartys. When fighting promised only mutual destruction, the white line rang and both parties brokered for peace.

"Diplomacy?" Scotty snickered.

Emory shook his head.

"Not diplomacy. An influence operation. I'll make the call and get ahold of a Velasco captain hopped up on hope and belief that Ivan is the answer to what's broken in that organization. They've bested us. Gio is dead. A few of our men turned rat. I'll concede those victories.

"But here's what else I'll tell them. Ivan is more monster than man. He doesn't hide it. He doesn't know how. No one knows that better than I do. Soon, they'll know it too. I'll remind them that war is hell, and we never wanted this. War is death, and they'll lose good men too. War is watching the people you love get torn apart, and their innocents aren't safe either.

"This isn't diplomacy. It's planting the seed. When they're battered and broken and barely holding on, when they see who

Ivan truly is, when they want an off-ramp, the white line will ring, and we'll be here to answer with our terms. If Ivan wants to hide in the shadows, then we shine the light. But first, we need to find him. That is the only thing that matters right now."

At the far end of the table, Pete leaned forward to get Emory's attention.

"One of my street soldiers, Zulu, can help with that. The kid is a genius. If anyone can track down Ivan, it's him."

Emory had heard Pete wax poetic about the kid before. He was up-and-coming and marked as one to watch. The men called him Zulu; short for Bravo Zulu, a job well done and a term of endearment because the kid kept his head down, wits about him, and came to the Moriartys a blank slate, all but his tech savvy. Pete had spotted his talent and recruited him as the go-to for technical exploitation.

"Good. Get him on it," Emory said. "That's all I have. Get home safe. Ears to the ground, I want any leads you find."

The men disbanded, some with approving nods and others with under-the-breath commentary as they cleared the table. Marcus and Scotty left with Sal and two others. Pete, Corey, and the rest stayed a few steps behind the other faction. The division resembled a gaping chasm.

"Stay," Emory commanded when Eli stood. "You too, Johnny."

After the room emptied, Emory stared at Eli but didn't speak. So brave earlier, Eli succumbed to the silence and slumped in his seat.

"Look, I meant no disrespect. It's just..." He chewed his bottom lip and sighed. "We take care of our own, right? I have a hard time wrapping my head around that girl being one of our own now."

That girl. It came slathered in so much unfounded loathing.

"Her name is Amelia, and that's not your concern," Emory said, but the pressure in his chest rose, and his pulse flooded his ears. "We have street soldiers in this organization, some in your crew, who would do us dirty before she would. You fucking know it too. Save me the bullshit about taking care of our own when you can't seem to manage your own crew's loyalty. If you ever do this shit again, I'll bury you myself long before Corey gets out the shovel. Now go."

Eli shot from his seat, all too eager to scamper off and tell the others, no doubt. Emory rested his elbows on the table and cradled his forehead in one palm.

"Johnny, you have a status update?" he asked.

Big Johnny, captain of Portland post, nodded and switched seats next to Jack. He more than earned his nickname, though "Gentle Giant" would've been just as apt. He stood as tall as Emory but possessed an affable and easygoing demeanor no one would ever attach to Emory.

He took out his phone and slid it across the table. "Cal was spotted in southern Oregon last week. One of my guys got these."

Emory swiped through a half dozen photos of Cal looking frazzled and out-of-sorts.

"He was staying at a bed-and-breakfast but left early," Johnny explained. "Someone else was trailing him, probably the Velascos. They must've spooked him."

"Not surprising," Liam said. "Cal was damn close to nailing down Ivan. I'm sure Ivan would like to snip that loose thread for good."

Emory agreed with a nod. "Where's he heading?"

Johnny shrugged and scratched his beard that grew in thick and patched with red.

"Hard to say. California maybe. The Portland police are done with their courtesy calls and wellness checks. Unless someone raises hell, they'll wash their hands and move on. There's one other thing. That kid from the motel was moved out of the ICU. His doctors think he'll pull through. If you wanna handle that, we have to do it soon."

On either side of Emory, a torrent of disquiet overtook Jack and Liam, but for different reasons. Liam admonished needless violence. Jack exalted it.

"I appreciate the heads up, but no. Leave the kid alone."

Emory ignored Jack staring a hole through him as he stood and shook Johnny's hand. "Great work. Keep me updated."

After Johnny left and Liam puttered off to the bar, Jack stood and shoved his chair into the table so hard the wood slats crackled. He stormed off with nothing left to say. Funny for a man who had so much to get off his chest earlier.

On the ride back from the funeral, Jack had passionately proselytized focus, commitment, and seeing the forest for the trees. He spoke in idioms and expected Emory to understand. And Emory had, but only because Jack and Mirabelle shared the same talking points.

"You going to see Miri?" Emory shouted at Jack's back.

He expected a lie. Mirabelle and Jack had been lying for months and did it with the same vague excuses. Jack's shoulders rustled with a bitter laugh. He spun slowly on his heel but wasn't smiling.

"What the fuck is that supposed to mean?"

Emory stepped out of the spotlight at the head of the table and crossed the divide between them.

"You know what it means. I'm neither blind nor stupid."

"You going to see Amelia?" Jack asked with the same animosity as half the captains. "C'mon, Em. It's not like people haven't noticed, and Sal makes a good point. What the fuck is she in all of this?"

Emory reeled with the unusual sting and met Jack in the middle of the room.

"Mine," he seethed and stared down Jack with a threat. He'd killed men for less than this. "She's mine, and don't you ever fucking forget that."

Emory drew a line in the sand and sent out the tide because somewhere up above Amelia nursed a broken heart and for what? A double-standard where Jack and Mirabelle could act with impunity, but Emory could not. *Fuck that.*

"It's a mistake," Jack said and backed away. When he reached a safe distance, he turned around and pounded up the stairs.

Emory slipped a finger between his shirt collar and the black tie still coiled around his neck. Relief came with a hard yank and the oppressive tightness loosened. It was just him and Liam. *Just like the old days.*

Liam used to hold his own court with Emory. He'd sling advice across the bar while Emory mulled it over with a drink. Liam fell into that familiar rhythm as he set out two glasses and pulled bourbon from the shelf. Emory perched on a stool as Liam whistled a Sinatra tune and fixed Manhattans.

"Jack's drunk again," Liam remarked and offered Emory the first glass.

He sipped his drink and savored the warmth filling his chest. "You agree with what he said?"

Liam's tune trailed off. Glass in hand, he circled the bar and sat next to Emory.

"I've seen what a mistake shaped like a woman looks like, even held it in my arms once or twice. It ain't her. Amelia will love you right, but she needs to adjust to our world, prove her loyalty to the organization, to *you*."

Make her one of us. Emory stiffened with deep unease. It wasn't that she couldn't belong in his world, but that she shouldn't. He saw that clearly after all that had happened.

"The captains have been split down the middle before," Liam continued. "It's nothing new. We always fall back into a unified whole."

"That's what worries me. This feels different." Emory glanced at Liam, who seemed content as he chomped on a brandied cherry. "You can't tell me you've never thought about what the first crack in the foundation might be."

Liam brushed it off with a shrug. "I don't dwell on it. Neither should you."

"I'm only asking what this would look like if it came apart. We need to be prepared."

"And you think it looks like *this*?" Liam lifted his glass to the table behind them. "Some back-talk over your new girlfriend? Our men wanting to avenge Gio's death? Their blood is up.

Emotions are running high. That's nothing, a blip. What are you afraid of, Emory?"

The question caught him off guard. Emory's instinct was to claim fearlessness. Perhaps that would fly when he needed to be their brave leader. In reality, the past few nights, fear got into him like a fever, burning him up as he laid awake while Amelia slept in his arms.

"I'm beginning to think someone else inside our organization is telegraphing our moves to Ivan. He knew Amelia was with me in Vegas. He knows she's here now. He knows..."

Emory was content to let the rest go unsaid, but Liam continued where he couldn't.

"He knows how much she means to you. Your brother will come out of the woodwork eventually. When he does, you have this whole organization to back you. And there's always a disgruntled street soldier somewhere willing to turn rat. That doesn't mean our world is falling apart. We've dealt with it before and will again. Your instincts are your strength. Don't dilute them by overthinking."

Get outta your head, son. The echo of his father hit Emory hard with a wave of grief he hadn't felt in years. Liam downed his drink and slid from the stool.

"My show's coming on." He squeezed Emory's shoulder and let his hand remain there for a fraught moment until he frowned and said, "I wonder sometimes if you regret choosing this life, if you wish you could leave it behind."

Liam stared at Emory in earnest. It wasn't a curiosity to ponder, but a call for reassurance.

Emory patted Liam's hand. "Don't ask me that question tonight."

"Fair enough. Get some sleep. No burning the midnight oil. You need a break."

Alone at the bar, Emory sipped his drink, but it soured his stomach and turned bitter on his tongue. The release he needed rested upstairs, and long ago he might've hated how much he craved her. It wasn't just sinking between Amelia's thighs and dissolving his worries in the pleasure she'd bring.

Amelia beckoned with far-off nostalgia, some golden memory that came like a dream. The sound of her buttercream voice, the way her mouth moved, the stories she told, the dreams they both shared. Where she spoke of wants, he suffered from need. Yes, he needed her; needed her in a way that promised pain, needed her even if it meant his undoing. Glory to the victor, she had him on his knees.

"What the fuck am I doing?" Emory muttered to himself.

He hopped from the stool and tossed out his drink in the sink. With his heart in his throat, he raced up the stairs and ignored the throng of people crowding the foyer. They said goodbye and hugged one another, exchanged clammy handshakes with insincere smiles.

Mirabelle hurried toward him and snatched him by the forearm. "Em, honey, you did the right thing. I know it hurts, but you gotta let her go."

"No." Emory yanked his arm free and rushed up the stairs.

Resolve weakened his knees but set his heart ablaze. Heroes always ran. No one ever said, *"The fireman strolled into the burning building"* or *"The soldier moseyed into battle."* Cowards ran too; from broken homes, busted hearts, the messes they made. The only thing separating the craven from the brave was the direction they ran. When it mattered most, Emory ran to her.

Down the hall, he nearly barreled into her room but stopped outside her bedroom door. Words would surely fail him, but his touch had a language all its own. It'd speak his desire not just for her body, but her heart.

He knocked with no answer then twisted the knob. Locked. She'd locked him out, and he couldn't have predicted the way it hurt. Heart heavy, he knocked again.

"Amelia, it's me. Open up."

Emory listened for sounds of her stirring. Nothing came, and no light spilled from beneath the frame. With the crowd gone, the house was at rest, and so was she.

Defeated and wholly dejected, Emory settled in across the hall for uneasy sleep. He'd see her tomorrow and tell her then what rested behind his palisade of the unspoken, the words he couldn't manage until then.

Every moment with her was making up for lost time. A comedy and tragedy of wasted years, it enthralled and gutted. Though the past couldn't be undone and his future was a tangle of uncertainty, he'd carve out his own fate and a place for just them two; side by side and free from this hell.

He'd tell her tomorrow.

THIRTY-THREE

AMELIA

In Mirabelle's passenger seat, Amelia eyed the clock. Twenty-five minutes ago, Mirabelle claimed their jaunt would take them down the road. She measured distance like Amelia's mom, though. "Down the road" could mean the next street over or halfway across town. For Mirabelle, it meant just outside Las Vegas where her friend owned a boutique.

Ten miles back, a detour led them off the highway and onto a back road. Mirabelle almost missed it and would've blithely blown past the end of the world, but Amelia had pointed out the signs and hollered that they better heed the warning. Mirabelle had laughed like a bell and took the detour as if she knew all along.

"You alright?" she asked Amelia. "You've been quiet."

"I'm fine," Amelia said, a detour of her own because there was nothing insightful to say.

"I know what happened between you and Emory last night. If you want to talk about it—"

"There's nothing to talk about. He made that clear."

Emory's empirical argument had been flawless and left no room for rebuttal. He'd neatly tidied up his heartbreak while Amelia's pillow soaked up tears throughout a sleepless night. Done and dusted, that was the end.

"This is a lot farther than you said. You're sure Emory is okay with this?"

Mirabelle flicked off the radio. Big black sunglasses obscured her eyes, but her lips pursed with prickly affront.

"I told you he was. I don't need his permission for everything I do. Besides, Thomas is with us."

Amelia peered out the rear window at Thomas's sedan behind them. She'd already discerned the strata of Emory's trust—those who had his ear, his heart, his suspicion. Thomas had been with Emory at Richard's party. Surely, that meant he belonged in the trusted cadre of reliable men.

"You know Em took care of things, right?" Mirabelle asked. "While you two were together, he dealt with the rat. Does that bother you?"

Mirabelle took off her sunglasses and glanced at Amelia. The woman had clearly choked on her share of bitter pills and seemed to relish administering the same hard medicine to others. Amelia had no illusions left to shatter, though, so she shrugged, far less scandalized than Mirabelle might've hoped.

"Makes sense he'd want revenge."

"I meant that he handled business while he was with you. These men will whisper sweet nothings one minute then order an execution the next."

Amelia didn't respond. She'd gnawed on that morsel until her stomach ached. It wasn't what she saw of Emory that concerned her, but what she couldn't see. He lived in plain sight, but the eclipse came with phone calls taken in the hall and meetings in the basement lounge. If she wanted the man, she'd have to accept the chief.

Off the highway, Mirabelle navigated the streets of a tiny desert town where shops and restaurants dotted the main drag. They parked in front of a storefront with a sign reading "La Boheme" in vibrant Tiffany glass.

Mirabelle's friend, Natalie, met them at the door. A sapphire chiffon dress overwhelmed her petite frame, but the gold chain around her waist accentuated an hourglass figure. Like Mirabelle, every detail of her appearance was polished.

"You must be Amelia," Natalie said and offered her hand. "It's nice to meet you."

"You as well. I feel underdressed." Amelia stared down at her cut-off shorts, a raglan shirt, and blue Chuck Taylors. The outfit served for the advertised purpose—a quick trip down the road to pick up a dress.

Natalie dismissed the comment with a wave. "Oh please. You look gorgeous. I'd be right there with you if it wasn't for this."

She gestured to the boutique. The place hearkened back to the muted delicacy and floral femininity of the art nouveau era. Everything was lush in its beauty, soft and swirling in its lines, right down to the patterned wallpaper and antique furniture displaying the merchandise. With leather and lace, gossamer and denim, it was a mashup of vintage pieces and modern staples.

Mirabelle plopped down on a velvet settee and beckoned Amelia with a pat. Natalie settled in a wingback chair across from them.

"What's with Rambo?" she asked and jutted a thumb at Thomas standing watch by the door.

"Shit's been a little hot and heavy lately," Mirabelle said rather seriously but quickly diverted with a red-lipped smile. "Enough of that. Tell me *everything*. We need to catch up."

Per usual, she expertly dodged the darkness and steered toward levity. Amelia didn't know if the quality was worthy of admiration or concern.

The afternoon wore on as they tried on clothes that smelled of vanilla and incense. Mirabelle and Natalie giggled over gossip and inside jokes. That was the point of the outing, Amelia realized, as a lightness returned to Mirabelle. It wasn't about the dress, but a reminder that an ordinary world existed with normal people living mundane lives.

For Amelia, the excursion into normalcy only made her more aware of life carrying on without her in it. Outside, even the desert sky she'd grown accustomed to looked different and she felt lost again. *I want to go home,* she thought. Whether her home or Emory's, she didn't know anymore.

After a while, they reached a natural end, the perfect time to say goodbye and head back. Instead, Mirabelle ordered food from a Thai restaurant up the street, and the conversation continued with small talk over a meal too late to be lunch but too early for dinner.

"Tell me again how you two met," Natalie said with curious eyes roving between Amelia and Mirabelle. "You both breezed past that part."

Amelia cleared her throat and answered with purposeful ambiguity. "Through Emory."

"And how did you meet him?"

Mirabelle glanced at Amelia, a quiet cue to tread carefully. Deflecting would only get her so far, though. If she and Emory had any kind of future, they'd have to tell the tale with either an adapted truth or coordinated lie.

"I met him at a party. I saw him across the room and hoped he might talk to me."

With her chin resting in her hand, Natalie grinned. "Did he?"

"Sort of. He got pulled away. We both did. Later that night, he helped me out of a tough situation. I'm incredibly grateful to him."

Though technically the truth, the retelling still tasted like a lie. Amelia's gratitude came well after simmering hatred. It was a wonder they'd ever come that far and a tragedy they might go no further.

"You seem more than grateful," Natalie said and twirled noodles around her fork. "Smitten, more like. Are you two together?"

Amelia shook her head. "It ended before it truly began."

Arms crossed, Natalie eased back to evaluate Amelia. A pillar of sunlight stretched across the floral rug between them.

"I can see it. You and Emory have very similar energy. You're both old souls. I hope it works out between you two."

The ache in Amelia's chest returned. She'd received that same gesture after past breakups. With the best of intentions, it twisted the knife as sad eyes consoled with the same words on repeat: "I'm sorry, Amelia. You'll find someone else." Beneath the charitable sympathy was a mountain of pity. Poor Amelia, the lovelorn little fool.

The shop phone trilled behind the counter. Natalie pushed from the floor and pointed at Mirabelle.

"Now, if only we could find you someone. This girl has been single forever."

Natalie fluttered off to answer the phone. Mirabelle dug into her curry but refused Amelia's stare. If the tables were turned, Mirabelle would have plenty to say. She liked to spout faux enlightenment in pithy quotes probably scavenged from Instagram. "Live your truth" was one of them. Mirabelle treated her truth like a dirty secret and lived in fear of its discovery.

"My freshman year of college, I was with this guy," Amelia said. "He was my first serious relationship, first love."

"That's sweet," Mirabelle replied with a half-hearted smile.

"Well, that's the thing. It wasn't sweet. He was a lot older than me and more experienced in just about everything. He used that to his advantage and was awful to me. Of course, it never starts that way. It's like quicksand. You sink a bit each day. By the time you realize the trouble you're in, you feel powerless to pull yourself out and ashamed to ask for help."

Amelia glanced at Natalie with the phone pressed to her ear, eagerly nodding as she scribbled on a scrap of paper.

"I withheld a lot from my best friend. I think I was afraid to hear the truth, so I suffered and I sank, and no one really knew."

Amelia had never relayed the story so succinctly before. She'd only ever vented it in pieces, so no one had the full narrative, only her. Mirabelle didn't know that, though, so she looked flustered and perhaps even slightly embarrassed on Amelia's behalf.

"I'm sorry that happened to you," she said and neatly packaged up her unfinished lunch. "Why are you telling me this?"

"Miri, you know why. I hope Jack is good to you. You deserve a good man."

Mirabelle's cheeks flushed almost the same love-bitten red as her lips. With a deep breath, she smoothed down the lace overlay of her skirt.

"Does Emory know about Jack?"

"Not from me."

"You cannot tell him," she insisted with requisite fear of her mercurial man, one who'd hang his failures on her. "Jack will lose his shit if you do."

"My loyalty isn't to Jack, and I won't keep secrets from Emory. Why can't you just tell him? He probably already suspects something."

"It's complicated, and Emory wouldn't understand. Jack knows every facet of me; the ones I hide, the ones I'm certain are hard to love. It's hard to walk away from someone who sees you so completely."

Amelia nodded sympathetically but knew damn well men like Jack liked to keep their women broken. The lies he must've told to crush a woman as vibrant as Mirabelle.

"My first night here, you told me I wasn't alone," Amelia said and reached for Mirabelle's hand. "Neither are you."

"You're a good girl." Mirabelle closed her eyes that glistened with tears and pulled her hand away. "I'm sorry, Amelia."

"For what?"

With a sigh, Mirabelle scrubbed her palms over her face. "Fuck. I feel like I'm losing it. Can't sleep. Can't eat. I just want to feel normal."

Mirabelle knuckled away the tears before they fell and exhaled a shaky breath through pursed lips.

"I said something to Emory yesterday before Gio's funeral," she confessed. "I told him I wasn't sure if you two were right for each other and that he should let you go."

Amelia stared at Mirabelle, certain there was something else, an admission that she'd gotten it all wrong. It didn't come. Instead, cumbersome silence grew between them as Amelia nursed the sting of what felt like betrayal. Then again, Mirabelle divided her loyalties in unequal parts. She was Amelia's friend, yes, but Emory's sister first.

"Why would you tell him that?" Amelia asked.

Mirabelle responded with a pitiful shrug. The thoughtless interference was worse than deliberate meddling. At least then, Mirabelle could claim good intentions, that she only wanted what was best for Emory. She'd instead done the cruel bidding of others, mindlessly and without question.

"If it's what you think, then stand by it," Amelia insisted.

"It's not what I think."

"It's what Jack thinks." Arms folded and cheeks burning, Amelia sat back in a huff. "Tell me I'm wrong."

Mirabelle wasn't foolish enough to deny it, so she defended a man who wouldn't do the same for her.

"This isn't about Jack. Leave him out if it."

"You're right. It's not about Jack or Emory. It's about you twisting yourself into knots to appease the men in your life while you tell yourself it's what any good Moriarty woman would do. It's bullshit, Miri, and you know it."

"What I said to Emory—"

"Emory is a grown man. You aren't responsible for his actions. If he doesn't know his own heart well enough to tell you you're wrong, then maybe you've done me a favor."

Mirabelle released an astounded breath. She had no right to look as wounded as she did.

"Don't say that. He loves you."

Amelia shook her head with a joyless laugh. "I don't think that's true."

She wasn't being coy or fishing for comfort because the cruelest consolation might've been that he loved her and it wasn't enough.

A shadow momentarily obscured the column of sunlight streaming through the window. Amelia turned as Thomas approached the table.

"I'm sorry to interrupt," he said. "Miri, it's getting late. We should head back. Jack just texted."

Mirabelle paled as her eyes snapped to Thomas. "What did he say?"

"He asked if I'd seen you. I haven't replied yet."

"Don't!" Mirabelle hopped to her feet and gathered her things as Natalie circled around the counter. "I'll call him. I'm sorry, Nat. We gotta go. And fuck! I gotta get gas too."

They left in a hurry of hasty hugs and shouted goodbyes. If Mirabelle intended to pick up a dress, that was summarily forgotten. She sped down the sleepy street and peeled into a gas station near the highway. Parked at the pump, she dug a card out of her wallet and handed it to Amelia.

"Can you handle this for me? I need to pee."

"Sure," Amelia said and circled to the pump as Mirabelle jogged across the lot to the mini mart. Thomas followed her in to buy cigarettes.

Leaned against the car, Amelia surveyed the station a world away from the one she and Brian had pulled into the night they fled Portland. As she stood beneath the overhang, the feeling that washed over her was the same, though, and a shuffle of footsteps approached from behind.

"Amelia?"

THIRTY-FOUR

AMELIA

The familiar voice hardly registered until Amelia turned around to Richard Dauer. The last time she saw him, he'd looked the part of a dapper and charismatic lawyer in a finely tailored suit. The man before her was the shadow of his former self in ratty clothes and with dark bags beneath his eyes.

"Oh God." Richard pulled Amelia into a hug, but she went limp in his arms. "Your dad and I have been looking all over for you."

Amelia squirmed out of his hold. "My dad? Is he here?"

The question came low and slow, as if being played back on a recording, and Amelia was floating somewhere outside of herself.

"He misses you so much," Richard said and, with shaky hands, pulled a piece of paper from his pocket and unfolded it.

On it was a picture of Amelia and her father at her graduation. The Xerox copy mollified the uncertainty behind her smile. Printed beneath the photograph was:

Amelia Havick
Age: 23
DOB: 3/17/2003
Auburn hair, Brown eyes
5'6" 130 lbs.

With breaths hard won, tears welled as she thought of her father plastering up flyers and scouring the town.

"Honey, listen to me," Richard said and anxiously eyed the mini mart. "The people you're with, they're not who you think they are. They've lied to you. Emory knows Cal is looking for you. He's kept you from your family. Your dad is just down the street. Let me take you to him."

Richard tugged on her forearm, but Amelia refused to budge.

"Don't you want to go home?" he asked.

Such a simple question, Amelia could have sworn she already knew the answer. Of course, she wanted to go home. Of course, she did. Why wouldn't she? But something hounded her, screaming for her to understand. Mirabelle was inside the mini mart and would return any minute. What would she think if Amelia disappeared without a word? And Emory. It'd break his heart if she left him like that.

"Yes," Amelia said. "I want to go home. I just...give me a second."

With a grimace, Richard stared at the mini mart again as Amelia dug in Mirabelle's purse for a pen. She pressed the flyer to the window and scribbled a note on the back of the page but hesitated before tucking it beneath the wiper blade.

"Amelia, we need to go," Richard insisted and reached for her, but Amelia wriggled away.

Why was the decision suddenly so difficult? Her dad needed her. He'd been left alone to bury her mother. She was all he had. But another force pulled in the opposite direction. Emory, Mirabelle, Liam, Gio, Pete—none of them were bad people. They'd been kind to her. They'd been there for Amelia in her darkest hours, the ones she was certain she'd never survive.

Amelia shook her head. "At least let me say goodbye."

"Listen to me." Richard nervously licked his dry lips and cinched her forearms in a tight grasp. "I've already called the police. I told them I found you. If you don't come with me, they'll see you with Mirabelle. She could get into a lot of trouble. Emory too. If you leave with me now, the police won't ever have to know that Emory was involved in this. It'll be our secret. Don't you want to keep him safe, protect him like he's protected you?"

Amelia nodded. "I'd do anything to keep him safe."

"Of course, you would," Richard said and led Amelia across the parking lot to a silver SUV.

"Whose car is that?" Amelia asked and scanned the lot for one of Rich's cars. He only drove luxury vehicles. It should've stood out amongst the dusty pickup trucks and nondescript sedans.

"FBI. They opened a case in your disappearance. I've been helping them."

"But you said you wouldn't involve the police."

Something didn't add up. Why the hell did he look so disheveled? And why did he care so much that she'd disappeared? He'd never liked her. Amelia tried to yank her arm away. Rich tightened his grip and roughly steered her toward the vehicle.

"I know what I said," he muttered.

Amelia turned back to the mini mart. Inside, Mirabelle stood at the counter with Thomas. His eyes locked on Amelia as Richard shoved her into the back seat and climbed in after. As the car lurched backwards, Thomas bolted outside.

Amelia's heart sank as she gained her bearings. Two men sat in the front seat with weapons across their laps. The one on the passenger side turned around. She'd seen his face before. In a black hood and with one black eye, he'd lurked on the outskirts of Richard's party like death itself.

When he flashed a soulless smile at her, Amelia shrieked and yanked the door handle. Locked inside, she pounded on the window, and before she could scream again, Richard covered her mouth and nose with a cloth.

Something acrid seared down her throat and into her lungs.

Eyes watering, she struggled against him, arms and legs flailing until they became too heavy to move.

"I'm sorry, Amelia," Richard whispered. "I'm very sorry."

THIRTY-FIVE

EMORY

In the basement lounge, echoes of Emory's past cut deep. The fearsome four, as they were once called—Emory, Jack, Corey, and Pete—swapped stories at the far end of the table.

Jack hooted with laughter until tears streaked his cheeks. Corey deadpanned tales from their early years, and Pete filled in the blanks for Zulu. Barely twenty-two, the kid kept his black hair shaved close to the sides, all but the top that was hard parted and slicked back. Tattoos crept down his arms to the knuckles. He mostly stayed quiet, seemingly enamored with the lore circling the table.

In the years before Emory and Jack's rise to the top, Pete and Corey were their equals. The hierarchy hadn't busted them apart yet or hidden Corey's dry wit and Pete's goofy humor behind a wall of deference. Emory missed the days when Corey spoke freely and Pete could still be himself.

Nostalgia didn't just sting, though. Sharp as a knife, it cut Emory to shreds when he tried to hold on. By early evening, he excused himself to the great room when the reminiscence felt too much like grieving the past. Vacuous despite oversized furniture and minimalist in its absence of decorative flourishes, the space was simple and secluded. After a while, Jack drifted in and flopped down in the chaise lounge.

"I'm going stir crazy. I don't know how Liam does it."

"I think he likes being a recluse these days," Emory replied, insight gleaned through observation.

Liam had had his time in the sun and basked in that light as long as he could, but it drained him. In his early-sixties, the man wanted his oasis in the desert and mundane delights—reality TV, a hot-house garden, afternoon naps with yesterday's newspaper draped over his chest.

"I'd forgotten so many of those stories," Jack said. "It really was a better time."

Emory picked a bit of lint off his black jeans and crossed his arms. "There were hard times too."

Hindsight was shaded like grenadine and tasted just as sweet. But there were nights when Corey screamed for help in his sleep. Emory would rush into his bedroom and shake him awake. "It's just a dream," Corey would say and climb from sweat-dampened sheets, partly embarrassed but mostly sorry.

"Where are you going after all this?" Jack asked. "Back home to Vegas?"

After all this. A mournful smile played on Emory's lips.

Time in the Moriartys was a continuum. All origins before were wiped clean and everything after was endless, expansive, and consuming. There was no "after this," but Emory knew what Jack meant; after Ivan was dealt with, after the dust settled and they fell into a familiar rhythm again.

Necessity, not glamor, drew Emory to Vegas, and it'd be a frigid day in blistering hell before he ever called it home. Home would always be Northern California. His place there sat high on a bluff that overlooked the craggy coast and was nestled amongst a grove of cypress and pine. He toiled over the house he'd built, raising it from his own vision of what a true home should be. Irony of ironies, he never stayed long.

"What I really want is to go home, back north."

Emory cleared a catch in his throat and let the rest go unsaid; that it'd be a one-way trip. He'd take Amelia, and they'd start over there, construct a life worth living and mark his time in the Moriartys as a strange interlude.

Jack cast dodgy eyes to an empty hall and lowered his voice, a precaution against blasphemy perhaps.

"It's okay to be tired of this life sometimes, Em. I can't imagine Liam loved it every second."

Emory shook his head. "I wouldn't underestimate him. This is his namesake, his legacy."

"It's your legacy too. You'll do right by it. You always have."

For Emory, it wasn't about love or legacy but duty. He chained himself to the organization and gave Liam his word that he'd usher the Moriartys into a new era. Love was reserved for family, but they were his family. In that way, the line blurred and competing instincts were braided too tight to unwind.

"Don't you get tired of it?" Emory asked.

Jack flashed a smile that left Emory awash in childhood memories. Brave Jack—riding his bike like a madman with busted up knees—every so often had a thoughtful streak. He'd look to the sky with wanderlust and speak slow and soft with a dazed grin.

"Not really, but I do wonder what we'd be doing if it weren't for this. Maybe we'd still live in that same neighborhood in Sacramento, right next door to each other. We'd have some gig turning wrenches or fitting pipes. We'd end up with beautiful women. Make babies and they'd grow up together. Barbecues, camping trips, holiday parties."

A dull ache ripped through Emory. He grieved for a life he'd never live and dealt with the loss of something he never had in the first place. He yearned for a future he could stamp his name to, a legacy that would make his father proud. Shame filled him up something fierce whenever he dwelled on what his old man might think of his life.

Emory subdued it lest it spread like wildfire, but a thought rose with dawn that morning and gained importance throughout the day. His father would've adored Amelia, would've told Emory she was right and to listen well and good to a woman like her, to hold her tight and not let her slip away.

"Sounds like heaven," Emory said, though he and Jack both knew the truth. If not for the Moriartys, they'd both be dead; Emory from Ivan and Jack from trouble to be found.

"Does that make this hell then?" Jack asked.

Emory watched him in peaceful repose, soaking up the sun like a cat that got the cream. It was easy living for Jack, lobbing jabs from the high ground and waltzing in there like Emory could forget last night. He'd slept on what Amelia said and found it more concrete in the morning. Meanwhile, Jack's last stand seemed toothless in comparison, and now he was the emblem of quiet dissent, the mouthpiece for whatever stirred in the ranks.

"You can call it whatever you want," Emory said, "but *you* were the one with a choice, not me. Don't ever forget that."

He delivered the barbed remark with an icy stare. Jack took the blow on a stiff chin and shifted to the edge of the chaise.

"I haven't. We don't talk about it much, but after you and Miri left, my world fell apart, not that I had much of one to begin with."

Jack licked his lips and ran his fingers through greasy hair. He only ever told the story with whiskey on his breath. He'd erupt with laughter and tell the tale of the shit-stain who married his mother.

For some, starting over meant wiping the slate clean. When his mom learned about the baby girl growing in her belly, she'd sent Jack to live with his grandmother in Nevada and washed her hands of him. He'd found Emory again and talked as if he'd orchestrated it all. In reality, he'd begged and pleaded to follow Emory into the Moriartys. It wasn't about brotherhood or belonging but righting the wrong of being unwanted.

"Life here makes sense," Jack said. "There ain't shit for me if I ever left. But if you or Mirabelle left, it'd feel like the end of the world again, and I tend to go crazy when I think about that."

Jack stopped short of apologizing, but the sentiment still

shaded his words. Emory accepted it and repaid the gesture with a little white lie.

"I'm not going anywhere."

"For now."

"For now," Emory agreed and reached for his phone vibrating in his pocket.

Mirabelle calling...

Emory answered and went to speak, but a hiccupped sob cut him off.

"Mirabelle, breathe," he said and shot from his seat. "What happened? What's wrong?"

"She's gone! Amelia's gone."

THIRTY-SIX

EMORY

Emory staggered around the side table but nicked his knee against the edge so hard the lamp nearly toppled over. He ignored the jolt of pain and hurried to the foyer with Jack close behind.

"What do you mean she's gone? I thought you two were here. Where the hell are you?"

Mirabelle dissolved into a fit of tears again. Unable to speak, her cries faded as someone else took the phone.

"It's Thomas. We're about thirty minutes south of Liam's at that commuter lot off 95. Rich Dauer has her. Two other men were with him. At least one was a Velasco guy."

A chill spread through Emory. He stopped halfway up the stairs. Highway noise crowded the line before a heavy sigh crackled through.

"Emory, I'm so sorry. The other was Ivan."

On rubbery legs, Emory groped for the wall and sat on a step. A flash of gold invaded his vision.

Blonde hair. Bloody face. Light breaking through the trees.

"I trailed them as long as I could," Thomas said. "They were heading east in a silver SUV. I got the plates."

"You're sure it was her?"

"Yes. She's with them. Amelia's gone."

"Gone," Emory whispered in a dumbfounded little echo, still suspended in horrified disbelief. "Gone." Louder that time, he snapped into focus and stood from the stairs. "Call Disco. Have him run the plate. Tell him to call me with anything he gets. You and Mirabelle stay there. We're coming."

Emory hung up and bolted down the steps. He grabbed his keys and Glock from the kitchen and cut through the foyer.

"Get the others and meet me out front," he told Jack. "Tell Zulu to bring his gear and Corey extra mags."

Jack sprinted up the stairs and hollered for Liam and the others. His voice blared through the foyer but faded as Emory took the steps to the circle drive two at a time. Liam and Pete raced out the door as Jack relayed what little he knew. Zulu and Corey followed not long after, and the men gathered around Emory.

He felt himself drifting away, the way he had in the woods; in the golden hour when the air smelled of blood and dew. Long ago, his brother promised revenge. Emory knew how it ended, could recite it in his sleep, and said it with haunted detachment.

"Ivan has Amelia."

Liam released a shaky breath, and Corey mouthed "Jesus Christ" to the sky. Stunned into silence, Pete gaped at Emory, and Zulu must've known enough because he paled and shook his head. Jack eyed Emory with the same fear that, even as boys, they reserved for Ivan alone.

"No one comes back, not a soul, until we find her," Emory said shakily, on the cusp of coming undone. "I don't care how long it takes."

They split up into two cars—Liam, Emory, and Zulu with all his gear in one, and the rest in the other. Reckless and reeling, Emory sped down the highway. The miles melted away, but the road never ended, and Emory's heart hammered in his chest with every silver SUV they passed. Eventually, he spotted Thomas's car parked on the broken patch of asphalt that passed as a commuter lot.

With a jerk of the wheel, Emory veered off the road and

slammed to a stop in the lot. The other car screeched behind him, halting inches short of collision. Emory kicked open the door as Thomas hopped from his car, ashen-faced and wide-eyed as Emory bounded toward him.

"How the *fuck* did this happen?" he bellowed as the setting sun burned hot at his neck.

Mirabelle scrambled from the passenger seat. Mascara stained her cheeks, and her eyes were red and swollen. Like hurtling herself in front of a freight train, she threw her weight into Emory who lurched toward Thomas.

"It's not his fault. I lied to him!" she cried and pulled a piece of paper from her pocket but struggled to unfold it. Emory snatched it from her and read.

> *I'm sorry. I have to go home.*
> *Please tell Emory that I'll miss him and to find*
> *me again when the time is right.*
> *Thank you both for everything.*
> *Amelia*

Emory flipped over the page. Amelia smiled up at him, so tenderhearted and sweet; everything he wanted and all he really needed. *The last you'll ever see.*

He closed his eyes and asked on a broken breath, "You're sure she wrote this?"

Only the afflicted indulged in lies like that; lies to make it bearable, to sleep at night, to live with themselves. Emory's lie might've been that she didn't want to go and Richard took her unwillingly. But the polished manners and swooping handwriting belonged to Amelia and smothered the lie before it took hold.

Mirabelle balked at the question. If she weren't so consumed by grief, maybe she would've laughed. They all might have laughed at his expense, and good on them. What a fitting end for a fucking fool. Call in the clowns. It was a heartbreak riot, a story for the ages. He brought her there to keep her safe but instead baited the hook for a beast.

"I told Thomas and Amelia that you said it was okay for us to leave. I lied," Mirabelle said again as if honesty was the currency to buy back trust.

The note crumpled in Emory's fist, his anger simmering toward explosion.

"You're going to get her killed! Do you have any idea what Ivan will do to her?"

None of them truly knew. They read it in the paper and said how very tragic. Cal Havick and his vendetta against evil couldn't vanquish the monster, so pretty girls with dazzling smiles were ripped apart and everyone asked, "Who rapes a corpse? Who cuts out their tongue so they can no longer scream?"

The instinct to retch nearly knocked Emory off his feet. He covered his mouth with a balled fist and stared at the expiring sun to burn away emergent tears. Mirabelle quietly cried and clutched her middle. Uncertain who to comfort, the men gathered around but didn't pick sides.

Emory's phone chimed with a text from Disco. ***Nada from the plates be there in 20.***

"Nothing from the plates," Emory announced.

Frustration coursed through him and coiled on itself with gathering pressure. They should be moving, doing something, not standing on the side of that fucking wasteland. Jaw clenched, his breaths shortened to ragged huffs, and his teeth ground together. Emory hurled toward his car. His fist smashed into the window and the glass starred beneath the brutal force. Pete wrangled him by the shoulders before Emory could deliver another hit.

"We're gonna find her," he said with certainty he had no right to.

Emory searched for doubt in Pete's eyes, that fracture in faith he could point to and justify the dalliance in darkness.

"Zules," Pete called out. "If you can trace Dauer's cell, you can get a location, right?"

With all eyes on him, Zulu stood tall and squared his

shoulders. He was so young, Emory noticed for the first time. The boy's combat boots, camo shorts, and torn-up Motörhead t-shirt did little to give the appearance of age.

"Yeah, that part's easy, but if his phone has been off..."

The thought hung in dead air.

"If his phone is off, what?" Corey asked. "We got nothing?"

Zulu shook his head. "Not necessarily. I could try to link devices that've connected to the same network as Richard's cell. It'd help expand leads."

With renewed promise, Emory waved Zulu to the car but didn't wait for him to jog over. He pulled pieces of gear from the trunk—laptop, switch box, cables, and an assortment of other shit that didn't mean a damn thing to him as long as it worked.

"I don't care how you do it," Emory said, "but I need you to find Richard Dauer. Can you do that?"

"Yes, sir."

Zulu made quick work of setting up his gear. Leaned against the car, Emory evaluated the sun skimming the horizon. They'd lose light soon, and that meant losing time and a whole host of other precious things. If he thought of it too long, the frenzy would begin again, so he quarantined that part of himself as Zulu pecked at the keyboard.

Liam settled next to Emory. Jack consoled Mirabelle, who sat on the ground and cradled her knees. Pete paced in front of the car, and Corey chain-smoked through a pack of Marlboros. When Disco showed up, he and Thomas agreed to take Mirabelle back to Liam's and wait there for orders.

"Alright, his cell was pinging nearby," Zulu said not long after Disco left. "Shit. That was hours ago." He tapped at the keyboard and waited, fingers hovering over the keys and eyes glued to the screen. "Fuck," he sighed into one palm.

"What's the matter?" Corey asked.

Zulu pulled his hand from his face, but it was Emory he stared at with big brown eyes full of fright, reminiscent of how Emory used to regard Ivan as a boy. He recognized something of his younger self in Zulu—a Latino kid grown up all wrong and rising fast in the underworld.

"His phone is off," Zulu said. "I can't get anything from it. I could try other things, but that'll take time."

They didn't have time. Emory could rail against reality and torpedo morale, but to what end?

He squatted in front of Zulu. "What's your real name?"

"Sam."

Emory rested a hand on his shoulder and gentled his voice. "Sam, you gotta keep trying. That's all I need from you. Just keep trying. I know you can do it."

"You got this, baby!" Pete shouted from behind Emory.

Zulu broke with a smile and set in with a flurry of keystrokes. By the time the sun disappeared behind jagged hills, the night menaced with a chill, and the wind whipped around them. The laptop's dull iridescence illuminated Zulu's face in a murky glow. He continued the task, but the frequency of taps slowed, and by the way he kept shaking his head, Emory knew they were reaching a dead end. The men knew it too. One by one, each of them slumped against the cars and faded fast as Emory paced in silence.

"Son, it's been hours," Liam said, quiet enough the others wouldn't hear. "We need to regroup. Zulu can keep working. It doesn't mean you're giving up. I just think we need to settle for a bit and think through alternatives."

Defeat battered Emory, and the doubts rolled in dense as fog. For all he knew, Amelia may not even be with Richard. He could've handed her off to Ivan and split. Emory meant what he said when they left, though. Days, weeks, months, it didn't matter how long it took to find her. He'd tear the world apart to get her back. His men must've taken it as a hyperbolic declaration born of passion but little resolve. Liam should've known better, though.

"I'm not going back without her. I don't care how long it takes. I'm not leaving her."

Emory glanced at Zulu. The kid shook his head with a forlorn smile. Nothing. They had nothing.

"I'm sorry, Emory," Liam said with premature condolences and a pat on the shoulder.

Emory was thankful for the night, if only for the way it obscured how he unraveled. There was no relief in the release. The loss came down swift and heavy and with indiscriminate cruelty.

Yet again, he'd deal with the loss of something he never had in the first place and wasn't his to keep—the life he'd like to lead and the one he wanted in it.

THIRTY-SEVEN

AMELIA

A warm breath on her cheek roused Amelia from the dreamless dark. The grogginess receded enough that skull-splitting pain set in next. She cracked her eyes, and a cinder block wall came into focus. A shadow hovered over her but retreated when she wheezed with a dry cough. Amelia rolled over on a thin mattress crusted in filth and mottled with stains.

In a small, humid room, brackish light seeped from a single fluorescent bulb. The one-eyed man sat cross-legged on the floor next to the mattress. Tall and sinewy, he didn't move, only stared with disturbing vacancy. Chin-length black hair framed a gaunt face of sharp bones and papery skin. His one eye looked like a black marble, and the lids of his missing eye were fused together in a line of puckered skin that'd healed glossy pink.

It's just a nightmare, she tried to console herself, but why then did the scent of mildew and damp rot fill her nostrils? *And the blood.* She tasted it in her mouth from a busted lip and, when she recoiled, thin rope cut into her bound wrists and ankles.

The man patted his knees before standing and crossed the empty room in airy shuffles. Amelia opened her mouth to scream, but her sandpaper throat produced only a yelp.

In a dark corner of the room, the man fussed with something then returned to the mattress with a metal toolbox. He placed it on the concrete floor and crouched in front. The toolbox groaned on its hinges when he tossed open the lid.

He stared at Amelia as he did it. *Look away.* She couldn't. *Look away.* His maniacal gaze wouldn't allow it as he pulled out tools.

Pliers. Hammer. Wrench. Ice pick.

Fear slid like an icicle to settle in Amelia's heart, and cold dread gutted her next. She licked the tears off her lips and dry heaved at the saltiness. The violent urge to be sick sat at the back of her throat but went no further.

The man placed the tools in a neat row then settled back on his knees. With a hand propped beneath his chin, he surveyed the assortment. His fingertips were grimy and caked with what looked like either dirt or dried blood.

I can't breathe. Amelia eyed the windowless metal door behind him and struggled in her binds. She could come out of her fucking skin. Itchy. She couldn't scratch. Crawling. The mattress and its filth. *And this man. This man.*

Amelia whimpered. He didn't respond, just admired his tools. Each and every one. The cold abandoned her, so Amelia burned alive right before his eyes. Her chest on fire. Her wrists ablaze. That nauseous heat. She came apart so predictably.

"Please," Amelia cried. It was too polite. Why couldn't she produce the panic turning her insides to pulp? "Please." Too thin. Too breathy. Too *fucking* late. She was never strong enough. "Please!"

Her scream echoed damply in the room. The man shushed her with a finger to his lips and shook his head. As he did, the dim light carved shadows beneath his cheeks and eye sockets.

"Not yet."

Like a cruel echo, the rasp of his voice wrecked in its familiarity. It wasn't just his voice, though. There was the slope of Emory's nose, the shape of Mirabelle's eyes; jet black hair and bronze skin.

Ivan.

He didn't have to say his name. She already knew and, with

that silent knowledge, came a foggy memory. She'd left a note for Mirabelle. Emory had undoubtedly seen it, and maybe he'd resigned himself to letting her go. *No one is coming for me.*

Amelia squeezed her eyes shut and buried her face in the dirty mattress. A sob escaped her. It sounded unearthly and foreign to her own ears. She'd never heard that sound; not from anyone, let alone herself. But then there was another sound; the ice pick scraping across the floor. Ivan jabbed the sharp end into the hollow beneath her chin and forced her to look at him.

He studied her face with cold fixation. It stirred something sinister, but Amelia couldn't place what it was; hatred or desire or some abomination of both.

"I can see why he likes you," Ivan said as the ice pick sunk painfully into her skin. "Get on your knees and pray."

Amelia shook her head. It wasn't defiance. He'd gotten her confused with someone else, someone brave. He'd tell her to put up a fight and make it count. *I'm not polite. I'm not brave. I'm not who he thinks I am. I'm not.*

"I'm not," she muttered, but the nonsense didn't phase him. He smiled because he expected it and had done it all before, so clearly a master at his craft.

Her eyes darted around the room. Mold. Light. Dust. Dirt. She was smart but only focused on stupid things. The pipe in the corner. A chair in the back. The rest distorted at the edges like a fever dream. Maybe she wasn't so smart.

"You're not what?" the man asked and narrowed his good eye. He expected an answer and would wait for it all night.

Amelia didn't respond. She curled in on herself with her knees to her chest and closed her eyes to disappear. That agency— so precious little—infuriated him. Ivan grabbed a fistful of her hair and violently forced her up. His teeth sunk into the fleshy corner where her shoulder met her neck.

Amelia screamed as he ripped into her skin. "Stop! Please! God!"

Ivan pressed the ice pick to her temple, and his single eye

darkened with lunacy and rage. "There is no God. Only me. Now, pray."

More animal than human, his bloodied teeth gnashed with a guttural growl, and his hand shook furiously, as if he battled the urge to drive the pick into her head. With a piercing scream, he threw it across the room just as the metal door flung open and two men strode inside. One dragged in a bound and bloodied Richard and tossed him against the wall opposite Amelia. The other gestured to her.

"You fuck her?" he asked Ivan, who fetched the ice pick and calmly wiped the blood from his mouth with the back of his hand.

"No." He turned to Amelia and lightly stroked the barrel of the pick. "My brother will want to watch."

Ivan winked at her, and his thin lips slithered into a hideous smile. Amelia slumped against the wall and pressed her cheek to the cinder block. Maybe she'd fall through to the other side and could float away. *Just float away.*

Ivan retreated through the door, and the two others followed. After they left, Richard stirred. Sweat and dirt stained his wrinkled clothes, and dried blood flaked from his forehead. There he was—the man who donned designer suits, drove luxury cars, and lived in a mansion with a ridiculous name—looking as though he'd been through hell.

Amelia lifted her bound hands to her neck and probed the bite mark that weeped blood. Pain seared down her arm and throbbed in her fingertips. Her limbs felt far heavier than they had any right to be and, if she closed her eyes, she swore she might even sleep. If her soul wanted to float away, then her body wanted to shut down.

She jabbed her thumb into the wound, enough to anchor her senses to something. It worked, and the room came into focus. Clumps of dirt gathered in the corners, and scuff marks littered the dingy, off-white interior walls. Overhead was a low drop ceiling with yellowed tiles. Most were missing, but rings of mold splotched the remaining ones. The place wasn't just rotting. It was abandoned. *No one will find me here.*

Tears brimmed, and Amelia bit her lip to cease its quivering. The room was sticky and hot, and she wanted to go home. What a pathetic want. Survival should've been the ultimate ambition. All she thought of, though, was her favorite blanket and the mug that fit so perfectly in her palm, even though a chip in the rim had once sliced her lip. She bit down forcefully where the scar used to be. It only made her cry harder.

"Stop that," Richard snapped.

With his legs kicked out in front of him, he groaned as he worked his way to the wall.

Amelia could have laughed at the audacity but instead demanded on a voice whittled thin, "Why did you do this?"

Restless quiet filled the room, all but the fluorescent hum and the soft scuffle of Richard's shoes against the floor.

"They have my wife. They'll let her go, but only if I brought you to them." Richard contemplated Amelia's wrists in binds and her neck bloodied from Ivan's bite. "It's nothing personal. Your father would've done the same."

"No, he wouldn't have!" Amelia cried, the salt from her tears itchy on her cheeks. "He's not a coward like you."

"Really? Then tell me why he bolted. He left Portland after your mom's funeral, and no one's heard from him since. If he's so brave, he would've stuck around and faced what's coming."

A painful breath hitched in Amelia's chest. "What do you mean? Where is he?"

Richard barked a bitter laugh. "I don't know where he is, but I do know Ivan will find him."

Regret plowed into Amelia. It stole her breath and ushered more tears. On a stormy night in Portland, her foolish heart had yearned to escape a life that was full of love and hope and all the precious things that'd be torn from her. *I won't survive the night.*

"You take after your father so much," Richard said and evaluated her through glassy eyes. "Same stubbornness. Same righteousness. You know, after law school, Cal wanted to open up a firm with me. Some humble place that did honest work. He ever tell you that story?" Richard gazed up at a water-logged ceiling tile. "God, I almost agreed too. You know why I'm as successful as I am?"

Amelia glared at him. She didn't care, but her silence seemed to unnerve him. Rich's lip twitched into a scowl, and he answered anyhow.

"I don't live and die by the rule book. Nothing is black and white, and corruption exists everywhere—judges who can be bought and sold, cops who make evidence disappear, prosecutors who broker deals under the table. I'm resourceful and clever. That's how you make money and a name for yourself; not doing what your dad does, toiling away for some greater good. That shit doesn't exist. The world is built on darkness. You either embrace it and thrive or die trying to reach the light."

"If you're so fucking clever and resourceful, how did you end up here?"

Rich smiled. He didn't seem to grasp his misfortune.

"When I took Philippe on as a client, everyone warned me it was a mistake and that I'd pay for it eventually."

Richard quieted and stared at a crack in the floor before continuing.

"Philippe was my friend, but I saw him for what he was—a has-been looking to coast into easy retirement. He didn't care about his business anymore. He slaughtered the goose that laid the golden egg when he agreed to Liam's peace deal. It didn't matter. He'd already collected his fortune and then closed the door behind him. It created the perfect opportunity for someone like Ivan to turn the screws of discontent.

"Ivan had connections to a few Velasco captains, those two men in here just a minute ago. He saw the Velascos as force multipliers for dismantling Emory's empire, and the Velascos seized the chance to achieve parity with the Moriartys, a first for them. So, they made a deal, but Philippe found out.

"The Velascos have kompromat on me. It'll end my career. Then there's Charlotte, the things they'll do to her. Ivan wanted

Philippe's whereabouts, so I gave it. I couldn't do anything about Burt, though. Dumb fuck. If it's any comfort, he did try to protect you. He refused to tell the Velascos that you'd seen the folder."

"How the hell is that supposed to comfort me?" Amelia demanded. It wasn't a comfort at all, but an absurdity of fate, all the inconsequential decisions that lead to disastrous ends. "If Burt didn't tell them, how did the Velascos know?"

Bound and beaten, Richard scoffed, scornful even then. "Burt went to Martin Kranski for help. He was worried for himself, but mostly for you. Kranski was a sloppy drunk. The information wasn't hard for me to wrangle out of him."

Amelia reeled from a sharp shock of brilliant hatred. "You told them! You sent them after me!"

"Oh, get off it. They would've gone after you anyway. Ivan's interest in you is as much to terrorize your father as it is to eliminate you from the pool of people who knew he'd taken over. And now you've given him a third reason."

Rich's eyes raked over Amelia. She tugged her shirt up her shoulder to sop up the blood.

"I saw how you hesitated at the gas station. I saw the torment in you, the way Emory's manipulated you into believing he gives a shit. And worse, you care about him. In fact, I'd say you're in love with him, aren't you?"

Amelia refused an answer, though it was obvious to her and anyone else around them and Richard too. He shook his head with a lurid grin.

"God, I'd love to see Cal's face when he finds out you spread your legs for Emory Holt. If it weren't so pathetic, it'd be hilarious." Richard tipped his head to the metal door. "You know Emory's just as violent and ruthless as them, right? He came to my party for payment. I'd say he collected, wouldn't you?"

At the lewd suggestion, Richard stared at Amelia's bare thighs pressed together.

"You don't know him," she said in a feeble attempt at defense.

Emory was brave and strong, and he'd come for her soon. *I won't make it through the night.*

"I know him far better than you do. I know the hatred the Holt brothers harbor for one another. I know how it fuels them both, how they'd tear this world apart just to watch the other bleed."

Richard winced as he shifted against the wall, and his visage darkened with deep unease.

"You were at my party. You saw what Ivan did. He turned my home into his slaughterhouse. That should be a testament to how little he values human life. It was a shot across the bow for Emory to see. Ivan wants his brother to suffer. Like it or not, that agenda of misery now includes you."

They both sat up as sounds rustled beyond the metal door. Ivan breezed in with three other men Amelia recognized from Richard's party. Knees pulled to her chest, she coiled into a tight ball to make herself small, as if she might disappear that way.

Ivan snatched her by the forearm and dragged her from the mattress. She squealed and tried to wrestle her arm away, but his fingers only clamped tighter as he hauled her across the room.

With surprising strength, he tossed her at Richard. Amelia slid across the grimy floor and slammed into the wall. The impact knocked the wind out of her. On her forearms and knees, she gasped for breaths but still scarcely managed to fill her lungs. One of the Velasco men pulled a phone from his pocket while another unbound Richard's hands.

Ivan shoved the phone at Richard. "Call him."

For what felt like ages, Richard fumbled with the phone and tapped at the screen. He handed it to Ivan just as Emory's voice, muffled and deep, filtered through.

THIRTY-EIGHT

EMORY

A mile from the commuter lot, the Moriarty men regrouped at a truck stop diner aptly named Crossroads. They piled into two adjacent booths and nourished scant appetites while Zulu went to work.

Across from Emory, Liam perused yesterday's newspaper. Ink stuck to his fingertips and transferred in sooty prints to his coffee mug. Next to him, Jack avoided Emory's stare as he tapped the filter end of an unsmoked cigarette against the table.

Disgust overwhelmed Emory. The table was dirty and cigarettes filthy. And why was his nose buried in his phone? Why wasn't he at the other table poring over leads like Corey, Pete, and Zulu? At least Liam put up a front of relaxed nonchalance, his own attempt at comforting Emory.

It might've worked, except the kitchen grills filled the diner with stifling heat. Emory would burn alive in there and be happy for it, anything to stem the anxious thoughts. He stared out the window, though there wasn't much to see.

The parking lot was mostly empty save a handful of eighteen-wheelers lined up in rows. Drivers hopped from their cabs and walk bowlegged across the lot. Inside, they greeted one another with stiff nods and plopped down at the counter. They'd grind their eyes with the heels of their hands and grumble demands for coffee, black and hot.

Emory sipped on his own coffee loaded with cream and sugar to mask the bitter taste. Wanda the waitress wandered over and slung a worried look at the lot of them.

"You sure everything's alright, hon?" she asked Liam but eyed Zulu with his gear scattered in the adjacent booth. She'd graciously run an extension cord from behind the counter and, until then, understood not to ask questions other than if they needed more coffee.

"Quite sure," Liam said with a terse smile that sent Wanda on her way.

"I was texting Miri," Jack explained and tucked his phone away. "She said they made it back to Liam's."

"I see." Emory gestured to Jack's empty hands. "For someone so well-connected to my sister, it seems strange you didn't know where she was today, had no idea she'd slipped out."

Jack huffed an offended breath, but his eyes teemed with hurt. It was the most emotion Emory had seen from him all night.

"You think I had something to do with this?"

Emory shrugged but stopped short of voicing accusations. He could take back allusions, which were often filled with weasel words and double talk. An accusation of treachery couldn't be laughed off later as a misunderstanding. It had to be proven and dealt with or debunked without a doubt.

Liam pointed to the picked-at muffin on Emory's plate. "Shut the fuck up and eat."

"I'm not hungry."

"You will be, and you'll need your strength."

Emory almost rebuked the assumption—there'd be a fight he might not handle—but couldn't marshal the wherewithal to argue. He shoved the plate aside and slid down the booth.

"I'll be out front if anyone needs me."

Outside, he walked the building's perimeter and perched against a sun-bleached mural painted on the side. Once upon a time, it exalted Nevada's flora with prickly pear and cholla brightly framing an electric sun. Beneath the light of a full moon, it looked lusterless.

Across an empty expanse of sand and rock, headlights flickered in the distance, and black mountains silhouetted the night sky. After a few minutes, Liam's familiar cadence manifested on a crunch of gravel. With it came the peppery scent of his cologne as he rounded the corner.

"Can't smoke anywhere these days," he quipped with a flick of his lighter and a drag off his cigar. Fragrant wisps of smoke curled from his lips as he squinted at the horizon. "Remember what I told you about the desert?"

Emory nodded. "You said it was like a woman. Beautiful but deadly."

His early days in the organization were a blur of memories that often bled together, but that conversation dog-eared a page in his past. It was one of the first heart-to-hearts he'd had with Liam, a man who, back then, Emory swore was trying to replace his father. He'd been a teenager, capricious and difficult with a hair-trigger temper.

"Beautiful but deadly," Liam said. "I told you not to get sucked in. That's the problem. People are so infatuated by the allure, they set off. Before they know it, they're lost and dying amongst the beauty they so desperately sought."

Emory folded his arms and soured on the reverie. "Is this meant to be an analogy? One about Amelia? If so, save it."

Liam's brows lifted, and he dropped his smoking hand before the cigar reached his mouth.

"No, just reminiscing on our first meaningful conversation." Liam shook his head with a laugh. "God, you were a little asshole then and filled with so much anger. Like a hurricane, I watched you destroy everything in your path—relationships, friendships, yourself. I knew the rage would blow over, and it did, but I still see glimpses of it sometimes."

Liam jutted his thumb at the diner where Jack probably sat alone with his hurt. "You shouldn't have said that."

"I know," Emory conceded with a sigh. "I'm coming unstitched."

"That's fair." Liam quieted and seemed to stew on his thoughts. "It's interesting you assumed you were getting a lecture about Amelia. What criticism were you expecting from me?"

"You saw what happened last night. How did Sal put it—the on-the-fence shit will end in tragedy for everyone?" Emory gestured to the desert around them. "Lo and behold."

"Whose tragedy is this? To most the men, Amelia's life is a rounding error in our business and nothing more."

Liam took a long pull on his cigar and sent rings of smoke to the silver-dollar moon. Emory watched them disband as they drifted away.

"Let me tell you a story," Liam said. "I swear it has a point. It won't seem like it, but it does. I used to have this fountain pen. I saw it somewhere and coveted it long enough that Francisca told me to shit or get off the pot, so I bought it, used it a few times, then lost it. I looked for that thing in the obvious places—pockets, desk drawers, couch cushions. Eventually, I called it a loss and moved on. Francisca loved pens, though. You remember that?"

Emory shook his head. Francisca died only a year after he arrived in her life, not long enough to learn her quirks.

"Well, she did. For Francisca, pens had to feel a certain way. The right tip and grip, ink like silk on the page. We went to our lawyer one day to draw up her living will. When we left, she got in the car giggling like a little girl and pulled a pen from her purse. It was our lawyer's pen. She'd signed something and walked off with it. She claimed it was perfect in every way. The thing was hideous. A glittery, plastic abomination.

"From that point on, though, it was her pen, the pen to end all pens. I'd tease her about it, and it became an inside joke. Whenever the pen was out, I'd give her a hard time about finding perfection in something so mundane. When she passed and I was handling her things, I came across it. I couldn't get rid of it, so I kept it on my desk. Whenever I saw that pen, I thought of how much I loved her, the things that made her happy, our life together."

Liam glanced at Emory. Heartache burdened his gaze.

"I lost the pen. I used it one day, and it was gone the next. I didn't cry much after she died but broke down when I lost that fucking pen. It was ridiculous to everyone else. It was just a pen. I had pens, more pens than I needed and much nicer ones too. Hell, I even had a fancy fountain pen once. They didn't get it. No one did. It didn't have to make sense to others, though. The pen meant something to me, and I lost it. Whether or not they understood didn't change how I felt."

"Did you ever find it?" Emory asked and shivered against the night's subtle chill. It'd displaced the heat and burrowed beneath his skin.

"No, but I still look for it sometimes. Here's my point. You lost something meaningful to *you*. It's a tragedy to *you*. Just because the men don't understand doesn't mean you can change what Amelia means to you. That girl is your calm sea."

"My what?"

"Your calm sea. When I was a young man chasing the wrong kind, my father told me, 'Look for calm seas.' People wondered how a delicate creature like my mother managed a son-of-a-bitch like him, but she was always the backbone, the strong one. She stilled the storm inside him. A calm sea. Amelia is your calm sea."

Emory nodded, though it took no great deal of introspection to know what Amelia was to him. The thought was beautiful, but Liam left out a crucial part. The sea was at the mercy of the sky. When storms rolled in, calm waters suffered the surge.

"Your mother and Francisca," Emory said, "they endured, but would you say they flourished? Or did they live their lives in service to an organization that robbed them of normalcy and peace of mind?"

Overhead, a floodlight flicked on and left Liam faintly stunned in its light. "They made sacrifices. All the spouses do."

"But our world consumes people. You think a future of

sacrifice is what I want for Amelia? Look at what I do for a living. Look at what's happened now because of it."

"We've all done awful things in our time. You're a good man."

Emory expelled a caustic laugh. "Am I? Sometimes, I have these dreams where my sins are weighed against Ivan's, and the scales come up even. Same darkness. Same monstrosity."

In those nightmares, Emory chased salvation, but the beast lived in him, and when it broke free, it thrived with Ivan by his side, two brothers bonded in blood.

"Bad men don't bother with atonement," Liam said. "I promise you Ivan doesn't worry about that. You are not your brother. You saved Amelia's life. You could've left her at Dauer's, but you didn't. I'm not stupid, Emory. It wasn't opportunistic heroism, was it?"

Liam cast a pointed look at Emory, the answer already in hand, it seemed, but some things needed to be said out loud.

Emory shook his head. "It was more complicated than that."

"Then tell me. Why her?"

A nervous breath passed Emory's lips, an overture to a story seldom told. Denial would be futile, and they were alone in the desert, the secrets they shared between them and the moon riding high.

"When I was ten, Ivan murdered our babysitter. I found him raping her dead body in the woods. He forced me to watch. Most of it's a blur, but I've never forgotten her eyes. I thought people looked peaceful when they died. She didn't. Even in death, she looked helpless and terrified.

"When he was done, we buried her beneath dead leaves. The whole time I felt like I was erasing her. On the way back home, Ivan kept saying, 'You and I, we did this,' like it bound us in some unbreakable way. She wasn't found for months, basically bones by then. I wasn't responsible for her death, but I felt responsible for her disappearance. If I hadn't covered her body so well, maybe they would've found her sooner.

"At the party, I knew Amelia was in danger even before the killing began. I had my chance to get out, but I saw her on the ground, just lying there amongst the dead. I thought she was dead too, but then she opened her eyes and looked just as terrified and helpless as the girl in the woods."

Emory swallowed hard to dismiss the lump in his throat and, with a deep breath, drank in the cool air.

"I can't change the past but thought maybe I could atone for the time I'd been too late, done too little, played a part in erasing someone else. I know a singular moment of morality doesn't pay for a lifetime of sins. The debt doesn't work that way, but she wasn't dead, and I couldn't leave her."

Emory leaned against the wall and stared up at the sky dusted with stars. When he spoke again, it wasn't to Liam. If something up above was listening, he hoped it might hear him.

"I just want her back."

"You're in love with her," Liam said plainly and didn't bother spinning it into a question. There wasn't much need.

"Yes," Emory whispered, the confession aching in his chest, and he'd gladly give his next heartbeat to turn back time. If only he'd told her sooner, it might not have happened.

Liam rested a hand on his shoulder with a slight pressure that encouraged Emory to face him.

"I always wanted a son and prayed he'd be half the man you are," Liam said, his eyes glistening in the moonlight. "Then you came along. A son to me, a good man, more than this world deserves. You were never meant to claim my legacy. I realize that now, and I'm sorry I ever asked you to. Once Ivan's gone and the war is over, I'm setting you free."

Emory laughed. "You say that now."

Liam didn't hold his sentimental musings well. Like too much whiskey, they went to his head.

"I mean it. You want your freedom or not?"

"The oath I took…"

Liam snorted and stubbed his cigar against the wall.

"That oath is meant to keep shit-stirrers in line. 'Lose your way, you lose your head.' Not you. You," he said and pointed his smoldering cigar at Emory, "you are the exception. I brought you into this. I'll find you a way out."

Emory searched Liam's face for a bluff, but the fervor had already started with the promise of freedom, and his head swam with a flood of questions. There'd have to be plans, contingencies, a way to do it safely.

"How though?" Emory asked because so often his dreams orbited just out of reach. Until it was in his hands, he wouldn't trust it. "It's not that simple. What would I tell the others?"

"I never said it'd be simple, and there's a catch, of course. I need you to lead this organization through war. Once we put things to rights, I will build you an off-ramp. You'll be the hero I put to pasture. That's how we'll sell it to the others."

Liam offered his hand. Deals like that existed in word first and legend later, never inked in anything real.

"You really mean it?" Emory asked and cautiously took Liam's hand.

"My integrity lives and dies by my word. What else do any of us have if not that?"

Locked at the eyes, they shook on it and started for the diner. Giddy in such dire times, Emory's first instinct was to tell Amelia. The flash of her smile lit up his thoughts, but the punishing darkness prevailed again. *She's gone,* he reminded himself as his phone rang in his pocket. Emory dug it out and stumbled to a stop as he stared at the screen.

Dauer calling...

A flurry of activity erupted in the diner. The others hovered around Zulu battering his keyboard.

"Where is she?" Emory demanded. "You can have whatever you want. I will give you everything I have. Just give her back to me."

A puff of breath rustled on the other end of the line.

"Little brother," Ivan said in a slow exhale and depravity Emory remembered well—the thrill of the taunt and the chilling way he elongated his words. "Don't speak. Just listen."

Emory's pounding heart plummeted to his stomach and cold

sweat slicked his brow. Dizzy on his feet, his vision blurred at the edges. Through the window, Pete gestured to Emory with a twirl of his finger. *Keep him on the line.*

"Remember that day in the woods, Emory? I've never felt closer to you, more proud to share your blood. She can bring us together again, just like that day. I want to be close to you. I want to taste what you've tasted, feel what you've felt."

Ignited with sterling hatred, Emory's knuckles popped as his hands curled into trembling fists.

"Where is she, you *fucking* psycho? I will tear you apart!" he raged, but the call had already ended.

Emory froze with the phone to his ear. The world moved around him, a million miles an hour or more as he stared in a daze at the screen. He palmed the outside wall to steady himself as grief slackened his frame and saliva filled his mouth. He'd be sick soon.

Inside the diner, Zulu shoved pieces of equipment into bags, and Jack tossed cash to the table. Pete bolted out the door with Corey hastening behind.

"Got it!" Pete hollered and sprinted for the car. "We got a location."

The numbness dissipated and left Emory unsteady on his feet. He removed himself from the wall as the other men hustled from the diner.

He turned to Liam, who smiled softly and said, "Let's find those calm seas."

THIRTY-NINE

AMELIA

Ivan hurled the phone at the wall. Amelia shielded her head as it smashed to pieces that scattered around her. Scraps of hope, so very few, shattered with it. Did Emory even know she was alive? She'd meant to scream so he'd have no doubt, but her voice failed her when it mattered most.

With her nose buried in the crook of her arm, Amelia couldn't even summon tears. A stillness washed over her as the men moved about the room. That stillness quieted the voices in her head, and a memory stepped out of the void.

Years ago, a broken man had barricaded himself in her father's office with a gun to his head. He didn't want to live anymore, and somehow Amelia's father was wrapped up in the man's courtship with death. Her father had reasoned with the man, who left not quite whole but a little less broken. Months later, he thanked her father for saving his life.

"What did you say to him?" Amelia had asked her dad after the ordeal. It was the only good question that came to mind; not why or how or what any of it had to do with Callum Havick. That seemed to matter less.

"I said he was strong," he'd told her. "That he was at war with a loss no father should ever have to endure. It tore him down. He rallied against it. In the trenches, he fought. It raged. He prevailed. Every breath he took, every beat of his heart, was a victory. I said I admired that, strength in the so-called broken. Truth is, he saved himself. I just threw him the rope."

Amelia had listened to the tale in breathless wonder—nothing so riveting had ever happened to people she knew—but her father's remarks slipped through the slats of her ribs and burrowed in her heart. It was there she preserved his words, even after the story itself faded away. A part of her knew she'd need it someday.

Someday had come.

"I need to work," Ivan said ominously and popped his neck.

The men vacated the room but left Richard behind. Amelia came undone with a gasping sob and her heart thundering in her chest. She tried to gain her feet and scramble after. They weren't her saviors but still the only hope she had left. When the door closed, Amelia collapsed to the floor with that same cry, the one like before. It still sounded like someone else; someone already broken, though Ivan hadn't yet started.

He hauled her back to the mattress by her bound wrists. Writhing and screaming, Amelia fought, her body contorting so violently she was certain bones might break. She tried to bite him and almost succeeded in the vicious tussle, but Ivan's hands squeezed around her throat as he forced her to her back. Amelia thrashed beneath him with what little strength she had left until Ivan's ice pick hovered dangerously close to her eye.

"You will die tonight. That's already certain. But if you don't stop, I will make your death slow agony."

With a knife, Ivan sawed through the binds at Amelia's ankles. Only then did she begin to pray. She wouldn't give him the satisfaction of her spoken words, so she kept vigil within her heart. She thought of Gio's prayer card and the Virgin Mother.

Amelia prayed to her, but not to be saved. She was too far down this path, so she prayed instead to float away; for some part of her to drift with the stars until it was over. And if it was going to end for good, she prayed it would be quick and that her mother would come fetch her.

Float away. Just float away. Amelia closed her eyes and willed it to happen.

True to his word, Ivan was the only God with her tonight. He answered her prayer but only because he craved slow torture. He left Amelia unscathed on the mattress and seized on Richard instead.

"Watch," he commanded.

Amelia refused. She had no choice but to listen, though. Time wore on at a glacial pace, and she couldn't say how long it lasted as Richard screamed through the assault. Too petrified to move, Amelia laid against the mattress, her cheek pressed to the damp fabric. Only once did she crack her eyes open. That'd been a tremendous mistake. Ivan stared at her as he thrust into Richard and had probably been watching her the whole time. She squeezed her eyes shut again and cried just to drown out the noise.

When he was done, Ivan pulled over the rusted rolling chair from the back of the room and sat. With his lanky limbs crossed, he chain-smoked cigarettes but didn't speak. The pain in Amelia's shoulder spread to the base of her neck where a headache grew until it throbbed in her temples, and her eyes ached despite the drab light.

"Let me go," Richard wept on the floor and coughed up spittle flecked with blood. "I brought her to you. You can do anything you want with her. Just let me go."

Ivan crawled from the chair and laid down beside Richard with his cheek to the floor. "Of course, I can, but you don't get to decide that. I do."

With each intermission of Ivan's attention on her, Amelia studied the room and committed its layout to heart. At the back, where the fluorescent light didn't reach, was a white door. No one had come or gone from it. With no locks or chains, it lacked the hardware of an important egress.

The toolbox was next to Richard. Before the assault, Ivan had inventoried the tools again and selected his favorite, the ice pick. A heavy-bottomed ash tray littered with cigarette butts sat at the base of the chair. Across the room, a pipe—a foot-and-a-half and dense by the looks of it—was propped against the wall.

"Richard," Ivan said and pushed from the floor, "you were Larry Bickford's defense attorney."

Out of tears, Richard pressed his nose to the ground with a dry heave.

"He was a suspect in Mindy Cartwell's murder," Ivan continued as he paced with the ice pick pressed against his index finger. "You reviewed the evidence and said Larry was an amateur, too inexperienced and stupid to pull off something that heinous. Whoever did those things to her was smart, capable, an expert at their craft."

Ivan stalked to the mattress and knelt beside Amelia. With a frantic whimper, she writhed away.

"Expert at their craft," he repeated mindlessly but seized Amelia by the throat and squeezed hard enough a bone popped.

Float away. Pressure immense, her windpipe crushed. Another pop. *Oh, God.* Nothing numbed. No amount of self-talk could pull her from her body. Mouth agape and panic absolute, Amelia choked for a breath. She kicked her legs and clawed at his hands.

Ivan released his grip. Her first full breath powered another sob. On forearms and knees, Amelia scrambled from him. The ropes seared into her skin, but she ignored the pain. Ungainly in her effort, she managed mere inches.

"Listen to this." Ivan yanked her toward him and jabbed the ice pick at the base of her neck. "Just listen."

Belly down, Amelia laid still. Her master plan went to ashes. *Float away.* It didn't work that way. She felt *everything* just like he knew she would. Ivan crawled on top of her again and licked the tears off her cheek.

"Baby, don't cry," he soothed in a mockery of Emory and had even perfected his voice. It crushed her, the heaviness in her chest diabolical. Ivan would violate her, but why did he have to break her heart?

Float away. He wasn't coming for her. *Float away.* He wouldn't make it in time. *Please let me die now. I think I'm ready.*

Ivan flipped her to her back. Amelia didn't try to fight and couldn't tell if that frustrated him. He grimaced and called out to Richard.

"Describe her body, the condition they found her in."

Amelia stared into the lights that buzzed above. Silence stretched on where Richard didn't speak. When he finally did, it was on a hoarse voice that sputtered a few disjointed recollections.

A heart ripped from her chest. Tongue from her mouth. Body rotted beyond recognition.

"You're all pathetic," Ivan told her and abandoned his ice pick for the folding knife in his pocket. "The screaming, the pleading, the promises you make." He sliced through the binds at her wrists. "When there's nothing left to do, you pray."

Violent trembles wracked Amelia's limbs as Ivan climbed on top of her. His weight crushed her chest and siphoned the air from her lungs. There'd be no floating away from a monster like him. Amelia tried to bite him, buck him off her, scream for help. The effort earned her only pain—in her shoulder, her head, her thighs where his fingers dug into the flesh and pried her legs apart.

"I'm the closest thing to God's love you'll ever know," he told her as his dirty palm slid up the inside of her thigh.

"Please don't! No!" she screamed, but that only delighted him more. He licked his lips and held the knife to her throat.

"Emory should've been here by now. I gave him plenty of time. Remember that when it all goes black. He left you for me. He left you."

The knife blade grazed the inside of her thigh until the sharpened end menaced between her legs, threatening a horror no imagination but his could conjure. The metal door exploded open and slammed into the adjacent wall so hard the warped studs shook. Two Velasco men hurried through.

"You need to come quick," one of them said, winded and with sweat dampening his temples.

Some foul mixture of disappointment and delight surfaced on Ivan's face as he climbed off of her.

"Stay here and watch them," he told one of the men.

Gunfire echoed inside the building as Ivan rushed from the room.

FORTY

EMORY

Atop a hill shrouded in darkness, the six Moriarty men evaluated the building below. They'd backtracked twenty minutes north then cut east down a dark country road. For all Emory knew, they'd driven into the abyss. A smattering of stars above—more than he had ever seen—begged to differ. Beauty like that didn't exist in that diabolical void. Then again, what did he know about the abyss?

The metalworking factory sat forgotten at the end of a gravel road overgrown with brush. A fence ran the perimeter, but the "private property" signs weren't enough to keep the vagrants and junkies out. Human-sized holes punctured the chain-link.

"Did we come this far just to stare at it?" Emory asked. "Let's do the damn thing."

They'd waited long enough and hadn't drawn any attention that Emory could tell. The inaction could make him sick. Next to him, Jack's silhouette itched and twitched for a cigarette. In nicotine-deprived annoyance, he voiced what the others surely thought.

"We don't know the situation in there, their numbers, where they're positioned. We can't just go running in."

Emory surveyed the building again and enumerated the ground they'd have to cover. Six men. Thousands of square feet.

The doubts leeched into his blood and threatened to poison his resolve.

"There are two vehicles," Pete said and pointed to the black SUVs parked near a loading dock. "It's not a guarantee, but that should give some indication of relative numbers. No one has come or gone either. That's a good sign."

Liam moved down the line and slotted himself between Jack and Emory. "We're not gonna know until we get inside."

"What do you suggest?" Emory asked Corey. His battle-savvy paid dividends in these situations.

"We split up inside. Jack, Zulu, and Pete break left at our entry point. You, Liam, and I break right. We enter at the door by the loading dock."

When the others nodded their assent, Liam turned to Emory.

"Are you ready for this?" he asked, his face half in shadows so the others couldn't clock the subtext underscoring the question. Perhaps they hadn't even considered it. Emory had.

Are you willing to die by his hand tonight?

Liam could never ask him directly, not even then, so he shrouded the question in ambiguity and hoped Emory understood. And he did; better than anyone, because long ago he accepted that facing Ivan meant facing death.

Emory gnawed his lip and glanced at the full moon riding high, smaller than it'd been an hour ago but brighter too.

"Yes," he said with a decisive nod, "let's go."

Corey tore into a duffle bag in the trunk and doled out extra ammo along with his age-old homily of making it count—head and chest shots, no indiscriminate firing.

The men split off into their designated groups, and the cars crawled down the hill. Emory winced at the crunch of pea gravel as they rolled through an open gate. They parked alongside the building beneath the shadow of a corrugated steel overhang. The men moved in fluid silence out of the vehicles and crouched between the engine blocks and the outside wall. There was no way the commotion hadn't announced their arrival, but nothing stirred; only the singing of crickets and his men shifting in their squatted positions.

"We stick to Corey's plan," Emory said to the huddle. "Jack, you lead your side. Corey, it's all you for ours, man."

Corey mumbled a "yes, sir" and Jack gave a perfunctory nod. In the back, Zulu stiffened with wide eyes.

"You good?" Emory asked as a measure of solidarity. It didn't rightly matter. They were doing it, no time for self-reflection or pep talks. The kid exhaled a shaky breath and nodded.

"Say your prayers if you got 'em," Corey muttered before leading the way in swift movements that took advantage of the shadows along the wall.

They crept up the metal stairs to the building and gathered at the top. Emory scanned the faces of his men contemplating what lurked behind the metal door. It didn't need saying. They all knew this was the most dangerous part. He gripped his Glock and steadied his finger along the trigger guard. Corey turned to him, panting and giddy with an adrenaline rush.

"Ready, Chief?"

Emory nodded and Corey whipped open the door. Silence swallowed up the echo as it collided against the outside wall. With an all-clear, they spilled inside with weapons drawn.

The gutted-out space was vacuous with exposed beams and cinderblock walls. A row of empty metal shelves lined the middle and transom-like windows near the ceiling offered meager light.

Emory followed Corey to the right with Liam behind. Jack, Pete, and Zulu broke left. The place smelled of mold, and the building gave a haunting, metallic sigh as a breeze picked up outside.

With his eyes adjusted to the dark, Emory scanned for movement as they collectively swept toward twin doors, one on each side of the space. Every breath hitched hard in his chest as they approached. In a mirror image, the two groups of men stood with their backs against opposite walls. Corey counted down on his fingers and stared at Jack, who palmed the doorknob on the other side.

Three. Two. One.

Emory lifted his gun. The doors flung open in unison, and both Corey and Jack recoiled with backs flush against the wall.

Still nothing, just an empty corridor on Jack's side with no signs of life and surely the same on their side too. Emory's jaw clenched as he bit back a slew of expletives but refused to voice the fear rattling in the back of his head. *She's not here.*

"You're clear," Jack mouthed. Corey nodded the same.

They paused a beat before Corey slipped into the empty hall. Emory followed and stared down the front sight of his weapon. The corridor reeked of decay. Water-rotted walls buckled from age, abandonment, and the assault of the elements, and brown stains splotched what was left of the drop ceiling. Gunfire rang out in the distance behind them.

"Sounds like Jack got himself a warm welcome," Corey said and eased around the corner at the end of the hall.

The gunfire oddly comforted. It meant they were in the right place, at least. Down another corridor, they slipped toward a door where a jaundiced glow emanated from a square door light.

"Who the fuck is that?" Corey asked about the bald man's head perfectly framed in the glass pane.

He sat on a fold-out table, blithely unaware of their approach as he bullshitted with someone else in the room. Next to the table, another door opened to an area stacked with pallets and boxes.

"Velasco," Emory said and recognized the man by his fleshy jowls and sweat-soaked temples. At Rich's party, he'd barely kept up with his cohorts.

They knelt when they reached the door and Corey turned to Liam with a shit-eating grin. "You good, old man?"

Liam rolled his eyes. "I wrote the book on this, boy. Quit your talking and let's go."

Corey bolted up and delivered one violent kick to the wooden door. It splintered as it exploded open and half of the bald man's head bathed the wall behind him with Corey's shot. The other man fumbled with his weapon as Emory buried a bullet between his eyes. He collapsed, dead before he hit the floor and blood streaking the wall behind him.

Chaos erupted on cue. Bullets ripped through the open area, splitting wood as they tore through empty pallets. At least five Velasco men spilled through doorways on an uproar of shouted orders. The mishmash of tactics sent their men scattering in opposite directions.

Corey laid down cover fire as Emory and Liam hurried into the fray and ducked behind a stack of pallets. Jack and the others barreled in and picked off Velasco men who scrambled for cover.

Emory's pulse thundered in his ears. The hair on his arms stood on end. He might've chalked it up to the way his body hummed and blood pumped, senses singing on high alert.

Beside him, though, a corridor enrobed in darkness housed a shadow. One cold winter's night so many years ago, Emory deciphered that same presence. It had sickened with unnatural dread, the same dread that afflicted him now with a cold sweat slicking the back of his neck. Tonight, that presence would force Emory to meet it in the abyss.

"Go!" Liam nudged Emory toward the hall. "We'll take care of this. Go."

FORTY-ONE

AMELIA

Amelia scrambled to the wall. With her back against it, her heart hammered in her chest as her eyes darted across the room. The pipe was between Richard and the back door. It was her best option, but the window of opportunity was closing fast. Soon, it'd slam shut altogether.

No one's gonna throw you the rope. She'd have to do it herself. The notion loosened her fear. Bit by bit, she broke from its hold and rejected the lies it told her. She could save herself and was strong enough to try.

In small, innocuous movements, Amelia eased from the wall. The Velasco man turned to her. She froze and let her gaze fall to her lap, but the weight of his stare pressed into her with silent warning. Beyond the metal door, noises came closer, just creaks and groans at first. Before long, though, they echoed through the hollow belly of the building.

The guard shifted uneasily on his feet and poked his head into the hall. Amelia eyed the pipe and rallied against a sharp splinter of doubt. One hit—one hard hit—would put the man down long enough for her to run. She might lose the battle, and with it her life, but no one would ever say she didn't fight.

More commotion and the all-too-familiar sound of gunfire grew louder. Men shouted dissonant orders—go there, head there, don't come any closer. Confusion steadily surmounted as chaos made its way toward the room. The Velasco man clung to his gun with a white-knuckle grip, but his hands shook.

Amelia zeroed in on his fear. She held her breath, counted silently to three, and bolted from the wall. Shaky legs almost took her down. Across the room, she scooped up the pipe just as the guard rushed toward her.

Amelia swung hard as he lifted his gun. The pipe cut through the air. By instinct, he dropped his weapon, and the pipe collided against his palms. He yanked it and Amelia toward him. She lost her footing and tumbled to the ground but clung to the pipe for dear life. The violence of her fall sent the guard down with her. Her chin hit the floor hard and busted open her lip again. As her mouth filled with blood, the pipe rolled away.

On her hands and knees, Amelia clambered after it. The guard cinched her ankle and ripped her backwards. On her stomach, reaching, stretching, arm howling in pain, her open palm pounded the concrete. Amelia flipped to her side. Her unburdened foot smashed into the man's face. Stunned, his nose gushed blood, and he let go of her ankle.

Amelia dashed for the pipe. She grabbed it up and spun around. The pipe cracked against his temple with a spray of blood. He crumpled to his knees before the upper half of his body toppled over.

Bedlam rocked the building as Amelia ran for the back door. Richard gaped at her and the utter audacity that she might survive and of her own volition too, strength in the so-called broken. He'd written her off as a victim—the sad girl who could hardly speak up for herself, let alone fight for her life.

On his knees, he reached for her with bound hands, his face puckered with swollen wounds and his mouth warped in fear.

"You can't do this! They'll kill me. Do you want that kind of blood on your hands?"

"Get fucked," she said and ran for the white door at the back of the room as Richard cried out.

"Amelia! *Fucking* cunt!"

The white door hid the great unknown. It could be anything, a closet or some other dead end. That didn't matter. She'd take her chances before she'd ever accept certain death. With the pipe in hand, Amelia rushed through and into a short corridor line with windows to the outside, some busted out.

She sprinted to the end of the hall, through another door and into the night. A blast of humid air bathed her skin. Her senses dulled as she fled down a flight of metal stairs to the ground below. Along the building's perimeter, headlights pierced the night and closed in quickly as she fled.

FORTY-TWO

EMORY

With blind wrath closing in, Emory sprinted after the shadow. His legs, faintly numb, moved of their own accord, propelling him forward as he followed the shadow into a room off the hall. Once inside, the door slammed shut and delivered him into the darkness.

What did Emory know of the abyss? Everything.

He knew how it consumed with an inexorable hatred that ripped at the soul. He knew its violent allure, the gruesome promise it made. And, as the shadow approached, he knew the internal fury it provoked.

Emory's hands shot out in front of him but groped dead space. A maddening silence devoured all sound, all but the frantic beat of his heart, until a heaviness slithered up next to him.

"Little brother," Ivan whispered, his fetid breath warming the shell of Emory's ear. "You can't know how much I've missed you."

Bony fingers gripped Emory's shoulder, the sharp nails digging in. Emory whipped around. Blacker than black, the shadow moved through the void again.

"Where is she?" Emory bellowed and charged forward, colliding into a table and upending items that clattered to the floor. His knees locked, suddenly stiff and ungainly as he righted himself.

Ivan issued a horrid laugh, unchanged after all these years. The same laugh had taunted Emory through his childhood and in the nightmares since. Pressure built in Emory's chest, and his throat ached.

"You brought Amelia into your world," Ivan said and cast a circle around Emory as he spoke. "You knew this would happen. I think you wanted it to."

"No," Emory whispered.

With his heart in his stomach, he spun around to keep up. Images of Amelia flashed in his mind—her smile, her touch, the other ways he might've kept her safe without going so far. *I can't do this.*

"You never take me at my word. What did I promise you?"

Another taunt, Emory couldn't keep up. Winded and dizzy, though they had only just begun, his breaths came ragged.

"Stop," he commanded but lost his nerve as he fired a shot. It buried in the wall somewhere behind him. *Make it count.*

As ever, Ivan remained one step ahead. "Piece by piece, limb by limb, I tore her apart, just like you knew I would. You set 'em up. I knock 'em down." Ivan shuffled to a stop and spoke again. "Another life we destroyed together. I wanted to be close to you. Deep inside, you wanted it too."

Emory inched forward until the tips of his boots met another pair of feet. In the darkness, he stood face-to-face with his brother.

"You're lying," he said hoarsely and licked the sweat from his upper lip. "Tell me where she is. I'll give you anything you want."

"Anything?"

"Yes."

Ivan hovered close to Emory. The noises beyond the door dampened, and silence grew as thick as the darkness until Ivan spoke again.

"I want you," he whispered, "because your soul is wrecked, just like mine. You and I are kindred in that way. You bury your instincts, but it keeps you up at night, never knowing when you'll lose control. You took your little blood oath, but when you're burning up for all the wrong you've done, you know who you're bound in blood with. It's not them, Emory. It's me. Bloodlines will always trump blood oaths."

Don't let him in, self-preservation warned, but it was too late. The reckoning had begun; sins weighed and evil doled out. Emory backed away, groping in the dark for something to hold on to and guide him out of there. His chest constricted, each inhale more labored than the last, and he faintly registered the wetness of tears on his cheeks.

A click ushered in the light and Emory squinted against a single bulb swinging from the ceiling. He studied his brother's face up close for the first time in years. He'd committed it to memory, searched for it around every corner in waking life and in nightmares too.

Only then, Emory barely recognized it. Hollow cheeks and sharp bones protruding from thin skin gave a skeletal effect, but the black of his good eye was the worst of it. With placid lunacy, it housed the knowledge of his wicked deeds but none of the burden or anguish.

"You look like our father," Ivan said and contemplated the tears on Emory's cheeks, "cry like him too."

Ivan approached, his hand lifted in a mockery of tenderness. Muscles tensing, Emory flinched when Ivan's palm met his cheek and collected the tears there.

"On his dying breath, he begged for my help. He didn't want to die, didn't want to leave you and Mirabelle alone with me. So, he cried and he begged. They always do."

A ghastly smile unfolded on Ivan's thin lips. Forgotten pain burned in Emory. He'd always believed his father died alone. That would've been a kindness.

"You left him to die?" Emory asked, incredulous, as he steadied himself against the wall.

Ivan stood several inches shorter than him and was noticeably much thinner than Emory remembered. Why then did he seem so larger than life and impossible to defeat?

"No. I watched then left. Later, I came for you, but you'd packed up our sister and sought sanctuary in false brotherhood. It can't protect you or her forever. You know that."

Ivan circled to Emory's side and forced him to retreat from the wall. Emory lifted his gun that wavered in trembling hands.

"Where is Amelia?" he demanded tremulously.

"She was the wrong kind, but I made do," Ivan said and leaned in close, his lips brushing Emory's cheek. "My God, she was sweet."

A familiar scent wafted from Ivan's shirt. Something floral. Something sugary. *Ice cream in a rose garden*. It shattered the spell.

In a savage eruption, Emory launched himself at Ivan and slammed hard into his bony frame. Together, they collided to the floor. Emory's shoulder padded the fall but screamed with a sharp, splintering pain. A struggle ensued of thrown elbows, knees, and fists, but neither gained anything as strength met strength in an entanglement of limbs until Ivan flipped on top of Emory.

Emory adjusted the gun in his sweat-soaked palm. He tried to lift his arm, but Ivan's fist cracked across his face. The hit stunned. Emory's eyes watered, and the iron bite of blood filled his mouth with another hit. Arms raised, he shielded himself from the assault, but, with the heels of his hands, Ivan clamped Emory's temples and squeezed hard until his vision blurred at the edges.

Ivan slammed Emory's head against the concrete floor, once and then twice. The black vignette tightened as Ivan lifted Emory's head again. One more smash, and lights out. With his last bit of strength, Emory thrust his hips and thrashed his legs. Blood pooled in his nose, making it hard to breathe until Ivan's grip slipped.

Emory toppled Ivan and climbed on top. His hands coiled around Ivan's throat. Rage commanded his grip until he felt bones pop. His teeth gnashed with the satisfaction. *More*. He squeezed harder with primal instinct coursing through him. *Kill or be killed. Do it.*

"Where is she?" he raged and smashed his fist into Ivan's mouth. Another brutal hit shattered his front teeth. The broken bits sliced Emory's knuckles. Ivan choked on the blood filling his mouth as he squirmed out from underneath.

Emory grabbed his gun and sprung to his feet. When Ivan dove into him, they collided through the door and into the hall. The spindly lunatic had no right to his strength, and each of Emory's punches seemed to register no pain, only grunts. They wove around one another, slower and panting as they swung their weight into each other.

Ivan hurled himself at Emory again but crashed into the wall as Emory darted out of the way. *End it.* He trained his gun on Ivan. Panting on the floor, Ivan stared up at Emory but made no move to defend himself, so his hands fell to his sides.

"You can't do it, can you?" Ivan spit out a mouthful of blood at Emory's feet. "If you kill me, something dies in you too, the part of yourself you cherish the most; the hatred that's become your purpose."

Emory squatted in front of Ivan and, like a serpent's strike, violently seized him by the throat. He pressed his gun to the middle of Ivan's forehead.

"Where is she?"

Are you ready for this?

Emory swallowed hard. He'd spent so many years hunting the wrong answer to the question. Delighting in the hesitation, Ivan laughed as shouts sounded from a room farther down the hall.

"Amelia's getting away!" Richard Dauer yelled. "Someone come get her!"

Emory hopped to his feet and blindly started down the hall but stopped halfway. He lifted his gun and spun around. Ivan limped along the wall. Another glob of blood filled his mouth, and he flashed a crimson smile.

"Me or her?" Ivan rasped and edged farther away. Behind him, the open area had cleared out, all but a few dead bodies sprawled on the floor. "You can't have both."

Their eyes met with common knowledge passing between

them and the only thing they'd ever agree on—it ended when one of them was dead.

Emory didn't move in either direction. Time slowed as Ivan shuffled backward. Gun lifted, Emory followed, unable to look away or change course. If only a handful of moments in life truly defined one's fate, this was surely one.

"You hate me more than you'll ever love her," Ivan said as he stood at the far edge of moonlight streaming across the floor. Shadows gathered at his back. With another backwards step, he beckoned Emory to join him, drawing him once again into the darkness.

Emory could follow him there and into the depths of depravity. Perhaps it was where he belonged. He strode toward the edge of madness, closer to his brother who looked in raptures as the gap closed between them.

End it.

Stopping short of the shadows, Emory pulled the trigger. The recoil ripped through him, sending a shockwave of pain through his shoulder. He ran for the room down the hall and looked back the moment before he careened inside.

Blacker than black again, Ivan's silhouette hobbled around the corner, not dead but evidently injured. Like a phantasm, vaporous in the way he evanesced back into the abyss, Ivan was gone.

FORTY-THREE

AMELIA

Amelia raced down the rusty staircase. She nearly lost her footing as she jumped from the second-to-last step and hit the ground with shaky knees. Her ankle tweaked with a shock of pain, but she righted herself and remembered her mettle. She couldn't quit now, not when she'd come this far.

She rounded the building's corner and sprinted its length with a chain-link fence to her right. Her legs burned, pumping hard as she hurled toward freedom before stumbling to an abrupt stop. At the end of the building, the fence blocked her path.

Amelia steadied herself with another sip of air and hoped like hell it was just a trick of the moonlight. As she got closer, though, the fence remained, a culmination of her fears woven together with a curl of barbed wire on top.

There was nowhere to go but backwards where pain and death awaited her. *I can't turn back.* For the past month, she hadn't chosen how she'd lived, but she could choose how she died. It wasn't there and not like that.

"It's okay. It's okay. It's okay," she muttered in fast succession and a surge of adrenaline.

She'd have to climb. The barbed wire could do its worst, but torn to shreds would be a blessing compared to what Ivan had in store. Amelia sucked in a hard breath and approached the fence.

Gravel crackled behind her, and dread pooled in Amelia's gut, her stomach roiling. Someone had followed her. She wouldn't get out without a fight. She sidelined the urge to vomit and gripped the pipe.

This is it.

All she had to do was hold on and swing hard. She'd done it once. She could do it again. With her heart slamming in her chest, Amelia turned around. She lifted her eyes from the ground in a hesitant sweep to Ivan, who'd found her, no doubt.

She didn't register who she saw instead. He'd come for her. He didn't have to. He could've read her note, called it a loss, and let her go. The pipe hit the ground, and a knot ached in her throat as Amelia groped the fence beside her.

Emory stood there as if ripped from a dream. His chest heaved with something between exhaustion and exhilarated relief. Pain tore across his face smeared with blood. Eyes to the sky, he mumbled something to the moon before his hands went to his knees and he doubled over.

Amelia closed her eyes. Maybe it really was just a cruel dream, and she'd wake staring at that cinder block wall with a shadow bearing down on top of her.

Another crunch of gravel came, though.

Then another.

More still, faster, almost running.

Amelia opened her eyes as Emory rushed toward her.

She set her legs in motion too. Where her steps staggered, Emory's were forceful and determined, and the distance between them melted away until they collided. Face buried against Emory's chest, Amelia breathed him in; dirt, sweat, blood, and, somewhere beneath, his familiar scent. His heart thrummed a frenzied rhythm against her cheek as he wrapped her in his arms.

"You came," she whispered, dizzy as her fingertips lightly clawed at his chest. "You came for me."

Amelia lifted her head to meet his astounded gaze. Emory cradled her face, his palms warm and sticky with blood. His bottom lip was busted open, and blood smeared his cheek and stained his white t-shirt.

He exhaled a baffled breath as he searched her face. "Of course, I did. I was never gonna leave you. Not now, not then, not ever."

Emory dipped his head just as Amelia rolled to her toes. The kiss they shared tasted of blood and home and everything she craved. He must've craved it too and pulled her deeper into the embrace. One hand pressed to the small of her back, and the other cradled her head, his fingers sinking into her hair.

A car approached at the end of the building, its headlights cutting a path across the dirt. Jack climbed out, and another vehicle pulled up with more Moriarty men spilling out.

"We need to get out of here," Emory said and scooped her up.

He carried her to a car where Liam climbed into the back. Amelia studied him up close—the slope of his nose and cut of his jaw. If she looked away or let him go, he might vanish, so she kept her eyes on him. As he moved to lower her into the car, Amelia snaked her arms around his neck.

"You have to let go of me long enough to get in," he laughed, warm and deep, the sound like being submerged in hot water after having been out in the cold for so long. The sensation tingled up Amelia's spine. She unwound her arms as he placed her in the passenger seat.

Emory sped away from the warehouse and onto a back road that eventually dumped them onto the highway. The moon hovered outside the window, a silver chariot racing alongside and granting safe passage home.

Amelia held Emory's hand and watched the movements he made—the way his left wrist draped over the steering wheel and right arm leaned into the center console; the way he'd periodically narrow his eyes at the rearview mirror.

"You look at me like it's been lifetimes since we saw each other last," he remarked as highway lights spilled into the car.

Hadn't it been? Their first encounters were a distant shore of strange memories. That past life of fear and frustration bent the knee to the unexpected and indescribable. They'd crossed oceans of fear, mistrust, and uncertainty to reach this place with one another.

"I didn't think I'd see you again," Amelia said but tucked away the rest. She'd come close to a brutal end, and the what-ifs would gladly devour her if she let them.

Emory watched the road, his face impassive as ever, but raised her hand to his lips and kissed her knuckles.

"Here I am," he said. "Here we are."

When he glanced at her, Amelia glimpsed in Emory what he must've seen in her too—the rapture of reunion after a veritable lifetime apart. She scooted against the center console, and Emory draped his arm around her, as close as they could get.

Here we are.

FORTY-FOUR

EMORY

Empty roads led the way back home. Halfway there, the night rescinded its light as low clouds crowded out the moon. Emory punched the gas on a charcoal stretch of highway and eyed the clock. *11:33.* They'd be on the wrong side of midnight soon.

The superstition had started after his mother died. Emory's father kept the peace in their household well enough for a widower. After work, he'd scrounge up dinner and shoo Mirabelle and Emory to bed after dessert and a little TV. For the rest of the night, the radio would croon in the living room until Ivan came home. The fights started then, always after midnight.

Huddled against his bedroom door, Emory would listen to the chaos unfold. He'd heard all sorts of ugliness—arguments, accusations, threats. Somehow, his old man always sensed his presence.

"You're on the wrong side of midnight, boy," he'd holler down the hall. It sent Emory back to bed but never to sleep.

"What's on the wrong side of midnight?" he asked once, serious enough that his father understood he wasn't being flippant.

"Nothing good. Bad dreams and bad ideas. Stay on the right side of midnight and life will treat you well."

At a quarter 'til, they pulled into Liam's circle drive. Emory collected a shell-shocked Amelia from the car and led her by the hand inside. The foyer was dark save the parlor's light seeping across the floor. Emory collapsed to a settee against the foyer's far wall and pulled Amelia down with him.

Relief drained him, the fatigue all-consuming and painful in its own right. He nursed the urge to fall asleep with Amelia in his arms and wake when the nightmare ended. It didn't work that way. The only way out was through.

"Where are you hurt?" he asked and surveyed her injuries.

Before she could answer, he pushed the blood-soaked shirt from her shoulder. Earlier, he'd noticed the stain and its coppery scent but not the gruesome bite beneath.

Amelia yanked the shirt back in place. She wrapped her arms around his middle and burrowed her face into his chest. On the ride back, she'd been alarmingly calm. Safely home, she came apart with a shuddering cry. The bite was just the beginning. Ivan branded her with something else—the same terror he'd planted in Mirabelle, the kind Emory couldn't seem to chase away.

"I got you. You're okay," he soothed. The tighter he held her, the harder she shook. "We made it."

Emory loosed a sigh that ached in his chest. The house stirred around them as the men clambered in and Mirabelle rushed down the stairs. They ignored the others and held onto one another.

"The things he was going to do to me," Amelia whispered. Tears clung to her lashes and broke free as she shook her head. "What if he comes again? What if he—"

Emory pressed his mouth to hers to stop the flow of words. Her bottom lip was busted, just like his, so blood laced the kiss.

"Listen to me," he said. "I'd set the whole goddamn world on fire and watch it burn before I'd let anyone hurt you. Not him, not anyone."

In his periphery, the parlor light ebbed and flowed as Corey paced the floor. The other men had gathered there too. Pete dipped into the foyer, his face a mask of dread.

"Chief, sorry to interrupt. We need to talk to you."

This shit never ends. "Do we really have to do this now? Whatever it is can wait."

"It's just—"

"It can fucking wait!" he snapped, ready to come out of his skin again if it meant finding an escape.

Amelia had him on borrowed time and glanced at the parlor where the others waited. Pete retreated, but his intrusion had already poisoned the well.

Emory rested his forehead against hers. "They can wait," he whispered.

But for how long? The parlor stirred with unrest, and Liam's voice rose with atypical heat. *I don't want to be here.* Emory stiffened and squeezed his eyes shut. With the adrenaline wearing off, pain exploded at his cheek and radiated across his shoulders.

"You're hurt," Amelia said softly. He nodded. "Where?" she asked.

Heaviness grew in his chest. It was always there, never really went away. He learned to live with its gravity and all the ways it weighed him down. He didn't dwell on where it came from or when it started. Some part of him already knew.

"I can't do this anymore. I can't." His voice cracked with age-old hurts, the rotten things he buried so they wouldn't eat him alive. In the foyer, in the dark, they devoured him. "We need to leave. We need to get out of here."

Emory eyed the front door. Why had it never occurred to him to set himself free? No one expected him to bolt. They never would. He patted his pocket and his car keys there. Phone in his back pocket. Wallet in his car. Amelia in his arms. Everything he needed was within reach.

"Let's just go." Emory took her hand and went to stand, but Amelia held onto him with surprising strength and forced him to sit.

She lifted her hands to his cheeks, her touch soft and honey in the look she gave. Everything about her came slathered in that sweetness. Even now with a busted lip and mangled shoulder, smelling of blood and sweat, and with mascara streaking her cheeks, she treated him tenderly in spite of the horrors she'd endured. The world needed strength like hers. He needed it too.

"Emory, what are you talking about? We can't leave."

He shook his head and covered over her hands at his cheeks with his own. Since when did she invest in the lie that he couldn't walk away? *Since you brought her into this. Since you made her believe.*

"Run away with me. Please. We'll go somewhere he can't find us."

The frenzy started up again, an animal pacing the cage. Desperation clouded his judgment, and he had no business hatching plans so close to the wrong side of midnight. He didn't care and would gladly disregard logic just to be set free.

Amelia licked the blood off her lip and combed her fingers through the hair at his temples. It soothed him, she already knew. In their nights together, she did it when he couldn't sleep.

"We can't. Not right now."

Shoulders slumped, Emory dropped his eyes to her chest rising and falling in steady rhythm. His calm sea, what he wouldn't give to rest a bit on her quiet shores. Strong as she was, she couldn't shield him from the inevitable, though, and a silhouette filled the parlor door's frame.

"Emory, now," Liam demanded. Shadows shrouded his face, and the parlor clock started its midnight chimes. "Something else has happened. This can't wait."

FORTY-FIVE

EMORY

Emory arrived in the parlor on the wrong side of midnight. The men quieted as he slid shut the pocket door. Liam stood at the fireplace where flames crackled and sufficed as comfort. The rest opted for the warmth of whiskey. A bottle traveled the circle that included Thomas emptied of apologies and Disco sullenly avoiding Emory's stare. Jack, Corey, Pete, and Zulu perched throughout the room.

In an unintended homage to the shadow walk, Jack stepped aside to let Emory into the circle and waited for him to join. It wasn't enough that Emory had left Amelia to come in here. They needed him back in the fold and committed to the brotherhood.

What more do they want from me? Everything, it seemed.

Emory stepped forward, the circle complete. Like those desert nights gathered around sacred flames, something powerful existed there but so too did the sinister and unspoken.

"What happened?" he asked.

The men exchanged ashen-faced glances that entreated someone else to speak. Jack finally did.

"Three street soldiers from Disco's crew were dumped outside our headquarters in Vegas. They were missing hands. Their cocks were cut off and stuffed in their mouths."

Emory drew a breath and closed his eyes, but the vision in the dark was no less vivid. The Velascos had always been violently inventive. Ivan would sharpen that flair, give it purpose and place, and dead bodies would pile up, brutalized in ways that'd sour the stomach and boggle the mind.

"War's here," Corey remarked to no one in particular, perhaps just himself, but for the benefit of the room too.

The burden of leadership landed at Emory's feet. He'd shoulder that responsibility if nothing more than for the expectant and faintly fearful eyes peering at him, battle weary though it was just the beginning. The road map of past precedence ended, and they would travel off the page. *The only way out is through.*

"Enough is enough," Emory said with scant composure and his heart pounding in his ears. "I won't tolerate our own being ripped to pieces and dumped on our doorstep. If the Velascos want brutality, they'll get it in spades. We will define a whole new meaning for them."

"There's more," Corey said and turned to Disco. "Give him the ground truth."

Disco cleared his throat and pinned his eyes to the floor. "Some captains think our organization won't survive a war and maybe it's better to break off now."

Emory drew a deep breath. "How many?"

"Five that I know of. Eli and Scotty are the most vocal, but Marcus, Sal, and Nate share the sentiment."

Disco shook his head as if it were a crying shame, as if he hadn't fudged the numbers and counted himself out. Emory turned to Jack, whose cheeks flushed red. Treachery must've never crossed his mind. Good time Jack, boozing and bantering, wouldn't notice the divide, not until the earth split and swallowed them whole.

Emory fetched the whiskey bottle from Pete and took a swig. Only on rare occasions did the men see him drink—shadow walks, funerals, weddings. He marked the milestones but scarcely the road between. They watched him as he held the room in silence.

"That tracks with what I've seen." Emory swished another slug of booze on the inside of his cheek to dull the pain. "I would've said six, though."

He stared at Disco in a winged-back chair too large for his slender frame. He'd always carried himself bigger than what he was and had the stuffy, bespectacled appearance of a scholarly man. He'd never looked the part. Disco said nothing but pressed his lips together and clasped white-knuckled hands in his lap.

Emory returned the bottle to Pete and presented the door with an outstretched arm. "Thomas, Disco, you're free to leave."

The circle tightened after the two men left, as if the walls might soak up secrets shared there. Emory noticed how battered his men were. Blood matted Pete's golden curls from a nasty cut to the scalp. Half of the knuckles on Corey's right hand were busted. A bullet graze split open Zulu's forearm. It wouldn't need stitches, but the cut mangled a bit of tattoo work.

"We can't go to war if we don't trust our own brothers," Emory said, though he knew damn well war wouldn't wait for loyalties to align. "We have to put a tourniquet on this. It's the only way we'll have a fighting chance. We'll focus on Scotty and Eli. Marcus, Nate, and Sal will fall in line with some persuasion. Corey, I want you to keep an eye on Disco."

"It's Scotty, man," Pete said and chewed a hangnail. "Eli's just a hothead. He'll come around. Scotty's got the chip on his shoulder."

Emory might've guessed as much. Grievances always boiled down to three things—money, women, pride. Years ago, Scotty fancied himself a shoo-in for captain of Las Vegas post. When Liam appointed Emory instead, Scotty cried nepotism to anyone who'd listen. Few did, and the stunt landed him a post in cakewalk territory no one else wanted.

"We need someone trusted inside Scotty's territory," Jack said. "Do we have anyone who can blend in and go unnoticed?"

Emory surveyed the circle, and each man shook his head, all but Pete.

"Zules, how do you feel about Northern California?" Pete asked but looked to Emory. "What do you think? It's not uncommon for green soldiers to move crews. I'd be willing to loan him."

Emory mulled it over. Trust broke down the ranks. If he couldn't trust Scotty, then he couldn't trust Scotty's inner circle either. He needed an embed.

"If I send you to Redding post, can you be my eyes and ears?" Emory asked Zulu.

The kid nodded. "I'll be there as soon as you need me."

"Thank you. You came through tonight, and I owe you," Emory told Zulu and then the broader room, "Same goes for the rest of you."

Corey brushed aside the kudos and asked, "What about the white line operation? Do we bother with that now?"

Emory glanced at Liam. Still entranced by the flames, he rubbed his chin but offered no sage words. Emory already knew what he'd say. *Keep your head.*

"Yes," Emory said. The men would want blood—and rightfully so—but they couldn't lose sight of broader strategy. "We need to create stress fractures in the Velascos. We hit them where it hurts first—their longest-serving captain, their Gio. When morale's low, we feed discontent in the lower ranks. We send the message none of this would've happened if it weren't for Ivan. We never wanted this and have a common enemy. With any luck, they turn from the bottom up."

"With no luck, we risk escalation," Corey said.

"True," Emory conceded, "but that's always a risk, and we can't roll over on what happened tonight. They'll keep pushing boundaries if we do. We hit back hard and signal we'll negotiate only if they give up Ivan."

The men concurred with a round of nods. Emory ran his fingers through grimy hair crusted with sweat and dried blood.

"That's all I have," he said. "Stay safe. We'll get through this."

The last part tasted bitter rolling off his tongue. *We'll get through this.* He'd said it as much for himself as the others, and when the men filed past him and said goodnight, he couldn't rightly tell if they believed it either. For the time being, it'd do.

After Corey, Pete, and Zulu left, Emory sunk into the sofa and Jack into the winged-back chair. Liam remained at the fireplace where the flames popped and hissed. He'd been uncommonly quiet but turned to Emory and Jack.

"You boys came here as a precaution. This place isn't a safe haven anymore. Bad things are bound to happen if you stay."

Jack puffed an offended breath. "What are you saying?"

"That you and Emory need to leave."

"I'm not running away scared—"

"And I'm not asking!" Liam pounded the mantle. A porcelain vase, ancient and undoubtedly irreplaceable, wobbled close to the edge. Liam paid no attention to it and leveled furious eyes at Jack. "War is here. The armistice with the Velascos is over. It won't be reinstated. Ivan will be back. These are certainties that promise bloodshed and death. You're leaving, and I'm not negotiating terms."

To Jack's obvious dismay, Emory agreed. "He's right. We're sitting ducks if we stay here."

"And what do you suggest?" Jack fired back.

Emory stood, knees popping and cheek smarting. Sooner or later, he wouldn't be cut out for this shit anymore, and his body would fail long before his mind.

"I'll head to California with Amelia," Emory said but left out the rest. It'd be a one-way trip. "I'll set up headquarters at my home there. It's well enough off the grid, and the Velascos don't have reach into that territory. If I can pull Ivan out of the woodwork, he'll have less backing there than in Vegas. I'll deal with Scotty. Pete will come with me and keep an eye on Zulu."

"And Miri?" Jack asked with a hopeful ring that seemed to both thrill and sicken him. He never attached himself to one woman for long. To Jack, love was a liability.

"You and Miri will go back to Vegas. You'll oversee Corey's

takeover. If Disco steps out of line, you do the needful. You and I will handle war plans. Pete and Corey will rally the rest of the captains. We need to mind the morale and make sure the men and their families are taken care of."

Jack chuckled, pulled out a cigarette, and rolled the filter between his thumb and index finger. Emory studied him, the dirt caked beneath his fingernails and the childhood scar from a broken arm. Brave Jack, where did he go? The man in the chair had hair that hung in strings and hunched as if he were chilly. More likely, his vices had him in a stranglehold.

"If you can't handle it, I'll take Miri with me," Emory said.

Jack's eyes snapped to him. "When did I say I couldn't handle it?"

"When did you show me you could?"

"How about tonight? Risking my life to save her *fucking* hide again!"

Jack flung a hand toward Amelia's bedroom upstairs. A wave of anger seized on Emory. His blood coursed hot with savage visions of squeezing Jack's neck the way he'd squeezed Ivan's.

"Enough!" Liam barked and inserted himself between them. "I can't have you two squabbling over trivial bullshit." He swung around to Jack. "Amelia is one of us now and Emory's queen. You'll respect her as such and shut the fuck up about it. End of story."

"And you." Liam turned to Emory. "It's embarrassing it took you this long to realize Jack and Mirabelle are together. Your sister is a grown woman and could do far worse than Jack. Count your blessings, and quit your bitching."

In the subdued light, Emory and Jack locked eyes. He looked remorseless and vindicated. For what, Emory didn't know.

"You two will leave tomorrow afternoon," Liam said. "We can't be scattered forever, so this is just until we sort out our own."

"What about you?" Emory asked. "You pulled it out tonight, but you're not a young man anymore. You need to be with me or Jack."

"This is where I belong. If that little shit shows up here, I'll kill him myself."

Liam's eyes crinkled at the corners with a hollow laugh. It momentarily dispelled the tension until a knock sounded at the door and Mirabelle peeked inside.

"Sorry to interrupt," she said. "Emory, can I talk to you?"

With nothing left to discuss, Emory waved her in as Jack and Liam said their goodnights and left. Mirabelle stood at the room's center as Emory took up Liam's spot at the mantle.

She'd washed off her makeup and changed into pajamas, her hair still wet from the shower. Something in her hesitation and doll-like features—big eyes laden with regret and a mouth drawn into a pitiful frown—reminded Emory of when they were kids.

"I'm sorry," she said carefully, as if dipping a toe into turbid water.

When Emory refused a response, Mirabelle stamped her foot and halved the distance between them.

"I said I'm sorry!"

He glared at her. "I heard you the first time."

"And you won't forgive me. Amelia's upstairs, afraid but alive, and you won't forgive me."

"I owe you nothing!" Emory bellowed and slammed the mantle with his fist.

The vase tottered off the edge and shattered on the floor. Mirabelle swatted away tears with a shaky hand.

"How can you be this cold?"

"I can't forgive you right now, so stop saying you're sorry if that's all you're after."

Mirabelle knew him better than that. He wasn't surly for sport, just quick to anger and slow to forgive. For her, a rebuffed apology was an open wound she'd pack with bandages and wonder why it festered. *"You gotta let things breathe,"* Emory often told her. Forever her folly, she never listened.

Emory toed the vase's porcelain pieces into a pile. Remorse would come later. The only shame he felt was for the perverse satisfaction of breaking beautiful things.

"You saw him?" Mirabelle asked, her morbid fascination entirely transparent.

She wanted a post-mortem of grisly details, but the night came back to Emory in ink-blotted memories, misshapen at the edges and parts of it haphazardly redacted altogether. He didn't care to run down the gaps.

"I did. He got away before I could kill him."

The lie took the air out of the room. Mirabelle's gaze sharpened, and her duality emerged; the childlike need for protection juxtaposed with an ability to peer into him with cutting clarity.

Kill Ivan or save Amelia. One or the other, he'd had to choose. The others didn't know and hadn't seen that he could've had both.

Mirabelle knew, though. Somehow, she knew. She inched closer and Emory stood tall, poised to defend himself against the accusations he deserved. He'd had his chance to end it but didn't.

"He'll be waiting for us, Emory," Mirabelle said ominously and, though it wasn't all that revelatory, her resigned certainty chilled.

"You think I don't know that? Of course, he will. What do you think he was doing those years we thought he was dead? He planned this, all of it."

"Not all of it. There's a part you don't want to talk about."

Emory rubbed his cheek that throbbed worse than before. At least his teeth weren't broken.

"Say it then, Mirabelle. What is it?"

She hesitated and made herself small again. He hated how she did that—waxed when she pleased with pointed declarations then waned sheepishly in anticipation of his response.

"He's found a vulnerability in you. As long as Amelia is here, she's a risk."

"To who? You and Jack?"

Emory barked a laugh, but Mirabelle shifted uncomfortably on her feet. He'd struck the lode and followed that vein to the crux of the matter.

"She figured it out, didn't she? She knows about you two, saw it before I ever could, right? No wonder you both want her gone."

Emory cantered off to fetch the dustpan from the kitchen. The questions still rang when he returned to the room. He didn't need Mirabelle's answer. The silence alone said what she couldn't.

"How long have you two been sneaking around?" Emory asked.

He liked to think he knew. It'd become obvious earlier in the year when they couldn't exist in the same room without tension that stifled. Around that time, Jack's foul moods held a stunning correlation to the days Mirabelle wasn't around.

Mirabelle cradled her elbows and blew out a hard breath. "Seven months. I was gonna tell you. I just didn't know how."

A volley of cutting remarks welled up inside Emory. He bit his tongue to ward them off. Despite his best effort, the hurt still masqueraded as anger.

"Don't fucking talk to me about risks or keeping secrets. I'll shoulder the blame if this goes south, but Amelia belongs with me. End of fucking story. I don't wanna hear shit about it from them." Emory ripped the brush from the dustpan and pointed the bristled end at Mirabelle. "And I certainly don't wanna hear shit about it from you. I will walk away with her and leave this place in ashes if I have to."

His threat echoed in the room and the foyer beyond. *Good,* he thought bitterly. *Let them all hear.*

Mirabelle lifted a hand to mollify. "I've only ever wanted what was best for you."

Emory squatted with the dustpan in one hand and brush in the other. "This can't be the thing that tears us apart, Miri."

"It isn't. You're my brother, and I love you."

"Then why do Jack's bidding?" he asked and swept the vase's broken pieces into the pan. "Why lie for him and keep his secrets?"

"Same reason you put your secrets into her," Mirabelle said, awfully brave when he wasn't looking.

"You love him?"

Mirabelle considered the question for far too long. Love was a litmus test. Yes or no, the answer immediate.

"I do," she said but added on condition, "not when he drinks, though. He's different then."

Emory set the dustpan aside and sat on the floor. The fire warmed his back as he stared up at Mirabelle. She looked too sad for a woman in love and garnered no giddiness for having admitted it.

"I knew the day would come when I'd have to let you go," Emory said. "I just never wanted it to come like this. We're leaving tomorrow. You'll go with Jack and Corey back to Vegas. Amelia and I will head for California."

Mirabelle drew a long breath as if enduring a blow but didn't protest.

"I told you not to get involved with a Moriarty man not because I want to meddle in your love life, but because they don't make for good partners."

"What does that say about you then?"

Emory had already thought it through and pardoned himself as the exception. He had an off-ramp, in blueprints, but an off-ramp still.

"Nothing. I deal with my bullshit and keep things squared away. I don't want you cleaning up after someone else's mess or having to answer for their choices. You can't fix whatever is broken in Jack. Don't lose yourself trying."

"You were supposed to end up like our dad—a simple man, a family of your own, a quiet life. How squared away can you be saddled with all of this?"

Mirabelle gestured to the mansion around them, the enduring symbol of a crumbling empire. How fitting it wasn't really Emory's. He didn't want Liam's house, no more than he wanted his legacy.

"I have to live with the cards I've been dealt," Emory said and left it at that. Mirabelle's irony wasn't intentional. She didn't know that the only simple and quiet pleasures their father ever knew were in death, not life.

"Maybe someday you'll fold."

"Maybe," Emory agreed but felt the clouds roll in again, on-call to cloak the light. "Go to bed. All will be well."

He had a lot of nerve saying something like that on the wrong side of midnight. Mirabelle stooped down to kiss his cheek and did as she was told, but clearly didn't buy it.

Neither did he.

FORTY-SIX

AMELIA

Fearlessness didn't exist in a girl like Amelia. Her mother told her so when she was five and got stuck in the white oak in their backyard. Brian had climbed it with courage burning so brightly that Amelia stood at the bottom in blind awe of her little friend.

On her turn, Amelia had made it only six feet off the ground. She wrapped herself around a branch, closed her eyes, and wailed for help. Her mother got her down and, after the ordeal, consoled Amelia with homemade cookies and a worried smile.

"You're fearless in other ways," she'd said, but it stuck like a thorn in Amelia's side as she waited for her brand of fearlessness to show up.

It did tonight.

When she wasn't looking, it blindsided her. Perhaps it should've made her proud or relieved, but Amelia's body was wooden and aching and her mind snowy with static as Mirabelle followed her into Emory's bathroom.

"You were so brave," Mirabelle said with misplaced effusion that echoed amongst the glazed tiles.

It reminded Amelia of the recommendation letter her English professor had sent to Harvard. It'd been stuffed to the gills with thoughtful hyperboles. A fictional Amelia existed more exacting and assertive and braver than she had any right to be.

Amelia shook her head and started the shower. "I wasn't brave. I was lucky."

Mirabelle stared at Amelia as if it never occurred to her that bravado made no guarantees, that luck was dumb and heroes often failed. She opened her mouth for the million-dollar question—did Ivan do to her what he did to those other girls?—but Amelia bluntly grounded that conversation before it took flight.

"I'd like to clean up now," she said. "I'd also like something other than a t-shirt and underwear to sleep in. Maybe one of Emory's flannels."

Mirabelle nodded but sniffled with misty eyes. She needed comfort Amelia couldn't give and didn't have to begin with. That well ran dry and might not function the same again, so Amelia turned her back on a crying friend, a moment she'd surely torment herself with later. With nothing else to say, Mirabelle left.

After her shower, Amelia toweled off and wrung out her hair but didn't take inventory of her injuries. She felt them just fine; every bruise, scrape, and cut accounted for. Then there was the bite mark still screaming with pain too loud to ignore. Mirabelle had dug out a red flannel shirt and left it on Emory's bed with a pair of leggings. No one wore flannel in Nevada, but in some outpost of Emory's closet, his sweaters and fleeces hung like a homesick wish.

Amelia dressed with the desire to burrow beneath bolts of fabric, layers and layers as thick as armor, until she disappeared. Even that wasn't enough, though, so she sought comfort in her and Emory's sanctuary on the third floor.

The room enchanted with its strange trinkets and paintings of lunar-drenched seas and boats seeking harbor. She'd almost forgotten about the black phone there and couldn't remember why it'd once fascinated her. It just looked ordinary, its sheen dull beneath a layer of dust.

Cross-legged on the floor, Amelia flipped through a book of

short stories. She skimmed the words but mostly admired the intricate gold-leaf illustrations. Emory found her there and sat beside her with blood still on his cheek and dirt staining his jeans. He brought an ice pack and medical supplies that laid in a heap next to him.

"That was my grandmother's," he told her and gestured to the book in her lap. "She kept a bunch of old toys and books in her basement from when my dad was a kid. Whenever we'd visit, she'd send us down there to play. I didn't care about the toys. I only ever wanted to look at this book. I liked the pictures and some of the stories."

Old books had memories; the parts where the spine was worn and glue cracked from revisiting the same page. After a while, they opened there of their own accord, committing to heart the most well-loved parts. That book was no different. It flopped open to an illustration of a raven carrying the moon.

"This was your favorite," Amelia said, and it felt as though she was reaching into Emory's distant past. So little of it existed at Liam's. Perhaps just that book.

"Is it that obvious?" he chuckled, and Amelia skimmed the story.

In it, a raven and a dove made an odd couple. Every evening at dusk, the dove mourned the loss of day. Distraught by the dove's grief, the raven fetched his most cherished stone—pockmarked but brilliantly silver—and hauled it to the night sky to resemble the sun. And so it was said that the raven hung the moon for his dove.

"Why this one?" she asked.

Emory shrugged and studied the page as if unearthing the memories there. "It has the happiest ending, the kind I wanted for myself."

"And what kind is that?"

"Finding someone worth hanging the moon for," he said sweetly and smiled at her nestled in a cocoon of his flannel. Pain sullied that smile as he opened his arms. "Come here. I need you."

Amelia eagerly crawled into his lap. With her body against his

—heart to heart, cheek to cheek—she felt the uneven, shuddering quality of his breath. The more it labored, the tighter he held on. She clung to him, the only comfort she needed, but when she closed her eyes, that cinder block wall and stained mattress filled her vision.

"I never thought I'd see you again," she whispered with her throat aching.

"I know. I was crawling the walls without you."

Emory placed his hand over her heart as if counting each beat. The meaning transferred in his touch. He needed a sign of life to know it wasn't a dream.

"I'm okay," Amelia assured him.

Twice, she'd told him that because if she said it enough, then it might be true. Did she believe it? Only time would tell. In their sanctuary, neither had to pretend, though, so they came apart where no one else could see. The others wouldn't know how they trembled against one another or the tears that wet both their cheeks.

"What happened down there?" Amelia asked and motioned to the foyer far below.

Emory ran a hand over his face and exhaled a heavy breath. His eyes darted to the shadowed edges of the room that seemed to stretch further across the floor.

"A few street soldiers were murdered tonight. I guess one declaration of war wasn't enough."

He snickered at the last bit and shook his head. Amelia searched his face for artifacts of how he'd come apart, the hurt he shared right there in the dark. Ever the master of restraint, Emory had brought to heel whatever overtook him in the foyer. She'd already seen it, though, and was bound to again.

"I meant you," Amelia said and gently walked a line that seemed to be shifting beneath her. "You were ready to leave here and run away."

"I still am," Emory said with a joyless laugh. It rung hollow in the space between them. "You were right, though. This shit has to end, and I can't run from Ivan forever."

Resolute as ever, he lifted his chin and put up his defenses with stoic reserve. A pit grew in Amelia's stomach. The fire still burned in Emory, no matter how often he tried to ice it out. Sooner or later, he'd lose the ability to contain the blaze.

"It's okay to come apart," she told him and rested her palms against his chest that rose with sharp breaths.

"For now, I need to keep it together," Emory said. He combed his fingers through her hair, but his jaw clenched and brow hardened. "You don't have to tell me anything you don't want, but did Ivan..."

When he couldn't manage the question, he abandoned it altogether. Amelia shook her head but spared the details, including Ivan's assault on Richard.

"He would have but didn't. You came just in time. I did recognize him, though."

Emory's eyes snapped to her with dread that surfaced as swift and fierce as the storm-battered seas in Francisca's paintings.

"What do you mean? How?"

"I saw him at Rich's party. He came after me and Brian. I thought you knew."

"Fuck. No, I didn't." Emory bit his bottom lip but must've forgotten the cut there. He winced but only clamped down harder until his bite drew blood. "I should've known, should've seen this coming."

Of course, he'd blame himself, but it wasn't a lapse in observation. Amelia remembered well how Emory had scoured the outskirts of Rich's party and noticed danger long before anyone else. If Ivan had wanted to reveal himself, he would have.

Emory slipped the flannel off Amelia's shoulder and scrutinized Ivan's bite. She declined to look at it. She'd derived bitter satisfaction at how it stung with soap and hot water in the shower but resolved herself to ignore it forever.

Troubled, Emory looked for a distraction. Amelia admired that quality in him, how in trying times he couldn't withstand idle hands. He fetched a tube of ointment and warmed a glob between his thumb and finger. When he dabbed it on the wound, Amelia held her breath against the sting.

"I didn't kill him," Emory confessed in the small shelter of space between them. "I had the chance, a few actually. I could have, but I didn't."

He glanced at her haltingly as if afraid of what he might find in her eyes or perhaps to hide the shame in his. It struck Amelia then, though not for the first time, how viciously his time in the Moriartys warped his reality. She cupped his cheeks to force his gaze.

"Emory, taking a life is no small thing. You hesitated because it's not easy for you nor should it be, even with someone as deserving of death as Ivan."

"I know. I let him get under my skin. It's just..." Emory shook his head. "It's more than that, though."

"Tell me."

"Ivan thinks there's something kindred between us, a bond deeper than brotherhood. It's like he knows how to convince me of it. The hatred I feel for him is diabolical. That same hatred, that same darkness, it's in him too."

Another wave of worry besieged Emory as if she might see echoes of Ivan in him. Amelia tucked a strand of Emory's hair behind his ear and kissed his cheek.

"There's nothing kindred between you and Ivan," she whispered. "You don't have to inherit what he says as the truth. You get to decide who you are, not him."

Emory nodded and, in another distraction, unspooled a bit of medical tape and affixed a gauze pad to her shoulder.

"We'll need to keep an eye on this," he said and kissed the bandage.

The "Royal We" comforted with endearing solidarity. Amelia burrowed into it like down bedding, another layer to keep her safe. Up close and in the light, she inspected the lesion reddening his cheek. It'd surely mature into a nasty bruise, so she fetched the ice pack and held it there.

At the contact, Emory closed his eyes. "Feels good."

His lips parted with long, peaceful breaths, the kind that precede sleep. Amelia removed the pack and pressed her lips to his cold cheek then his mouth. She minded the cut there with kisses that still tasted faintly of blood.

"And that feels even better," he said with a smile as his fingertips grazed her spine. "Amelia, there are things I need to tell you, things that will probably be hard to hear."

She stiffened, and her heart picked up its beat. She couldn't take much more bad news, and whatever Emory meant to say, he looked primed to deliver it gently. His eyes softened and so too did his words, as much as his deep voice would allow.

"Your dad isn't in Portland anymore."

Amelia shook her head, though she had no grounds to reject it. Richard had already delivered the news. Then again, she couldn't discern the dividing line between Richard's truths and lies.

"Are you sure?" she asked, faintly hopeful Richard had gotten it all wrong. Emory wouldn't bring that to her unless he was certain, though.

"Yes, I'm sure. I wanted to tell you, *meant* to tell you tonight. He's heading south. I don't know where. California maybe."

"If your brother is after him..."

Amelia ushered out the thought before it squatted in her mind and refused to leave. Instead, she wanted to plead with Emory and ask the unthinkable, to bring her father there and make him understand.

"He did the right thing. It's better that he left. I do know he's alive, and I have someone looking out for him."

"One of your men?"

"No, but someone I trust, a good man."

"Oh," was all Amelia could manage as guilt bubbled up from strange depths.

Not so long ago, she'd been all too eager to blaze a path away from her father. Instead, she'd destroyed the road behind her, no home to return to. Rotten irony would say, "You got what you wanted." She never wanted it to come like that, though.

Over his shoulder, Emory fixed his eyes to the window where a lonely moon illuminated the sky and streamed cold light through the pane.

"We're not safe here anymore either, are we?" Amelia asked, but tears occluded her vision and not because the bite mark stung or her back ached from slamming into the cinder block wall. It wasn't the phantom feeling of Ivan's fingers clamping around her wrists or his palm running up her thigh. He'd marked her as his own and would come again; for her, for Emory, for everyone she loved.

Emory licked a bead of blood from his bottom lip. "No, we're not. You and I are leaving for California tomorrow."

"Leaving," Amelia repeated and shifted in his lap.

She glanced at the table where they'd played cards and sipped sweet wine in the golden hour. If anyone asked, she'd say it was there in their sanctuary where they fell in love and found a shred of peace.

"For how long?" she asked, though timelines seemed more arbitrary than ever.

"I don't know. Weeks, months, maybe longer." Emory toyed with a loose button on the flannel shirt, rubbing the mother-of-pearl between his thumb and forefinger. "Look, I know you didn't choose to come here and now you're not given a choice on how to leave, but—"

Amelia pressed her index finger to his lips. Stunned, Emory's eyes widened at he stared at her.

"No."

"No, what?"

"Don't do that. I didn't choose how I came here, but I can choose how I leave, and it's with you. I choose you, Emory. Everything you are now, not what you might become one day. *You.* That's it. That's my choice. It will always be you."

Amelia expected a protest from him but found none. She'd made up her mind and there was no talking her out of it. She would walk the path with him deeper into the underworld where, in the sweetest of ironies, she'd found belonging.

"What do you want, Amelia?"

The answer was him.

Always him.

Emory kissed the pad of her finger still at his lips. "About last night, those things I said in the parlor."

Amelia had almost forgotten. It seemed trivial and hardly worth relitigating. Emory gathered her hands and held them to his chest. His heartbeat fluttered against her palms.

"I fucked up and said the wrong things because I have a knack for that. What I should've told you then because God knows I felt it well before now is, I love you, Amelia. I don't know what my future holds, but I know I want you in it, and I know we belong together, now and always."

"Now and always," she repeated, faintly quizzical and dazed because love never came easy for her nor had it ever ended well.

When it came at all, it was always with a great deal of convincing; convincing herself that it felt right or convincing others that she was enough. There'd be none of that, and she found in Emory a mirror to herself—the earnestness in which he offered his heart and the gravity of that moment when he made it known.

The path ahead would be difficult—that much she knew—but loving him, loving each other, would not be, and she took solace in that. Soon, she'd extract from it her strength and perhaps that was where she'd derive her fearlessness; fearless enough to love a man like him, fearless enough to let him love her too.

Amelia twisted the loose ends of his hair around her fingers and kissed the scar on his top lip.

"I love you too," she said, her body finally rid of the chill she couldn't seem to chase away.

A devilish smile unfurled on Emory's lips. "I know you do."

Amelia laughed. "Okay, cocky."

"No, it's not ego talking." Beneath her, the tension in Emory's body released like a knot coming undone as he contemplated her. "It's the way you look at me. I wish you could see yourself in those moments. Don't ever stop looking at me that way."

"I won't. I promise," she said, her lips grazing his in another soft kiss.

Emory's tongue slipped into her mouth, and Amelia relished his familiar taste and the warmth of his body beneath her.

"What is it?" she asked when Emory pulled away enough to look at her.

"I'm getting out. *We're* getting out. Together."

"How? I thought..."

"If I see the Moriartys through war, Liam will find me a way out. This will all be over, and we'll have our simple life together, the one we both want. I just need you to trust me."

Wild with hope, Emory spoke on a hush the secret they'd share. He was less manic than he had been earlier but still convinced they could walk away and leave this all behind.

He entreated her to pour faith in him and endure. But it wasn't about endurance. It was the duality of trust. Like her father used to say when Amelia learned to drive, *"I trust you, but not the loonies you'll share the road with."* Amelia trusted Emory implicitly, but not the organization where snakes and rats and other duplicitous creatures lurked.

While he might escape his blood oath, who was to say the Moriartys would survive the war? Perhaps that was what her father meant by big death. The institution was doomed to fall eventually. She let that go unsaid. It'd only spoil the moment where Emory wove their wants together and offered an escape.

Buried in his flannel and safe in his arms, Amelia nodded. "I trust you."

With a deep sigh, Emory relaxed against her and Amelia rested her head on his shoulder. He caressed her back and spoke slow, his breath humid against her forehead.

"You know, Liam calls you my queen."

"I do. I think it's sweet."

"I need you to know that you'll always be my queen. In here and out there." Emory tipped his head to the window and the world beyond. "It's going to get hard for a little while. There will be no shortage of things that try to tear us apart."

Amelia sat up in his lap and coiled her arms around his neck.

"Let them try," she said with determination her mother might've called fearlessness. "It'll always be you and me."

"You and me," Emory repeated, a solemn vow spoken between them and a pillar of strength they'd surely need for the storms ahead.

FORTY-SEVEN

EMORY

The night passed with dreams so strange the morning light couldn't burn off the delirium. Emory's subconscious conjured things that would've made Dali envious; not nightmarish but disturbing in a hypnogogic way. With Amelia snuggled against his chest and her breaths coming long and slow, the uneasiness drained away. Emory brushed aside a fall of hair, kissed her cheek, and went back to sleep.

They woke for good an hour later. As Amelia showered, Emory packed. The soft-sided suitcase lay open on the bed, his clothes stacked or wrapped in taut bundles, their complementary shapes jigsawed for efficiency.

You could tell a lot about someone by their luggage. When he traveled, Emory made a game of matching suitcases to the assholes crowding baggage claim. Next to the conveyor belt, they threw javelin elbows to snap up monstrously large or hideously patterned suitcases.

Emory would stake out some space in the back and wait as his bag—solid black with a grey tag—puttered along. He'd snag it when convenient and be on his way. What did that say about him? Nothing of consequence and that was the point.

He gave Amelia his good bag, a large oxblood weekender that traveled by car and car alone. She packed in under twenty minutes, everything she'd amassed there fitting in a bag meant for weekend get-aways.

Emory found that deeply confronting. It wasn't the statement of his innocuous black suitcase looming next to hers, but the punishing sense that he'd failed her.

They weren't zipping up the coast to breathe in the salt breeze and make love by moonlight. They weren't driving into pine-swaddled mountains or a sun-washed vineyard for a weekend of romance. She deserved the world, and he gave her far less, just a leather bag for their somber journey.

Amelia took that bag without complaint. In the room across the hall, she carefully folded each garment and placed it inside with the same quiet faith she'd placed in him.

And what did that say about her?

Everything he already knew. Everything he loved.

In the kitchen, Liam prepared breakfast with the stubborn notion that Emory should brief their plans to Corey, Pete, and Zulu over a hearty meal. Liam served up thick slices of garden tomatoes, crispy bacon, and a steaming pile of scrambled eggs. Mirabelle made blueberry muffins that ballooned over their baking cups, the sugar granules on top sparkling like fresh snow.

They gathered around the dining room table and, as the others ate, Emory detailed the plans. Corey, Zulu, and Pete took it well but read the tea leaves. It wasn't tidying up loose ends for a cold spell but weatherproofing for a hard freeze. Weeks would turn to months. Summer would collapse into autumn that perished with winter.

Emory reached for Amelia's hand resting beside her teacup. In the rosy light, her profile was serene and stunning. She'd need warmer clothes. Sweaters and flannels. Boots, socks, jackets, scarves. She could have everything she wanted, but one day her vessel would run dry, emptied of the grace she'd given him. She'd want the things she already owned or perhaps just the chance to tidy up her own loose ends.

At the far end of the table, the sun streamed through the blinds and laid slatted shadows over Jack's face with carceral effect.

He hadn't spoken much, just a few grunts of agreement as he picked at his breakfast. Earlier, as bacon sizzled in the frying pan, he jumped with a startle at a pop of grease. It wasn't like him to be spooked by paper tigers.

After breakfast, Corey headed for Vegas to unseat Disco. Zulu and Pete returned to LA and would join Emory and Amelia in a week. The rest of them rounded up the last of their belongings.

Where Emory treated his room at Liam's like a billet, Mirabelle had nested in hers with framed photographs and personal mementos. She packed with frazzled emotion as if being evicted from her sanctum. Amelia helped where she could while Emory hauled their bags to the garage.

Afterwards, he joined Liam in the basement lounge to wait for the others. By day, the space lost its saturnine charm. Purged of celebration, it stank of stale smoke and spilt beer. He and Liam settled across from one another at the oblong table typically reserved for holding court.

"It was nice having everyone at breakfast this morning," Liam said and reached for a heavy-bottomed ashtray. "Don't you think it was nice?"

"Very," Emory agreed, though he didn't find it odd that they'd shared a meal or spoke freely, sometimes meandering off-topic and ripping with laughter. Families did that every day. The only bizarre thing there was treating it like a novelty.

Liam lit the end of a cigarette and savored the first drag with eyes lightly shut and a hand resting on his belly. He would've dozed off, a perfectly good cigarette reduced to cinders between his fingers. *He's getting older,* Emory observed for perhaps the first time.

"What the hell are you gonna do here all alone?" he asked, more pleading than curious.

Liam opened his eyes and ashed his cigarette. "I'll be fine. It's not exactly a shithole."

With a chameleon quality, Liam looked less frail than he had a mere moment ago. Emory suspected he'd only ever catch glimpses of Liam's helplessness. If pride was a boulder, then time was the wind. When a man reached old age, time should've eroded pride to just a pebble in his palm, a bit of dignity to take into death. Time hadn't touched Liam's pride, only made it more onerous for his aging bones to carry.

"I came across a busted vase in the kitchen trash," Liam said wryly with smoke issuing from his lips. "Know anything about that?"

"I lost my head," Emory admitted. "I'm sorry."

Liam chuckled. "I think I started it."

"I think you did too."

"A lesson for us both then. Keep our heads."

Liam's residual smile evaporated as he examined Emory. The attention unnerved. Did he notice something Emory couldn't see in himself, something malignant spreading uncontrolled? *"Your soul is wrecked. Just like mine."* He almost asked, but Liam put out his cigarette and pushed the ashtray aside.

"Well, my boy, shall we leave it on the table?"

Emory nodded. "Seems fair."

Only Liam ever used that phrase. It'd sound too much like a cheap imitation coming from anyone else. "Leave it on the table" meant no question was off limits and Liam expected no bullshit either.

"Do you regret this?" he asked and tipped his head to their surroundings but kept discerning eyes on Emory as if the truth might sneak by when he wasn't looking. "I think you must."

"I don't regret the past," Emory answered honestly. "I just want a better future."

"Does Amelia know about the deal we made?"

"She does. I think she's afraid it's too good to be true."

"Maybe it is," Liam ventured carefully, as if minding bubbles liable to burst.

Heat spread at the back of Emory's neck, and his fingers curled beneath the table. *Then why dangle the fucking carrot?*

"It's not."

Patience waning, Emory bit his tongue to clip the rest. *Keep your head.* Liam's gaze flicked over Emory, his musings transparent. *"This world doesn't coddle idealists,"* the look said.

"I only meant our darkest days are ahead of us, not behind."

Emory had no response. The hackneyed statement didn't need his commentary—he'd heard that fatalist drivel before—so he pressed his lips together and gave a shallow nod.

The door at the top of the stairs opened with what sounded like a struggle. Someone slapped the doorknob and fumbled with something heavy that clomped down each step. *Ka-plunk, ka-plunk, ka-plunk,* it went and left a chorus of giggles in its wake.

With his duffle bag thrown over his shoulder, Jack wheeled Mirabelle's large suitcase across the room. The girls followed with Mirabelle's other bags, each more bloated than two months ago when they first arrived at Liam's.

What did Mirabelle's luggage say about her? That she could tolerate living out of suitcases better than most and had gained expertise in a nomadic existence. It cost her some shine, though. She sparkled less, her smile as wide as ever but her eyes sullen.

Liam refused to see them off in the garage, so they each took their turn saying goodbye and needling him with final appeals to leave with them. Graciously, he refused. After Jack and Mirabelle left for the garage, Liam thrust his hand in Emory's with a business-like shake.

"We'll be in touch."

"If you need anything," Emory said, "I want you to call."

Liam rolled his eyes. "Quit fussing. I'll be fine."

As with Mirabelle, he reserved his affection for Amelia and pulled her into a tight hug.

"You take care, love." Liam rested his hands on her shoulders and motioned to Emory. "Keep him in line. We'll see each other again very soon."

"I hope so," Amelia said and took Emory's hand.

He led the way along the bar where sorrows had been drowned and triumphs toasted. With a twinge of nostalgia, Emory passed the pool table in the back. God only knew how many nights he spent sinking stripes into the pockets as he and Jack pondered their existence.

Emory reached the heavy door at the back of the room, but Amelia hesitated at the threshold. Her grip on his hand tightened, and they started down the concrete corridor. The musty air was cool and dry, and the amber light struggled to fill the space.

"There aren't any spiders in here," Emory assured, half a joke, but he couldn't promise that scorpions or other critters hadn't wandered in seeking reprieve from the heat.

Amelia squeezed his hand. "It's not the spiders I'm scared of."

She didn't elaborate. With her head down, the dark hid her face but couldn't obscure the worry lacing her voice. Emory almost asked what she feared, but the question seemed both trite and obvious. Before he could reframe it, they reached the garage.

Emory squinted against the fluorescent lights. Liam kept the space free of clutter. Carved into a slope at the back of the house, it functioned as a staging area where Moriarty men could covertly come and go.

Jack crammed his and Mirabelle's suitcases into the trunk of his car. Shapes mismatched, they didn't quite fit. Jack forced the problem suitcase in place with a violent kick and slammed the trunk shut. With worried eyes, Amelia peered up at Emory, and the color drained from her cheeks.

"I know," he whispered then approached Mirabelle. She returned the hug he gave her with the stilted rigidity he knew to be fear.

"I love you," Emory said and rested his chin atop her head. "If you need me, call. Day or night, I'll come running."

"I know you will," she laughed, nervous and tinny, and rolled to her toes to kiss his cheek. "I love you too."

Amelia spirited Mirabelle to the corner where they could speak in private. Emory turned to Jack and issued a warning.

"Remember what I said."

Jack stared reproachfully, as if Emory had fleeced him of joy. Poor Jack, swindled in a snake-oil scheme. Never his fault. No, not him.

"Care to clarify?"

"If my sister isn't being treated right, I'm coming to get her. There will be no more of this."

Emory gestured to the trunk and the suitcases forcefully wedged inside. With baleful insolence, Jack snickered at the suggestion.

"I would never hurt her."

"You gonna stay dry then?"

"As a desert," Jack said with a wink, but his face registered maudlin hurt.

Emory couldn't smell the boggy peat of scotch or barrel smoke of whiskey on his breath, but, even stone sober, the drink had its reach. He edged closer, feeling as though they teetered on the knife's edge of a breakthrough. One misstep could gut them both.

"I need you to take care of yourself."

"I won't let you down, boss."

"I'm not talking about my deputy, Jack. I'm talking about my best friend."

Jack stared at the floor between them, his hair hanging limp around his sallow face. He'd stopped greasing it back, and untamed growth sprouted in the hard part.

"I'm fine." Jack popped his neck and stretched his arms overhead. He glared at Amelia, who sounded an alarm to Mirabelle in hushed but urgent tones. "We'll be fine. Back to normal soon enough."

"Normal," Emory repeated, though the concept was lost to them, or perhaps they'd never known it at all.

Jack dug the keys from his pocket and flashed an ephemeral smile. "Well, see you on the other side, I guess."

Emory didn't like the finality of the statement or what it might suggest.

"You'll see me soon," he corrected but didn't exactly know how long that might be.

The arrangement would surely accelerate what had already started; the two of them pulling apart in different directions.

Like a rubber band stretched to its limit, sooner or later, it'd snap.

With no love lost, Amelia didn't say goodbye to Jack. It wouldn't have mattered. Jack climbed into his car, and Mirabelle did the same.

Emory started down the long drive from Liam's estate and set a meandering pace through the neighborhood of colossal mansions that'd always struck him as nonsensical and gaudy.

I'm going home, he thought with a smile touching his lips. His elbow sunk into the center console, and he rested his hand on Amelia's thigh. She shifted nearer, her cheek nuzzled against his bicep and her free hand caressing his forearm.

"What did you tell Miri back there?" he asked.

Amelia stirred against him. God, how quickly he'd come to know her body, the subtle movements that telegraphed her needs. She'd crawl into his lap there in the car if she could and rest her head against his shoulder. Instead, she craned her neck to kiss his jaw, the playful affection masking her palpable unease.

"I told her what I'm afraid of."

At the neighborhood's gated entrance, Emory turned left onto the two-lane road winding toward the valley.

"Well, are you gonna tell me too?" he laughed and slinked his arm across her shoulders.

He stroked her hair and counted her sharp breaths, three and then four. He knew her mind too, the heaviness she carried with secrets she'd rather not keep.

"I think you already know," Amelia said.

Emory followed her eyes to the rearview mirror. In the reflection, he watched Jack's car creep down the road in the opposite direction and disappear around a shadowed bend.

"I think I do too."

FORTY-EIGHT

CAL

The cold snap would set records for Las Vegas. The weatherman said so from the television static in Cal's motel room just the other day. Portland burned, Vegas froze, and Cal was caught in the middle because a chill to desert folk still felt balmy to him.

For the past week, he'd kept his head down, but strangers looked askance whenever he ventured out in shorts and a t-shirt. "You gotta blend in, Cal. Bland as unbuttered toast," was Kingsley's advice, so Cal picked up a canvas jacket and cargo pants from a consignment shop up the road. Discretion had a price, though. Toasty, indeed, he was burning up.

He'd traveled from Oregon through high desert along rain-shadow terrain that was an arid echo to his hollowed-out heart; the best of him scooped out the middle and the rest of him struggling to survive. Along the way, he encountered little more than jackrabbits and Joshua trees and vibrant skies set against the vermillion desert. It would've stunned in other circumstances, but Cal couldn't shed the feeling that he was retracing Amelia's steps across empty land so far from home.

He put down shallow roots at a motel on the southern edge of Las Vegas. Cash was king in that kind of place. No one asked for a credit card or probed for his home address. He'd slid the clerk a wad of bills that bought him a room for the week. "It's got a nice view. A *real* nice view," the clerk said and smacked his lips.

Beyond the room's rubber-coated curtains, the window overlooked The Strip Mall, a titty bar wedged between a tanning salon and a Chinese restaurant. The restaurant advertised "The Wanton Special" after midnight—orange chicken, a side of cream cheese-stuffed wontons, and a soft drink for $12.99. *Clever,* he'd thought, and yanked the curtains shut.

The first few nights, the neon bleed still reached his window, and Cal reasoned if he couldn't beat them, he ought to join them. Not the strip club, of course, but orange chicken after midnight. Some leaky valve in his chest nagged, though, at the prospect of greasy food that late. Probably for the best.

In the morning, Cal woke, shrugged into his cargo jacket, and drove to the local diner. Along the way, he passed a billboard that advertised bus tours of Vegas' old mobster haunts. Tourists could follow in the footsteps of Meyer Lansky and Moe Dalitz and hear the blood-soaked tale of how Bugsy Siegel put the gilded city on the map for mafia elites.

You're in gangland now, Cal thought but didn't need a billboard to tell him that. The hostile specter loomed, dangerous and wild. While everything back home was velveteen and lush, there things seemed brittle and menacing right down to the sun-bleached bones on the side of the road.

Cal pulled into the diner as the sun triumphed over McCullough range. A smattering of storm clouds rolled in from the west and would soon snuff out the light. He'd add that to the pile of oddities. Rain was a novelty there, and the locals treated storm clouds with the same hushed reverence as bible-thumpers receiving the good word on Sundays.

Even as Cal settled into a corner booth by the window, he watched as diner patrons climbed from their cars and pointed to the black mass on the horizon. It left his stomach in knots, so he gazed down into the coffee mug snug in his palm and watched a nebula of cream swirling inside.

Kingsley turned Cal onto the place. Greasy-cheap, he called

it. That meant good eats on a budget, indigestion the real cost. The place was old enough that a defunct cigarette machine collected dust in the corner. They'd probably make out like bandits filling the machine's coils with antacids and milk of magnesia.

Out the window, Kingsley's truck backed into a parking space. He'd arrived in Vegas three days before and worked out of the FBI field office in town. They gave him a hot-desk and left him alone to run down leads. How long would it last? "Long enough to matter," Kingsley had said, but Cal still didn't know how to bookend the statement.

Kingsley crossed the diner's sticky checkered floors, his rubber-bottomed shoes squelching as he went. Everything was slightly misted in grease and covered with grime. Kingsley slid into the red vinyl booth across from Cal and peered out the window at the aberrant sky.

He didn't comment on the weather or opt for other mainstays of small talk—how Cal slept, if he caught that last inning of the Dodgers game, what looked good that morning.

Instead, Kingsley said hello and perused the menu longer than usual. Ultimately, he ordered the same thing as yesterday and the day before—western omelet with a side of bacon, tomato juice, and coffee. They made light chatter until the waitress arrived with an oversized tray balanced on her shoulder and expertly slung a half-dozen plates to the table.

"I've got good news and bad news," Kingsley said as he salted his eggs, "but the good news has to come first. The motel clerk woke up. He was lucid for a few hours."

"And the bad news?" Cal asked, though the past tense spoke for itself. He didn't suspect the clerk was lucid for a few hours and then watched Jeopardy or ate a bowl of Jell-O or asked to call his mother.

"He's dead. The hospital claims the night nurse accidentally fudged the dose of his pain meds. Stopped his heart like that."

Kingsley snapped his fingers, shook his head, and dug into his omelet. Cal stared at the short stack of pancakes in front of him.

It sickened with the pad of butter melting on top and the syrup already soaked in.

"Don't tell me you believe that," he grumbled and sawed off a bit of the stack just to occupy his hands.

"I don't, but something isn't adding up. Emory Holt is decisive, and the window to act was weeks ago, so why would he deal with this now?" Kingsley plucked a slice of bacon from his plate and pointed it at Cal. "Someone else called this shot."

"A decision like that would only come from Emory."

"And what if his decision was to leave it alone? That means someone went behind his back."

Kingsley chomped on a bite of bacon and stared out the window. As even keeled as he was, his eyes, deep brown and expressive, gave him away. Like staring through the looking glass, they always reflected what weighed on his heart. At that moment, they registered unease. Cal had seen that in Kingsley before and recognized the pattern.

"You've met Emory, haven't you? You talk like you know him or something."

Kingsley nodded, and his eyes traced a reluctant path back to Cal. "He helped with a case once."

Cal waited to hear what else. It seemed odd that the chief of the Moriartys would play ball with a fed. Then again, those men routinely padded the pockets of law enforcement, a small price to pay for cops to look the other way. Kingsley wasn't like that, though, and Cal sensed there was more to the story.

"What was the case?"

"We had an arrest warrant for one of his former captains," Kingsley said as he tried to corral a chunk of bell pepper onto his fork. "Child molestation and solicitation of a minor. The guy caught wind of it and disappeared. All our leads dried up, so I reached out to Emory on a long shot. He pulled the piece of shit out of the woodwork and turned him over."

"Am I supposed to believe that makes him a good man?"

"You can believe what you want and you'll hate to hear it, but he *is* a good man. Smart, determined, humble. Embattled, though. Men like that..." Kingsley paused and let the bell pepper go as he chased down words instead. He shook his head and glanced at Cal. "I pray for his peace."

"Not his salvation?"

"No man is beyond redemption, Cal. Not even him."

"Whose side are you on?"

Cal meant it as a joke, but Kingsley answered dead serious, "The right side. Wherever that may be."

"Fair enough." Cal popped a chunk of pineapple into his mouth. "Is there any actual good news in all of this?"

"The pliers collected near the motel came back from the lab. We got a hit for Damon Presnick. You know that name?"

Cal nodded. Damon was a hired hand for several organizations and slippery as hell. His eccentricities and vagabond habits made him good at his job but hard to pin down.

"His last phone call was with Jack Armstrong," Kingsley said. "Whatever happened at that motel, the Moriartys were involved."

The pineapple turned sour in Cal's mouth. He chewed slowly but couldn't look at Kingsley. He might find the agony of irony there, never mind the truth. He could bury his head in the sand, but it made no difference. Reality prevailed.

"They have her," Cal said, so plainly and evidently unaffected that he felt a stranger to himself. An odd rush of relief momentarily subsumed his heartache. It was progress, at least; a compass pointing due north after spinning out of control for weeks.

"Occam's razor would say so." Kingsley sipped from his mug and peered at Cal over the rim. "Unfortunately, there's more. The Nye County sheriff's office responded to a call about some unusual activity at an abandoned warehouse. They went to check it out this morning and found several Velasco members a few days dead. Clearly, something happened out there."

There it was again. The black hole of blinding truth, as inescapable as it was crushing. An unknown variable had inserted itself between the Velascos and the Moriartys, and the two organizations clamored for the same thing.

Outside, the wind caterwauled against the cinderblock bones of the building, and the sunlight faded, throwing long shadows across the parking lot. With the dim light, the diner looked especially dingy; the floors dull, the patrons sickly.

"War's started. That's what happened." Cal shoved his plate of picked-at pancakes aside. "So, what now?"

"I'll follow up on leads and figure out what happened at that warehouse. You know the game, though. It's their jurisdiction, so the sheriff's office will call us in if they need assistance."

Cal huffed a derisive laugh, bitter for having witnessed bureaucracy in all its stunning ineptitude.

"They won't," he said. "It'll get reported as a dust-up between rival organizations. No one will bat an eye or remember in a few weeks. No leads and no one to claim the bodies. I've been in this business a long time. That's how this goes, and it's how they slip through our fingers."

"How do we bring them down then?"

Kingsley shifted forward in his seat. His chest rested against the edge of the table with no concern for how his dress shirt might sop up bacon grease.

A lifetime ago, Cal would've been flattered to indulge a young gun like Kingsley with enough career ahead of him to run with the time and opportunity he had left. Sitting in a diner booth in a rundown town, far from home and with nothing much to his name, Cal wasn't the man he used to be and probably never would be again. Shit out of luck, he had no good answers.

"We don't," he said. "We never will."

Thunder rumbled outside, and lightning cracked the sky. A few booths over, an old couple rubber-necked out the window.

"You talk about them as if they're a supernatural force we can't vanquish."

"I never said they couldn't fall. Just that it wouldn't happen from the outside. My brother Mitch pounded his head against that wall his entire career. He tried everything to bring the Moriartys to their knees, and I do mean everything. You know what it got him?"

Kingsley shook his head.

"An early grave."

When Cal saw his brother last, Mitch had gained years on his face he hadn't yet lived. On a warm spring day, he stood on Cal's deck in his church clothes, the khaki and pastels so at odds with the darkness that'd followed him by then.

"Betrayal is the only thing that's going to break the Moriartys apart," Mitch had said. "It'll be someone on the inside who does them in. By the time anyone notices, it'll be too late."

The scent of fresh mowed grass and Easter ham had lingered in the air. With Helen and Amelia, barely a teenager then, dying eggs at the breakfast table, life was sweet, but Mitch was haunted, and Cal was at a loss for how to chase away the demons.

He'd assumed his brother was only eulogizing a long career. Mitch had talked about hanging up the hat for years, only waiting to watch the Moriartys fall so he could rest easy in retirement.

"Our world is no different, Cal," his brother had said. "There are enemies on the inside too. Be careful who you trust. The only thing I've ever respected about the Moriartys is that they don't hide their evil behind a badge."

At brunch, Mitch had picked at his food and responded mostly in hums or distracted grumbles. When he left, he'd hugged Cal long and hard, as if some part of him knew it was the last time.

Kingsley stared at Cal and looked just as thunderstruck as Cal had felt standing on his deck that Easter Sunday with fresh death on the horizon. Cal motioned to the steak knife next to Kingsley's plate.

"Let's say someone cuts me with that knife. I stuff it with gauze, stop the bleeding, and wait for it to heal. When it does, I move on and don't make the same mistake twice. But let's say I get knocked down hard, the kind of fall that tears up my insides. I get back up and go about my life unaware of the trauma until it's too late. I'm bleeding out on the inside and don't even know it."

Cal dropped his voice and prodded the table with one finger. The silverware rattled with each jab.

"Let's cut the shit. We both know Emory has Amelia. We hemorrhage the Moriartys from the inside and watch them crumble. When they do, I'll be there to get my daughter back."

"Hemorrhage from the inside," Kingsley repeated and took a swig of tomato juice. "An informant?"

"No. Informants are like thorns. The Moriartys will pluck them out, one after the next. We get someone close to the top, someone in Emory's inner circle. A personal betrayal will make him question everyone and everything around him. He'll set fire to his own organization and watch it burn just to drive out the treachery, and, when he's done, he'll have nothing left but an empire of ashes."

The vinyl crackled as Kingsley slumped in the booth with a sigh. "Jack?"

"Closer than that."

Understanding bloomed on Kingsley's face. He nodded slowly and whispered, "Blood's thicker than water."

"Precisely."

With his appetite returning, Cal reclaimed his plate of pancakes. Though cold and soggy, he savored them more than when they were hot off the griddle. Kingsley seemed to have lost his appetite and surrendered his half-eaten meal to the waitress when she fluttered by.

Some things were sacred and Cal would know. One balmy June night, a storm scattered his family to the four winds and across the great divide. Family was sacred, but Emory crossed the Rubicon first, and it was only fair that he should suffer the same storm.

With an enemy inside—and family, no less—the tower would fall.

JOIN MY NEWSLETTER

Want exclusive behind-the-scenes content, updates on my latest works, and pictures of my adorable cats? Sign up for my newsletter, and you won't miss a thing!

As a token of my gratitude, you'll receive a FREE spicy mafia romance short story, *One Last Shot,* set in the *Bloodlines* universe.

Sign up on my website (link and QR code below):

www.cesarrow.com

You can also follow me on social media to catch the latest.

Email:
cesarrow@cesarrow.com

Instagram:
https://www.instagram.com/ce_sarrow/

BlueSky:
https://bsky.app/profile/cesarrow.bsky.social

Tumblr:
https://cesarrow.tumblr.com/

ABOUT THE AUTHOR

C.E. Sarrow discovered her passion for writing while earning her chemistry doctorate. While experiments bubbled in the lab, she found a different kind of chemistry on the page and has spent the years since honing her writing craft. She lives in the US with her fiancé, a coven of cats, and far more books, plants, pens, and candles than she'll ever need.

ACKNOWLEDGMENTS

Many hands and hearts helped me bring this story to life. I am so grateful to them all.

To Jay, my partner in life and cat parenthood, who has supported me through every moment of this journey.

To my best friend, a true creative and muse, who has been hyping my writerly endeavors from the start.

To Sam, who believed this story had the legs to go the distance and offered so much encouragement as it took its first wobbly steps into the world.

To Kate, who saw this book in its earliest stages and offered helpful feedback, as well as Alix and Rebecca, who did the same after I'd rewritten this book numerous times. To Amber, who helped me steer this story toward its ultimate destination.

To my editors, Beth and Amanda at Beth Hudson, Ink, who gave this book a good polish and were endlessly encouraging in the process.

To Naoru Suisou, whose talent I've admired for years and who brought Emory and Amelia to life through her gorgeous artwork.

To Ellie at LoveNotes PR, who patiently guided this nervous debut author through the ARC process and is just an all-around delight.

To my ARC readers, who showed so much enthusiasm for this book.

To the writers I've met along the way, who have graciously offered their advice, encouragement, expertise, and support. I have so much respect and admiration for you.

And to you, dear reader, you have my sincerest gratitude for giving this book a chance. May our paths cross again very soon.

My sincerest thanks—

C.E. Sarrow

9 798994 255810